Bitter Sweet Encounters

L H Morrow

Bitter Sweet Encounters

Author: ©L H Morrow

All rights reserved. No part of this publication may be reproduced, stored in a retrieval system, or transmitted in any form or by any means, electronic, mechanical, photocopying, recording or otherwise, without the prior written permission of the author.

This novel is entirely a work of fiction. The names, characters and incidents portrayed in it are the work of the author's imagination. Any resemblance to actual persons, living or dead, events or localities is entirely coincidental.

National Library of Australia Cataloguing-in-Publication entry

Creator: Morrow, L. H. (Linda H.), author.

Title: Bitter sweet encounters / Linda Morrow.

ISBN: 9780987439321 (paperback)

Subjects: Courage--Fiction.

Australian fiction.

Dewey Number: A823.4

Published with the assistance of

www.loveofbooks.com.au

Dedication

This book is dedicated to all the victims of crime.

For all those who have suffered from the hands of terrorists, rapists, murderers and arsonists worldwide.

May the heart of humanity embrace you and offer up support and comfort, to all those in need.

Chapter One

After refuelling, the jet sped up the runway, quickly climbing into the evening sky and banking to the left, before heading swiftly to its destination. Kath peered out the window. Far below and sprawling out into the distance laid a mish mash of twinkling lights. Probably the outskirts of outer London, she assumed.

Her heart was racing, knowing she was drawing closer to home, closer to her family, closer to the devastation she left behind over two decades ago. With a heavy heart, she sat twisting her diamond ring around and around, recalling her brutal rapes and the death of her two brothers. Agonising thoughts dominated her mind, as she reflected upon the bomb she detonated, killing five notorious Irish Republican Army members, namely Finbar Ward. This prevented the execution of her immediate family and Marcus's family as well. People, she truly loved.

It now seemed strange sitting next to Marcus in his private company jet, making the homeward journey. All those years ago, she fled Northern Ireland with a broken heart, completely and utterly alone. Leaving Marcus and her family behind, all believing she was dead. Believing she was killed in a horrendous bomb blast, leaving the people in the North absolutely devastated. She made her solitary journey to Australia, crossing the treacherous Irish Sea on a ferry late at night, before continuing her long and arduous train journey down to London. She finally boarded a plane at

Heathrow Airport, to complete her journey and begin a new life in Sydney Australia.

Kath stretched across, gently lowering her hand on top of Marcus's. This was the man she left behind, all those years ago.

He was an extraordinary human being, who was the love of her life. Marcus had been truly devastated at that time thinking he had lost his beloved Caitlin, her name, as she was known back then. Yet, through a twist of fate, destiny allowed Marcus to find his first true love, once again. Marcus's father moved with his family to America and ended up merging with an Australian company in Sydney. Ironically, the very company he chose was the same one that Kath was General Manager of.

After Kath recovered from losing her husband Rod in a horrendous accident, eventually Kath and Marcus managed to get back together again. They then found themselves in the midst of continuing their great love for each other, both catching up on the many years they lost together.

Initially, Marcus was inconsolable, after discovering Kath had lied to him and by faking her own death, Marcus felt she had abandoned him and all her family. After a major confrontation, Kath was traumatised and overwhelmed with immense remorse and tried to take her own life. Marcus succeeded in rescuing her, only minutes before she would have plummeted to her death. Reunited and still very much in love, Marcus was completely overjoyed, discovering he had a twenty year old daughter named Margaret.

Kath flinched, immediately filled with enormous guilt. Thinking, it was only twenty-four hours ago when Marcus got the opportunity to speak with young Margaret, for the very first time. It was only twenty-four hours ago, when life was grand. Rachel her youngest daughter accepted her mum's newly fledged relationship with Marcus, totally unaware of their past, when Kath told Margaret about him on the phone. Margaret laughed and was extremely pleased for her mother; she was also completely oblivious she had been speaking to her real father, a few moments earlier. When the phone rang, Marcus picked it up on passing, delighted to hear young Margaret happily dispensing the beauty and history she was discovering, during her holidays in Ireland.

She had been holidaying there for six weeks and was heading back home again in twelve days time. She had rung home to give the final details of her arrival. Kath clearly recollected the happiness etched upon Marcus's face, while he made idle chit chat with his daughter. The smile he clearly embraced, before handing the phone over to her.

Unconsciously, Kath tightened her grip when she mentally revisited the last conversation she had with Margaret. Her heart plummeted, as she recollected screaming to Margaret, instructing her to get out of the building. She swallowed hard as tears crept down her cheeks, recalling the deadly blast. Kath sat silently, reliving the insufferable devastation she felt when the bomb exploded. Remembering how the line of communication was instantly cut, leaving her with no way of her knowing, whether her daughter was dead ... or alive.

Marcus gently swept away the tears streaming obliviously down Kath's cheeks, instantly drawing her out of her reverie, as she gulped back more tears, appearing extremely pale and totally exhausted.

"Will you be okay, my love?" Marcus enquired tenderly, searching her face, recognising the pain etched in her eyes, before stretching forward and taking her into his arms.

She exhaled; letting out a huge sob, wishing things could have been different. Wishing she hadn't bought Margaret, the bloody plane ticket in the first place. Wishing, they didn't have to make this god-damn, awful journey back home.

Peering at him terrified, she replied, her voice barely a whisper. "It's ironic, don't you think? I left Northern Ireland after detonating a bomb and now I'm returning home, because our daughter was in a building when a bomb exploded. Do you think its karma Marcus? Do you think this would have happened, if I hadn't caused those deaths and destruction all those years ago?" she agonised.

"Hush now darling" Marcus interjected "you must stop beating yourself up and blaming yourself. Of course it's not your fault; it's simply fate. Our destinies were written a long time ago!" he replied decisively, appearing both strong and calm.

The seatbelt sign came on, flashing ominously as the undercarriage dropped down. Marcus gave her a quick kiss on the forehead, before strapping her in safely. He buckled up; grasping her hand with his 'everything will be fine Kath, I promise' look, smiling across at her reassuringly.

A cold chill suddenly ran down his spine and within a split second, his heart plummeted in distress. He found himself worrying excessively, hoping and praying his young daughter Margaret, would be one of the lucky ones, as the plane touched down in Belfast.

Taxiing along the runway, the jet slowly turned and headed towards the arrivals gate. Both Kath and Marcus were avoiding direct eye contact, trying desperately to keep their inner demons tightly under wraps. Gripping each other's hand tightly and bracing themselves, both were petrified of the news that awaited them, as they entered the airport terminal.

Three hectic days later, the undesirable journey had to be endured by many. The sky was set with dark heavy rolling clouds, mixed with a light drizzle. It was a gloomy morning, raining down upon the mourners arriving and congregating at Roselawn Cemetery, all wishing to pay their last respects.

Making the headlines, the media splattered the atrocious news of the tragic slaughtering all over their front pages. Men, women and children attending a birthday party in a pub on the outskirts of Belfast perished, along with other patrons. The North was in deep mourning and as Marcus stood with his hands encased in Kath's, the past suddenly came rushing back to him, haunting him once more.

Peering over at the many coffins, draped in rain sodden lilies and pure white roses, he clearly remembered the day he attended Caitlin's funeral or Kath's, as she is known as now. He knew within his heart, the devastation these mothers and fathers, brothers and sisters, felt. He recognised they would never fully recover, understanding the huge gap which would exist in their lives, fully conscious the void could never be filled. He exhaled; recognising they would never be as fortunate as he has been. Discovering almost two decades later, Kath misled everyone by faking her own death and had taken on a completely new identity in another country, in order to protect him and their respective families.

Prayers were sent heavenward, as bagpipes droned methodically in the background, playing Amazing Grace. Huge ruddy faced men stood isolated, hunched over in grief, blowing their noses as they wiped away their heartfelt tears, with sheer misery etched upon their beaten brows.

Kath gasped in loathing, tears escaping down her cheeks, as she stood dressed in a heavy black dress and overcoat, worn to protect her from the bitter cold wind. She shivered despondently, trying hard to internally comprehend the sheer horror of it all.

Margaret's young friend Heather was one of the first coffins to be lowered reverently into a freshly dug grave. Twenty-three years of age, a young woman cut down in her prime, abruptly taken from her family and friends, in a despicable act of violence.

Kath was extremely emotional, swallowing hard and crying uncontrollably, gulping for air, thinking about Margaret and her excruciating loss.

Chapter Two

"Hurry up love," Brigee called out to Rachel, who was rushing around getting ready for school.

Plonking down at the breakfast table, Rachel groaned "how come mum and Marcus get to rush off, to an emergency meeting in London? Margaret is having a great time travelling around Ireland. Yet, I'm the one left behind attending school, having the dullest and most boring existence ever?"

Brigee chuckled loudly. "Rachel darling, you can hardly say your life is boring, it's anything but. God willing, you'll have a lot to look forward to and experience when you grow up."

Rachel sighed, before gulping down her last spoonful of cereal. "I guess you're right Brigee. I just wish I was grown up now!" Rachel retorted, sounding frustrated.

"Don't go wishing your life away pet, you've got all the time in the world, now if you could do me a big favour, go fetch your schoolbag and we'll be on our way."

As Rachel rushed off, Brigee stood quietly thinking about young Margaret, praying with all her heart, that she survived the massive explosion. Hopefully, Kath would ring her this evening with some good news.

After dropping young Rachel off at school, Brigee made her way to St Vincent's Hospital. The traffic was a nightmare at this time of the morning but she would be glad when she caught up with Valerie. She needed to explain everything to her dear friend face-to-face, knowing she would be as shocked and concerned as she was.

After parking, Brigee slowly walked towards the reception area, letting her guard down, no longer having to save face for Rachel's sake. She found herself fighting back tears, as the devastating news impacted on her. The receptionist paged Dr Valerie immediately, as Brigee fidgeted anxiously in the reception area, waiting with bated breath.

Valerie appeared shortly afterwards, dressed in her white doctor's coat with a pale green dress beneath, complete with a stethoscope draped around her neck. Upon sighting her, tears welled up within Brigee, causing Valerie to rush over to her good friend immediately.

"Brigee darling, what on earth has happened?" grabbing her hands and caressing them in hers straight away.

Brigee gulped "it's Margaret, things are up in the air at present and I'm waiting for Kath's call. I hope and pray the wee critter's still alive; I couldn't bear it if Margaret hasn't made it. God Valerie … everything's in a big mess," Brigee gasped, with tears spilling down her cheeks.

Valerie instantly hugged Brigee, before taking her to the office for privacy, determined to find out, what exactly was going on. She got Brigee seated and rushed off quickly to fetch two coffees from the vending machine, before sitting down beside her. Gently encouraging her to take several sips of coffee, Valerie finally managed to calm Brigee down. Looking up tearfully, Brigee gradually began revealing the whole story to her, allowing Valerie to fully comprehend, what exactly had taken place.

Valerie gasped in horror, after Brigee explained the severity of the situation, fighting back her own tears.

Brigee took another gulp of her coffee, swallowing hard before looking up, all pale and drawn.

"Do you think young Margaret is okay Valerie? Do you think she's still alive? I couldn't bear it if she was murdered."

Valerie calmly reassured Brigee. "Of course she's fine, you only have to look at Kath. Don't forget, Margaret's her daughter and we both know how resilient our Kath has been, over the years we've known her."

Brigee brightened up instantly, reflecting immediately upon Kath's life. "Gosh, I never thought of it like that, you're right you know. I must remain positive and believe she's a survivor, just like her mum," releasing a huge sigh of relief.

Valerie arranged to take the rest of the day off to be with Brigee. She sent her back home again, explaining she would join her within the next couple of hours, insisting they would have lunch together, which instantly raised a smile from Brigee. After Brigee left, Valerie quickly rang her husband Matt, informing him of the dire situation in hand. He was equally stunned and completely shocked. He completely agreed that Valerie should stay with Brigee, until she received the phone call from Kath and then decide afterwards what action should be taken.

The rest of the day passed uneventfully. Rachel was pleased to see Valerie when she arrived back home, automatically filling her in on all of her latest activities. Brigee gratefully prepared the dinner, appreciating that it gave her something to do. By keeping physically and mentally active, meant that it momentarily kept all terrifying thoughts at bay. After dinner, Rachel disappeared off to her room to relax and watch some television. Valerie went to the fridge to retrieve a bottle of white wine and leisurely poured out two glassfuls, before settling down next to Brigee on the sofa.

They sat and talked about the day Margaret was born at St Vincent's Hospital, reminiscing about the antics she got up too, while growing up.

Both were confiding how proud they were of Margaret's achievements and acknowledged she would make an excellent doctor one day.

It was almost nine o'clock in the evening when the phone rang abruptly. Startled by the loud ringing, Brigee's heart missed a beat and Valerie instantly jumped, as their conversation was suddenly interrupted.

Brigee automatically rose and went to retrieve the phone, with Valerie following closely behind, filled with trepidation. "Hello," Brigee whispered down the phone. "Is that you Kath?"

"Yes it is," Kath replied, sounding extremely tired.

Brigee stood nervously listening attentively to Kath, acknowledging everything verbally as well as nodding in reply, with Valerie standing pressed up against her, listening in. "Oh t-h-a-n-k god," Brigee announced, breathing deeply, tears filling her eyes immediately. "Yes, yes, I'll tell Valerie, in fact, you can tell her yourself," automatically handing the phone over to Valerie.

Valerie straightened up, forcing herself to focus, before taking the receiver. "Hi Kath darling, I was listening in and heard the good news. Thank the lord Margaret's safe; now don't go worrying about anything over here. Brigee's a force to be reckoned with and she's taking care of everything, as we speak."

"Heather's gone," Kath stammered. "Margaret's dear friend, who was so young and innocent, like so many of the others Valerie," Kath sobbed.

Valerie interrupted firmly but compassionately by saying "we must concentrate on the positive Kath, try not to think about the what if's and be extremely thankful for a positive outcome, regarding young Margaret. Brigee only told me about the bomb this morning and I couldn't believe it. With Matt and I being away on our mini-break, we didn't watch any news and simply relaxed."

After successfully managing to get Kath back into a positive mindset, Valerie hung up shortly afterwards. Immediately she let out a huge whoop, before giving Brigee the biggest hug imaginable. Tears ran down their cheeks, tears of joy, tears of relief and above all, tears for those who were less fortunate.

In the meantime, Rachel continued watching television upstairs, totally oblivious to it all and this was the way it would remain.

Brigee and Valerie clinked their wine glasses together, both cheerfully celebrating. "Here's to good health, happiness and families," Valerie announced, breathing easier and grinning widely at Brigee, both enormously relieved at the overall outcome.

Chapter Three

The atmosphere at Roselawn Cemetery was dismal, like the weather. During Heather's service, Margaret clung to her mother, wrecked with grief, trying to come to terms with having lost her dear friend, trying to comprehend how she was one of the survivors. Her mind reverted back to the incident, the moment when her mother screamed down the phone, to run. She obeyed; she did exactly what her mother ordered. Her gut instinct kicked in and she ran immediately to the exit. She stood sobbing, saturated in overwhelming guilt, riddled with anxiety, knowing she didn't go looking for Heather. Tormented with extreme regret, Margaret bowed her head low, acknowledging she fled with the others, running for her life, thinking only of herself. And there she stood, confused and tortured, guiltily peering down at the grave site, suffering immensely from survivor's remorse.

Marcus drew closer, gripping both Kath and Margaret within his arms, trying his upmost to offer them both comfort and solace. He was solemn but inwardly relieved. Thankfully, Margaret his daughter survived and was very much alive, on this cold damp miserable morning.

The proceedings began to break up and mourners surged forward, offering up their heartfelt condolences to the immediate family members. Grim dark hearses were seen leaving the burial ground. Twelve heart wrenching burials took place today, due to the senseless bombing. May god bless the souls which lay within. The forlorn mourner's began to disperse shortly afterwards, as Marcus gripped Kath and Margaret's hand and began making his way back to the car.

Margaret sat in the front passenger seat, directing Marcus how to get to Heather's parents house, which lay on the outskirts of Carrickfergus.

Kath sat silently in the back of the car, proud her daughter was trying her best to ease David and Maureen's pain, after losing their only daughter. Kath agreed to let Margaret stay at the farm and extended her holidays until the end of the month, allowing her an extra two weeks than was previously arranged, due to Heather's untimely death.

They travelled up a long winding lane, shielded by hedges of hawthorn, honeysuckle and rambling blackberry bushes, all appearing dormant and colourless. The fields stretching out before them appeared like a huge green multi-coloured, patchwork quilt. A large grey farm house soon came into view, with a large red tractor parked in the yard, standing adjacent to the left hand side of the building.

Filled with trepidation they exited the car slowly, breathing in the fresh country air before entering the home, situated on the outskirts of town. More cars were beginning to arrive, presumably to offer up there heartfelt condolences, to the remaining family members inside. Heather also had two brothers, Alex and Daniel. At least two sons had been spared death, caused by violence, raiding the North, yet again.

Margaret entered the home, quickly introducing Marcus and her mum. Maureen and David were pleasant in their mannerisms, easy going country folk, who were immensely enamoured by their Margaret. Maureen had become attached to young Margaret during her stay in Northern Ireland and the love bestowed upon her, was equally reciprocated by Margaret.

Joining in with a proverbial cup of tea, Kath and Marcus relaxed more; both amazed at the platefuls of homemade biscuits and array of cakes, baked and supplied by considerate friends.

Soon it was time for Kath and Marcus to leave. Maureen lovingly hung her arm around young Margaret's shoulder, reiterating it was no problem for them at all, for young Margaret to stay at their place. Maureen smiled down at her with tears in her eyes, before looking up.

"I know what she's doing Kath and you must be extremely proud of her. And yes, she is bringing me comfort, knowing she was so close to our dear Heather. May god rest her soul," she said, smiling weakly. "Hopefully some time spent together, will allow us to bring some closure to this whole dreadful affair," Maureen added wearily.

Kath and Marcus left and headed back to the Europa Hotel, situated in the heart of Belfast. It was an iconic hotel, remaining after several bombs had been planted in it and one sensed it would continue to do so, throughout these troubled times. This hotel was mainly chosen because it was close to Margaret if she needed them but far enough away from the home of Kath's parents, not to get recognised.

Arriving back, Kath instantly retreated to the bathroom. She stripped off and stepped under a hot steamy shower, trying her best to wash away the immense sorrow, lying seeped within her soul.

Gravely concerned, Marcus called out to her through the misty steam, requesting Kath's presence, as he wanted to head downstairs for dinner. The evening meal was a quiet affair, as they both sat mundanely contemplating their horrific day. Both were fully aware of how close they came to losing their daughter. Both overwhelmed by the immense suffering caused, by such a brutal and reckless act of terrorism.

Marcus stretched tenderly across the dining table, holding Kath's hand, peering deeply into her eyes. "Let's have an early night darling, you look absolutely exhausted," he appealed.

Kath nodded slowly in response, silently rising from the dinner table suffering from a headache. Marcus was soon tucking her into bed and gave her a gentle kiss on the forehead, before she drifted into a deep exhausted sleep.

The next morning the sunlight shone through the hotel window, as they both devoured their breakfast, delivered to their room earlier. After a second cup of coffee, Marcus told Kath to get dressed quickly, explaining she needed warm clothes as he intended to visit Bangor.

Later walking hand-in-hand along the promenade, the huge grey waves pounded against the solidly built stone wall, keeping mother nature at bay, when she was at her worst.

The shop fronts displayed tiny buntings hanging from their awnings in various colours, apparently used for a local celebration the previous week. They drifted aimlessly in and out of the local shops, before stopping for lunch at the Savoy.

Later in the afternoon, they both slowly wandered up to Ward Park. Sitting on a wooden bench in quiet reflection, both were sipping on hot coffees as they took in the sights, cherishing the total calmness.

Little mottled brown ducks were meandering along the muddy banks scurrying for food, as the odd one came in to land, gliding gracefully across the huge glass-like pond and coming to rest, before joining the others squawking nearby. The glossy prickly holly bushes were out in full bloom, adorned with vibrant red berries, punctuating the air with a magnificent fresh aroma. Next to the war memorial, an old U-Boat gun stood perched at the top end of the park, dominating the landscape, overlooking the neat green manicured lawns, lying serenely below.

Marcus rested one arm over Kath's shoulder, extremely pleased he decided to visit Bangor. He had intentionally made the effort to leave the Europa Hotel, to instil some peacefulness back into their lives.

Early evening they ate dinner, both ravenous from having spent the day outdoors walking around.

After retiring to their room, Marcus filled the bath up enticing Kath to join him; wanting her to relax. He was enormously pleased when she did.

She lay back resting languidly upon his torso, after stretching forward and retrieving her glass of wine. She closed her eyes, thankful for this quiet moment with Marcus.

He tenderly massaged her shoulders, easing away the high level of anxiety that had been built up, since receiving Margaret's excruciating phone call from Ireland.

She relaxed into him more, as he slowly brought his hands around to sooth away the tension in her tummy region. She moaned softly, grateful for his tender touch. His hands drifted higher and ever so gently, he began caressing and massaging her breasts. Leaning forward, he kissed her tenderly on the lips. Kath responded, closed her eyes and sighed peacefully, her body melting in sheer anticipation.

Easing out of the bath slowly, he took hold of Kath's hands gently in his, helping her out. Immediately wrapping her up in a large fluffy towel, he gradually began pampering her. Firstly, by drying her body, while placing tantalising kisses upon her erogenous zones. Fully aroused, he raised her chin upwards, allowing him to peer lovingly into her eyes, before kissing her slowly and seductively. Without another word spoken, he swept her up into his arms, swiftly making his way into the bedroom.

Resting her gently upon the bed, he continued his slow and sensual love-making, watching her relax and unfold, before his very eyes. She gave a whimsical sigh, as he went down on her. Her body rose up to meet his gentle seduction, as she nestled into the soft warm sheets. His love-making was deliberately leisurely and tantalising, driving her over the edge, before wrapping her up in his arms and taking her. She welcomed his manhood and immediately began moving in unison, appreciating his fullness and seduction. Filled with immense desire, Kath feverishly sought out his moist mouth, capturing his intense passion and yearning, while welcoming and meeting his desires.

He pressed into her more and she accepted him graciously and gratefully, wrapping her arms around him tightly. Their climaxes were proving to be unstoppable, with both rapidly losing control, their heated bodies pulsating and rising together as they came, forging their immense love for one another. Tears began streaming down Kath's face as she swallowed hard, feeling the pent up tension and fear seep out of her body. Elated, she peered up at Marcus. "Thank you my darling ... I needed you so badly."

He responded by kissing her deeply and she melted into his strong, masculine arms.

Soon afterwards Marcus tucked Kath tightly into bed, kissing her gently upon the nose. She gave him a blissful smile, totally relaxed and serene. He glided around to his side of the bed and climbed in, quickly switching off the bedside lamp. Turning around and wrapping his body neatly around hers, he nestled into her, discovering Kath was already sound asleep, causing Marcus to smile inwardly and relax. Hopefully, she had put this major tragedy behind her, he thought, before falling asleep.

Chapter Four

Kath could feel the warmth of the sunlight trickling in through the bedroom window, as she yawned and stretched lazily in her bed, before slowly opening her eyes. She was surprised to see Marcus sitting up on one elbow peering down at her, with a massive grin etched upon his handsome face.

"May I enquire Mr Garofoli, why you're so happy at this time of the morning?" she joked sleepily.

"I was watching you while you slept and you appeared so serene and angelic. I am truly blessed you love me so much," he responded sincerely.

She smiled. "My, my, Mr Garofoli, what fine woman could resist your irresistible charms, hmmm especially after last night's performance," she replied, laughing lightly.

Smiling, he teased her. "By the way, you were talking in your sleep last night, young lady."

"Oh was I indeed?" she purred. "I'm sure it was all good."

He frowned slightly and said "not really my love; you were tossing and turning a lot, calling out for Mary ... your mother."

Kath's smile instantly disappeared and she moved quickly to get out of bed. "What's happening with breakfast this morning?" she enquired lightly, changing the subject on purpose.

"Well, I took the liberty of ordering room service, if that's okay with you?"

"Great," Kath replied. "I'll go and take a quick shower to freshen up, before it arrives."

Completely naked, she strolled over to the bathroom door, flaunting her body provocatively. Her finely tuned mind, sensed he was watching her every move, making her glance over her shoulder straight away.

"Don't even think about it," she giggled.

In an instant Marcus was out of the bed bounding towards her. She quickly ran laughing into the bathroom and promptly locked the door.

"Aah and here I thought we could have continued on from where we left off from last night," Marcus said, as he chuckled from the other side of the door.

"You're a sex maniac," she declared jokingly. "Go and read a newspaper or something, while I have a shower," she laughed, turning the taps on straight away.

She climbed in amongst the hot steam, relieved to have the moment alone. Silently, tears began sliding down her cheeks as she stood, allowing the hot water to cascade and wash over her body. Anxiety was rapidly building up from within again, as she gulped back a sob, thinking about her parents. Thinking of the grief she had put them through. Reflecting upon all the lost years she missed, as she stood under the shower and cried some more.

Marcus retrieved the delivered newspaper, automatically shocked after opening it up. All the victims from the bombing peered up at him, young Heather included, with their names and ages scrolled beneath. Utterly gutted, he intuitively scrunched up the front page, before throwing the whole bloody newspaper in the bin. This was the last thing he wanted Kath to see, especially when it could have been so easily young Margaret's face, embellished on the front page of this morning's Belfast Telegraph. Damn the reporters to hell, he thought, the newspapers were making a real meal of it. His heart automatically went out to the parents and loved ones, after sighting the front page, along with its appalling headlines. Remembering only too well how it felt, having to deal with Caitlin's death displayed on the front pages of the Belfast Telegraph, many years ago.

Strolling across the room, a light knock on the door drew his attention immediately.

"Room service," a small voice echoed on the other side.

Immediately he opened the door to reveal a young uniformed maid behind a huge trolley, adorned with large silver trays. Fresh coffee aromas permeated the room, as the maid wheeled the trolley in; she smiled and closed the door quietly behind her as she left.

Marcus sung out, "hey Kath, breakfast has arrived!"

"I'll be there in a moment," she called out, reaching down to turn off the taps.

Marcus set up the small table beside the window, pouring out the coffees as Kath strolled across the room; she gave him a quick peck on the cheek, before sitting down.

"This smells delicious," she announced, lifting the lids off the silver trays. The bacon and eggs were scrumptious, along with the tomatoes and mushrooms, while not forgetting Denny's Cookstown sausages which were her favourite, smothered in HP sauce. They both tucked in eagerly, washing down the tasty breakfast with several cups of coffee.

"That was absolutely delicious," Marcus announced, rubbing his belly.

"If I keep eating like this, I'll be as fat as a fool in no time at all," Kath replied laughing.

Having shared breakfast, shortly afterwards, they both got dressed in warm winter clothes. Peering out the window, Kath acknowledged it was a blustery day outside, spotting some wrappers twirling and swirling up the street, driven by the gusty wind. Quickly tying her hair up in a pony tail, she put on a heavy coat and exited the room along with Marcus.

"Well Mr Garofoli, what sightseeing expeditions have you in mind for us today?" she enquired, smiling up at him.

"I thought we might take a trip to Newcastle and pay the Mourne Mountains a visit."

"Well, that would be grand," she declared, imitating an authentic Irish brogue while tucking her arm within his, as they quickly descended the stairs.

They journeyed by car up Belfast Road and on through to Carryduff, before passing through the lower end of Saintfield. This was a quaint little village, lying halfway between Downpatrick and the notorious Belfast. They drove past the huge stone hand-built wall belonging to the Crossgar Monastery, as they made their way towards Downpatrick. It was here, Marcus noticed Kath becoming extremely quiet.

Stopping at the traffic lights he glanced at her sideways, before cautiously broaching the subject. "It will have to be done my love, it's only fair and it's better sooner rather than later."

"I know, I know," she growled at him without warning, through clenched teeth. "What the hell do you expect me to do Marcus? Do you think I can just waltz in there and say, hi mum and dad, I'm your daughter and I'm very much alive after all? Oh and by the way, all those years ago were utter bullshit, just lies, so many bloody lies," she shouted, breaking down in tears.

Marcus immediately pulled off the road, removing both seat belts straight away, instantly wrapping her up in his arms. She clung to him sobbing and whimpering like a small child, overcome with extreme grief.

"I'm sorry for shouting at you Marcus. I'm frightened and scared ... I don't really know what to do. I don't want to give the pair of them a heart attack for Christ's sake, yet my heart's aching and I'm dying to see them both."

He kissed her softly on top of her forehead. "I'm sorry Kath; I really didn't mean to upset you. You know that, don't you?" She nodded in response. "Don't worry anymore about it my love. I'll take care of it and we'll get it sorted over the next few days." He gave her another reassuring hug, comforting her before passing her a handkerchief.

Starting up the car he continued to make his way up to Newcastle, leaving Kath to sort out her thoughts, in silence.

The countryside was immensely green, the cream woolly sheep with their blackened faces were striking, scattered throughout the picturesque landscape.

Soon they arrived; the main street hadn't changed much over the years. The bright blue of the Bon Bon shop was as vibrant as ever, displaying its bucketfuls of colourful windmills twirling manically in the wind. The rowing boats were tied up in the park opposite, with the Mourne Mountains towering over them in its entire, green clad splendour, appearing majestic.

Marcus immediately pulled over and parked kerbside, before whisking her out of the car. She was practically dragged across the road and taken into Barry's Amusements. She laughed out loud, as Marcus purchased a handful of tickets and took her around to the dodgem cars. She couldn't help but smile as they swirled around the circuit, laughing as they happily bumped into each other, both reminiscing about days spent in their early childhood. Days when nothing was ever taken seriously, days when they were both carefree. Seated in their digitally make-believe racing cars, both were laughing as they inserted their coins into the hungry waiting slots. Kath broke into squeals of delight, heavy handed when pulling down on her steering wheel to swiftly take the corners, as both manically raced towards the finish line, before their times dropped out.

Cuddling up together, they endured the steep dips and sharp curves of the big dipper, screaming loudly as they went. Both of them ended up thoroughly spent, laughing happily while sharing a massive pink candy floss between them.

Marcus was pleased it lifted Kath's mood immensely, eliminating the uneasiness experienced on their journey on the way up and it was exactly what they needed.

They got into the car shortly afterwards, deciding to visit Tollymore Forest Park for old time's sake. As they drove down the Deodar Cedar Avenue, they both admired the spectacular scenery, making a striking feature as they entered the park.

They parked their vehicle before purchasing some sandwiches and coffee at the little kiosk, both deciding to wander down to sit upon the old stone built bridge, with the Shimna River rushing frantically beneath them. The air was fresh and crisp as they sat sipping on their coffees and munching into their amply filled sandwiches. They took in the outstanding natural beauty of the conifers and the broad leafed woodlands which lay before them, while eating and sitting in silence together.

Taking each other's hand after lunch, they followed a trail descending down to the tree lined riverbank. Wandering along they came across a deep rock pool and a magnificent cascading waterfall. As they continued walking, the sunrays would intermittently burst through the treetops along their path, dispersing a little warmth. The sun was highlighting the magnificent and all encompassing Himalayan cedars, with their wide spreading branches accentuating their blue-green foliage, adding to the enchanting atmosphere and serenity, which mirrored their frame of mind. It was indeed a perfect ending, to a fun filled day.

They arrived back at the Europa Hotel much later in the evening, after having stopped off at the Burrendale for high tea on their way home. It was a reasonably new restaurant and they enjoyed the fresh salmon, served up upon a bed of crunchy vegetables and garnished with a mouth-watering sauce. They both indulged in a yummy dessert, before finishing off with an Irish coffee.

The smell of pine drifted throughout the restaurant, with the logs in the huge stone built fireplace burning merrily away, crackling and sparking under the immense radiant heat.

Soft Irish music was playing in the background, adding to the ambience created within the room. It was true, as Kath sat thinking about how the Irish were known throughout the entire world for their welcoming hospitality. Tonight was simply perfect, proving to be extremely therapeutic, as she smiled compassionately across at Marcus, thoroughly relaxed.

The next few days were spent shopping for Brigee, Rachel, Valerie and a few more friends. Kath laughed, she would never be forgiven if she arrived home without a present for Rachel, with Marcus readily agreeing.

The days of various sightseeing expeditions helped Kath immensely, allowing her to settle down and recover from the initial shock of almost having lost her daughter. However, the dilemma in relation to her parents hung over her like a huge grey cloud, yet to be resolved.

On Thursday evening while lying in bed together, Marcus raised the subject gently. "Please don't get angry with me Kath but I thought we could possibly visit your folks tomorrow?"

She looked up at him, his face appearing gentle and compassionate in the lamp light. "Mmm it's a possibility but what's the plan?"

Marcus smiled, instantly sliding down on his pillow. "I thought if I visited your parents tomorrow, I could explain I was passing by and decided to drop in for a few minutes, automatically giving me an opportunity to gauge their reaction."

Kath nodded sedately. "But how do I fit into the equation and how will you introduce me?"

Marcus paused momentarily before saying "initially, you could wait in the car and if they appeared receptive, I could come out and fetch you, before formally introducing Kath Blake to them both".

Tears welled up in Kath's eyes. "It will be extremely difficult, when I first meet them again," she gulped.

"I know darling," Marcus interjected "but I'll be there helping and supporting you."

"And then what?" Kath questioned.

"Well, you can judge the situation and decide whether or not to tell them who you really are."

Kath looked relieved and Marcus was confident his plan would allow Kath to at least move forward. Perhaps this way the issue would finally be resolved. He leaned over giving her a goodnight kiss and she reciprocated, before stretching over and switching off the bedside lamp.

Morning arrived much too quickly for Kath. She had a restless night and woke up agitated, knowing what lay ahead.

Breakfast was eaten quickly by Marcus and he noticed Kath only toyed with her food. He didn't mention anything, because his main objective was to drive her to Downpatrick and hopefully get her to communicate with her parents.

The journey was slow and arduous for Kath, her heart was racing and her palms were hot and sweaty by the time they approached Crossgar.

"STOP Marcus, stop the car," she urgently shouted, instantly startling him. "I need a cigarette for god's sake ... I'm feeling awfully sick." Her demeanour was portraying panic and tension, visibly etched across her pale waiflike face.

Marcus persisted. "Look, I'll run into the bottle shop and pick up a bottle of your father's favourite whiskey. Chivas Regal, isn't it?" Kath reluctantly nodded a reply. Marcus left without delay, not wanting to strike up a conversation, knowing full well she would attempt to sabotage his plans, coaxing him to take her back to the hotel immediately.

Arriving back at the car he noticed Kath was sitting inside, pale and withdrawn. He immediately switched on the radio, before driving off. Soon, they were driving up her parent's, long and winding lane. Rounding the corner, he noticed Kath anxiously fighting back tears. His heart went out to her but he knew this challenge had to be met head-on. Driving into the yard, an old collie dog came rushing out, yelping, barking and kicking up a real stink.

Marcus stopped the car and a voice called out "stop that Patch, come here boy."

Kath turned around and instantly recognised her father. He looked much older, rounder and was still wearing a tweed cap, his proverbial trait. She swung around nervously to Marcus, literally green in colour. "Go Marcus; go quickly for god's sake before he comes over here."

Marcus quickly grabbed the bottle of whiskey and briskly jumped out of the car. Walking swiftly around to the back of the vehicle, he instantly began striding hastily towards Joe.

"How on earth have you been?" Marcus called out. "I was in town and thought I would pay you a visit?"

Joe let out a loud gasp. "Well in the name of heavens, is that you Marcus? Mary and I were only talkin' about you the other evenin'. How in the hell are you lad? You're lookin' grand, might I add."

Marcus gave him a heartfelt hug, as tears of gratitude welled up in Joe's eyes.

"Well come on in lad, our Mary will get a big surprise. This is great; I still can't believe you're here."

They both wandered through the back door, as Kath sat in the car ever so still, with tears trickling down her cheeks, falling on to her lap.

Mary was delighted and utterly gobsmacked when Marcus walked in on her. Instantly, she ran over and hugged him, with tears streaming down her cheeks. "Ach isn't this grand Joe, isn't he lookin' powerful well, in the name of heavens Marcus, you've hardly changed at all."

Before long, they were chatting excitedly away, exchanging news and laughing like old times. Mary offered to make a pot of tea and Marcus explained he had Kath sitting outside in the car, waiting for him.

"Why didn't you say lad, sure I'll go and fetch the wee lass."

Before Marcus could object, Mary was gone like the wind.

Kath was startled when the car door suddenly bolted open.

"Well hello Kath, I'm Mary. Sorry for leavin' you out here for so long luv but that big lad of yurs only just told us you've been sitting out here all on your own. He's a silly oul ijet," she laughed. She grabbed Kath by the hand. "Holy Mary mother of god, your hands are freezin' child dear. That Marcus one should get a fair clout across the ear hole, for leavin' such a fine lookin' lass out here all on her own."

Kath couldn't help but laugh, as she was being led by her mother across the yard. She hadn't changed a bit, Kath mused but I wonder how she will react when she finds out, who I really am.

Entering the house Kath was totally amazed, as it seemed like time had stood still. With very few changes having been made, Kath instantly melted, discovering it was ever so comforting. Gaining her senses, she glared across at Marcus, who instantly shrugged his shoulders and pulled a face. She automatically sensed there was no way he could ever stop her mother. She smiled over at him; laughing inwardly, her mum was like a tornado, she thought and when she got something into her head, there was no stopping her.

"In the name of Jesus Marcus Garofoli, you gotta get a good beltin'. This young lady is frozen stiff sittin' out there all on her own, the poor wee thing."

Joe automatically rose from his seat, offering Kath his chair. "Come and sit yurself down here luv and get some heat back in yur bones."

Mary disappeared into the kitchen. You could hear the banging and clashing of the cupboard doors, as cutlery and cups were being brought out, before she sung out to whoever would listen. "I'm just putting the kettle on luvs and I won't be too long."

Joe smiled across at Kath, she looked a nice sort of a wee lass, he thought. He was glad Marcus met someone, although he noticed there was no ring on her finger, mores' the pity, he sighed.

"Marcus said he met you in Sydney luv, at least it's a hell of a lot warmer over there than it is over here, ay."

Kate smiled up at him. "It most certainly is Joe, although it can become extremely hot and sticky in the summer months" using the thickest Australian accent she could conjure up. She didn't want to take any chances in getting recognised. Although, she didn't think they suspected her at all, which allowed her to relax a little bit more.

Mary then came charging into the living room, setting down a plateful of sandwiches on the coffee table, before quickly disappearing and returning swiftly with biscuits and a homemade cake.

"Mary, a cup of tea would've been fine," Kath announced.

"I don't think so young lady. You being all the way out from Australia 'n' all, besides I can't have our Marcus talkin' bad about us," Mary laughed, disappearing again to retrieve the teapot no doubt.

Marcus sat down next to Kath holding her hand in his, while peering into her eyes. She smiled and nodded. Marcus sunk down into his chair more and relaxed; very pleased things were beginning to work out.

Idle chit chat took precedence and a wonderful time was had by everyone present. Kath noticed how familiar they were with Marcus and she was pleased how easily Marcus fell into the way of things. She sighed, looking around and surveying the whole scene. It seemed like old times, except her two brothers Michael and Declan were missing. Nostalgia was kicking in speedily and tears began welling up in her eyes; Kath rose quickly heading towards the door, on the pretence of needing a toilet.

"Just run upstairs luv and it's the second door on the right once you reach the top of the landing," Mary called out after her.

Kath ran the tap, after cupping her hands together; she managed to splash some cold water on her face. She peered into the mirror contemplating on how well she had been doing but was annoyed at herself, for suddenly becoming overwhelmed. She desperately wanted to wrap her arms around her mum and dad, telling them how sorry she was, how she missed and loved them both so much, explaining the constant yearning in her heart.

Marcus enquired cautiously from downstairs. "Are you okay darling?"

"Yes, I'm coming now and we really have to go," she emphasised to Marcus, calling out to him nervously.

Arriving back downstairs, Marcus instantly rose to his feet. "Joe and Mary, we both had a truly marvellous time but we really need to be making tracks. I was supposed to only drop in for a few minutes and that was over two hours ago," he laughed.

Mary immediately went over and hugged Kath. "It's been wonderful meetin' you 'n' all. Now make sure you look after that big lad of ours, 'cause he has a special place in our hearts" Mary confided, smiling across at Marcus.

Joe shook Kath's hand. "Now you have to promise to drop in again, before you head back to Australia and bring that big man with you. Sure, it was like old times for us, 'n' it would warm the cockles of yur heart."

Kath waved from the car, smiling and promising to visit again real soon, as Marcus manoeuvred the car and drove out of the yard tooting the horn, waving also. "What did you think my love; I bet you it wasn't half as hard as you anticipated?"

Kath beamed across at him, settling her hand on top of his. "Thank you my love, it was extraordinary and you were right Marcus, it was unfinished business, something that had to be attended to immediately." She lifted his hand up from his lap and kissed it.

Marcus immediately stopped the car in the middle of the lane and undid his seatbelt; leaning over straight away he lovingly kissed her. She surrendered, reciprocating his kiss tenderly, before shortly interrupting, by joking.

"You better get a move on luv or you'll have me da's tractor right up the arse of yur car any minute now," in the broadest Irish accent she could possibly muster up.

He immediately released her, laughing loudly. "To be sure, to be sure," he teased, swiftly buckling up his seatbelt and driving off.

The next few days were spent relaxing around the hotel and Marcus noticed Kath was extremely happy. She was absolutely delighted she had visited her parents; they frequently were mentioned in her conversations, without any difficulty. A wonderful advancement, considering less than a week ago, she couldn't bring herself around to mention their names.

Marcus waited patiently for her to recommend their next visit; this would demonstrate she was ready to move forward and perhaps divulge her real identity. He didn't want to pressure her. Kath inevitably would have to make the next move whenever she felt comfortable, which would allow her to progress confidently to the next level. On Wednesday after breakfast, Marcus got a surprise.

"How would you feel if we paid a visit to my folks today?" she enquired, smiling across at him over a cup of coffee.

He was inwardly pleased, his heart instantly churning in somersaults for her but decided instead, to act objectively. By doing so, he was relieving her of any pressure, inwardly acknowledging it was a major decision and one of which held so much potential.

Chapter Five

The journey to Kath's parents this time around, was a joyous occasion. Before they arrived at their destination, Kath requested Marcus to stop at Saintfield, allowing her time to gather up a few groceries to take over with them. Memories seeped happily through her mind, as they crossed the street to the home bakery. Smells of freshly baked soda bread saturated the air, as they entered the shop. Displays of dainty, delicate pastries were pleasing to the eye. Kath purchased soda and wheaten farls, along with two oven treacles, her father's favourite.

"I'll have a dozen of mixed pastries as well please," Kath insisted.

The young assistant dressed in a chequered pink overall smiled, while retrieving pink coconut haystacks, currant squares, along with some cream horns, chatting socially as she arranged them delicately in a box.

After leaving, they continued up the street to Kelly's Butchers. Kath smiled as she entered, the sawdust lay thick upon the tiled floor, instantly noticing it hadn't changed a bit.

Mr Kelly stood proud behind his counter of freshly displayed meat. He wore a dark blue and white striped apron tied around his midriff, which was noticeably pouchier than when she saw him last. His red ruddy face bore a happy demeanour.

"Can I help you young lady? You're not from around these parts, I see."

Kath was pleased no one had a clue who she was, she felt like a voyeur peeking in on people's lives, going undetected. "No, I'm visiting from Australia actually and decided to pop in to purchase some things for a friend?"

"Righty oh then, what will you be havin' " drawing out his large butcher's knife and sharpening it in front of her, an old familiar trait.

Kath quickly ordered the displayed pork fillet, along with some sirloin steaks, sausages, mince roll, lamb chops, liver and three huge pot roasts. She remembered her mum was an expert in cooking these for Sunday lunch.

"That comes to two hundred and five pounds and ninety-three pence," Mr Kelly declared, seemingly pleased with himself.

Well, why wouldn't he be, Kath thought. She had probably been equivalent to ten of his normal customers. She mentally took note and reminded herself how lucky she was to be living in Australia. At least the meat was one third of the cost over there.

Marcus retrieved the shopping bags as they made their way back to the car.

"One more stop," Kath mentioned, glancing across at Marcus as he filled the back seat of the car.

He smiled and said "the lolly shop no doubt," knowing her so well and raising an eyebrow, as they both laughed out loud in unison.

Entering Mullen's transported her back to her childhood days, as she stood at the old wooden counter peering across at the tall colourful glass jars, filled with the most delicious sweets imaginable.

Instantly melting with joy, she enthusiastically ordered Cinnamon Lozengers, Raspberry Ruffles, Liquorice All Sorts, Jap Desserts and of course, not forgetting the Brandy Balls.

She laughed while ordering these; she almost choked to death on one of them when she was a small child. She recalled quite clearly being told not to touch them. However, being the little rascal she was, she managed to climb up on to a chair and retrieve one from the bag on the sideboard. Needless to say, gasping for breath and blue in the face, her father soon had her dangling by her feet, shaking her upside down in order for the offending object to fall out.

Soon, both Kath and Marcus were making their way up to the homestead, both happy in their thoughts, both very much aware this was indeed a re-enactment of their yester-years. Patch the dog came running out barking, rapidly wagging his tail when Marcus happily bent down to pet him. Mary and Joe came out to welcome them very shortly afterwards, both were overwhelmed with the amount of grocery bags.

"In the name of heavens, what on earth were you thinkin' kids? Were you intendin' to feed the five thousand?"

Kath beamed at her mum. "We enjoyed your hospitality so much the other day; we didn't want to impose on your generosity. So we bought just a small handful of groceries."

"Aah there's no use in talkin' to them Joe, one's just as bad as the other," Mary laughed, guiding them both inside.

Kath followed Mary into the kitchen, noticing the old Aga stove was still sitting in the middle of the room, slowly smouldering away, creating a warm environment on such a cold wintery morning. Cupboard doors were flung open and closed again, as the groceries were dispersed into their rightful places and the kettle was filled up, for a welcoming cuppa. Mary suddenly turned around and hugged Kath deeply.

"You know Kath; you've just made my Joe so happy, as you have reminded us of one of our own. You certainly have brought this house back to life again," as tears filled her eyes.

Kath felt emotional, swallowing hard to keep her own tears back. She held Mary tightly, giving her a quick kiss on the cheek before releasing her. "Right, where do you keep the sugar Mary?" Kath enquired, grateful for thinking quickly.

Immediately it distracted Mary from her melancholy, intuitively making her spring into action straight away, much to Kath's relief.

A little later, the women entered the living room, Mary with a hot steaming teapot in hand and Kath with a plateful of pastries. The two men were sitting by the fire talking, both seemingly happy and content. Soon they were all sitting tucking into the cream cakes, enjoying the serene atmosphere and the great company, chatting amicably amongst themselves.

Marcus and Joe decided to take a stroll outside, leaving the two ladies to tidy up inside, both chatting away pleasantly with not a care in the world. Kath queried the toilet whereabouts again and Mary directed her upstairs.

Kath could hear the clattering going on downstairs in the kitchen and decided to peek inside her old bedroom. She inhaled deeply, as the door was opened. Everything was exactly as she had left it, when she moved out to her flat on the Ormeau Road, all those years ago. Old Raggedy Ann, her ragdoll, sat high on the top shelf above her patchwork quilted bed. The pale pink curtains had faded but the pretty white dressing table looked as dainty as ever. Aged books stood upright on the shelves in the far corner of her room and Kath found herself sitting upon the bed clutching Fluffy, her teddy bear from bygone years. Without warning, tears began rolling down her cheeks, as fond memories rapidly flooded her mind.

"Caitlin?"

Kath swung around instantly. Her mother stood above with outstretched arms, tears streaming down her face.

"Mum," Kath croaked, rising up immediately, wrapping her up in her arms. "I'm so sorry mum. I'm so sorry" she howled. "I didn't have any choice."

"Hush now my love, hush. I knew you would come back one day dear. I told your dad and he thought I'd lost the plot but a mum knows these things Caitlin." She dragged a strand of Kath's wet hair and tucked it behind her ear, before giving her a gentle kiss upon her cheek.

Kath smiled down, grabbing her mum more tightly around the waist, while more tears were banking up again, as she let out another huge sob.

They sat down on the bed together, hugging, kissing and laughing, before Mary announced "let's go downstairs and tell your father, although I think he has his suspicions."

"Does he ... know?" Kath questioned.

"Well, the first time you were here, you automatically put two spoonfuls of sugar in his tea for starters" she laughed. "Then you got up and told him to sit down in his favourite chair. Moments before you stood with your back to the fire warming your bum as you usually did before."

Kath smiled. "Well obviously I wasn't as smart as I thought," Kath declared, happily. "Here I am thinking I was clever and nobody suspected a thing."

Mary stretched over, taking Kath's hands in hers. "My dear, dear, beautiful daughter, when you know and luv a child as much as we did and you suspect they were acting out of character, you start willin' them to be safe, hopin' and prayin' they got away, not quite believing they're dead. You're always watching, wondering and thinkin' that maybe ... just maybe ... one day, they would come back home to visit."

41

Kath looked at her in complete surprise. "But what about my disguise, my black hair and everything?"

Mary chortled. "Well of course I would know you, even if yur hair was green, yur skin yella and you had one leg missin'," laughing heartily again.

As Kath and Mary made their way down the stairs, hand in hand, the front door swung open and Joe and Marcus strolled in.

"Dad," Kath shouted with deep felt emotions, bounding down the steps two at a time.

Joe looked up and cried out in joy. "Caitlin darling," as Kath jumped into his long awaited arms. "My, my, yur mum was right my dear child, she always swore you would come back one day." A huge and gut wrenching sob escaped his throat, as he wrapped his arms around his long lost daughter. They stood momentarily, bathed in each other's love, totally oblivious to the outside world.

Marcus stood transfixed, tears welling up in his eyes; totally elated with the loving sight unfolding before him. He peered up at Mary, who stood mesmerised upon the stairwell; tears were running down her cheeks freely. Marcus's heart felt as if it was going to burst, thinking about how he had longed for this day and how he wished it had come ten or fifteen years earlier. But he must be grateful, grateful now at long last; they were reunited once again. Together as they once were, together as a family.

Needless to say, the morning progressed quickly, Marcus noticed Kath touching, hugging and holding her parents spontaneously. Smiling constantly, she reminded him of his dear Caitlin a long time ago. Now she was known as Kath Blake a beautiful, intelligent, business lady and she belonged to him.

Kath took her time, to meticulously explain to her parents why she had to leave. They listened, enamoured by her resilience and bravery, both proud of her achievements in Australia, nodding in unison as she explained the gruesome bombing before she left. Both listened with solemn eyes, stretching forward and holding a hand each, when she filled them in on the horrific facts.

After a few hours of tears, laughter, sharing and divulging their lives and recapping on what they had missed, it left Marcus admiring Joe and Mary even more. A magnificent display of unconditional love was shown with such empathy, both parents automatically forgiving the anguish their daughter had put them through. Both truly grateful for her return and ever so thankful, she was home once again.

Soon mother and daughter were up again, flying into the kitchen to prepare a lunch for the ravenous bunch.

Joe stood up and walked over to the cabinet. Stretching in, he dragged out the bottle of Chivas Regal. Putting a nip into two glasses he wandered slowly over to Marcus. "Well son, here's to our Caitlin, oops I mean Kath's return and to a happy future for you both." Both clinked their whiskey glasses together, smiling as they toasted, before downing the lot in one go.

The women returned with the lunches made, followed by a steaming pot of tea and they all sat around the table chatting amicably amongst themselves, happy and content, like old times.

By the afternoon, Joe and Mary were fully aware they had two granddaughters; both were alarmed and appalled, recognising how close young Margaret had come to meeting her maker. They agreed they would meet young Margaret but Joe and Mary thought it was best to keep a low profile and for both of their identities to remain a secret.

"You never know what those buggers might get up to Kath," Joe exclaimed, shaking his head thoughtfully. "You did such a good job disguising everything when you left and we don't want to jeopardise anyone now luv."

Mary nodded frantically, agreeing. "Your dad's right luv, let's face it, Finbar has relatives and the talk for revenge 'n' all went on for a number of years over here, after the bombing."

They decided that Margaret would be told Mary and Joe were dear family friends of Marcus's family, explaining to her that he treated them as his adopted Aunt and Uncle, thereby protecting everyone adequately, with Marcus readily agreeing.

The evening arrived. "You look exhausted Kath, it's time we made tracks," Marcus suggested.

"I am darling," Kath murmured "but in a good way. I feel a huge weight has been lifted off my shoulders," glancing over at her parents smiling.

"Marcus is right luv, you best be going, we can catch up again tomorrow."

Kath fell asleep on the drive home, contented having divulged her identity to her parents. Happy she no longer had to carry the horrendous burden of guilt around anymore. Marcus escorted her to the elevator, before making their way up to their room. Slowly helping her to undress, Kath looked up and began giggling. "You'd think I was drunk Marcus but I'm truly euphoric and happy." Giving him the biggest smile ever, as he tucked her into bed.

"Goodnight my love. You braved the storm as usual my darling. I am ever so proud of you. It wasn't an easy task by any means," Marcus said and tenderly kissed her on the forehead.

She eased down into the bed gently and fell asleep immediately.

Marcus sat on a chair and lit up a cigarette, the red glow reflecting off the window as he peered outside, on to the streets of Belfast. A few cars travelled eastwards, wipers flicking over windscreens as the rain began to fall. Marcus sat silently smoking, reflecting upon Kath's life, enthralled and daunted by her sheer courage and stamina. Overwhelmed on how she turned full circle, piecing her life back bit by little bit, clawing her way through endless obstacles, in order to get where she was today. Tears filled his eyes, as he sat in his solitary silence, encased in the darkness of the room, as he drew down on his cigarette one last time.

He crawled into bed beside her, sliding over to her warm curled up body. He delicately wrapped his loving arms around her, embracing her, glad she had survived. Glad she made peace with her parents and above all, glad they could spend happy times together again, he mused, before falling into a well earned sleep.

The next day they decided to visit Margaret up at Carrickfergus, as they had only a week remaining, before heading back to Australia. Maureen and David received them with open arms, making them feel extremely welcome; both were singing the praises of young Margaret.

Kath surmised the extended stay had done wonders for her young daughter, as she wandered around the household confidently.

Marcus decided to take everyone out for lunch as it was a glorious sunny day. They sat around the lunch table, communicating happily amongst themselves. Kath watched Maureen subconsciously gaze at her daughter, frequently appearing almost as if she was lost in a world of her own. Obviously pining for Heather, having to face the brutal reality, she would no longer be coming home. It was decided, Kath and Marcus would pick Margaret up in two days, leaving a little time for visiting Marcus's relatives and for sightseeing as well.

Kath gave Margaret a reassuring hug. "Take care love and we'll be back to collect you soon. Oh by the way, I spoke to Rachel last night and she misses you like crazy."

Margaret smiled, a faraway smile, looking a little lost as tears filled her eyes. "It's going to be hard leaving," she whispered.

"I know darling but I'll be here to help, don't worry everything will be fine." Kath turned and walked towards Marcus, signalling to him it was time to leave. They said their farewells quickly and drove towards Belfast silently, both distracted by their fragmented thoughts.

A few days later they were heading up the dual carriageway again, both were looking forward to picking up Margaret. Marcus was especially glad; looking forward to the moment when he could spend time with his daughter, although mind you, that was another obstacle to overcome. Both Kath and he had decided that informing her that he was her father could be carried out later, when they got back home to Australia.

The goodbyes were made; inciting a tearful and emotional experience. Both Maureen and David affectionately conveyed their appreciation to young Margaret, for staying with them. They presented her with a gift and told her to open it up later, before giving her one final hug. "If you're ever over here visiting again, please drop in and see us," Maureen reiterated, with huge sorrowful eyes as they drove off.

Further down the road, Margaret was excited after receiving the news they were visiting Giant's Causeway, she previously hadn't had the time or opportunity to do so. The day was relaxing for them and Margaret was amazed at the hexagon shaped volcanic rocks ascending skywards, like huge giant steps, splattered along the spectacular jagged coastline.

She buzzed around taking photos; Marcus and her mum were given instructions to look seaward, knowing the massive waves behind them would create a superb backdrop. She had them standing together, facing each other, balancing precariously on a rock. "Now Marcus, you must give mum a romantic kiss so I can catch it on camera," giggling and instantly raising her camera into position to focus.

Marcus beamed down at Kath, "a man's gotta do what he's told." He immediately took Kath into his arms and kissed her tenderly. A crowd nearby expressed a loud roar of approval, as Kath blushed.

Margaret screamed out "cut." Chuckling loudly, obviously enjoying the moment, extremely pleased her mother was having a loving relationship with Marcus. Everyone enjoyed the day immensely and Margaret was fascinated by the Irish bus tour guide who explained the Ulster folk tale about Finn McCool and how Giant's Causeway came about in the first place.

The following day they decided to shop in Belfast, allowing Margaret to purchase some gifts for her friends back home. The little Irish dolls were quaint, so she got a couple of them for Rachel. The Aran sweaters were beautiful, so without hesitation, Margaret straight away purchased two for her best friends and one for herself, which would be perfect to wear at University, with a pair of jeans and boots in the winter time. Wandering along Royal Avenue everyone was chatting amicably, all of them deciding to stop for a coffee, before heading back to the Europa Hotel.

Without warning, a deafening and massive explosion took place. Instantly glass went shattering into the air, with debris and dust forcibly strewn halfway across the street, landing close by. A woman came stumbling out of the wreckage, pierced with shards of glass, mixed in with blood and grime, clutching a screaming toddler, splattered in blood. She stood trembling in broad daylight, utterly confused, shocked beyond comprehension. Her eyes were demon-like. Terrified, she started screaming, a blood curdling scream that reached and touched your very soul.

Kath stood still, traumatised to the core. Her legs began wobbling, as she clutched desperately for Marcus's arm, before bending over and vomiting straight into the gutter. Margaret stood deadly still, pale and lost looking, as huge blobs of tears streamed rapidly down her cheeks. Marcus was stunned; his ears still ringing as he hastily grabbed them both. "Come with me now," he barked, clutching them by the hand and leading them away as quickly as possible from the bloody scene, instructing them to look straight ahead.

Injured citizens were appearing on the street, completely disorientated and wailing uncontrollably. Limbs were missing on charred bodies, complete chaos and mayhem reigned, the area appearing very much like a war zone, while the screeching sirens drew closer, leaving a horrific chill running down Marcus's spine.

Hurriedly, they made their way up to Oxford Street to retrieve his car. He automatically pushed Kath into the back seat along with Margaret, driving off and accelerating as fast as he legally could, recognising a heavy grave silence hanging in the air. He quickly switched on the radio to be met with news and reports of the recent bombing. He began manically switching from station to station, sighing out loud in utter frustration, before abandoning the whole idea. He hurriedly decided to head up to Joe and Mary's place, pulling in quickly at a nearby petrol station, to refuel and to grab a packet of cigarettes. Passing over the money, he was startled to observe his hands were shaking terribly. Shivering involuntarily while waiting for his change, he fought back tears, knowing how close he had come to losing his family, yet again.

Mary and Joe were surprised to see them all so soon. Marcus, along with the others hastily made their way into the house, before offering up a greeting. Marcus explained very quickly what had happened. Mary froze automatically, alarmed by what had taken place, realising how close they had come to dying. Joe sat Margaret and Kath down beside the fire, thinking they were the colour of a livin' corpse, before scurrying off to get a few glasses. Quickly he poured Kath and Marcus a whiskey each; "it will help calm the nerves."

Kath nodded, peering into the fiery flames. She gulped down her whiskey, accompanying Margaret, with her watered down version. Marcus lit up a cigarette and passed it over to Kath, who took it gratefully, her hands noticeably trembling.

"Are you okay love?" Marcus enquired gently.

Swallowing hard she nodded, as large tears began to appear. "I'm beginning to hate this country Marcus. What the hell possess these people? Christ, we were nearly killed. For what, I ask you? Equal rights, power and religion, personally I feel it's a load of bullshit. Many countries from around the world have been caught supplying ammunition, contributing to the chaos and misery. I really don't understand. You've got beautiful people in the North and South; with a variety of nationalities, different religions and from all walks of life, ninety-nine percent of the population want nothing to do with these god-damn troubles. Yet, you've got small percentages that are cruel brutal animals, ruining it for everyone else, by bombing, killing and maiming. It doesn't make any sense, no sense at all," she sobbed hopelessly.

Mary flung her arms around her daughter. "There, there, luv, now don't go gettin' yourself all worked up and upset, the buggers aren't worth it. Besides, I believe in karma. Now why don't you have another cigarette and go for a nice walk with our Marcus. It will help you relax and unwind, while we look after young Margaret for you."

After Kath and Marcus exited the room and left the house, Mary went straight away to comfort young Margaret sitting quietly beside the fire, who noticeably hadn't made a single comment, during the heated discussions. Mary put her arms around her, drawing her closely to her chest. Margaret instantly expelled a huge sob, breaking down and crying profusely. Mary spoke gently to her, explaining she mustn't dwell on the incident and told her not to link the incidents together. As the other bombing was over three weeks ago and an entirely different situation.

Mary took her hands and peered into Margaret's pale, sweet, young face. "Now my child, you mustn't start blamin' yourself. Thinkin' you were the cause of this, 'n' that you possess some sort of bad luck or curse, because that's a load of old baloney, do you understand what I'm saying young lady?"

Margaret looked up through tear stained eyes and nodded. "Yes, I understand what you're saying Mary and yes you're right, it was all an appalling coincidence."

"That's my girl," Mary croaked happily. "Now let's go into the kitchen together and we'll make a nice wee cup of tea, before we drive ourselves roun' the ben' " Mary said smiling.

Marcus and Kath walked across the fields, both appreciative of the greenery, which was proving to be calming, as they inhaled the fresh country air.

"Kath, today's bombing obviously would have reopened old wounds and unpleasant memories from many years ago. However, you've got me here beside you this time around and a beautiful daughter back at the farm, not forgetting about young Rachel at home in Australia."

Kath nodded in retrospect. "I know love, it was one hell of a shock, those poor innocent people, the young mother and child and …"

"Stop right there Kath, you can't afford to buy into these senseless murders, don't go there, it will eat you up and destroy you. Let's try and put it out of our minds, especially for young Margaret's sake, as this is inevitably a major setback for her and she'll need our full attention."

Kath nodded in recognition, fully aware of what Marcus was saying, knowing he was absolutely right. "Okay love," she replied, giving him a watery smile, obviously still shell shocked from the horrifying ordeal.

Entering the house together, they were amazed to find young Margaret in the kitchen, laughing along with Mary. Their hearts melted, as they joined them.

Margaret swung around straight away, smiling. "Mary was telling me funny stories about when Marcus was younger and how he loathed his father when it came to the shooting season. Explaining to me how you took the dogs out at night, chasing every darn pheasant as far away as possible, on your father's estate." Her eyes dancing in delight, while relaying the story back to them.

Marcus and Kath smiled in unison. Indeed those were the days, the good old days, Marcus thought. Hopefully he would have many more in Australia with his new family, after he got Kath agreeing to marry him.

Mary and Joe insisted they stay at their place for the evening, allowing them to avoid notorious Belfast. "Besides, you can't go back to Australia without sampling the best soup in Ireland," Mary chuckled, as she fetched a large saucepan from the fridge.

Marcus nodded across at Kath in agreement.

"Okay we'll settle here for the evening. The country air will probably do us all a world of good," Kath announced, rising quickly to help her mum set the table.

Large bowls of delicious homemade vegetable soup, together with warm crusty rolls, were washed down with a glass of cider.

Soon, the three women were tidying up in the kitchen, while the men returned to the front room. "That was delicious Mary but I hope we're not putting you out," Kath sighed, hanging the tea towel over the Aga railing.

"Listen luv, Joe and I are enjoying the company and we want you all to make yurselves at home." Mary then glanced instantly across at Margaret. "The water is scalding luv and almost ready to jump out of the pipes. If you want, you can have a lovely hot bath and I'll hoke you out a pair of pyjamas."

"That would be great. Thank you Mary," Margaret answered, stretching over to give her a massive hug. Kath watched contently, smiling. Her heart was full.

Kath was soon up in her old bedroom, tucking Margaret into her old brass bed.

"This is real pretty mum, isn't it," Margaret remarked. Her face all pink and warm, matching the pretty pink flannelette pyjamas, Mary had loaned her.

"Yes it is my darling; you must get some sleep now, as it's been a rather exhausting day."

"I will mum, I am absolutely dog-tired and ready to fall fast asleep, especially after the hot bath," Margaret said, looking like a little cherub, peering up from within her warm bed.

"Well goodnight darling," Kath murmured, bending down to kiss her daughter on the forehead.

"Mum?"

"Yes love," Kath questioned.

"I want you to know, Mary helped me immensely today, by explaining and looking at things in her funny Irish ways. Don't say anything but I really love them both and do you know, they feel like grandparents to me mum. I know it probably sounds strange to you but they do."

Kath's eyes glazed over. "Of course it doesn't sound strange love; they're so kind and loving. In fact, Mary feels like a mum to me." She drew a deep breath. "Well goodnight love" swiftly turning her back on her daughter to wipe away her own tears, before leaving the room.

Later in the evening, tucked up in bed with Marcus, she retold him the story. He instantly wrapped her up in his arms and cuddled her tightly. Tears immediately sprang to her eyes, her emotions in turmoil.

"I've been thinking Kath, perhaps we should stay here for a few more days. Mary and Joe would love it and it would be good for young Margaret. We'll also get to spend some more time with your parents."

She nodded in response.

"I'll ring Sydney tomorrow and organise it, so that our company jet will arrive in Belfast on Friday. We can pop down to Downpatrick tomorrow and buy a few extra clothes, to carry us through the next couple of days. If that's okay with you love?"

"Fine," Kath murmured, smiling up at him. He was a good man, a strong resilient man and that's exactly what she needed right now.

Arrangements were made quickly in the morning, after everyone consumed a huge bowl of porridge, topped with sugar and milk. The women were heading to town to do some clothes shopping, while Marcus gave Joe a hand on the farm.

At the shops, Kath and Margaret had fun choosing warm woollen sweaters, along with jeans and fluffy socks, to keep themselves warm. They even purchased two pairs of wellies to walk through the fields with, later on. Margaret bought bright coloured beanies with gloves to match, for everyone.

"You would think we're going to the snowfields, like back home," Margaret joked happily with her mum.

Arriving back at the farm, they sat around the kitchen table and had a huge plough- man's lunch. The homemade chutneys went deliciously with the crusty rolls, along with an assortment of cold meats and cheeses, washed down with a steaming hot mug of tea.

After tidying up, Marcus hollered upstairs. "Come on Margaret, I'll take you for a country stroll and show you some of my favourite spots," smiling across at Kath.

Margaret came bounding down the stairs and quickly retrieved one of Mary's coats. Soon they were on their way, leaving time for Kath to converse with her mum and dad, without young Margaret around to overhear them.

Margaret enjoyed climbing over the old stone ditches and meandering over the stunning green fields, inhaling the fresh country air. She especially loved to follow the path of the swift running river, pouring itself noisily over large, smooth, weathered rocks and discovering to her delight that further upstream, the river flowed into some dark and deep rock pools. Laughing heartily, she was astounded when Marcus informed her he use to swim in these very same pools.

"My god, they would have been absolutely freezing," she exclaimed, amazed by the natural beauty surrounding her, while enjoying Marcus's pleasant and easy going mannerisms. She was glad he was dating her mum; she liked him a lot actually and hoped they would settle down together. They made their way back to the farm, both exhilarated and absolutely exhausted from their long country walk.

"Is that youse luv?" Mary bellowed out from the living room, after hearing the backdoor opening.

"It sure is," Marcus called out "and a steaming pot of tea would also go down real well," as both were heard laughing and giggling on the back porch.

Mary told Kath to sit with her father and quickly rose to make an afternoon cuppa, to be served up with a few homemade biscuits.

Margaret arrived in with rosy red cheeks, appearing radiant, settling herself down quickly in front of the fire, as Marcus slowly wandered in behind her.

"Mum it was fantastic. Marcus showed me some rock pools he used to swim in," she said, eyes wide with expression. "I don't know how he didn't manage to break an ankle or a leg trying to get in," she added, laughing. "And it's a wonder he didn't freeze to death, when he did manage to get in unscathed."

Kath smiled; glad she had time with her father, unbeknown to Margaret of course. It was wonderful to see that the pair of them getting on so well together. Fate brought them here and it had taken a turn for the better Kath mused, as Mary entered with a steaming pot of tea.

The next few days past uneventfully, proving to be wonderfully blissful and relaxing for them. Margaret helped retrieve eggs with Mary in the mornings; and later in the afternoons, she would help Joe fetch some bales of hay to feed the cattle. Margaret seemingly enjoyed the slow gentle farm life, thriving in the unhurried atmosphere.

Kath also noticed her mother was becoming restless, as she feverishly began baking and cooking incessantly, running around like a chook with its head cut off. Kath recognised it was due to their departure tomorrow, acknowledging they would be sorely missed by them both. Kath brushed the thoughts away from her mind, as it saddened her to be leaving her parents but maybe, they would visit them in Australia one day. Who knows, let's face it, they were still young, only in their early sixties and Marcus could arrange for the company jet to pick them up, making it a less arduous journey for them both. Time will tell, she mused.

Before they knew it they were at the car saying their goodbyes. Tears were streaming down the face of Kath and Margaret, as they hugged Mary affectionately, saying their final farewells. Joe shook Marcus's hand and told him to look after his girls, with tears in his eyes. They got into the car with heavy hearts and teary stained faces. Windows were instantly wound down, as they blew kisses and called out their love for the elderly pair, standing huddled together arm-in-arm, waving goodbye in the distance.

Marcus set his hand upon Kath's. "We'll be back to visit one day and besides; we can always bring them out to Australia for a holiday."

"Hooray," Margaret screamed out from the back seat, knowing full well this would happen, because she knew Marcus was a man of his word and she admired him a lot.

The rest of the afternoon was spent packing their bags in the Europa Hotel, gifts were stashed away in their suitcases and comfy clothes were left out to wear, for their lengthy journey home. Margaret was looking forward to travelling home; she had never been on a private jet before. Kath was pining for Rachel, Brigee and Valerie, as it had been one hell of a journey and thankfully, one which ended well.

The jet raced up the runway after receiving clearance from the air traffic controller, leaving behind the huge Harland and Wolfe cranes, wrapped up in a thin grey mist, standing overlooking Belfast. The jet veered to the right, heading eastwards towards London, with Margaret totally enamoured by the luxury fitted jet. The seats reclined making the journey much more comfortable, enabling her to sleep on her way home. A young hostess tended to her with drinks, pillows and blankets and even gave her a selection of movies to choose from. Kath and Marcus watched; as she played around with the reclining seat momentarily, before settling down to watch a movie. They both sat together holding hands, really glad they were heading home. They were extremely pleased they had visited Kath's parents and were given the opportunity to make their peace. Both sighed contently and were enormously grateful, acknowledging, Margaret was now out of harm's way.

Chapter Six

Kath was extremely grateful she wasn't cooped up like a battery hen and fully aware of the time saved opposed to flying commercially, even though they stopped off several times for refuelling. Touch down at Sydney Airport felt like heaven to Kath, the sky was endlessly blue as they taxied up the runway. Exhilarated and relieved to be home again, she would soon get to see Rachel, Brigee and Valerie, allowing her to slip back into a normal life, without the impending threat of a bomb.

Walking across the tarmac the sun felt warm against her skin, Kath appeared vibrant and happy as she removed her jacket, before entering the terminal. After Customs clearance had been made, they headed promptly to the arrivals lounge and were immediately greeted by a loud cheer. Rachel went racing across to her sister grasping a barrage of brightly coloured balloons, together with a 'welcome home' message, scrawled across a pink satin ribbon. She straight away hugged her sister, obviously delighted to have her back home. Valerie and Brigee greeted Kath, relief were written upon their faces, accompanying a genuine heart warming smile, both extremely appreciative they were back home safe and sound.

A convoy of cars headed back to Gladesville. Everyone was chatting happily, exchanging and catching up on the latest news. On arrival, Brigee immediately headed to the kitchen to put the kettle on, with Valerie following closely behind. Soon, they were sitting outside on the patio munching into a delicious lunch, already prepared by Brigee and Valerie earlier, before they collected them all from the airport. Kath was snacking on some smoked cheese and crackers, glancing around at her family and friends, enormously happy to be home again. Sitting in quiet contemplation, she acknowledged this was her home; this is where she belonged, where she felt implicitly safe and secure. She smiled inwardly, sighing leisurely, appreciating this much treasured moment.

Later in the afternoon, suitcases were opened and presents were retrieved from among the pile of crumpled clothes. Brigee and Valerie were thrilled with their gold Claddagh rings, immediately sliding them on to their middle fingers in unison, both swearing they would never be removed, before bursting into joyful laughter. Rachel adored the gold Celtic pendant, as Margaret fastened the gold chain around her neck. Margaret was presented with hers as well, sending her into squeals of happiness, as it was fastened around her neck by Marcus. All the trivial trinkets followed; the Irish dolls went down a treat, along with the Aran sweaters, tea towels and the typical Irish T-shirts, sending everyone into fits of laughter as they read the slogans.

The day moved quickly and soon they were sitting around the kitchen table, tucking into a beautiful lasagne and freshly made green salad. The girls crunched hungrily into the crispy garlic bread, as the adults sipped upon their delectable white wine.

Marcus stood up unannounced. "Here's to friends, family and a wonderful country."

"Here, here," Kath interrupted, clinking her glass amongst her dear friends, radiant, happy and extremely content.

The days unfolded slowly, allowing everyone to slip back into their normal routines. The girls would be starting back to school and university next week but Kath had already made her way back to work. Marcus told her to take a few weeks off but she disagreed immediately, she loved her job and enjoyed the challenges, working with her staff on a daily basis.

Brigee noticed Marcus calling around more frequently, staying for dinner and enjoying the girls company immensely. She hinted at Kath to make Margaret aware who Marcus really was but Kath put it off, not yet ready to divulge her secret. She was apprehensive and afraid of bursting the bubble of peace and joy, surrounding them at present.

Marcus arranged for Kath to come to his place for the weekend, under the pretence of a working environment. She was aware deadlines were drawing closer and was only too happy to oblige. Friday night was upon them and Marcus quickly suggested they should go out and get some dinner first, before getting stuck into the business dealings. She readily agreed and was very much looking forward to it, as it had been rather a hectic day. A quiet dinner was exactly what she needed, to help her relax and unwind, she thought, following him to the car.

Kath reapplied her lipstick as Marcus drove his car towards Darling Harbour; she noticed he was slightly agitated. Perhaps the sales team were not reaching their required targets, Kath thought. She heard cuts were being made in Melbourne, as she smiled across at him, hiding her concern.

Making their way across the paved walkway, Darling Harbour shone in all its glory. The restaurants were invaded by patrons chatting idly away, sipping their cool refreshing drinks, obviously enjoying the warm balmy evening. A few yachts were moored in the harbour, their huge masts pointing skyward, laden with heavy weather borne sails, bobbing tranquilly on the dark, silken water. Hand in hand they made their way across the impressively lit promenade, heading towards Jordan's Seafood Restaurant, one of her favourite eating haunts.

The head waiter approached and Marcus stepped forward.

"A table for Mr Garofoli has been booked for 7pm."

Smiling at them the waiter nodded, dressed in a pristine white coat, neatly pressed black pants, together with a white shirt and bowtie. "This way please," he announced in an authoritative manner.

Kath followed him as he made his way to the back corner of the restaurant and as she rounded the corner a loud "SURPRISE" greeted her instantly. She recognised Brigee, Valerie and her girls immediately, along with Marcus's father and mother who were fully aware of Kath's history and sworn to secrecy. She was absolutely speechless, peering quickly back at Marcus, her face a question mark, as everyone started laughing in unison. Intuitively gaining her demeanour, Kath gently enquired what everyone was actually celebrating.

Marcus smiled at her, his eyes twinkling in the candlelight. "I thought it would be nice to celebrate together with family and friends, considering the upheaval we had in Ireland. It makes me appreciate everything and everyone so much more."

She beamed at him, touched by his words, knowing exactly how he felt, because she felt the same.

The evening progressed beautifully; the food was mouth-watering, the wine delicious, everyone appeared relaxed, familiar and extremely contented. The soft music began to play and Marcus enticed Kath up for a dance. She rested her head upon his shoulder as he held her in his arms, moving to a slow number.

"I love you more than anything in the whole world. You know that don't you?" he murmured.

"Mmm, I most certainly do," she whispered softly, moving slowly to the beat.

"I never ever want to lose you again," Marcus continued more urgently.

"You won't. I'm yours forever my love."

He held her in his arms tighter, "that's what I hoped you would say," he whispered tenderly.

Peering across the room he nodded to Brigee, who disappeared without delay. Marcus held tightly on to Kath, as they danced slowly around the room keeping in perfect rhythm, both in touch with each other's feelings and both very much in love.

Arriving back at the table, the mood was peaceful and Marcus noticed the champagne had arrived. Suddenly the kitchen doors burst open; a huge cake decorated with sparklers was being hurried across the restaurant, held high on a silver tray catching everyone's attention.

"Must be someone's birthday," Kath whispered, bewildered when it arrived at their table.

Everyone sat perfectly still, smiling, as Marcus dropped down on one knee. Kath was taken back, swallowing hard when Marcus produced a red velvet box.

"Will you marry me Kath? I love you with all my heart, yesterday, today and for always."

Tears welled up in her eyes instantly. "Yes Marcus. Yes of course I will marry you."

The patrons sent up a roar of approval, as Marcus slid the engagement ring on to Kath's finger. The ring was immensely attractive; it was a huge five carat square cut emerald, surrounded by twenty-three diamonds, arranged in a high gold setting. It was perfect, dazzling beyond belief as Kath held out her hand for all to see, as tears joyfully cascaded down her face.

Marcus smiled across at her, whispering quietly. "The emerald represents Ireland, where I first fell in love with you. The twenty-three diamonds signifies the years when we were separated and the gold symbolises the golden years we'll get to share together."

"You're adorable," she cried, before being inundated by well wishers, headed up by her two girls who were absolutely ecstatic.

The evening passed like a dream. Kath was touched by the thoughtfulness Marcus had invested into getting her engagement ring, especially designed. Peering down at it, she wore it with pride, thinking of all the history that passed between them. Also thinking about their love in the early stages, later reconciling again in Australia and how their love had matured and stood up to the test of time in the most horrendous of circumstances. She snuggled up to him in bed later, exhausted yet exhilarated; the evening would remain with her forever, as she drifted into a deep comfortable slumber.

As planned, Marcus spent a relaxing weekend with Kath, alone at his place. They lounged around his penthouse soaking up the relaxed atmosphere, without a care in the world. Late Saturday afternoon, a loud knock on the door surprised Kath. "Expecting anyone?" she queried.

"Just some papers, sent over by dad probably," Marcus answered nonchalantly, heading towards the bathroom door. "Can you get the door?" he called out casually.

Kath opened the door and was immediately greeted with a huge basketful of red roses, as well as a large box draped in a red silk ribbon. "Oh my gosh," she exclaimed with joy; as Marcus quietly came from behind.

"A surprise engagement present for you," he smiled. Before she could even say a word, he kissed her tenderly. "Well, don't just stand there all goggle eyed. Open it up," he teased.

Setting the fragrant roses upon the kitchen table, she sat down and opened the box. Inside laid a sensational Giorgio Armani red satin dress, with tiny diamantes sewn along the hemline and also along the elegantly cut neckline. It was the most beautiful gown she ever laid eyes on, as she gasped in disbelief. A pair of red satin shoes also lay in the box matching perfectly with the gown, together with a small clutch handbag, further complementing the outfit. "Marcus what on earth have you gone and done ... this is far too much ... too extravagant ... and besides ... where on earth will I be able to wear this?" appearing wide eyed and completely astonished.

Smiling, Marcus responded. "Fortunately, we have an invitation to my parent's house this evening, as they are having a celebration in honour of our engagement. You know mother; it will most certainly be a grand affair, so I thought this would be very appropriate. I hope you like it? Valerie helped me of course."

"I should have guessed she would be involved, one way or another," Kath laughed, shaking her head. "Might I enquire as to what time this grand affair is?" leaning over and draping her arms around his neck "because I'll have to get my hair and nails done to match the opulence of this dress," kissing him affectionately.

"Mmm, keep this up young lady and we might not make it for 7pm this evening."

The remainder of the day progressed quickly. Kath had a long relaxing bath, pampering herself for this evening's celebration. Lying back in the luke warm water, inhaling the sweet perfumed bath salts, she recognised how fortunate she was, having Marcus back in her life. She truly loved him with all her heart, he was beautiful both inside and out. Caring, thoughtful, strong, resilient and yet the gentlest, kindest man she had ever known. She knew in her heart, she was truly blessed.

Slipping on the gown and peering at herself in the mirror, she instantly felt like Cinderella. The gown accentuated her perfectly curved body, falling beautifully at the neckline and divulging a little cleavage, while screaming sophistication and sheer elegance. She wore her hair up, fastened with a diamante clip which added to her overall appearance. Smiling broadly, this all felt so familiar to her, as she recalled getting ready for the ball in Portrush, all those years ago when life was simple.

Marcus called out "are you ready my love?" breaking her from her reverie.

"I'll be out in a second," she sung out, before taking one last glance in the mirror. Smiling, she left the room.

Marcus gasped when she appeared from the bedroom. The gown glittered in the dim lights and was absolutely stunning. "Magnificent," Marcus exclaimed, with sheer admiration written across his face. "Truly Kath, you look sensational and could pass as a princess right now."

She moved slowly toward him and gave him a tender kiss. "Thank you my darling, it is truly spectacular and I will feel like the belle of the ball this evening."

He took her into his arms. "I can't wait to make you mine Kath, to be man and wife forever," he whispered. Tears glistened in his eyes, knowing he couldn't live life without her. Already missing two decades together, there was no way he wanted to miss one more single, solitary, minute. "Come on then, we better go ... before I seduce you," he murmured, lovingly smiling down at her.

"Marcus Garofoli, it's amazing how some things never change," she said laughing, grabbing his hand quickly before leaving the penthouse.

Arriving at Vaucluse, the huge house was lit up magnificently. Entering the grand marbled hall, their coats were taken immediately by the butler, before being led into the main room. Huge chandeliers glittered in the softly lit room; elegant satin curtains dressed the patio windows, leading out on to a large terrace. The antique furnishings matched in perfectly with the expensive paintings, adding a grandeur and opulence, like no other.

Kath felt overwhelmed but was soon made to feel welcomed by Marcus's father Carlos. "My goodness you look lovely this evening Kath. Our Marcus is a very lucky fellow indeed," Carlos said, smiling across at her. "Eleanor my dear, Marcus and Kath have arrived."

His mother came across immediately, transparently confident within her domain and in her element, smothered in diamonds and satin. "Welcome dear Katherine and congratulations once again. I simply can't wait until the wedding. With Marcus being our only son, you simply must have it here my dear," she announced grandly, sweeping her elegant hand around the room.

"We've only got engaged Eleanor and we're in no immediate hurry," Kath stated quickly, raising an eyebrow.

"Not too long darling, I hope. We are longing for a grandchild."

Marcus instantly grabbed Kath's hand. "Mother we have to go; Kath hasn't been introduced to Uncle Bernie yet." Before waiting for a reply, he promptly whisked Kath away. "Don't say a word my love, it is mother's abrupt mannerisms. I don't want you to take any notice of her, because I certainly don't."

"God-damn it Marcus, she knows she has a grandchild but that wouldn't fit in well with her high society friends, now would it?"

"Kath ... at last, I've found you. My god you look fantastic" Valerie interrupted them smiling, instantly giving them both a heartfelt hug.

Rachel, Margaret and Brigee appeared next, all elegantly dressed and ready to have a pleasurable evening. The remainder of the night progressed satisfactorily, after the run-in with Eleanor earlier. The food was outstanding, the wine was superb and the dancing continued into the small hours.

Arriving back at the penthouse, Kath went to undress.

"No don't," Marcus whispered in a husky voice "let me," as he strolled across the bedroom floor. Slowly, ever so slowly he unzipped her gown, before letting it fall gently on to the carpeted floor, while he kissed her long elegant neck. Turning her around to face him, he reached up and gently released the clip, letting her hair fall down around her. He swallowed hard, enamoured by her sheer beauty, as he gently slipped the red silken camisole straps, gently down over her smooth satin skin. She caught her breath, as he bent down, taking her nipple into his warm sensuous mouth. He continued to tease her, as he removed her satin panties effortlessly.

Standing in the moon light, clad in her stockings and high heels, she felt hot, wanton and ready to be taken by her man.

Without warning, he swept her up in his strong arms and carried her over to his bed. Laying her gently upon the cool satin sheets, he began his gentle seduction. Exploring her mouth passionately, arousing her, elevating her more by massaging her breasts, before moving downwards. She felt her temperature rise as he delved between her thighs, bringing her to an instant climax, her body quivering involuntarily, as he expertly navigated his way around her body. He worked his way up her body again, smothering her in tiny kisses, before invading her mouth with his. His tongue invaded her mouth desperately, urgently, making her desire him even more. Without saying a single solitary word, he took her manfully, filling her completely, meeting her every need. She cried out, overwhelmed with passion, climaxing abruptly and uncontrollably, while kissing him passionately.

Bringing up her knees, she flicked him around suddenly, catching him by surprise. She buried her hands in his; stretching them high above his head, invading his mouth feverishly with her tongue. Bending down, she tantalised his nipple in her mouth, rasping her teeth over it, causing him to stir and rise up. She licked, bit and teased him, making him hunger and cry out for her. Only then did she place herself above him, slowly moving over his manhood, rubbing in a teasing manner against him, slowly, driving him closer to the edge. Silently and skillfully, she took him strong and hard, gasping loudly. She rode him wildly and indulgently, smothered in perspiration. She continued building, building his momentum, building his rhythm, until he could hold back no longer. He freed his hands instantly pulling her down on to him, drawing her closer and releasing into her, both writhing and groaning in ecstasy. Overcome with emotion he grabbed her, kissing her brazenly upon the lips with tears glistening in his eyes.

"God, I love you Kath. You're so sexy, so beautiful and I never ever want to lose you."

"You won't my darling; I'm yours, all yours my love, now hush." She lay in his arms contented, full and mellow as she snuggled in closer, smiling as she drifted into a deep sound sleep, before he kissed her goodnight.

Marcus lay awake momentarily, immersed in Kath's love, before he slipped out of bed and out of the room, to light up a cigarette.

On the rooftop, the city appeared magical at this time of the evening. The light drone of traffic could be heard in the distance, as the cars wormed their way through the streets, appearing bug-like, with huge yellow eyes following each other along the expressway, lit up like an airport runway.

Marcus drew down on his cigarette once more, thinking about his mother, thinking about the comment she made to Kath. He clenched his left fist as his jaw line grew taut; anguish was written in a frown across his brow, coming to the realisation that Margaret must be made aware of who he was, real soon. He didn't want to pressure Kath though god knows she's been through enough to last her a lifetime.

But he knew his mother could not be trusted, thinking of her vindictiveness this evening, made him instantly recoil. He knew his mother had high hopes for him when he dated the Prime Minister's daughter but nothing could ever fill the void of losing Kath. His mother was in her element mixing in with the aristocracy and made it blatantly known to anyone who would listen; he could have done a lot better. However, his father always adored Kath on a personal level, as well as admiring her as a respected business woman.

A crumpled paper bag blew across the rooftop drawing Marcus's attention, immediately pulling him out of his reflections. He stood up resolutely, deciding to do whatever it took to keep Kath happy. Before making his way back indoors, Marcus decided that one day, Kath, Margaret and Rachel would be a part of his family, on a permanent basis.

Chapter Seven

As soon as Kath arrived home Sunday night, she heard one of her girls call out to her from the kitchen. "M-u-m, we're in here having some ice-cream."

Entering the kitchen, Kath found Rachel and Margaret both tucking into a huge bowl of chocolate ice-cream. "Girls, what on earth are you both doing up? It's 11.30pm and I thought you both would be in bed fast asleep."

The girls groaned in unison and then Margaret explained. "Gosh mum, we're dying to have another peek at your ring and to get all the gossip from last night. We spotted Marcus pulling you away from Eleanor, rather abruptly shall we say," imitating a posh voice and pulling a face at the same time.

Sending Rachel into a laughing fit immediately, while she lifted her mum's hand and examined the engagement ring. "Wow, it's pretty spectacular, it must have cost a fortune," she bragged, smiling up at her mum.

Margaret drew closer to investigate. "Yeah mum, what was it Marcus said on Friday night, something about twenty-three diamonds for twenty-three years?"

Kath immediately felt her cheeks burning, before adding "he said it took over twenty years to find me, hence the pretty diamonds." She didn't mention how he had lost her in the first place.

The girls laughed and chatted with their mum until 12.30am. They were then both ushered off to bed, having to rise early for school and university the next day.

Arriving at work, the news of Kath's engagement had obviously leaked out, as most female staff members flocked to see her diamond ring. Congratulations were given whole heartedly, because everyone was pleased she found happiness again, having lost Rod without any warning was definitely a terrible ordeal for anyone to recover from.

Marcus and Kath had lunch together down at Birkenhead Point. As she sat sipping her white wine, Marcus gazed at her, amazed at her beauty, her elegant persona and her large green cat-like eyes. "A penny for your thoughts," he enquired, interrupting her thoughts immediately.

"Oh, I was thinking about the time when Valerie and I were having lunch here and you, along with your father and some other employees arrived." She laughed. "I remember doing a runner and leaving poor Valerie sitting at the table, totally flabbergasted, wondering what the heck just happened."

"I'm so glad I found you again Kath," reaching across, to hold her hand. "I really don't know how I managed without you in my life all those years ago but that's all changed now, hasn't it?" smiling across at her. "Although, the biggest problem which exists for me right now is how quickly I can get you down the aisle," he grinned.

The days meandered into weeks, Kath noticed Margaret ringing Ireland frequently, having long conversations with both David and Maureen. She surmised they were missing their daughter Heather, terribly.

However, the phone calls were concerning Kath, which initiated a phone call to Dr Gilchrist, her psychiatrist and explaining the situation to him. "Kath, please don't worry, it's quite normal for Margaret to maintain contact with Heather's parents. A void needs to be filled and she obviously misses Heather. Her parents are offering up a place of solace, where each of them can find comfort. It will pass Kath," Dr Gilchrist advised.

Kath instantly decided to let Margaret grieve in her own natural way, pleased she made the call to Dr Gilchrist, allowing her to understand what was taking place. She continued on with her daily tasks, heavily involved with the latest campaign for a new magazine launch, to be finalised at the end of the month.

On Saturday evening, Kath lay curled up on the sofa, relaxing and watching a movie.

Marcus suddenly sat up straight, immediately starling her. "Kath, I can't wait any longer," Marcus declared.

"For what?" she questioned, swinging round to face him.

"To get married of course," he responded, twisting a lock of her hair around his index finger.

"Oh that again," she sighed, sinking back down into the sofa, trying not to show her concern.

Marcus searched her face. "What is it Kath, what's stopping you from marrying me?"

She tried to avoid his gaze but he lifted her chin and pleading with his eyes, he whispered. "Don't you love me enough?"

"No, it not that at all, it's just ..." she faded out.

"It's just what darling?"

She gazed into his eyes, sensing his sadness, as tears welled up in her own eyes. "Every time I try to marry someone, something bad seems to happen and I end up losing them," she murmured, swallowing hard.

"You married Rod, didn't you?"

"E-x-a-c-t-l-y my point and look what happened to him," she sobbed.

He swept her into his arms immediately. "Kath my darling you can't go through life in fear. Our fates are sealed and we've gone through the worst, so let's just celebrate whatever time we may have left, TOGETHER."

Clinging to him, he leant down and affectionately began kissing her. She responded immediately.

Marcus spent the night with Kath and decided while they were eating breakfast together, to make the big announcement. "Well," he said, smiling across at Kath who grinned at him from the other end of the breakfast table. "Girls and not forgetting Brigee of course, Kath and I have decided to get married on the 21st December."

Rachel let out a loud whooping sound; spitting toast crumbs all over the kitchen table, immediately sending everyone into explosive fits of the giggles.

Brigee went around and instantly hugged Kath and Marcus. "About bloody time you two, I was beginning to give up," she laughed out loud.

Everyone was obviously delighted with the announcement and began chatting all at once.

Kath met up with Valerie the following day for lunch, breaking the good news and informing her of the wedding date. Valerie was extremely happy for them both, instantly enquiring as to where the wedding would take place.

Kath paused, squirming in her seat a little. "Well you know Eleanor, she wants the whole bells and whistles but quite frankly, I don't. I haven't spoken to Marcus about it yet but I want a simple intimate wedding, with only immediate family and friends present."

"Okay," Valerie replied, clearing her throat "leave it with me Kath. I'll think of something which will make everyone happy." Valerie found herself smiling after finishing her lunch and continued. "Don't worry Kath, give me a couple of weeks and I'll come up with the perfect plan," instantly kissing Kath on the cheek and hugging her, before she left.

Work was as hectic as usual; Margaret and Rachel were excelling academically and Marcus was constantly happy, now that a wedding date had been chosen. A call from Valerie, found Kath driving over to Leichhardt to meet up with her friend for lunch. After ordering, Valerie couldn't contain her excitement any longer. "I came up with an excellent idea which should please everyone," Valerie declared happily, when the waiter left with their order.

"Well go ahead and spill, I can't bear to think what Eleanor might have in mind," Kath sighed.

"An island wedding my dear friend," Valerie announced.

"What do you mean?" Kath questioned, intrigued and puzzled.

"Well, say you and Marcus decided to get married on Hamilton Island. Not many guests would be able to travel, plus it's almost Christmas and everyone is busy, r-i-g-h-t? Finally, they can't really cater for huge numbers like what Eleanor would have in mind, over there."

"Marvellous," Kath smiled "and Eleanor will have to cut down on the numbers. I'm sure Marcus will love the idea … because I certainly do." She laughed, seemingly much more relaxed than when she first arrived.

During lunch they discussed where the wedding service would be conducted, which was going to be Whitehaven Beach, an eight minute flight from Hamilton Island. The flowers, dresses, bridal party and all the other formalities which would take place, were discussed in great detail over lunch. An hour and a half later, Kath walked away a much happier woman. All she had to do was get Marcus's approval.

At the end of the week, Kath raised the topic while lying in bed with Marcus after an incredible seduction. Both were in a carefree mood, as the soft ambience lingered on well after their loving encounter. "Marcus?"

"Yes darling," he answered, after setting his glass of wine back on to the bedside table.

"In relation to our wedding, how would you feel if we had it on Hamilton Island?"

He sat up immediately. "I don't care where we have it my love. I'll leave it all up to you. As long as we're together as Mr and Mrs Garofoli, you can have it on the moon!"

Kath smiled. "I want approximately fifty people there, a small intimate wedding Marcus."

"That's fine with me baby," he whispered softly.

"But what about your mother?" she questioned.

"Don't worry about her I'll handle it. It's our day my love and she'll just have to go with the flow," he said casually, stretching forward to kiss her gently on the lips. Kath returned his kiss ardently.

It was soon on for young and old. Kath and Valerie were sending out invites, organising dresses, flowers, caterers and venues. The girls were wonderful with Kath, keeping her calm and centred, preventing her from becoming overwhelmed by the huge amount of organising which had to be carried out. The tasks were proving to be more difficult, due to the fact the wedding was taking place on Hamilton Island up in the Whitsundays. Valerie was to be her Matron of Honour, with Margaret and Rachel both being bridesmaids. Marcus's best friend Barry had a young daughter called Rebecca, who was going to be their flower girl. She was only four but the cutest little thing imaginable. She had a mop full of beautiful brown curls and the biggest, most gorgeous brown eyes, you ever did see. They were large and mischievous, mixed in with a complete innocence, which only a child could possess.

Everything was coming together and Eleanor eventually came to terms with the arrangements, because Marcus made it blatantly clear, there was to be no interference whatsoever. He informed Kath he had threatened his mother, telling her he would run off and elope with Kath, if she tried anything. It was all falling into place nicely, with only a month to go.

At last, Kath could finally take a breather. All the arrangements had been made, right down to the accommodation for the fifty guests. She was now looking forward to the wedding and both decided to spend their honeymoon in the Whitsundays, a perfectly renowned sun drenched holiday destination.

Marcus arranged to fly up a few days earlier, along with Valerie, Brigee and the girls, in order to check everything was running smoothly.

This gave Kath a few days at home alone, allowing her time to potter about, unwind and totally relax. She visited the Observatory Day Spa down in the city and had a luxurious day, being fully pampered from head to toe.

Rechecking her suitcases before the taxi arrived; Kath took one last look around, before locking up the house and heading for the airport.

The sky was a light pale blue, merging into the tropical azure ocean, as the plane came in to land at Hamilton Island Airport. Marcus was waiting for her at the arrivals, beaming from ear to ear. She was rather surprised Valerie, Brigee and the girls weren't there to greet her but they were probably lazing around the pool before lunchtime.

Her suitcases were loaded on to the golf buggy, before Marcus made his way up the steep hill. The aroma from the hibiscus drifted in the air as they made their way along the road, bordered with tropical lush green vegetation.

Arriving at the Qualia Resort, a concierge immediately parked their buggy and set Kath's suitcases on to a trolley, before leading her to the suite.

It was absolutely amazing, a tropical paradise hidden away on the northern tip of Hamilton Island, a jewel in the midst of the Whitsundays.

Marcus explained to Kath "this whole area is strictly for the wedding guests, so we can have privacy and an intimate atmosphere with everyone, over the next three days."

Kath sighed blissfully, totally overwhelmed and exceptionally pleased. "You've certainly outdone yourselves, it really is remarkable and I feel ever so relaxed already."

"Well, get yourself freshened up and I'll meet you by the pool for lunch along with the girls," Marcus advised, as he made his way to the door.

"See you in ten," Kath called out, before making her way into the bathroom to grab a quick shower.

Journeying down to the swimming pool area, Kath was completely chilled out, enjoying the Coral Sea views as she made her way down the steps. Rounding the corner and following the pool sign, she was taken by surprise when all the wedding guests were waiting for her with a glass of champagne in hand.

Marcus waltzed up with the girls, Valerie and Brigee. "Here's to tomorrow my love and beautiful surprises," stepping back and sweeping his arm wide.

Before Kath could question or query anything, from amongst the crowd, Joe and Mary appeared. She immediately choked back tears, overwhelmed with emotion, unable to speak, she simply held out her arms to receive them both.

"We wouldn't want to miss this for the world luv," Mary spluttered. Crying, laughing and hugging her all at the same time.

Joe stood there gazing at his daughter, as proud as punch. "Not for all the tea in China," he whispered, giving her a huge breathtaking hug.

Cheers arose from the remaining guests, before they all sat down at the tables and chatted harmoniously, during a scrumptious lunch. Joe and Mary were positioned on either side of Kath, as she looked around, smiling constantly. She was deeply touched and enthralled by her parents making the long arduous journey to Australia, especially for her wedding.

The only guests aware of Joe and Mary's real identities were Valerie, Matt, Brigee and Marcus's parents. The rest were under the illusion they were Marcus's adopted aunt and uncle from Ireland, which left Eleanor completely baffled but she remained silent, not wishing to incur Marcus's wrath.

"When did you get here?" Kath enquired.

"Oh about a week ago," Mary volunteered. "We were staying at Valerie's and Matt's," smiling across at them.

"And they spoilt us rotten," Joe piped up.

"So that's why I didn't see much of you Valerie," Kath screamed across the noisy table.

"I was busy sight-seeing with Marcus's adopted family," Valerie laughed, winking across at Kath and giving her a huge smile.

"That's right luv, after the jet lag we were taken to the Sydney Opera House and we also saw Bondi Beach. Mind you, Mary's not too impressed with some of those half naked lassies," Joe commented.

"Darn sure I wasn't," Mary interrupted "but I enjoyed being up in Centrepoint Tower, it was out of this world," her expressions divulging her excitement.

"Well, you've been busy by the sounds of things and tell me Marcus, did the girls know this was going on?"

"Yes they did. In fact they went with Joe and Mary to Taronga Zoo," Marcus exclaimed.

Kath raised an eyebrow, shaking her head in disbelief; it seemed everyone was in on the act but her, although it was the nicest surprise ever.

After lunch Marcus came over and kissed her. "I guess this will have to last me until tomorrow?"

"Yes, it most certainly will," Kath whispered, laughing.

It had been organised for them to have separate suites until after the wedding. Marcus was to have the remainder of the day with Joe, spending time on the golf course and then going out to dinner in the evening with the remainder of the guests.

Kath on the other hand was being pampered in the day spa, along with her mum, Valerie, Brigee and her girls. It was a beautiful relaxing day and Kath couldn't have wished for anything more. Marcus had given Kath the perfect wedding gift, by bringing her parents across for her special day. Spending the afternoon with her mother made her heart melt and she knew it would be something she would store and treasure in her heart, forever. She gave them one final hug, before returning to her suite at 9.30pm.

There was a huge day ahead of them tomorrow and now it was time to retire to bed, in order to be fresh and ready for her wedding day. She lay in bed alone, longing to feel Marcus wrapped up in her arms, to help calm her pre-wedding day jitters. She couldn't help smiling, thinking about her parents being here to witness her wedding, albeit to Marcus's meticulous and secretive planning. She glanced over at her wedding gown, wrapped up in layers of tissue paper and sealed in plastic, which would allow her look splendid on her special day. Butterflies swam around in her stomach, simply thinking about marrying Marcus tomorrow, her first true love. She was grateful how fate had brought them back together again and tomorrow, he will be destined to be her husband, until his dying breath.

Chapter Eight

At 11am, Valerie, Brigee, Mary and the girls were sitting in Kath's suite getting their hair and makeup done. Brigee and Mary were making cups of tea, both getting along like a house on fire. The mood was cheery and relaxed, as Kath sat down at the dressing table, ready to be prepped. Brigee was dressed in a pale lemon suit which was elegant, pretty and light for the occasion. Mary was wearing a delicate blue suit, a few shades darker than the bridesmaid's dresses, which would blend beautifully for the wedding photos.

Soon, it was time for them to leave; they would be flown out by helicopter to White Haven Beach, where the wedding ceremony was taking place. The other guests would have arrived there by now, taking a commercial catamaran hired for the occasion, to the stunning and unique location situated amidst the Whitsunday Passage.

Joe arrived at the door, in time to compliment them on their attire and gave Mary a quick kiss goodbye. Kath sat at the dressing table, the pale peach lipstick accentuated her perfectly formed lips, as she smiled up at her father radiantly.

"My, my, you look like a princess my love. Your mum's heart and mine, feel as if they're going to burst open with pride and joy."

"I'm so glad you're here dad, it means the world to me and I'm ever so grateful. You've made me the happiest bride imaginable."

"Hush now lass or you'll have the old man cryin' and makin' a mess of your dress," he said with pride, grabbing her hand and leading her to the door.

The helicopter flew towards the beach, an eight minute journey, highlighting the white sand and the clear blue water from above, before landing on the most beautiful beach in the world. They could hear the amplified ceremonial music when the engine was cut, although it was set in order not to impinge upon the marine life or any other national park users.

As Kath elegantly made her way up the beach with her father, to where Marcus and the wedding group were standing, the guests collectively sighed, stunned by the gorgeous bride.

Kath's wedding dress took their breath away; it was an empire, side halter styled wedding dress, with a chapel train. The white chiffon shimmered in the morning sun, as she stood beside Marcus, who had tears of joy written in his eyes. The 'A' line floor length sleeveless dress, had the strap joined together by a silk flower, positioned on one side of the sweetheart neckline. The empire waist bore a broad satin sash, allowing the vertical waves of the dress, to drape downwards.

The beautiful calm sea with tranquil waves, were lapping nearby, providing a magnificent backdrop for the wedding service.

Valerie, Margaret, Rachel and the little flower girl were dressed in pale blue chiffon dresses, with soft white ribbons tucked under the bust line, drawn softly around the back and tied. Each one was holding a posy of frangipanis, blending in beautifully with Kath's amazing bouquet of tiny white orchids.

All had their hair drawn up, with a matching frangipani clipped on to the side. While Kath's headpiece was simply elegant, a sophisticated comb, embossed with tiny pearls and decorated with petite white orchids, neatly clipped on to one side of her head.

Joe gave Kath a soft kiss on the cheek, before walking over to stand with Mary, Brigee and Marcus's parents.

The small and intimate service took place under clear blue skies, upon an unspoilt white beach, stretching for miles. Kath and Marcus made their personal vows, touching everyone's heart, before slipping their wedding bands on one another's finger.

The celebrant proudly announced "You are now man and wife. You may kiss the bride."

Marcus took Kath into his arms, whispering "I will love you forever, right up until I draw my last dying breath," before kissing her passionately.

The guests cried out in joy, all truly delighted with the union, before professional photos were taken of the pair. The guests left in the catamaran after group shots were taken and the married couple departed in the helicopter later, with the wedding party made up of both sets of parents and Brigee, who left in two separate seaplanes.

Returning to Hamilton Island, the reception was being held in Sail's Restaurant, located in the main resort centre. The veranda bar was already serving up brightly coloured cocktails, when Kath and Marcus arrived back. The white tablecloths adorned with gleaming silver cutlery and vases of frangipanis, offered elegant sea views, across Catseye Beach. The palm trees rustled in the balmy tropical environment, creating a meticulously intimate mood, for all who was attending.

The seafood platters were delicious, served with freshly baked rolls and scrumptious green salads, accompanying glasses upon glasses of Moet, easing everyone present into a tranquil and relaxed mood. Speeches were made; Matt had everyone in stitches and Marcus's father Carlos, welcomed

Kath into the family, along with her girls, adding a thoughtful kind gesture. Eleanor was in her element, pleased with the ceremony and the impressive reception; in fact she was getting a little tipsy by the end of the evening.

At 6pm, Kath and Marcus commenced dancing on the outdoor dance floor, decorated with soft lanterns hanging from the nearby palm trees. The sea breeze was sweeping in the sweet frangipani aromas, combined with the delicate French champagne; Kath was feeling giddy and exhilarated. She threw her wedding bouquet to her single female guests at 9pm and June from her office, was overjoyed when she caught it.

Kath and Marcus sang out their farewells, before departing on a golf buggy, the only means of transport available on the island. This one however, was covered in flowers and had tin cans tied to the back of the vehicle with ribbons, along with a sign 'Just Married' attached. They headed up the hill laughing together as the cheers faded into the balmy night air, as they made their way to the Qualia Resort, where they were staying in the 60th Pavilion, which offered deluxe packages of sheer extravagance.

Her soft, white, wedding dress lay deposited upon the natural timber floorboards, as Kath slowly made her way into the candlelit bathroom. Sliding gently into the rose scented spa, she glided into Marcus's strong awaiting arms, before retrieving her glass of champagne sitting on the side.

"Mmmm, what an absolutely extraordinary day," Kath whispered. "Everything went perfectly from the very beginning, right up until we left the reception," she smiled inwardly, relaxing further into Marcus's firm chest.

"And to think, the evening isn't over yet," Marcus replied huskily, while nibbling her ear.

"Thank you my darling, thank you for taking care of everything, especially for bringing my parents out. It was the most gorgeous day imaginable and I'll be forever in your debt." She then turned around and kissed him.

"Now lie back and relax Mrs Garofoli," he smiled. "It's been one hell of a day, which I will carry with me for the rest of my life. When you stepped out on to the sand after disembarking from the helicopter with your father, truly Kath, you looked like an angel sent from heaven above."

She smiled up at him, replaying the image through her mind, her face soft in the candlelight; she whispered "I felt like a princess."

He kissed her once more, turning her around slowly and began kneading her shoulders gently, then dropping his hands downwards he massaged her breasts tenderly. Kath made a soft sigh, relaxing down more into the rippling, soothing spa. Marcus's hand wandered around to her navel; massaging her firm flat stomach, before progressing further downwards. Kath lay wrapped up in his arms, enjoying the slow, sensual, teasing touch, raining down upon her. As he expertly delved in between her thighs, she soon began a rhythmic swaying, keeping in time with Marcus's touch. Soon she could feel her passion being ignited, her nipples erect, her body hot from desire as she began losing herself completely. Letting out a light guttural cry, she orgasmed. That was instantly smothered by Marcus's mouth, capturing her in a long deep passionate kiss, sustaining her heightened senses for longer. Tears filled her eyes, as Marcus slowly wrapped her in his arms. "Now, that's what I call a perfect ending" he said, kissing her gently upon the forehead.

The night was spent between soft satin sheets, each taking turns in pleasuring each other. The flimsy curtains floated in the balmy evening breeze, filtering through the veranda windows. They were both thoroughly exhausted and very much in love, extremely grateful and appreciative of one another.

"Good night my princess," Marcus whispered into the night, as Kath's peaceful body lay next to his. She was lost in a deep slumber and a million miles away, floating in amongst the striking moments she only just experienced, on her unforgettable wedding day.

The next couple of days came and went quickly, spent with their parents, Valerie's family and Brigee of course. Late breakfasts, lazy lunches and relaxed evening meals, allowed an intimacy to form amongst Kath's family and friends, which warmed her heart.

Visiting the local zoo, Eleanor and Mary both jumped back horrified, when a huge crocodile leapt a metre into the air to retrieve a chicken dangling from a rod, held high by a zoo attendant. Both were clutching each other's hands, eyes wide and shocked, before bursting into fits of laughter.

Joe and Marcus's father would stroll along deep in conversation, covering everything from the scenery to politics in a friendly banter, enjoying each other's company immensely.

The girls were enjoying the adult company as well and were getting thoroughly spoilt from all angles but took it all sensibly in their stride.

The day finally arrived, when Marcus and Kath were saying their farewells at the airport. The other wedding guests had already left the day before.

"Now enjoy yurselves luv," Mary cried out, waving goodbye from the departure gates. "We'll see you both when you get back."

"Valerie will have us thoroughly spoilt by then," Joe added merrily.

Eleanor blew them a kiss and grabbed Mary's arm, while the happily married couples headed to the small plane, waiting on the hot tarmac.

As it taxied down the runway, Kath turned around and gave Marcus a kiss.

"What was that for?" he questioned happily.

Kath grinned widely. "For making it all happen and for it being such a perfect occasion," she answered cheerfully.

They both headed back to the resort and relaxed around the pool for the remainder of the afternoon, retiring early to bed, as they had a busy schedule tomorrow.

At 7.30am the huge catamaran arrived at the jetty to take them to the Great Barrier Reef, which Kath was looking forward to immensely. The whole Whitsunday Passage melted into the sparkling, sapphire Pacific Ocean, as the catamaran made its way to the various islands, picking up more passengers.

They had morning tea up on deck, watching a pod of dolphins play on the starboard side, oblivious to the audience they had attracted. Teenagers were making great squeals of delight when the dolphins sprung out of the water, creating a sea spray on their descent.

Before arriving at the pristine reef, groups were allocated their scuba diving gear; this prevented wasting valuable diving time when they arrived.

Lunch was served. Marcus and Kath both tucked into their food hungrily, knowing they had an exciting and extremely active day ahead.

Finally, they were told to get changed into their gear, as they were only five minutes from their destination. Sam was their underwater guide and had been working the reef for the past five years. He was a young thirty year old, with blue eyes, tousled blonde hair and a typical Aussie marine biologist, who was extremely protective of his reef. He taught what signs he would use under water, like creating an X with his arms to warn everyone of danger, because what he could be pointing to could be extremely beautiful but also deadly.

The huge white catamaran shimmered in the sun as it was anchored on to the huge pontoon, standing as a sanctuary awaiting her visitors. The group of six followed Sam down to the lower deck, all checking their equipment one final time, before setting out on their adventure.

Kath entered the ocean staying close to Sam and Marcus. The water was amazingly clear and Kath was instantly delighted by the stunning coral reef. The colours and textures were astoundingly beautiful; a sense of serenity filled her very soul as they forged their way forward, on their epic watery journey.

A school of clown anemone fish darted past everyone, adorned with bright orange and white stripes, totally ignoring the intruders. As they made their way along the reef, diving deeper into the blue abyss, sea grasses in flowing tranquil meadows came into sight.

Sam signalled for the group to follow him down further, before pointing to a two metre dugong along with her calf, journeying along the depths of the ocean. Apparently these odd looking creatures are related to the elephant family. Giant clams sat in clusters upon the ocean floor, their wide mouths lying open, waiting patiently for their prey. Marcus tugged Kath's right arm and pointed to his left. A few metres away, a gigantic green sea turtle was making its way through the reef, her massive shell appearing not to hinder her, as she glided elegantly through the ocean in a nonchalant manner.

A huge school of parrot fish inundated the group. Sam signalled and everyone stopped to feed the beautifully coloured fish, donning the bright colours of parrots you would find in the tropical far north. They nibbled upon the food readily, obviously used to the excited tourists invading their warm watery world.

Travelling further along, Sam gave his group the warning sign, quickly pointing out a spectacular firefish, exquisitely reddish brown in colour, with gold and cream yellow bands embossed on its body. It had distinctive elongated fins and numerous spines. It was almost thirty centimetres in length, appearing beautiful, yet its' painful venomous fins could cause severe reactions in humans and sometimes even death.

Kath spotted tiny seahorses making their way slowly through the sea grass, passing the sea urchins and brightly coloured sponges, their brown imprinted skins camouflaging and protecting them from unsuspecting predators.

The day progressed rapidly and happily, as they made their way back to the catamaran; where Marcus swam much closer to Kath, after Sam pointed to a three metre reef shark, swimming away in the outlying area, instinctively aware of their presence.

Boarding the catamaran, everyone instantly burst out into a loud chatter, overwhelmed by the magical sights they encountered, having been truly mesmerised by the sheer beauty of the vibrant, underwater reef.

Towel drying Kath's hair, Marcus stretched around giving her a quick kiss. "Well, what did you think? Did you like it?" he quizzed enthusiastically.

"Like it! It was extraordinary Marcus. I have never seen anything so stunning in my entire life and it will stay with me, for always. Thank you yet again," she beamed up at him, before planting a kiss on his wet nose.

Soon they were happily tucking into hot cups of coffee and munching upon yummy biscuits, as they made their journey home. All of the passengers seemed exhilarated, touched by mother nature's beauty. Everyone more conscious and aware, as to why we should look after our natural environment, as the catamaran made her way slowly through the stunning archipelago of islands.

The next few days were spent kayaking and snorkelling down at Pebble Beach, which the Qualia Resort had exclusive access to, guaranteeing absolute privacy. In the late afternoons, they would lie rejuvenated beside the twelve metre infinity swimming pool, drinking delicious and brightly coloured cocktails, basking in the late afternoon sun, while lying beneath the swaying coconut palms. The intuitive service at Qualia Resort was marvellous and Kath would miss the quiet haven, when she left.

The last evening they had dinner out on the veranda, watching the dramatic sunset upon the horizon. The wine was mellow, the food delicious and both were filled with regret, knowing it was time to leave the tranquillity and head back to the real world.

They made love later that evening, slow and seductively, gently exploring each other's body one last time, in a part of paradise which they would remember for always.

Chapter Nine

Brigee picked them both up from the airport, bright, breezy and full of chat as usual. Valerie and the girls gave them a welcoming hug, when they arrived home. Mary and Joe took great delight in explaining how much Valerie and her family had spoilt them.

"This is a marvellous country Kath luv. Sure you have everything here, from beautiful cities to quaint country towns. You've got tropical rainforests, sandy deserts, mountains, glorious beaches and even snowfields, it's bloody unbelievable," Joe exclaimed.

"Sure you wouldn't be needin' to leave the place if you lived here," Mary butted in, laughing out loud with a twinkle in her eyes.

Kath and Marcus went straight back to work the next week, both catching up on the imminent reports required. During this period, the girls and Brigee kept Joe and Mary occupied by visiting tourist havens, thoroughly enjoying each other's company.

In the evenings over dinner, Marcus and Kath were filled in on the day's activities. Mary was fascinated by the aquarium down at Darling Harbour, while Joe was deeply moved by the War Memorial Museum in Canberra. They both enjoyed the ferry crossing on their visit to Manly, where they paddled their feet in the ocean and ate huge ice-creams "which were meltin' in the sun rapidly," Mary added. They both adored the sunshine; both fully aware it had been snowing back home and were extremely glad they were missing it. The week flew by quickly, while Kath and Marcus organised to take a few days off, to go sightseeing with her folks.

The following morning as the freeway came to an end; Marcus slowly made the uphill climb towards the Blue Mountains. The winding roads were edged with deep red bottle brushes and bright vibrant, golden wattle trees.

Kath smiled inwardly, when they passed the sign for the Norman Lindsay Gallery, reminiscing about the day she spent there with Valerie and the brief illicit affair they had.

They were stopping off for numerous cups of tea on the way up, which astounded Marcus, who had completely forgotten about the traditional Irish trait of tea drinking. A few hours later, they were searching for a parking spot near the lookout.

All having stretched their legs, they found the mountain air much cooler and fresher, as they peered across at the sandstone plateaus and the gum covered Jamison Valley, lying far below.

Following a particular walking trail, they clamoured down some stone steps carved into the mountainside, before crossing a small rope bridge, allowing Kath's parents to rest upon a small bench positioned on the first of the Three Sisters. These were three prominent rocky pinnacles, sitting on the edge of the escarpment at Echo Point, which had been eroded and separated by the wind and rain. This famous rock formation obviously had an Aboriginal legend attached to it; a mystical story which was told by guides to the inquisitive tourists visiting.

They spoke of the three sisters who lived in the Jamison Valley, members of the Katoomba tribe, who fell in love with three brothers from the Nepean tribe. Tribal law forbid them to marry and the three brothers captured them and caused a major tribal battle. A witchdoctor recognising the sisters were in danger turned them to stone during the battle. However, he was unable to reverse his spell, because he was also killed during the conflict. After hearing the story, the tourists would peer at the rocky pinnacles sadly, talking amongst themselves, keeping the legend very much alive.

They then climbed on board the scenic skyway, suspended on cables high above the Jamison Valley, which provided everyone who fitted into the airy cabin, a spectacular view.

The magnificent panoramic views of the surrounding mountains were breathtakingly beautiful, as they ate lunch in the revolving restaurant.

Afterwards, all four clambered on the tourist railway train; where passengers were tightly packed into the cage-like carriages, before descending swiftly down the mountainside at a 160 degree angle. They were immediately swallowed up by a dark steep tunnel; shrieks of panic rippled throughout the air, before everyone was shot out into the welcoming sunlight, coming to an abrupt stop.

Finally, they clamoured out of the carriage laughing, before following a windy path around to a majestic waterfall. Roaring thunderously in the afternoon sun, this great torrent of water cascaded down from over the mountain top approximately ninety metres above them, making its mighty descent and coming to rest in a large, crystal clear rock pool, surrounded by massive green ferns and moss covered boulders. They enjoyed wandering along the timber pathway, each taking in the natural stunning landscape, unfolding before them.

Later in the afternoon they visited the local shops in Katoomba, where Mary and Joe purchased thick woollen jumpers, ugg boots and woolly cushion covers, embossed with the proverbial koalas and kangaroos, made especially for the tourists.

In the evening they resided at the Fairmont Resort, a highly respected establishment perched on the edge of the heritage-listed Blue Mountains

National Park. The ambience of the rooms, equipped with fireplaces for the winter months, made Joe and Mary feel very much at home. The crystal chandeliers in the dining room added opulence and an old worldly charm to the hotel. Mary and Joe had the kangaroo steaks for dinner and were pleased with their choice. Kath and Marcus both selected the barramundi fillets, which were mouth watering and absolutely delicious. They retired to their respective bedrooms at 10pm, relaxed and exhausted from the day's adventure.

"I think they enjoyed the day immensely," Marcus commented, climbing into bed next to Kath.

"They most certainly did and tomorrow will be something quite different for them again."

They gave each other a quick kiss, before drifting into a deep sleep, tired from the day's shenanigans.

After an early breakfast, they climbed into Marcus's four wheel drive to commence another scenic journey. It was approximately a two hour drive out to Jenolan Caves, so they wanted to get there in plenty of time to complete a few tours. The journey took them through Lithgow and the majestic Hartley Valley, where they took a break and stopped for tea and scones.

Arriving at the caves, they put on their good flat walking shoes and made their way up to the kiosk to purchase the tickets. Joe insisted on paying and Mary readily backed him up, adamant they've been spoilt enough.

The tour guide, a young university student called Amy, greeted them with a hearty smile, before attentively leading them into a deep cavern. Inside, the limestone rocks were lit up strategically, with spotlights emitting a warm glowing ambience, creating a cathedral like atmosphere. Suspended from the high ceilings, long jagged stalactites had accumulated over thousands of years, collecting the soft limestone on its downward, moisture dripping journey.

They squeezed past stalagmites, entering a huge amphitheatre-like cave. This was brilliantly lit up; displaying warm yellow walls, constructed by nature, appearing like huge organ pipes, creating a serene and holy sanctuary.

Wide eyed tourists took photographs, capturing the underground rivers and cave formations, which are the oldest and largest underground cave system in the world. They visited three caves out of the eleven, with everyone appreciating the sheer beauty of the awe inspiring formations, which mother nature had beautifully created. There were many steel steps to be climbed that led them to enter different caves with their young guide Amy. Kath came to be pleasantly surprised by her mum and dad's agility and stamina.

After a few hours they filtered out into the bright sunlight again, exhilarated and enchanted by the tour. Lunch was eaten at the Jenolan Hotel, which was both hearty and wholesome, before making their journey back to Katoomba.

The following day was spent by Marcus and Joe visiting the Leura Golf Course, which was situated next to the Fairmont Resort, whilst Mary and Kath drove to Katoomba and wandered through the local shops to gather up a few gifts.

The break was ideal, giving the four of them time to reconnect, to speak openly about old times, without getting caught out by the girls. They laughed and chatted, fully aware Joe and Mary would be heading back home next week. Recognising it would be a sad day; however, they were all extremely grateful for the wonderful experiences they shared. The wedding had gone off gloriously; Joe and Mary got on well with their granddaughters and got to know Kath's friends intimately. Overall, their holiday had been an enormous success.

The following morning, they made their journey back down the mountain, taking the Bells Line Road route this time around. The road was twisty and bendy, a major hazard for huge trucks, although it was a spectacular scenic route.

They stopped off at the local orchards and handpicked some apples to take home with them. They sampled the homemade apple pies, along with a cup of tea of course, before continuing on their journey. The girls were delighted when they arrived back and made dinner for them all, along with Brigee's expert help of course.

The days meandered and blended into each other, as suitcases were packed for Mary and Joe's departure. Soon it was time; time to say their goodbyes, time to make promises to catch up again, time to give them a gigantic lasting hug and to wish them both well.

As the jet sped down the runway, Kath let out a huge sob, no longer able to contain her heartfelt emotions.

Marcus instantly took her into his arms. "I know it's sad my darling but you can't keep them here forever."

"Why not," she challenged, like a small lost child.

"Because my darling, they have their own lives and friends back home."

"I know," Kath replied "but there's no harm in hoping," peering up at Marcus, giving him a watery grin.

Hand in hand they left the airport, a little bit of their hearts tucked away, bruised and saddened. Although, their hearts were also swollen with love, from the precious time they shared with Mary and Joe.

Marcus settled into family life perfectly and was readily accepted by both Margaret and Rachel. Brigee was also pleased; Gladesville felt like a home again, continually filled with fun and laughter, similar to when Rod was alive.

Marcus kept the penthouse over at Bondi and even gave Margaret a key, who was completely thrilled. "You can use it when you're over at Bondi Beach with your university friends or when you're partying in the city at the weekend," Marcus whispered, so that Rachel wouldn't hear or there would be World War III.

"You're one spoilt young lady" Kath commented, raising an eyebrow, inwardly pleased Marcus and Margaret had managed to build up an amazingly close relationship. Recognising it would help immensely when they broke the news to her, Marcus was in fact her real father.

Everyone was back into a routine; Rachel was back at school, Margaret was attending lectures and tutorials at the University of Sydney and Brigee was at the helm of the household, organising menus and laundry.

Work was full on for both Kath and Marcus, the industry was becoming more competitive, demanding new innovative ideas in order to keep ahead. The days were long at times but extremely rewarding for them both. Kath and Marcus enjoyed the challenges. They were extremely disciplined and focused, each as equally relentless and driven as the other, when it came to getting deadlines met.

The employees respected them both; they were known to be tough but extremely fair and treated all their employees like family. They honoured every employee's birthday with a traditional birthday cake, along with a suitable birthday present. Christmas time was adored by the entire staff, because extravagant parties were held nationally, with gifts and bonuses given out, demonstrating their employer's appreciation. The staffs' loyalty and hard working ethics were renowned at Noblealert and frequently envied by opposing companies.

Margaret was excelling at the University of Sydney and the professors were enthralled by her enthusiasm and determination, glad she would complete her Masters, as it was well within her capabilities. Margaret initially saw this as an obstacle, mainly because it would keep her from working in surgery for another year but a trade off was made as to where she could complete her internship. Her drive was to be in the operating theatre as quickly as possible, in order to change lives and to save them, wanting desperately to make a major difference.

Kath and Marcus admired her dedication and didn't mind her having her twenty-third birthday party at the penthouse. She didn't want a long drawn out family affair, which was totally understandable. She simply wanted to hang out with her university friends, with finger food, wine and a casual party, allowing them to dance to the latest music.

Valerie consoled Kath at a luncheon the very next day. "Don't worry my dear. You're not losing her Kath. She's just growing up and gaining her independence, just like our son Richard who will make somebody a wonderful husband one day."

"Don't even go there Valerie," Kath groaned, picking up her glass of wine. "At present, I am simply enjoying the four of us together as a family, as it's been terrific, everything feels perfectly normal and I'm extremely happy," smiling across at her good friend.

"I'm glad," Valerie replied, placing a hand over Kath's in a caring manner.

The party was organised and Kath was prevented from hiring any caterers. "Everything's low key mum," Margaret repeated, appearing irritable. "We'll have cheese and crackers, chips, dips and simple finger food M-U-M," she added, rolling her eyes.

Marcus rested his hand gently upon Kath's shoulders. "Come on love, we'll leave and let Margaret get on with it."

Wishing she could stay, Rachel instantly gave a roar of protest standing amongst the brightly coloured balloons, she had just blown up.

"Thanks sis and everyone else for your help but I'll catch up with you all tomorrow at lunchtime," Margaret asserted, giving them a quick kiss and ushering them out the door.

Margaret changed into a glitzy silver top, jeans and silver sandals. Afterwards, she added some last minute decorations to the living room, before her friends started trickling in. Charlotte and Hilary were given a quick tour before the others arrived and were overwhelmed by the penthouse and its extravagant design. With thirty friends attending, the party got lively around 11pm. That's when the music got louder and the dancing kicked in. Some of the guys were lining up tequila shots and having a competition, which entailed licking salt, sculling a shot and sucking on a lemon, drawing great gales of laughter from the spectators. The doors were slung open on to the balcony as the night heated up, as more and more people started turning up.

Margaret relaxed, totally immersing herself into the party scene. The alcohol together with the marijuana hanging in the air was making her feel giddy, happy and slightly sentimental, when she was dancing with Ben, from the university.

The party got louder and rowdier, growing more out of control by the minute. Margaret was shocked to find lines of coke lying on the coffee table and immediately objected but was instantly told to butt out, by people she didn't even know. Glasses were being broken; people were piling into the bedrooms and one was even vomiting in a pot plant. A massive fight broke out and Margaret ran into the bathroom, swiftly locking the door behind her.

Hurriedly she rang Marcus on her mobile. "Hello."

Instantly recognising Margaret's strained voice, Marcus immediately asked "is everything okay?" Peering at the bedside clock, it read 2am.

"No it's not," Margaret shrieked down the phone. "I'm in the bathroom. There are gatecrashers, drugs, crazy party goers and a massive fight has just broken out. I'm sorry Marcus … I'm truly sorry but I desperately need your help."

Sitting up straight away, fully alert and awake, Marcus shouted down the phone "hang in there Margaret, I'm on my way. Stay where you are and keep your phone on you."

Marcus immediately hung up and jumped out of bed, explaining everything in a second to Kath, who was already wide awake, out of bed and getting dressed. Making their way across the city was much easier and quicker at this time in the morning. Thirty minutes later, they arrived at Bondi.

Making their way up in the elevator, Marcus rang Margaret and discovered she was much more hysterical than before. "We're only two minutes away love, don't worry, I'll sort everything out."

Opening the door abruptly, both Marcus and Kath were shocked. The penthouse was trashed and people were everywhere. A lot were dancing and swaying in the middle of the room, obviously stoned. The music was loud, pumping erratically in Kath's ears, as she shoved her way through the disorderly crowd, to find Margaret locked away in the bathroom.

"Take a deep breath and hold my hand, everything will be okay," Kath reiterated, as they made their way out of the bathroom.

Unexpectedly, the music stopped, immediately drawing abusive and irate complaints, from the obnoxious and unruly mass.

Marcus stood up on a chair. "Guys and girls, I hate to break it to you but this party is officially over. Unfortunately, the neighbours have made several complaints to the police, in relation to the noise and they're on their way over now."

A loud groan rose from the crowd and an immediate evacuation began taking place. Girls were quickly running for their handbags and jackets, while the guys were crazily grabbing their booze and drugs, all frantically heading for the door.

Minutes later a few of Margaret's friends came over to say goodbye, others to apologise for the mess and to quickly offer to help tidy up. Margaret was shell shocked at the devastation lying before her. Standing pale, withdrawn and silent, tears began welling up in her eyes.

Soon the room was empty, only the three of them stood in complete silence, peering at the broken glasses, food trampled into the thickly piled carpet and the smudged cigarette stains smeared across the cream suede furniture. The smell of alcohol mixed in with vomit, hung putridly in the air.

At Marcus's request, Kath fought hard to control her anger, although she was still enormously frustrated and disappointed, at the senseless trashing of his apartment.

Margaret broke down into huge uncontrollable sobs, tears of disenchantment streamed down her cheeks and Marcus pulled her into his arms instantly, holding her tight. "I'm so sorry Marcus. I'm so sorry. You're not even my father and yet you trusted me so much."

Marcus felt bad for her; it hurt him immeasurably to see his daughter so horribly distraught. He peered over at Kath; she too had tears in her eyes, experiencing the whole emotional scene, unfolding before her. Kath took a deep breath and nodded at Marcus, knowing in her heart, the time had arrived.

Marcus drew Margaret even closer. "It's okay, they're only material things and they can be easily fixed; besides it wasn't your fault. We should have organised security to prevent gatecrashers."

Margaret stared up at him, red eyed and full of tears. "You're always so nice to me and I don't deserve it, especially not now," peering dismally around the penthouse.

Marcus inhaled a deep breath. "Margaret darling, fathers' are normally nice to their daughters because they love them unconditionally, no matter what takes place."

Slowly comprehending what had been said, Margaret appeared shell shocked. "Do you mean, what I think you mean? Are you saying ... you're my father?" Margaret responded, apprehensively.

"Yes my love, your mother and I have wanted to tell you for quite a while but it never seemed to be the right moment. However, this is as good a time as ever." He hugged Margaret closely, before breaking down and crying, unashamedly.

Kath went over and wrapped her arms around them, letting go of a huge sob, mixed with overwhelming emotion and relief.

Margaret had a million questions for Marcus and her mother. At 4am in the morning, they comfortably sat crossed legged on the floor, drinking coffee together, before Kath told Margaret her life story. Explaining how her brothers were murdered, informing her how she fled and falsified her own death, in order to protect everyone. She stopped short of mentioning her rape, names of the gun runners and of course Jack Gillespie.

Margaret sat shocked and horrified by the whole story, finding it difficult to comprehend, how her mother even survived. A whole new respect grew for her mother and Marcus, as their stories unfolded.

By 6am they sat silently, watching the sunrise together. A brand new day and a brand new beginning, Margaret thought, which came with a father she never knew she had. Margaret was completely mature in regards to the whole new outcome, finding it endearing to have inherited a real father. Every so often in the midst of their cleaning frenzy, she would stop and glance across at him, smiling happily. Kath stood back and watched silently, her heart full and relieved beyond belief. Margaret knew at last about Marcus's true identity.

The carpet cleaners arrived at 9am and by twelve noon, the place looked as good as new, with no trace of the party from the night before.

They headed back to Gladesville, each happy in their own right, with only Rachel left to contend with.

Margaret's birthday lunch was a splendid affair, shared with Valerie and her family, along with Brigee. A huge chocolate cake topped with candles was brought out to the veranda by Brigee and everyone joined in singing 'happy birthday.' A huge hip hip hurray resonated into the open air, with the unwrapping of presents, following shortly afterwards. Margaret was especially astounded by the solid gold bracelet which her parents had bought for her. She adored the engraving inside, which read 'live long, love unconditionally and laugh lots.' A few hours later everyone left, leaving the four of them to tidy up.

Kath nodded at Marcus as she took Rachel aside, leaving father and daughter drying the dishes.

"What's up mum?" Rachel enquired, always a perceptive child from the day she was born.

"Well you know what happened at Margaret's party, don't you?"

"Yeah" Rachel answered, eyes wide and grinning. "I wish I was there, because I would have sorted them out," she declared seriously.

"Well something else happened love."

"What?" Rachel interrupted, giving her mum her full attention.

"Well darling, there is no other way of putting this but to come right out with it. I knew and loved Marcus a long time ago; in fact, he's Margaret's real father."

"Wow!" Rachel proclaimed. "I already thought so," she added enthusiastically.

"What do you mean?" Kath questioned.

"First of all, can't you see the similarities . . . look at the eyes m-u-m!" Rachel sighed, indignantly. "And remember when Marcus gave you the engagement ring, well I heard him saying to you how he missed you for the past twenty-three years!"

"Soooo," Kath enquired.

"Mum, how old is Margaret?" rolling her eyes skywards, completely exasperated.

"Well I never," Kath announced, nodding her head in disbelief.

Suddenly Rachel reached over, giving Kath a horrendous hug. "It's great mum and I'm really happy, because we're even more of a family now," jumping immediately off the sofa and running into the kitchen.

Marcus and Margaret looked up together, waiting in anticipation for Rachel's reaction. "I'm really happy for you Margaret and guess what? You found out on your birthday," Rachel babbled, rushing over and giving her a huge hug, followed by a kiss. She slowly strolled over to Marcus, announcing "I kinda knew a-n-y-w-a-y, just ask mum," she added joyfully, giving him a hug also.

Later in the evening Marcus and Kath retired to bed, feeling ecstatic. The two girls accepted the news, both equally as happy for one another, while Marcus and Kath felt their family unit had just grown closer, closer than ever before.

Chapter Ten

And before they knew it, Christmas had almost arrived. Last year due to the wedding up in the Whitsunday's, Christmas wasn't spent in the traditional manner. The girls returned home with Brigee, Mary and Joe, leaving Kath and Marcus to continue on with their honeymoon.

However, this year Kath was having a huge party and was inviting the whole of her family and friends. Brigee was up to her eyeballs, organising the traditional family festivities and was intending to pick up the turkeys by the end of the week. The girls were on holidays and they made themselves useful, by organising the decorations, as they waited for the Christmas tree to be delivered later that afternoon.

"Don't hang the mistletoe over the dining room doorway Rachel, as everyone entering together will have to kiss," Margaret screamed out to her from the staircase, as she added more tinsel to the banisters.

"Imagine, everyone having to kiss," Rachel called out giggling. "Especially if they want something to eat," she grinned.

"Exactly my point Rachel," Margaret sighed loudly. "A long queue into the dining room and Brigee will get mad as hell. Because the food will start getting cold and you'll know all about it," Margaret chided.

Rachel begrudgingly removed the mistletoe as the phone rang and Margaret immediately went rushing down the stairs to retrieve it.

"Hello?" she enquired politely. "Yes, it's Margaret speaking," she replied, drawing in a deep breath, waiting impatiently for the secretary to transfer the call through to the Professor.

"Good morning, I've been anxiously waiting for your call. Hopefully it's good news, because the experience I would gain would be absolutely marvellous," Margaret babbled excitedly, drawing in a deep breath and holding it, waiting in anticipation.

"Yes Margaret, I understand what you're saying. But I can assure you that it wasn't an easy task," Professor Thompson reported, in a bureaucratic manner. "However, getting quickly to the point, as I am sure you are extremely busy with Christmas almost upon you. The answer is yes. You may take up the position at the end of February Margaret and I wish you all the very best. Congratulations once again on obtaining such admirable results, you were truly an exemplary student."

"Thank you, thank you," Margaret reiterated down the phone. "I will make the University proud Professor Thompson and Merry Christmas."

"I'm sure you will Margaret and a Merry Christmas to you too," he muttered, before hanging up.

"Yippee," Margaret called out happily, obviously ecstatic, quickly heading back to the decorations sitting on the stairs.

"What are you so happy about?" Rachel enquired.

"Never you mind you little nosey parker," Margaret joked.

"Perhaps it's in relation to a Christmas present?" Rachel queried.

"Could be," Margaret teased, picking up the tinsel, aware she would have to notify her parents really soon. Something, she wasn't really looking forward to.

Marcus and Kath arrived home after lunch as planned, to help decorate the living tree. This was a normal family tradition for Kath, both here and back in Ireland. But this year in particular was a special momentous occasion, because she got to spend it with her four favourite people, as Brigee was definitely counted as one of the family.

Marcus lifted Rachel up on his shoulders to put the star on top, as everyone stood back, admiring the magnificent ceiling high tree, adorned with pink, mauve and golden baubles, accompanying pretty tinsel and hundreds of small intricate lights. "It's a truly superb and professional job you have done young ladies and I must add, a very special one, as I have my loving family around me," Marcus confided.

Kath leaned forward and kissed him, with tears of happiness in her eyes. "My sentiments exactly my darling," she added, as everyone wandered into the kitchen for a much deserved drink.

All the Christmas festivities had finished at work; thank heavens, Kath thought, as it was extremely exhausting. She couldn't wait to have the next two weeks off with her family.

On Christmas Eve, the girls were already up in bed, while Marcus and Kath sat in the front room sipping on a glass of red wine, both enjoying the tranquillity. The tiny Christmas lights twinkled serenely in amongst the pine scented branches, the tree stood majestically, coated in elegant decorations, with an abundance of large colourful boxes tucked in at its base.

Kath sighed "isn't this beautiful Marcus. I can't believe another year has flown by already and it's almost Christmas Day. Hmm ... it feels so special, so normal and so wonderful," her voice trailing off softly, as Marcus leant over and kissed her.

Without saying a word, he took her in his arms and carried her up to their bedroom. On Christmas Eve night they made love together, like two young couples, choreographed and synchronised in a slow, seductive manner. In no immediate rush, simply taking time to gently caress and please one another, before collapsing into each other's arms and falling asleep, under the moonlit sky.

At 6.30am the next morning, Rachel was up and bouncing on their bed, encouraging them to get up so they could head downstairs to open their pressies. Brigee stayed over and soon it was on for young and old, as wrapping after wrapping was torn off manically, followed by bountiful shrills of joy.

Brigee adored the gold locket and the matching gold bracelet, glancing immediately across at Marcus and Kath.

"Thank you so very much but it's far too much, you really have to stop spoiling me," she asserted.

"It's because you're worth it," Kath and Marcus chirped up in unison, both bursting into a fit of laughter.

Margaret fell in love with her new medical journals which Valerie helped Kath pick out, along with a black leather doctor's bag containing a stethoscope, surgical scissors and other medical equipment, impressing Margaret immensely.

"It's wonderful, thank you so much mum and dad," she cried happily, giving them both hugs and kisses, with tears of admiration and gratitude written in her eyes. Fully aware it was an extremely expensive and thoughtful gift.

Rachel jumped around excitedly, making sounds of happiness, discovering she received the latest state-of-the-art stereo equipment. Her young inquisitive eyes also admired the up-to-date beachwear, which was the trend at present. Billabong shorts, T-shirts and bikinis were opened up quickly as well and she loved the numerous pairs of sandals, Margaret had bought for her.

Marcus got a surprise when he began unwrapping new golf clubs, which were well disguised in a huge box. The Ralph Lauren T- shirts and shorts would also fit him well. He was enormously taken back, when he opened up a box containing an exquisite watch, made by the Swiss watchmaker Vacheron Constantin.

"Read the back," Rachel coaxed, well aware of the gift's engraving. Turning it around, Marcus read out aloud 'May you have time to enjoy your new family, today, tomorrow and always'. His eyes began to tear up. Swallowing hard, he instantly leant over and gave Kath a loving and gentle kiss.

Finally, it was Kath's turn to be mesmerised, everyone instantly gasped out loud when she retrieved a glamorous silver gown from amongst the packaging and silver shoes were unwrapped soon afterwards. "They're gorgeous," she confided, completely thrilled.

"Valerie helped," Marcus smiled, hinting it would be splendid for this evening's party. "Yeah," all the girls agreed in earnest.

Kath began to also unwrap a flat blue velvet box. She immediately held her breath, before prising it open. A pair of extravagant pear-shaped dropped earrings sparkled in the early morning light. The emeralds were breathtakingly beautiful. "They're absolutely stunning my darling. I have been thoroughly spoilt," peering up at him, smiling radiantly.

Marcus smiled happily. "They'll match the necklace which Rod bought you and also your engagement ring my love. May you have good health to enjoy them, for many years to come."

"Let's have some breakfast 'cause I'm starving," Rachel bellowed, startling everyone into immediate action. Wrapping paper was retrieved and dispensed into huge plastic bags, while presents were lifted and taken to their respective rooms. Brigee set about getting breakfast ready for everyone, with everybody setting about their tasks in a jovial Christmas spirit.

The party was a formal evening affair, where friends and family could catch up and enjoy delicious food and wine, dressed up in all their finery.

Kath emerged glamorous in her new silver evening gown, the emeralds complementing her outfit, adding to her elegant and regal persona.

When Marcus waltzed down the stairs with Kath, wearing his formal black tie and suit, anyone could have mistaken them for movie stars. Marcus's green eyes and dark chiselled Italian features, truly complemented Kath's sophistication and elegance. The champagne flowed and everyone mingled happily, enjoying the ambience and hospitality bestowed upon them.

The house was decorated magnificently; tiny lights accompanied extravagant decorations, hanging spectacularly outside in the garden, carrying the festive and relaxed atmosphere along with it.

"I feel like the happiest women on the planet right now," Kath confided, peering over the balcony and down upon her guests.

Marcus gently kissed her. "Merry Christmas my darling, you've been the best present anyone could ever wish for." They tinkled their champagne glasses together in a gentle loving gesture. "To love, harmony and family," Marcus whispered.

"Here, here," Kath replied, sipping on her champagne, deliriously happy and content.

The guests began filtering home from 1am onwards and by 2.30am Marcus was carrying Kath to the bedroom. She loved this man so much, he was everything and more a woman could ever ask for, she thought, drowsily melting into his arms.

The next morning everyone had a sleep in, not rising until 10am. Brigee was in a cheerful mood, while organising a continental breakfast. She stood momentarily, smiling and watching sunbeams dancing over Looking Glass Bay, reflecting tiny prisms of rainbow light upon the pristine white boats. It was indeed a beautiful day, for the family to watch the yachts leave Sydney Harbour, she thought. Soon, the yachts would be racing out through The Heads, tackling the notorious Sydney to Hobart annual Boxing Day event. Today, half a million spectators would converge on the Sydney Harbour foreshores.

Noblealert had an entry this year, along with ninety-five other entrants. James Woodridge, who was one of the company's directors, was in charge of the team. 'Sweet Emerald', the ninety foot yacht owned by Noblealert, would travel the six hundred and twenty-eight nautical miles. Glasses would be raised, with good luck sentiments given to the crew members, before they left. It was also a good time to catch up with various national staff members, wishing them all good fortune, before they sailed off into the horizon.

Over the years there had been many tragic deaths along the rugged Bass Strait, when crossing the treacherous Tasman Sea. The event was a huge tradition; large businesses invested millions of dollars into their yachts, in order to win the prestigious cup. Many of Australia's great sportsmen and women enjoyed the challenge, competing against their global competitors.

The next week passed by quickly, where lazing around and relaxing was the order of the day, primarily. The girls came and went with their friends, spending time mulling around the pool and snacking, before heading off to the movies later in the evening. Kath and Marcus got time to visit the theatre and to frequent a few French restaurants, down in the Southern Highlands. They went sailing with the girls on a few occasions the following week, out and around Church Point, which was a picturesque part of the world. Kath noticed Margaret was being much quieter than usual, she enquired if anything was wrong and was instantly reprimanded. Many a lazy lunch was spent with Valerie and Matt, which was enjoyable, interesting and stress free.

Arriving home late in the afternoon, Kath heard Brigee in the kitchen and went to retrieve a cool drink. "You better tell your mother soon. At least that way, she will have gotten used to the idea," Brigee sighed in exasperation.

"I better get used to what?" Kath interrupted. She was instantly met with huge green eyes and a pale shocked face, belonging to Margaret. A silence hung in the air, as Margaret clearly appeared uncomfortable.

Brigee decided to leave the room. "I'll leave you both to it then," she remarked on her way out.

"T-h-a-n-k-s Brigee," Margaret retorted, rolling her eyes heavenward, clearly unimpressed in getting caught out.

Kath made her way to the fridge trying to appear blasé; however her gut instinct was kicking in, warning her bad news was on its way. "Do you want a drink love?" she enquired lightly, hoping she was wrong.

"No thanks mum," Margaret replied, knowing there was no turning back, knowing it was time to fess up.

Kath casually wandered over to the kitchen bench and took a seat on one of the stools, opposite her daughter. "Well then, what's the big secret you've been keeping, it can't be that bad, surely?"

Margaret fumbled with her hands not making eye contact, before drawing a deep breath. "Mum there's no easy way of saying this, so I'm just going to come straight out with it and tell you. I'm going to Northern Ireland to finish my internship."

Kath sucked in air, trying her best to remain calm, trying her best not to panic, although deep down in the pit of her stomach, she wanted to scream.

It took her a few moments, until she was able to speak. "But why Ireland Margaret? Surely you have more than enough hospitals to choose from over here. Besides, if it's an adventure you're after, why don't you sign up with the Flying Doctors, apparently that's pretty full on?"

"Mum I hear what you're saying, however, I'm going to be a surgeon and what better place is there to practice in, other than the Royal Victoria Hospital in Belfast," Kath inhaled deeply.

"The last time we visited, was to fetch you after a bomb exploded, which killed many people Margaret, including your dear friend. And don't forget, we came deadly close to being injured ourselves, when we were out shopping in Belfast."

"Mum, you can't wrap me up in cotton wool you know. I'm a grown woman, I've made my decision and that's that." Margaret stormed off immediately, leaving Kath sitting in the kitchen on her own, thoroughly heartbroken.

Brigee wandered in slowly and Kath looked up, huge uncontrollable tears came flooding to her eyes, flowing down her cheeks profusely.

"I know, I know," Brigee began, wrapping her arms around Kath. "I've tried talking her out of it but she's dead set on the idea and she's as stubborn and determined as her mother."

"I know I can't stop her Brigee but I'm scared because I know what can happen. It's hard to imagine your daughter living on the other side of the world, constantly in imminent danger," she sobbed.

"Take a deep breath love, Marcus will be home any minute. Believe you me, he will speak to young Margaret and find a compromise to secure her safety and give you peace of mind."

"Okay, I hope you're right Brigee," Kath sniffed. "I'll grab a glass of wine and sit out by the pool to calm down, before Marcus arrives back home."

Kath sat beside the tranquil pool, sipping upon her drink, as her mind wandered back to her past, back to the terror and bloodshed, making her shiver instantly, in the late afternoon sun. Of all places for Margaret to choose, she couldn't think of anywhere worse, any place so dangerous, somewhere so brutal and callous, when it came to grabbing unsuspecting victims.

Marcus interrupted her thoughts, making her jump instantly, as he flopped down on to the sun lounger, directly next to hers. "Well sunshine, I take it you had a nice relaxing afternoon, when I was out working on our yacht?" he enquired gently.

"No," Kath blurted out, tears streaming down her cheeks.

Marcus immediately removed her sunglasses, only to be met with her red swollen eyes. "What on earth has happened?"

"Margaret is going back to Northern Ireland to complete her internship," Kath replied.

"W-H-A-T," he exclaimed turning pale, obviously shocked, taken completely by surprise by Kath's disclosure. It took him a few moments to gain his composure, before he continued. "My god of all places, have you tried talking her out of it?"

Kath sighed. "It's no use, as she's so determined and basically told me we can't stop her, which is true. She's twenty-three years old and quite capable of making her own decisions, no matter how much we object."

Marcus sighed heavily, lifting Kath's glass and sculling the last drop of wine, before commenting. "You're right Kath, there's not one damn thing we can do about it, except send her with our blessings. However, why don't you speak with your mother and father, as she could stay with them perhaps and travel into Belfast each morning from there."

Kath bolted upright, her eyes lighting up instantly. Maybe it wouldn't be so dreadful after all, she thought. "Darling dear you're a genius, what a marvellous idea. Mum and dad would be absolutely ecstatic and Margaret would get the opportunity to build up more of a relationship with the pair of them, as she really cherished them, when we stayed there last time."

"Well there you go my love. Although, please approach the subject cautiously with Margaret. See what she thinks, because if you try and force her, she'll buckle and go in the opposite direction."

Kath leaned over and gave him a quick kiss. "Thank you my love, what a wonderful idea." She instantly decided to leave it, not encroaching any further on the subject with Margaret, not at least until the following day, giving everyone ample opportunity to calm down.

Marcus took Kath out for an evening meal and left the girls at home on purpose, easing the tension immediately, giving Margaret time to inform Rachel about her transfer. Kath managed to eat some of her meal, acknowledging it was going to take some time adjusting to Margaret being overseas and residing in Belfast. Marcus tried his best to distract her, although he wasn't exactly thrilled with Margaret's choice either. However, he had to admit and accept there was nothing they could do.

The following afternoon, Kath approached the subject carefully with Margaret. "Did you get the opportunity to tell Rachel about heading over to Northern Ireland, when we were out for dinner last night?" she enquired gently.

Margaret looked up from her books momentarily. "Yeah mum and she was really happy and excited for me," her eyes wide and wary.

"Good, I'm pleased. Your father and I discussed it last night and recognised you're a mature young lady and we both want you to go with our blessing."

Margaret immediately rose from the sofa and gave Kath an enormous hug. "Thanks mum, I really appreciate it and don't worry, I'll be careful."

"Your father also ran an idea past me last night but I don't know what to think, to tell you the truth" she continued casually.

"What was that then?" Margaret queried.

"Well, he thought if you stayed at your grandparents, it would mean you could keep an eye on them and let me know how they're really managing over there."

"Thanks mum, that's a great idea. Mary and I got on great last time when we visited and it would be terrific company for me."

Kath smiled inwardly but outwardly she remained at ease and non-commital. "I can't promise anything but I could telephone them at the weekend and check it out."

"Yeah, that would be fantastic," Margaret interrupted, truly delighted. "It would mean a lot to me, as I wouldn't have to stay in the flats near the hospital grounds, therefore less parties and pub crawls to attend. This would also allow me to work even harder, study more and hopefully get better grades."

Kath smiled, proud and amazed by her young daughter's commitment. "Okay, leave it with me and I'll get back to you after I've spoken with mum," Kath announced, before exiting the room.

She hurried to the pool area and found Marcus stretched out upon the sun lounger. "Done," she announced proudly, extremely pleased with herself.

"What?" Marcus questioned, sitting up immediately, obviously startled, wondering what on earth was happening now.

"Margaret wants me to ring her grandparents, to see if she can stay with them, when she's over there completing her internship."

"Extremely diplomatic my darling," he said, raising an eyebrow and smiling. "Now ... are you happy?" he enquired, taking her into his arms.

"Much better," she purred and kissed him.

The phone call was made and everything was set. Mary and Joe were tremendously pleased, as Kath had predicted. Margaret would be flown over in the company jet and Joe would pick her up from the airport on 22nd February.

Kath decided to gather the girls up the following weekend, suggesting they go shopping and acquire some much needed winter attire, for Margaret's overseas trip. They acknowledged it was going to be an extremely difficult task, considering it was their summer and temperatures were averaging around thirty-eight degrees. The Southern Highlands proved fruitful, with alpaca woollen jumpers, ready for the tourists all year round. The following weekend they drove up to the Blue Mountains, to purchase some more winter clothes. The time slipped by rapidly and before they knew it, they were all standing at the airport saying their farewells.

Brigee had tears in her eyes along with Valerie, as they hugged and kissed Margaret goodbye.

Rachel couldn't understand what all the fuss was about. "It's not as if she's staying away forever," she announced loudly, in sheer frustration.

Kath and Marcus gave Margaret one final hug each, before heading back to the small group. They stood silently, watching the jet speed down the runway, before lifting off and heading into the vast blue horizon.

Kath was anxious for the next twenty-four hours, until she received the phone call from Mary, explaining Margaret had arrived and was looking well but obviously she was exhausted.

Margaret had a quick chat with Kath, confiding she was crashing after lunch to catch up on some sleep. Kath laid the phone down to rest, pleased she had a safe journey, pleased she was with her grandparents. Now all she had to do was to keep busy and hopefully the year would fly by quickly and hopefully without dramas.

Chapter Eleven

Sitting at the breakfast table the following morning tucking into her bacon and eggs, Margaret looked up. "Thank you both for letting me stay here, it means so much to me and I really do appreciate it."

Mary instantly smiled. "Ough for goodness sake child dear, sure, you're our granddaughter 'n' all and we luv you to bits, isn't that right Joe?"

"It is indeed darlin' and Margaret, we must always remember to stick with the plan. No connection can be traced back to your mother. Anyone who asks, tell them we're your stepfather's adopted uncle and aunt, 'cause we sure as hell don't want any more trouble."

Margaret nodded quietly in agreement; still astounded by her mother's history and the lengths she had gone to, in order to protect her immediate family, along with Marcus's.

Margaret spent the next few days pottering around the farm, helping Joe out in the fields and spending time in the warm cosy kitchen with Mary. She felt at home, relaxed and carefree; cherishing every precious moment with her grandparents, comfortably settling into the Irish ways.

Joe took her out a few days later to visit some car yards, as her parents had given her funds to purchase a second hand car, enabling transportation to and from the hospital to be much easier. Kath and Marcus were comforted, knowing she wouldn't be relying on the public transport system, it meant she would be spending minimum time in and around the streets of Belfast.

At the weekend, Mary went with them to inspect the green Mini Clubman, which Margaret was interested in. After endless haggling, Joe finally shook hands with the car dealer. Margaret and Mary were soon in the car following Joe and heading back home. The traffic was much lighter here than in Australia, Margaret thought, making her way through Carryduff, stopping briefly to fill the car up with petrol.

Everyone loved her Aussie accent and they were ever so friendly, frequently asking about her homeland. She would be starting her internship next week; and was really looking forward to it, along with the challenges which lay ahead.

Monday morning arrived and she was heading down Ormeau Road, edging her way towards the Royal Victoria Hospital, dressed in a warm lamb's wool sweater, jeans and long winter boots. She shivered, turning the heater up a notch. It was going to take a while getting used to this wintery cold weather, she mused.

Upon arrival, she was instantly taken to the Emergency Department and introduced to Dr Hagan. A young man approximately twenty-eight years of age, she estimated, with the most gorgeous deep brown, chocolate eyes imaginable. His dark curly hair had a mind of its own, with his unruly locks stretching down to his collar, creating a mischievous and sexy demeanour. She was greeted immediately with a huge smile.

"Aah Miss Blake, all the way from Australia I believe. Welcome aboard and please join the new recruits for the surgical ward."

Quick introductions were made, while everyone grabbed a coffee from the nearby vending machine, as Dr Hagan happily explained the rules and regulations. Margaret was instantly relieved, acknowledging the six in her group were bubbly and friendly, which included two girls, named Daphne and Hazel. Breathing a sigh of relief, Margaret couldn't help but smile, knowing she would fit in perfectly.

The day progressed quickly as they were shown around the hospital and taken to the stores; here they were taught how to fill in paperwork, allowing them to retrieve supplies later. They were guided to the various operating theatres and got to watch an intricately detailed operation taking place, from the viewing room above. Margaret watched, absolutely fascinated when a young male got his three fingers reattached.

Lunch was spent with Hazel and Daphne. Both were extremely inquisitive and enthusiastic, wanting to know everything about Sydney Australia. They had been childhood friends and were planning to travel to Australia when they completed their studies, before starting into full-time employment. They grilled and questioned her endlessly, frequently bursting into wonderful delightful laughter, as both were obviously enthralled, because they could retrieve relevant information from a real live Aussie, as they put it.

In the afternoon, Dr Hagan took his small group on his rounds to visit his patients, who were pleased to see him. His Irish charm, quick wit and jovial sense of humour, gave him an easy going bedside manner. The eyes of the little old ladies lit up when he perused their charts, as he gave his new team details on the pending operation, asking various questions haphazardly, keeping everyone on their toes. It was soon 3pm and time to leave, the day progressing extremely quickly for Margaret, because this was her vocation in life. Happily making her way towards the exit, she was surprised to be called back by Dr Hagan.

"I'm sorry for taking you away from your new friends," he smiled "but how are you settling in?"

"Great," Margaret responded, smiling up at him "or should I say grand, to fit in more."

He laughed along with her. "Have you been fixed up with proper digs yet, because I know there's a vacant flat coming up soon on the Ravenhill

Road. Dr Thompson will be leaving us next week, heading off to Africa apparently."

"Thanks for the offer," Margaret replied "but I'm staying at my stepfather's relatives out in Downpatrick and I'll commute in everyday."

She noticed that he seemed a little disappointed and wondered what that was all about.

"Right then, I just wanted to make sure you're fully settled. We must look after our Aussies, as we've got very few over here. We can't have you feeling like an outcast and saying we're an unhospitable bunch, now can we?" he smiled.

"On the contrary I love it here; I visited once before on holiday and immediately fell in love with the place," she replied.

"Well that's great," he smiled. "I'll see you tomorrow at 7am ..." His pager bleeped, interrupting their conversation instantly. Glancing down quickly he took of rapidly, calling out his goodbyes as he went rushing down the corridor.

Margaret made her way down the sterile corridor, preoccupied and lost in wistful thoughts, before being pounced upon by Hazel and Daphne. "Well, what do you think of Mr Dreamy, isn't he gorgeous?" they both squealed in excitement.

"He's okay," Margaret replied, acting casually, while her young heart raced at a hundred miles an hour.

"O-K-A-Y," the girls replied in unison, wide eyed and startled by Margaret's reaction. "Well my dear friend, you've obviously have high standards in Australia but over here, Mr Dreamy would get ten out of ten," Hazel chuckled.

Eleven out of ten actually, Margaret thought, as she made her way down the corridor with her new found friends, smiling inwardly.

The first week flew by and come Friday evening, Margaret was glad she refused the invite to go out drinking with her friends, as she lay soaking in the warm luxurious bath. It had been an extraordinary week, the wealth of knowledge she gained in such a short period was outstanding. Knowing deep down in her heart this is where she belonged; this is where she wanted to be. Working in a surgical ward, was definitely her calling in life.

As the weeks passed, she thrived on watching the emergency operations, pumped with adrenalin and able to meet the challenges efficiently, when directly put on the spot by Dr Hagan. She had grown to admire his skills; his intricate work was renowned throughout the hospital. He was known for his ground-breaking work, moving forward and introducing new advanced techniques to the other surgeons, which they eagerly embraced. Mostly she admired his humility, his happy demeanour and his gentle hands on approach.

On Wednesday evening she received another call from her mother, who seemed to be getting used to the idea her daughter was fairly safe and responsible, while working in the heart of Belfast. She would frequently chat with Rachel, who kept her up to date on what was happening at home. She enjoyed her talks with her father, who seemed happy, content and still very much in love with her mother. She hung up feeling a little gloomy, missing them immensely.

On Friday afternoon, she decided to visit the local pub, with her small group of friends from the Royal. They had built up a nice rapport and often helped each other out, especially when it came to studying for exams. Robert and Jim were the quieter members of the group but then you had Gordon and Michael, who made up for their quietness. They were constantly rowdy and always trying to attract the girl's attention. However, Margaret was always consistent and kept them both at arm's length, treating them like little brothers.

Later in the evening, everyone decided to visit the Royal Ascot for more drinks and something to eat, before making their way into the disco at 10pm. The smoke filled club was packed, as the patrons danced provocatively in the middle of the wooden floor, swaying in rhythm to the wild blaring music, as their group made their way to a table, on the far side of the room. Margaret knew she would be staying at Hazel's tonight and decided to let her hair down. It had been a difficult week with many exams taking place, although she felt she had done well and decided to relax this evening. She shimmied on the dance floor, laughing heartily while flirting with Robert. The music changed to a slow number, as it was now 1am in the morning and things were beginning to wind down.

She was making her way back to the table, when a hand grabbed her from out of nowhere. "May I have a dance?" She turned abruptly, startled to find Dr Hagan standing in front of her.

"Dr Hagan," she muttered in shock, completely surprised to see him there. "Paul is sufficient Margaret, you make me sound so ancient," he laughed.

"Oops, s-o-r-r-y," she laughingly replied, delighted to see him.

The music played softly while they danced to a slow number. Drifting into his arms she inhaled his woody cologne. He smelt so manly, so invitingly dangerous, as the shivers raced down the back of her spine. The song came to an end and he insisted upon another, which she gladly accepted, caught up in the moment, totally unaware of the people around her. Margaret felt safe and secure within his strong arms, relaxing further, as he drew her closer.

The music came to an end and Hazel rushed over. "Come on ... hurry up ... our group is heading to a P-A-R-T-Y," she screamed over the noisy room, quickly grabbing her hand.

Paul shrugged, appearing somewhat disappointed, before Margaret grabbed his hand. "Come on let's go," she beamed, dragging him quickly alongside her.

The party was at Knockbracken, a house which was rented out by four university students. The music was ear-piercingly loud when they arrived with additional booze, contributing to the already overfilled shelves in the fridge. Retrieving a wine for Margaret, Paul guided her to the other side of the room, immediately striking up a conversation with her. He adored Margaret's Aussie accent and found her large cat-like eyes, enchanting. As they spoke, he found her to be a remarkably intelligent and driven woman, and she was totally unaware of how beautiful she was. Her dark auburn hair accentuated her green eyes and flawless skin, her lips were full, soft and enticing, as he took in every word she said. He swallowed hard, knowing he found her extremely attractive, knowing he was falling in love with her. He slung back his scotch in despair, knowing a relationship between a doctor and a student was completely off limits. A sackable offence, he reprimanded himself and one which he completely agreed with. That was, up until now.

"Let's get out of here," Margaret shouted, breaking him from his trance.

"Good idea," he readily agreed, grabbing her by the hand and making their way towards the door. Outside the air was cool; he instantly removed his jacket and wrapped it around Margaret.

"A true gentleman I see," she remarked, somewhat taken back by his chivalry.

"Well, I have an ulterior motive," he quipped, laughing lightly, before suggesting she went back to his place for a coffee.

They walked a few blocks, before arriving at a doubled storied, orange brick home, with a huge cherry tree standing out front.

"A man of many means," Margaret remarked, raising an eyebrow, surprised by his residence.

"Did you expect a bedsit, filled with squalor," he replied happily.

"Mmm something like that," she instantly chirped back, as they entered his home.

Inside was immaculate, with a huge stone fireplace dominating the living room. He automatically bent down and lit the neatly stacked timber, before grabbing her hand and leading her into the kitchen. Plonking her down on a stool, he proceeded to the cupboard and fetched a couple of mugs out, before switching on the kettle. The banter was light and the atmosphere relaxed, as she watched him comfortably moving around his domain.

Grabbing her mug of coffee, he interrupted her thoughts.

"Come with me," he smiled "we'll head back into the front room; the fire should be blazing nicely by now."

The small lamp in the corner created a warm orange ambience; the fire was blazing and crackling, as yellow and red flames licked and devoured the logs, contributing to the overall tranquil atmosphere. They sat clutching their mugs, chatting in between sips, completely comfortable in each other's company.

"Well, how many young suitors do you have waiting for you back in Australia," he enquired gently, peering into the fire.

"None," she replied instantly, her heart beating faster.

"I'm rather surprised there's no one special," he murmured caringly.

"Why," Margaret whispered, turning around, peering into his soft brown eyes.

"Well, obviously you're very intelligent as well as extremely attractive," he replied huskily, meeting her gaze.

"Not attractive enough to kiss apparently," she murmured, dangerously.

Before she could whisper another word, he took her into his arms and kissed her. She instantly melted, reciprocating his loving embrace, allowing him to ravish her. She was soon on the rug in front of the fire being kissed passionately, instantly overwhelming her with deep pleasurable feelings. She responded urgently, slipping her hand up under his sweater, feeling his rapidly beating heart, before undoing his belt buckle.

He stopped straight away. "Margaret we can't."

"Shhh," she murmured, pulling him down, willing him to continue, willing him to take her. He sighed heavily, no longer able to contain his hunger, no longer able to withhold his passion; leaning in, he drew her in much closer, kissing her deeply.

At 4am as the ambers in the fire grew dim, Paul quietly bent over to retrieve Margaret from amongst his crumpled clothes, lying scattered upon the rug. He carried her soft naked body upstairs to his bedroom, laying her gently on his bed, before climbing in beside her. Wrapping his arms around her, he fell into a deep satisfied sleep, feeling strong, able and whole again.

It had been a long time since he held another woman in his arms; it had been a long time since he felt like this. He had sworn he would never let anyone get close, swearing never to become emotionally involved again but with Margaret if felt right, he knew from the moment he set eyes upon her, he had fallen for her instantly.

By 8.30am the sun was beginning to filter through the venetians, creating a dancing, rippling effect upon the ceiling. Margaret lay silently for a moment, gazing serenely over at Paul, as he lay sleeping. His unruly dark locks spread out over the crisp white pillow, made him appear god-like. His dark long eyelashes were closed tightly, shutting him out from her loving gaze, of sheer appreciation.

He made love to her, ever so passionately last night, exploring her body gently, while drenching her in soft erotic kisses. Seducing her tenderly and making her climax frequently, before letting go and reaching levels of uncontrollable bliss. He was a beautiful and considerate lover, guiding her gracefully, before his final release. She never experienced such tenderness or devotion, in her young entire life. When sharing their precious loving moments together, both tenderly losing themselves in each other arms; their emotions were intense and electrifying, both merging together as one.

She could feel herself blushing, as she thought of last night. Feeling alive and allowing her emotions to bubble over, she responded to his every move, in a seductive and uninhibited manner. The alarm clock buzzed and she immediately reached over to switch it off, not wanting to disturb him, as he appeared so innocent and tranquil.

A dark haired girl peered back at her, large blue doe-like eyes were laughing at her, from the wooden picture frame sitting next to his alarm clock. She cried in great dismay, tears springing to her eyes and without saying a word, she quickly gathered up her clothes and exited his room. Downstairs dressing quickly, Margaret was noticeably upset when she hastily left, closing the door behind her.

Quickly making her way back to the Belfast Road, she hailed a taxi immediately to take her to the Royal Victoria Hospital in order to retrieve her car. Making her way home, her head started pounding, deteriorating rapidly into an excruciating migraine. Damn it, she shouldn't have drunk so much last night, she reprimanded herself. Tears began spilling down her cheeks, she shouldn't have slept with Paul last night either, it was so out of character for her. What a fool, what an absolute fool, she thought, while driving home, letting her heart rule her head.

"Shit, shit, shit," she screamed out loudly, banging the steering wheel, sitting stationary at the traffic lights. What was she thinking? That was it, she probably wasn't. Imagine sleeping with your boss on your first evening together and to add insult to injury, he had a girlfriend, some dark headed beauty staring at him from the bedside table. My god, what had she done? She was completely devastated, angry, disappointed and confused. Did she read him completely wrong, were his feelings real or not? Now she wanted to hit him and ask what the hell was he playing at? She inhaled deeply, before driving off again, completely humiliated and heartbroken.

"Well, did you have a lovely evening with the girls?" Mary enquired, when she arrived in through the door.

Margaret immediately put on a brave face. "Yes, it was a great evening," she replied, purposely not making eye contact with her. "I'll just head upstairs and have a shower, as I didn't want to impose on my friends this morning," she murmured, making her way towards the stairs.

She cried hard, spilling tears of disillusionment as she stood under the hot steamy shower, allowing the water to cascade down her body. She had never met anyone like Paul before and from the very first moment she met him, she felt strongly attracted to him. She felt strongly drawn to him immediately, all of a sudden feeling awkward and shy, whenever he was around.

At the disco he was fun and light hearted, yet at the party she got to see his serious side, especially when it came to talking about medical research and the difference he wanted to make. Leaving the party, his kind and gentle mannerisms were exposed, when he wrapped her up in his coat. She couldn't figure it out; he didn't seem like the type of guy to use a girl. His love making was exemplary and she thought he had feelings for her. Sincere, deep, loving feelings, as she had for him. Yet, she had seen the photograph with her very own eyes, a laughing, smiling, female in a wooden frame, prominently sitting upon his bedside table.

"Are you ready for lunch yet?" Mary shouted, from the other side of the bathroom door.

"Yes, I'll be down in a few minutes," Margaret replied, immediately broken from her disjointed thoughts.

The rest of the day passed uneventfully, as she had spoken to Hazel later in the afternoon, explaining she left the party and went home, due to a migraine. She hated lying but what else could she do. She could hardly confess she slept with the boss and was a dim-witted idiot, because he obviously had a girlfriend.

On Sunday, she spent most of the day upstairs studying, due to her forthcoming exams. Mary and Joe left her alone and went out visiting for the day, which suited Margaret perfectly.

Monday morning arrived and Margaret was absolutely frantic, dreading going to the hospital. She pulled up into the car park; her palms were sweating and her heart was racing. How on earth will she be able to look at him? He must think she had no morals after a few drinks, she thought. She could feel her face flush, as her mind raced erratically.

Thankfully, she saw Hazel and rushed over immediately, grabbing her by the arm, before waltzing in through the main entrance together. Safety in numbers, she thought, making her way up the hospital corridor.

Everyone was chatting about the party and exchanging stories when Paul marched in. He straight away scanned the room seeking out Margaret, before his gaze fell heavily upon her. Their eyes met and she visibly flinched, sensing the tension between them. Blushing, she immediately bowed her head, struggling to choke back her emotions.

He appeared angry and began lecturing everyone on hospital protocols, explaining how he expected his team to behave responsibly at all times, staring directly at Margaret, who instantly cringed.

Morning teatime arrived; Margaret was standing in line for the cafeteria, when she spotted Paul heading towards her. She immediately panicked and fled to the toilets, avoiding a major confrontation. At lunchtime she left the building on purpose and didn't reappear until lunch was over. The task of avoiding Paul all day had taken its toll on Margaret and when she rushed off to her car after completing her shift, she was physically and mentally exhausted.

Fumbling around for her keys, she was startled when a hand fell upon her shoulder.

"Margaret!"

Swinging around, she cried out in horror, finding Paul standing directly in front of her.

"Do you usually do a runner when you spent a night with a man and leave with no apparent explanation?" he queried sarcastically.

She stood there dumb founded, hardly able to breathe. Even when he was angry he was gorgeous looking, she didn't know whether to slap him for his arrogance or simply kiss him, as her adrenalin pumped mercilessly inside.

"Do you normally take women to bed, when you already have one?" she replied angrily.

"What do you mean?" he questioned, appearing confused.

"Look, you've already made a fool of me," she exploded, as tears began to surface. "So don't try and act all innocent now, thank you all the same."

"I don't know what you are talking about Margaret or who you're referring to?" he shouted.

"Oh don't you indeed. Well, who the hell is the dark haired, blue eyed beauty in the photograph, sitting on your bedside table then?" she spat back immediately.

"That's Violet" he answered swiftly, turning extremely pale, appearing quite shocked.

"Well, I hope you're real happy together," she cried, as she jumped swiftly into her car and drove off erratically, preventing him from saying another word.

She got a mile up the road, before pulling in at the local shopping centre. All of a sudden she burst into tears, enormously distraught as she sat in her car trembling, feeling terribly alone. An hour later, she made her way back home.

Mary put the kettle on when she saw her driving into the yard and was concerned, when she spotted her tear stained face. "Are you okay luv?" she questioned, holding out her arms straight away to offer comfort.

Margaret fell into them and immediately began sobbing.

"Now, now, it can't be that bad young lady? Mind you, I'll bet you it's over a man" Mary muttered, flicking her hand at Joe as he waltzed into the kitchen, unannounced. He instantly exited through the back door, automatically recognising it was 'women business', after Mary gave him the signal to clear off.

Dinner was a quiet affair and Margaret retired to her bedroom soon afterwards, under the pretence of studying. Deep down, she was utterly exhausted and felt like an absolute idiot.

About 8.30pm, Mary came knocking on her door. "Come in," Margaret called out, grabbing a book.

Peeking her head around the door, Mary smiled broadly. "I have someone here to see you, to cheer you up," she piped up, opening the door a little further. Half expecting Joe to be standing there, Margaret got the shock of her life.

Paul stood in the doorway holding a bunch of red roses, appearing rather solemn.

"There's no use in apologising," she immediately stated, her ego badly bruised.

"Now that's no way of greetin' a fine young man, who's obviously sorry for hurtin' you," Mary interrupted. "Now, I'll leave the pair of you on your own, to sort things out properly," she said, leaving without saying another word, softly closing the door behind her.

"May I please explain," Paul requested ever so gently, taking her totally by surprise. He sat down next to her on the bed. "I didn't mean to hurt you Margaret. I'm terribly sorry; I should have thought and moved the photo earlier." Before continuing, he lifted her head up to peer into her dark, sorrowful eyes. "Margaret, Violet was my fiancée and we were engaged to be married but two years ago, she died from leukaemia. She fought bravely to the bitter end but we both knew what the final outcome would be."

Margaret instantly felt horrible, before reaching over and hugging him tightly. "I'm sorry Paul ... I'm really sorry. I had no idea and I thought ..."

"It's okay Margaret, it's my fault and I'm stupid ... I always meant to put the photo away but I never got around to it. You see, I don't normally sleep in that room. I hadn't been with anyone else since Violet. I normally sleep in a single bed, in the bedroom next door," he shrugged. "I didn't think there would be enough room for the both of us there," he smiled, as huge regretful tears gushed down Margaret's cheeks.

"Now enough of that young lady," he whispered. "I missed you," he confided emotionally, tears in his eyes as he leant forward, kissing her gently on the cheek.

As Paul said his goodbyes to everyone, he leant in quickly and gave Margaret a kiss, which pleased Mary and Joe immensely. "See you tomorrow," Paul called out from his car, as he waved goodbye.

"I knew it was over a man," Mary laughed, shaking her head, as Margaret walked back inside. "Now you get to bed young lady and get a good night's sleep and not one word to your mum or she'll drive us all mad."

"Goodnight," Margaret announced, laughing halfway up the stairs, pleased with the overall outcome.

Chapter Twelve

Back in Australia, Kath couldn't believe Margaret had been gone for five months. Her frequent telephone conversations helped her comprehend and get used to the idea, that her daughter was becoming a fully fledged, independent young lady. Margaret sounded confident and extremely happy on the phone. Mary and Joe reiterated many times, how she was excelling academically at the Royal Victoria Hospital and was acting responsibly. Kath and Marcus were pleased she wasn't out partying in the evenings, which meant she was keeping well out of harm's way, therefore decreasing her chances of endangering her life.

"You're very quiet today young lady," Marcus chirped up, peering behind his Sunday morning paper.

"I was thinking about our Margaret and how much I miss her around the place."

He smiled knowingly, completely and utterly aware of her feelings, because he felt exactly the same. The very next day Marcus spoke to his father, who was in favour of Marcus's plans, agreeing it was time they both had a relaxing holiday. The company was excelling rapidly since the merger took place and with his son and Kath's input, he couldn't wish for anything more. Marcus organised the company jet, deciding to surprise Kath later on in the evening, when he got home.

Brigee was in the kitchen preparing dinner, chatting with young Rachel who was settling in nicely at her new school and maturing beyond her years.

Kath wandered in and kicked off her shoes, before making her way over to the kettle. "Fancy a cuppa Brigee," she called out over her shoulder, while fumbling around in the fridge for some chocolate biscuits.

"Don't mind if I do," Brigee answered, continuing to dice up the carrots.

"What's on the menu for this evening?" Kath enquired gently.

"Marcus's favourite, beef and mushroom casserole," Brigee piped up, as Rachel left the kitchen to phone one of her friends. "What's up?" Brigee asked "You seem a little down of late."

"I guess I can't wait until Margaret's back home again, I've been missing her a lot lately," Kath countered, filling up the cups.

"I know what you mean, as she and I use to have long leisurely chats in the afternoon and the place is certainly a lot quieter when she's not around."

Marcus was extremely happy at dinner time, appearing as if he had been up to all sorts of mischief, Kath intuitively thought, as she cleared the dinner table. "Well, what deal did you crunch today my darling?" recognising he was enormously pleased over something.

"No extraordinary business deals took place," he replied casually, intriguing Kath even more.

"M-A-R-C-U-S, I know you've been up to something because you're running around like a cat that swallowed the cream. So out with it," she declared laughing.

"How would you like to take a break?" he enquired thoughtfully.

"A holiday break," Kath enquired.

"Yes, to escape work and get some much needed therapeutic R and R," Marcus replied.

"It sounds wonderful darling but what would your father think of his two senior executives disappearing for a while?"

"I spoke to him today actually and it wouldn't be a problem at all, as it's much quieter at this time of the year."

"Sounds tempting," Kath mused, wandering into the living room, to finish off her wine and put her feet up to relax. "Have you a particular destination in mind?" she queried, settling down into the sofa.

"I thought Rachel could join us. She gets two weeks school holidays in July and we could take an extra two weeks, making it four weeks off in total," he suggested.

"Somewhere warm would be nice I guess," Kath casually mentioned. "I hate the winter as you know, although I shouldn't complain coming from Northern Ireland," Kath replied thoughtfully.

Marcus chuckled, knowing Kath hadn't a clue where he had in mind. "Okay then, that's settled, we'll leave on the 6th July and get back here on the 7th August," he announced happily.

"Okay count me in," Kath added, now sitting up and taking more notice. "May I ask, exactly where are we going?" she enquired.

"You most certainly can," Marcus teased. "I thought Northern Ireland might be a good destination."

Kath screamed in delight, her eyes huge and smiling. "Are you serious?" she questioned.

"Most certainly am," Marcus laughed. "I was getting the jet organised today, so I'm simply waiting on your reply my darling."

"Yes, yes, YES," Kath blurted out quickly, overwhelmed with great joy. "I love you," she beamed at Marcus. "You always seem to surprise me in the nicest possible way," stretching over and giving him the biggest hug ever.

As the time drew closer, Rachel could be found packing her suitcase with enthusiasm, totally excited because she was looking forward to seeing her sister as well as being delighted at the opportunity of visiting Ireland. She was the envy of all her friends at school, who quickly gave her a list of all the things she had to bring back for them. Irish Claddagh rings were in huge demand, she noted.

Brigee waved them off from the airport; pleased Marcus had come up with the idea. He was so in sync with Kath, totally aware she was fretting for her eldest daughter and immediately set about solving the problem. Rachel was fascinated by the private jet and couldn't wait to tell her friends about what it was like when she got back home in a month's time.

Finally arriving at Belfast International Airport, the sky was a vivid blue, scattered with white fluffy clouds hovering overhead. Joe was waiting for them at the airport, while Mary was at home cooking up a storm, completely in her element and deliriously happy. Margaret on the other hand remained totally unaware of the surprise visit.

Upon their return to the farm, Mary was out in a flash hugging her daughter tightly with tears of joy streaming down her cheeks.

Rachel took to Patch, the dog, instantly. He was swishing his tail manically and lapping up the attention, as he was being cuddled affectionately.

Mary quickly put the kettle on and soon they were all congregated around the kitchen table, tucking into sandwiches and homemade cakes.

"These are yummy," Rachel declared over the noisy banter taking place.

"Mum makes the best currant squares in Northern Ireland," Kath piped up, smiling across at her mother. Marcus glanced around the table, pleased he had organised the trip. Everyone had picked up from where they left off previously, catching up on all the latest gossip, the air filled with happiness and sincere love.

Around 4pm, the Mini Clubman drove into the yard while Marcus, Kath and Rachel instantly fled out of sight, into the front room.

Margaret walked into the kitchen from work and had only just put the kettle on, when Mary popped up from behind her.

"And how was your day luv? You look a little tired. I hope you're not overdoing it," Mary chided.

"It was great and the best news is, my exams are over until September."

"That's grand," Mary replied. "I'll make us both a wee cup of tea and you can fetch me the newspaper from the front room. I think Joe left it there this morning."

Margaret crossed the hallway, totally oblivious as to what lay ahead. Opening the door, she was immediately greeted by a huge resounding S-U-R-P-R-I-S-E echoing throughout the room. Margaret stood speechless, totally shocked, not believing her very own eyes.

"Oh my goodness, it's so great to see you," Kath tearfully murmured.

"Mum, dad and Rachel, I can't believe it," Margaret screamed, rushing over immediately and giving them all heartfelt hugs.

That's when Mary popped her head around the door. "Ready for that cuppa now luv?" she teased.

"I think I'll need a scotch after this lot," Margaret retorted happily.

Dinner in the evening was very much a family affair. They heartily tucked into their roast beef, served with freshly baked wheaten bread and delicious salads, followed by a scrumptious homemade trifle and ice-cream.

The women congregated in the kitchen afterwards, clearing away the dishes and chatting amicably amongst themselves. Joe and Marcus were in the front room having a quiet drink, reminiscing about the years gone by. Everyone was in a happy demeanour, laughing and joking amongst themselves, when a loud knock on the back door, drew their attention. Margaret stared across at Mary, wide eyed, instantly blushing, as Mary cleared her throat and nodded. "That'll be for you pet."

Without saying a word, Margaret immediately rose and went to the back door, opening it up cautiously, before proceeding outside quickly, closing the door behind her.

"Who's that?" Kath enquired immediately, hearing a male's voice outside.

"Oh, you'll see in a minute," Mary answered subtly.

Margaret very shortly afterwards re-entered the kitchen, accompanying a tall, handsome, young man. "Mum, I would like to introduce you to Paul my boyfriend," clutching his hand and smiling radiantly.

Kath stood up, walking over instantly to shake his hand. "Very please to meet you Paul, I bet you didn't think you'll be meeting us lot, this evening. We decided to give her bit of a surprise."

"So I've heard," Paul replied happily, not in the least bit intimidated.

"Well, you best take him in to meet your stepfather," Mary interrupted "and get it all over and done with lad," giving Paul a quick wink of understanding.

Margaret grabbed his hand and led him into the front room. "How long has this been going on for?" Kath gently enquired.

"I would say about four months now," Mary chirped "and you couldn't meet a nicer big lad if you tried," she added hastily.

They had supper in the front room and Marcus was quite taken by Paul. He was extremely intelligent, focused and besotted with his daughter. Kath sat back watching them all interacting happily, realising her daughter was all grown up and made a wonderful choice in befriending Paul.

Climbing out of his chair to leave at 11.30pm, he whispered "see you tomorrow."

"Sure will," Margaret replied, her eyes sparkling and full of love.

"Bye everyone and it was lovely to meet you all. A total surprise but a grand one at that," he added smiling.

After he left, Kath decided to tackle Margaret cautiously. "Paul was a surprise this evening. Were you keeping him a secret for any particular reason?"

"No mum, I just wanted to see how we would work out, that's all," she replied directly.

"Well, I think your father has taken a shine to him. I'm certainly impressed and your grandparents can't find fault in him. I'd say you've done very well young lady and certainly picked a winner."

"Thanks mum," Margaret laughed, instantly rushing over to give both her parents a massive hug. Extremely delighted they both liked Paul and approved.

Margaret and Paul had the next two weeks off, due to the July holidays and it worked out exceptionally well. Marcus hired a mini bus and they all went exploring Donegal, then they travelled to Waterford and visited the Waterford Crystal factory. The guys also thoroughly enjoyed visiting the Guinness Storehouse in Dublin, while the ladies went shopping in the Brown Thomas store. Rachel had everyone in stitches, when leaning out to kiss the Blarney Stone at Blarney Castle, built over six hundred years ago by one of Ireland's greatest chieftains, Cormac MacCarthy. The Stone itself is said to give the gift of eloquence to those who kiss it. This was one of Ireland's beautiful tourist spots and a fun day was enjoyed by everyone. They stayed in hotels, guesthouses and rustic old pubs, where the Irish hospitality was splendid.

Chapter Thirteen

On the third week, Margaret was back at the Royal Victoria Hospital again, working alongside Paul. Their romance had been kept under wraps, both acting totally professional and clinical, whenever anyone else was around.

After the 12th of July, a string of bombings and shootings erupted throughout the province. Up until now it had been reasonably peaceful; however Margaret could feel the tension building. The emergency rooms were beginning to fill with innocent victims suffering from brutal mutilations.

On a busy afternoon Margaret was bandaging up a young child's arm, caused by falling into a hay turning machine, when all hell broke loose in the reception area. Screams could be heard filtering down the corridor. Margaret being close by immediately went to investigate. Before she realised what was happening, she was savagely grabbed by the arm, by a man disguised in a dark balaclava clutching a gun.

"You'll do," he screamed at her. "We've got a mate John ... who needs a doc," he bellowed, dragging her towards the exit.

"I'm not a doctor," Margaret shouted. "I'm only an intern," trying her best to explain but it was obviously falling upon deaf ears.

"Come with us now bitch and cause no more trouble or there'll be more casualties, GOT IT," the assailant muttered angrily, roughly pushing her forward.

Swallowing hard, consciously worrying about her patient's safety, Margaret promptly followed their orders, in a state of shock. Hastily escorted out of the building, she was viciously tossed into the back of a van, complete with driver who kept the engine running, ready for a quick get-a-way. Taking off aggressively, screeching tyres filled the air as the vehicle frantically swerved, narrowly missing several cars on their exit. Margaret flew forward, brutally smashing into the side of the vehicle. Crazily turning around in a mad panic, she could have sworn she had seen Paul rushing out the main entrance and into the car park, through the filthy back window, as tears fell from her cheeks on to the grubby bloodstained, floor.

Paul drove erratically, in total despair, to personally deliver this distressing news to Margaret's parents. Paul preferred they find out from him rather than them seeing it on one of the nightly News programs.

"What do you mean she's been taken," Kath screamed hysterically at Paul, tears washing down her face. "I knew she shouldn't have come here. God-damn it, I should have put my foot down. Who were they? How many were there? What did they get away in? Why in the hell did they take our Margaret?" Kath exploded, in amongst tears.

Marcus was beside himself, sick with worry, wondering what course of action to take.

"The police have taken details from the witnesses involved," Paul volunteered weakly, devastated by the event. "They'll want her to patch up a wound on one of their comrades, releasing her when she's finished," he added.

"But she's not a doctor for Christ's sake Paul. What will happen if the piece of shit dies?" Kath screeched. "What then? They wouldn't be too happy would they? Will they let her go, do you think? Or will they kill her out of frustration. Let's face it; they don't have a bloody conscience do they?"

"Kath that's enough, you're getting yourself all worked up and it's not doing anyone any good," Marcus stated bluntly.

Mary and Joe sat watching the debacle, white and withdrawn, remembering all those years ago when they lost their two sons and Kath.

"Look, I'll go to the police station with Paul and you stay here in case they ring with some news. At least this way we're being proactive," Marcus stated firmly.

Paul and Marcus swiftly headed out the back door, wearing stern faces and slumped shoulders, lost in fearful thoughts, both hoping Margaret was safe, both praying she would be soon released.

In the meantime Margaret was in a hideout, situated god knows where. There were three cronies and the injured one, going by the name of John. He was only a young lad about twenty-two years of age, Margaret surmised, when she was taken into the bedroom to inspect the damage done. He was lying in bed clutching a blood saturated shirt, groaning in agony and bleeding badly from the abdominal area.

"Don't worry John; we've got a doc here to fix you up. You'll be as good as new in no time lad," the tallest of the three stated. Turning around abruptly towards Margaret, he hissed "right bitch, do yur job 'n' fix up my little bro or you'll regret it if you don't."

Margaret acknowledged there was no point in arguing. She was a doctor in their eyes, standing there shivering, wearing a white coat with a stethoscope wrapped around her neck. She was brought here to repair a badly injured man, a young man, who was a god-damn terrorist.

Both Marcus and Paul were gutted, after leaving the police station. The witnesses had barely any information, because the two hostage takers had worn balaclavas. The only possible clues were; one had said "'grab any doctor to fix up John." Whoever that was? Also the receptionist had noticed the tallest one of the group, had a Union Jack tattooed on the top of his right hand, leading from his thumb area and reaching up to the base of his wrist.

Their identities were unknown, according to the police. However, a loyalist group had been involved in a shoot-out on Falls Road earlier that morning and according to eye witness reports, one was badly injured. The Royal Ulster Constabulary said they would carry out an investigation.

Marcus was horrified, finding it difficult to comprehend that daily assaults and brutal sectarian killings, were still taking place. Innocent victims were frequently maimed and innocent bystanders similar to their Margaret, were frequently dragged into the whole sorry affair.

Meanwhile, Margaret removed the crumpled blood stained rag. Immediately, blood came seeping out and she instinctively plugged the hole back up again. A bullet was obviously buried deep within his abdominal area; she would have to remove it and stitch him up. She had watched a similar operation being carried out by one of the surgeons only a few weeks ago, which helped instil some confidence. Intuitively she knew she must remain calm, making it appear she knew what she was doing, recognising if they doubted her, she could pay with her life. Looking around and immediately surmising the scene, Margaret quickly took charge.

"Okay. I'll need boiling water for sterilisation, a needle and some fishing line will be required to stitch him up. Have you any surgical equipment at all?" she enquired firmly.

"Friggin' hell, what do ya think this is bitch, a god-damn 24 hour medical centre. Of course we don't have any bloody equipment; you've gotta improvise. Holy shit, we weren't expectin' our John to take a bullet," the leader snarled.

Marcus contacted Kath to keep her informed and enquired if anything was happening at her end.

"Absolutely nothing," Kath reported, pacing the room, having only calmed down a little since they left.

Paul took Marcus across to a local pub for a quick drink and over a pint of Guinness, he decided to speak up.

"Marcus I don't know if this will help but I have a friend who knows a bloke involved in some loyalist group. I thought if I contacted him and got him to offer some sort of a reward, maybe we could track Margaret down."

Marcus's eyes immediately lit up. "Bloody hell lad, that's a terrific idea … and it might just work. I'll arrange for funds to be withdrawn immediately. How much do you think it would take to gather vital information?" he enquired, sitting up straighter with a glimmer of hope.

"I don't know Marcus, maybe five thousand pounds," he shrugged "I really don't know but it would certainly grab their attention. As long as it doesn't hinder or sabotage the pending investigation," Paul added in earnest.

"What investigation?" Marcus rolled his eyes in frustration. "Damn it, I'll get ten out in case, surely that should get a positive result. Let's face it, Margaret's life is at stake here and I'll pay anything and I mean anything … to get her back," Marcus stammered, his eyes filling with emotion.

Margaret had no anaesthetic to knock John out with, before trying to remove the bullet. His brother suggested getting him drunk. That way he would be numb and completely out to the world. After forcibly sculling some whiskey, John became agitated and incoherent.

"Right then, he's almost ready for ya," the eldest stated. Turning around abruptly and without hesitation, he punched his brother smack bang in the face, causing John to instantly collapse back on to the table, out for the count. "Right you can go ahead now. I think, I've knocked him out good 'n' proper."

Margaret used the kitchen knife to make the incision; it was as sharp as any scalpel she had ever used. Opening up the wound, allowed her clear access to extract the bullet, buried deep inside. The other three cronies standing over her watching, turned green, appearing somewhat squeamish, which was ironic and an utter contradiction, she thought. Here they were, some loyalist group, willing to take lives by pulling a trigger or detonating a bomb but obviously couldn't stand the sight of blood. Perspiration was breaking out on her forehead, as she navigated her way cautiously in amongst his internal organs, with her bare hands. Panic was rising up and choking her, until she located the offending bullet, causing her to sigh automatically, in total relief.

At 6pm, Paul and Marcus were sitting quietly in the back room of some club, situated off the Ormeau Road in East Belfast. Jimbo, as he was known to his comrades, checked out the bag of money. "Wow Mr, you must really want yur step-daughter back, that's quite a haul of dough," he sniggered.

"We haven't got much time," Marcus replied firmly. "She was taken at 2.30pm and if she can't save their mate, god knows what will happen," Marcus stammered, filled with resentment.

Jimbo glanced across at Paul. "Well it seems the story is legit. We've heard a group of renegade Ulster Volunteer Force lads were out on a reprisal shoot-out up on Falls Road this morning, with one of them copping it badly in the guts. Did you get any descriptions at all?" Jimbo grunted. "It may help the lads and me to track them down."

"Yes, one's got a tattoo of a union Jack on his right hand," Marcus added swiftly, extremely irritated, anxious to get his daughter back, alive.

"Was he on the tall side of things?" Jimbo persisted in earnest.

"Yes he was, according to the eye witnesses," Paul interjected.

"Okay then, leave it with me, I think I know the group involved," Jimbo bragged, shifting his chair and rising from the table. "Go home and wait Paul. I'll ring ya once we've located her. OKAY."

"Thanks buddy, try and make it as quick as possible though. She's enormously precious to us and I love her deeply."

Marcus glanced across at Paul; a lump forming in his throat, as his heart immediately went out to the young lad. They were both shown to the door by the other two associates, who were kitted out in paramilitary camouflage and the proverbial balaclavas.

After extracting the lethal bullet, Margaret started stitching John up, using fishing line and a domestic needle; the only make shift equipment on hand. John was carried into another room and left there to recover, while Margaret stripped down the bloody sheets and tidied up.

"What now?" Mark enquired, nodding at the room next door, referring to Margaret.

Ray growled, "Nothin' yet solider boy, we'll wait and see if our John recovers first."

It was getting dark outside, Margaret noticed, instantly wondering how Paul and her family were handling the situation, at their end. Her initial fear dissipated and she was immensely pleased how the operation went. Providing John got through the night, with his antibodies kicking in and no infection taking hold, he would be well on the mend and would make a full recovery. It felt bizarre saving a terrorist, a pathological inhumane being who had no regard for life, yet expected to be saved when death came knocking at his door. Her thoughts were hastily interrupted.

"Okay girlie, we'll get you something to eat and you can kip down here for the night and we'll see what our John's like in the morning."

Haphazardly divulging their identities, Ray, Mark and Sam plonked down at the table, discarding their masks carelessly.

Margaret instantly gripped the back of a nearby chair, catching her breath, trembling internally, recognising and acknowledging this course of action was not good. No good at all, she thought, trying to maintain her composure.

"What do you think the chances are, of getting Margaret out?" Kath queried, after downing her umpteenth cup of coffee.

Marcus and Paul sat around the kitchen table, their faces serious, both appearing worn and haggard, while glancing up at the clock. At 6am, the sun was breaking dawn and the rooster embraced the early morning light with his daily awakening call.

Joe and Mary stirred upstairs, both exhausted, having little to no sleep last night. They got dressed slowly in the small waking hour, preparing themselves the best way they could, knowing the next few excruciating hours could mean life or death, for their young innocent granddaughter.

Rachel on the other hand, was totally unaware of the imminent danger her sister was in. She was staying over at the next door neighbour's house, having fun with their two daughters who had befriended her.

A loud knock on the door of Margaret's captors, startled everyone. "Who the hell is it?" Ray called out, automatically grabbing his gun from his belt.

"It's me ... Jimbo," a frantic voice called out from the other side.

"Open the door," Ray ordered immediately, not wanting to raise any suspicion on the street. "What the hell are you doin' here lad, when all good Prods are in their beds sleepin'?"

Jimbo smiled, automatically casing the joint out, noting there were three scoundrels in total. "I'm on a rescue mission Ray; I believe you have a young lady called Margaret held captive here."

"What's it to you?" Ray spat back defensively, not liking anyone knowing his god-damn business.

"Well some of my mates are prepared to offer a ransom and a pretty good one at that, I might add," Jimbo claimed enthusiastically.

Ray slid his revolver down on the table appearing a little more relaxed; especially after discovering he could make some dough, as it could come in real handy right now to purchase more guns and ammo.

"What's their personal interest in the lass," he grizzled, his eyes narrowing, full of suspicion.

"Let's just say there's a romantic interest and he doesn't want his girlfriend all cut up and disposed of, dumped in some isolated wasteland."

"Hell Jimbo, you askin' a lot lad. She's seen us and could squeal like a pig, if you get my drift man."

Jimbo was anxious, perspiration built up and oozed out on to his forehead. He didn't want any trouble, especially not a shoot out but he did promise Paul he would get her back, alive.

"Jesus Christ Ray, she's only a young lass out from Australia and she'll be heading back home straight away."

"Are you sure about that?"

"One hundred percent," Jimbo expanded, keeping a beady eye on the other two hovering.

"Well, how much are we talkin' about here?" Ray gruffly enquired.

"Seven thousand big ones," Jimbo emphasised. "Her parents have a bob or two apparently."

Ray exhaled a high-pitched whistle. "Geez, it could come in real handy, it's quite a good haul man."

"That's what I thought," Jimbo eagerly interrupted, sensing the tension easing.

"Well it all sounds promisin' but when could I expect the drop?"

"In exactly one hour from now," Jimbo added quickly.

"Okay ... I'm in," Ray barked decisively, rising from his chair abruptly. "Get here within the hour with the goods," he demanded. Ray walked immediately towards the door, making it blatantly clear to Jimbo that it was time to go.

"Can I see her for a moment," Jimbo hurriedly requested, swallowing the bile catching in his throat.

Ray nodded and he was quickly shuffled down a dark corridor, before a bedroom door was unlocked. Inside, Margaret was lying on a bed, her hands and feet bound tightly, her mouth sealed shut with duct tape. Her eyes grew wide, appearing startled and fearful, when Jimbo entered the room.

"It's okay luv," he comforted swiftly. "A ransom's been paid and before you know it, you'll be back in Australia safe and sound, with your family." Margaret appeared relieved and nodded in recognition, before he was shuffled from the room and led back to the front room.

"Okay, see ya in an hour," Ray snapped, shoving Jimbo out the front door, closing it hastily behind him.

The phone rang at 6.30am, immediately startling everyone in the kitchen. Marcus instantly retrieved it, drawing a deep breath. "Just a moment, I'll put him on," Marcus drawled, before passing the phone to Paul. The seconds seemed like hours, before Paul broke the silence.

"Great, I'll head down there now." Paul hung up, everyone was waiting goggled eyed, holding their breaths in suspense.

"Great news, Jimbo's sighted Margaret and she's fine."

"Thank heavens for that," Kath interrupted, exhaling a huge sigh of relief. "Where are they holding her?" Marcus queried diligently.

"All I know is, about forty-five minutes from now the money is being handed over in exchange for Margaret's well being."

"Then what?" Kath butted in.

"I've been instructed to pick her up from the club," Paul relayed. Pleased the whole ordeal was nearly at its end.

"I'll come," Marcus and Kath replied quickly in unison.

"No ... Jimbo wants no fanfare. I'm sorry, but as soon as I have her, I'll come straight back here."

Marcus nodded "Okay lad, go fetch her and bring our daughter back home. Safe."

Arriving at the door, Jimbo knocked. A dark figure was lurking nearby, watching from within the shadows.

"Hurry up," Ray muttered ushering him through the doorway, quickly scanning around outside, before closing the door. P-e-r-f-e-c-t he thought, grinning from ear to ear as he followed Jimbo up the hallway.

"Well, did you bring the dough," he grunted automatically, pulling a chair up to the kitchen table.

"Hell yes," Jimbo piped up; confident everything was going to plan. Opening up the brown paper bag, he hastily shook it, discarding the tightly bundled notes precariously across the table.

Ray's eyes grew wide, filled with greed. "Good job Jimbo. No one followed you, did they?"

"Nope, I'm on my own as promised earlier this morning."

"Great lad, 'cause we don't want any stuff ups, that's all," Ray added, peering across at the other two, standing maliciously close by.

"You can count it if you want to," Jimbo declared cautiously, pleased everything was running to schedule. "Right then, where's Margaret? We'll have to get going straight away," he added eagerly.

Ray grimaced. "There's a bit of a problem I'm afraid Jimbo, as we don't know how our John's doin' and if he'll survive or not."

"Look … I've kept my end of the deal Ray; you're not going to renege on me now, are you?" Jimbo questioned, his palms growing clammy.

"Nah! We just gotta rouse the girl and get her to check him out first, that's all," Ray grizzled, leaning back in his chair and laughing.

"Okay, let's get her up so we can get movin' right away," Jimbo responded nervously. Anxious for them to get out of there, he deliberately rose from his chair.

Ray got up slowly, leading the way down the dark narrow passageway, to where Margaret was held captive.

Upon entering, Margaret appeared relieved after sighting Jimbo.

Ray went over to her. "Listen carefully," he hissed loudly, while untying her. "Don't make any noise, all we want you to do is to check on John and then you can go."

Margaret nodded in response, rubbing her freed wrists immediately, noticing the rope left a deep indentation.

Jimbo removed the duct tape, signalling for her to be quiet. "Listen luv; just do your job so we can get the hell out of here as quickly as possible." Helping her up, it took a few moments for her to steady herself; her legs were stiff and cramped, caused by being tied up all night.

Slowly, all three made their way down to the bedroom. Margaret apprehensively approached John, who seemed deadly pale. She immediately felt for his pulse and was extremely relieved to find one. "Can someone get me some cold water please?" she requested calmly, more calmly than she felt.

Ray barked out a few orders and soon she was bathing John's forehead, with a cool damp cloth. Gradually he began to come around, appearing drowsy and incoherent. Suddenly he grabbed Margaret's hand, causing her to jump back in alarm. "What happened, where the hell am I?" he questioned groggily.

Ray gave a hearty laugh, pleased his brother had made it. Jimbo breathed a sigh of relief, looking much more confident.

"Okay," Margaret announced taking charge and talking to Ray. "You'll need to change the wound regularly to prevent it becoming infected and keep topping him up with painkillers every four hours for the next week. Make sure he avoids any stretching, because we don't want the stitches breaking open. If you do all that, he should make a full recovery without any complications."

"Okay young lady, let's go, your boyfriend is waitin' patiently for you," Jimbo prattled on, reaching for her hand quickly, making his way to the door. They left Ray speaking to his brother, seemingly oblivious of them leaving.

Outside the room and making their way back up the passageway, Jimbo was met by Sam. "You can't leave, she's friggin' seen too much," he growled spitefully, taking Jimbo by surprise. Before he could protest, the butt of a revolver was slammed violently into his head, immediately causing Jimbo to black out and crash to the floor.

Margaret tried to make a run for it but was rapidly hauled back by the hair, causing her to cry out and whimper loudly in pain. Dragged viciously by the arm, she was pushed into the next room. Within minutes she was tied up and her mouth quickly duct taped again, as large tears began bubbling down her cheeks. Choking back her debilitating fears, huge sobs escaped with a heavy heart. This was it, she thought. I'm going to die.

Ray abruptly entered the room and brutally dragged Jimbo's unconscious body across the floor, before dumping him unceremoniously into the corner of the room. "Tie him up Sam . . . just in case," he instructed forcibly.

Turning around slowly, to face Margaret, he smirked. "Sorry princess but as Sam said, you've fuckin' seen far too much but I'll make your execution quick, seein' you saved my brother's life," Ray coldly remarked as he quickly turned around and while making his exit, gave Jimbo's foot a vicious kick, before slamming the door behind him.

Margaret sat in the musty cold dark room, conquered by fear, fully aware she didn't have much time left. Shivering violently, her mind flickered back to her mother's story and only now did she fully comprehend the extent of terror her mother must have suffered. She thought of her family and Paul. Her beloved Paul, who she treasured, adored and loved so much. Massive sorrowful tears formed and flowed down her cheeks, splattering down upon her jeans as she sat helplessly and emotionally overwhelmed. She heard shuffling noises coming from the room next door, as she struggled with the ropes tied tightly around her wrists. She was trying frantically to free her hands but it was utterly useless, as it dug deeper and deeper into her flesh, causing her wrists to chaff and bleed. Although, she had managed to pull the duct tape off, alleviating the overwhelming and suffocating feeling, allowing her to breathe much easier.

From the corner of the room, Jimbo made a loud groan, immediately drawing her attention to him.

"Jimbo, it's me ... Margaret ... Are you okay?" she stammered.

Opening his eyes slowly, sharp barbs of excruciating pain shot down the right hand side of his head, as he gradually came around. Taking a few moments, he absorbed the dank miserable surroundings, before he shuffled around to face Margaret. "What the hell happened? Who hit me?" he asked shakily.

"It was Sam with his gun ... he was the one who knocked you out," Margaret confided quietly, appearing hopeful. Glad, she had someone to talk to.

"I'm sorry luv. I should have brought backup but I trusted the buggers. The dirty pack of rotten traitors," Jimbo snarled angrily, struggling to get up into a sitting position.

Out of nowhere, they heard a sharp tap on the bedroom window. Margaret gasped, as a dark figure in a balaclava pressed his head up against the glass, signalling not to make a sound. Slowly, ever so slowly, the window was jimmied open, allowing the intruder to push the window up, before swiftly climbing in.

"I have the place surrounded," he whispered. "I'm here to get you both out. Remain calm ... and do exactly what I say."

Another intruder entered the room stealth like, via the window. Making his way quietly over to the door, he was fully alert with a gun in hand and immediately kept guard. Swiftly, Margaret's hands and feet were freed and the tape removed, before the first intruder moved across to Jimbo. Margaret stood petrified; trying to comprehend what was going down.

Within minutes, Jimbo forced her closer to the window. "Okay, I'll climb out first and check for the all clear, you then follow directly behind, 'cause we're getting the hell out of here, as originally planned."

Swinging around before leaving, Jimbo grabbed the bloke's hand after noticing the tattoos on his arm and was immediately troubled. "How did you know?" he questioned.

"It's my business to know. I owe her mother a big favour from a long time ago."

Jimbo nodded respectfully, thanking him quietly, before leaving through the window.

Margaret was quickly helped out and instructed to follow Jimbo, who was ordered to run to his car and never look back.

Running stealth like up the street, the pair of them raced past parked vehicles, avoiding bins ready for collection, parked haphazardly on the pavement. Margaret ran for her life, pumped with adrenalin, totally relieved, gasping the fresh morning air with a laboured breath.

Arriving at Jimbo's car and about to get in, a thunderous explosion took hold, shaking the ground from where they stood. Glancing back, a huge cloud of smoke could be seen rising into the skyline, approximately six streets over, from where they made their escape. Her eyes widened in recognition, acknowledging what had taken place.

"Jimbo," she cried, stunned and horror-struck.

He shrugged swallowing hard, almost out of breath. "Well it's either them or us. Now let's get the hell out of here."

Chapter Fourteen

A mile up the road, Margaret started to breathe normally, thankful to be alive, grateful to be heading home to see Paul and her family. Out of nowhere the drama caught up with her, causing her to burst into tears, her emotions shattered and in turmoil. Thoughts of almost being murdered, her body dumped in some isolated spot, came flooding to the forefront of her mind, causing her to dry retch.

Jimbo automatically pulled the vehicle over, before stretching across to give her a heartfelt hug. "It's okay luv, it's all over. Now take a deep breath and try to relax, don't let the bastards get to you," he warned.

Realising she'll be with Paul in approximately fifteen minutes, she panicked. "Please don't tell anyone what really happened," she pleaded. "Mum would go absolutely ballistic; after discovering the ransom didn't work. She'll send me back to Australia and I don't want to go. I don't want to leave Paul," she begged tearfully, staring across at Jimbo helplessly.

Giving her a weary smile, he cupped her hands in his and announced "don't worry luv your secrets safe with me, we'll keep it simple. They took the money and we left, end of story ... R-I-G-H-T."

"Thank you," Margaret cried, relieved her mother wouldn't be told the full story, because if she was, Margaret would be on the first plane back home.

Paul smothered her with hugs, overwhelmed with joy when she walked into the club. Immense emotional tears were mutually shed, before heading off to her grandparents.

Arriving back at the farm, everyone came rushing out at once. Margaret was covered in kisses and given massive hugs, as tears of joy were openly expressed.

Jimbo was congratulated on a job well done, his hand shaken with gratitude by Marcus, immediately followed by a tearful thank you, from Kath.

Moving inside, Mary began making tea for everyone, keeping busy, as the whole situation left her quite shaken. It had opened up old buried memories from her own personal torment, having suffered with her boys and Kath.

"Are you okay luv," Joe interrupted her thoughts, aware of the toll it had taken on her.

"Yes luv, I'm fine," Mary said, putting on a brave face. "Now stop fussin' and get some whiskey out to celebrate our Margaret's safe homecoming," she added quickly.

Margaret hugged Paul affectionately in the front room, feeling safe again, wrapped up in his loving strong arms.

"I love you and I thought I lost you forever," he whispered, his eyes searching hers.

"You can't get rid of a bad thing ... right" she replied, trying to lightly brush the anguish away.

Nevertheless, he recognised the terror and pain etched in her dark green eyes. Now wasn't the time to talk; he would wait until later, when they were both on their own.

Kath refrained from giving off and emphasising what the outcome might have been, having been pre-warned by Marcus.

"She's been through enough already darling, let her unwind and relax, there's plenty of time to talk later. Thank god," he admitted, as they made their way to the kitchen table.

Paul suggested Margaret have a few days off work, allowing her to recover from the initial shock.

"I'm fine," Margaret announced, as stubborn as ever.

"No you're not, besides you must listen to your doctor," he teased, giving her a quick kiss on the nose.

"Paul's right," Kath interrupted.

"Damn right, I'm having the rest of the bloody week off," Jimbo announced loudly, causing everyone to break down into fits of laughter. Shortly afterwards, Jimbo left with Paul, after he had given Margaret a good night kiss.

"See you tomorrow my love," he called out as he drove off.

On the way home, Jimbo stopped off at the Ivanhoe Pub, to have a pint of beer with Paul. It was here while having a drink; he decided to divulge the true version of events, which had taken place. Paul's face visibly turned white as the story unfolded; the realisation kicking in on how damn close to death, Margaret really came.

"Shit, she made the transaction sound so bloody easy at the dinner table this evening," he protested.

"She loves you Paul and she didn't want to be sent back home. She made me promise not to say a word," Jimbo confessed, before taking another gulp of beer. "Look Paul, I suggest you let it drop, I told you the full story so you can comfort her. The other guys took care of the scoundrels,

159

believe you me. In fact, they won't be causing any more trouble, ever again," he expressed heavily.

Margaret found it hard to close her eyes, as every time she tried; all she could visualise was Jimbo being knocked out and dragged along the floor.

Kath and Marcus individually peeked in on her on several occasions. Each time she pretended to be sound asleep, not wanting to worry them.

Paul lay in his bed alone, tossing and turning, unable to sleep. Horrified by what Margaret experienced, wishing they had taken him instead. It would have protected her from experiencing the terrifying ordeal.

Marcus and Kath lay talking into the small hours, grateful their daughter was back at her grandparents, alive. They were appreciative Paul had intervened and met up with Jimbo to offer a ransom. Both blatantly aware it had saved their daughter's life, both totally oblivious as to what really took place.

In the bedroom next door, Mary clung to Joe; with large silent tears flowing down her cheeks.

"She's home safe and sound luv, now there's no point in worryin' " Joe whispered, giving her a kiss on her forehead.

"I know luv but it was frightening, so like before," she gulped.

"I know darlin' but that's in the past and it's best leavin' it there or you'll drive yurself insane pet. To tell you the truth, I wasn't quite sure if I was comin' or goin' meself, durin' the whole damn ordeal," Joe murmured.

She smiled up at him, he was always so strong, so resilient and she didn't know what she would do without him. Switching off the lamp, he cuddled up close and both fell into a troubled sleep, absolutely exhausted from the whole ordeal.

Kath had a chat with Margaret the following morning, voicing her concerns about her well being, as diplomatically as she could. Emotions were running high, when Marcus entered the room.

"Dad, tell mum she's being completely ridiculous and extremely over protective, will you?" she pleaded.

"Have you two eaten breakfast yet?" Marcus enquired, trying his best to diffuse the heated argument, having walked straight into the middle of it.

"Marcus, there's no getting away from the facts. Our daughter was kidnapped and is lucky to be alive. Wouldn't you agree?" Kath countered.

"What I agree on is for the pair of you to take a deep breath and calm down; have some breakfast and then we can work things out logically, in a much quieter and peaceful manner."

Mary hearing the argument taking place, purposely wandered into the kitchen "everyone's ready for bacon and eggs, I take it," she smiled energetically, automatically softening the atmosphere.

After breakfast, Paul arrived and Margaret rushed off, deciding a country walk was exactly what she needed.

"Let her go," Marcus pleaded, resting his hand upon Kath's arm. "Paul and Margaret need time alone … to talk things out."

Kath nodded in response, immediately agreeing with him. Hopefully Paul will be able to talk some sense into her, she mused, walking off to make another cup of coffee.

The rambling blackberry bushes were out in full bloom, laden with large juicy berries, ready for the picking. They wandered over the green pastures together and Margaret could feel the tension slowly dissipating.

"Did you get any sleep last night?" Paul casually enquired.

"Not too bad," Margaret responded quietly, avoiding eye contact.

"I'm surprised, going by what Jimbo filled me in on last night at the pub."

Margaret swallowed hard, knowing the game was up and there was no point in lying. "It hadn't turned out the way we expected but I'm here now," she snapped.

"You're extremely lucky to be here by the sound of things. My god Margaret, you're lucky to be alive ... you could have been murdered," he bellowed.

"Calm down Paul, you're getting as hysterical as my mother and on that note, I don't want her to know what took place or she will go utterly ballistic."

Paul sighed heavily. "I'm sorry for yelling but I love you so much and h-e-l-l, I don't exactly like the idea of you being in so much danger."

"Quite frankly, I would rather forget about the whole god-damn scenario and I'm sure Jimbo informed you, the rogues won't be bothering a-n-y-o-n-e ever again."

"That's probably the only thing saving you from me telling your parents," he declared. "Let's face it, there was no way on earth in keeping you safe, if they hadn't been taken care of" he responded defiantly.

They carried on walking, climbing over stone walls and jumping over ditches, before they came upon a small river. They sat down on the riverbank together wrapped up in each other's arms, silently inhaling the tranquillity, both lost in their solitary thoughts. The stream was meandering and winding its way around a corner, the current rippling gently as it flowed and gurgled over the jagged edged rocks, creating a peaceful ambience, as it continued on its journey.

Primroses were clustered on the adjacent bank, pretty pale lemon flowers tucked up in dark green foliage, adding softness to the picturesque landscape. Nearby, the weeping willow boughs were lunging forward, its willowy branches cascading downwards towards the rippling stream.

Lying with her head resting upon Paul's lap, Margaret was mesmerised by the fluffy white clouds, visibly changing, as they were blown across the iridescent blue canvas.

Lying idly and creating shapes from the overhead clouds, Margaret was at peace, basking in the sunlight with her lover.

"You're determined to stay," Paul taunted, breaking into the silence while twiddling with her hair.

"Certainly am," Margaret replied casually, seemingly with not a care in the world.

"You promise to be more cautious in the future?"

"Most certainly do," Margaret answered, rising up and wrapping her arms around him, giving him a passionate kiss.

"Okay then, let's head back so you can sorts things out with your mother."

Strolling back to the farm house hand-in-hand, their moods were serene. All what had to be said had been discussed and resolved amicably. The next major task ahead of them was to convince Kath. When they entered the kitchen, Mary immediately began making lunch, asking Kath, Margaret and Rachel to help out. Marcus discreetly took Paul into the front room to have a man-to-man chat, in relation to Margaret's well being and safety. Lunch was eaten together as a family; the atmosphere was light and cheery with the normal bantering taking place. Afterwards, Mary gathered Rachel up for a long walk, leaving Margaret and Kath alone together, allowing them time for a much needed discussion.

"You know what I'm going to ask, don't you?" Kath enquired, looking directly at Margaret.

"Yes I do mum but it's not possible. I want to stay at the Royal Victoria Hospital and spend Christmas here, with my grandparents. I want to spend more time with Paul. I love him mum," she said with conviction, as tears flooded her eyes.

Kath stretched over and took her into her arms. "I know my love but can you promise to be more careful in the future, now that you're probably more aware than most, of what can actually happen."

"Mum, I promise to be extremely vigilant and to ring you twice a week, if that helps," she blubbered, stumbling through sobs.

"Your father and I have discussed it at great lengths and YES you can stay but if there's one more incident, you're straight home on the first available flight," she emphasised strongly. "Your father is speaking with Paul at present, advising him to be more protective of you and to keep you out of harm's way as much as possible." They both hugged each other affectionately, before leaving the kitchen.

Margaret enjoyed being back at work, as it kept her busy and took her mind off being kidnapped and almost murdered. Paul didn't let her out of his sight and acted like a personal bodyguard. He drove her home in the evenings, to have dinner with the family as Kath, Marcus and Rachel would be heading back to Australia really soon.

Rachel was spending the last few days shopping with her mother, gathering up presents for her friends at school. In the afternoon she would laugh and giggle in the kitchen with Mary, who was teaching her how to make various homemade biscuits. In the evenings everyone would sample Rachel's efforts and was somewhat surprised at the delicious treats.

On Saturday morning, it was time to say their goodbyes. Paul went to the airport with Margaret and stood watching as the jet took off down the airstrip, flying off into the distance, until it finally disappeared. Joe and Mary gave them both a heartfelt hug, before turning around to head straight back home again.

"Do you fancy going to the pub?" Paul enquired lightly.

"Sounds like a good idea to me," Margaret smiled, grabbing his hand and leaving the airport together.

Chapter Fifteen

Kath and Marcus were glad to get back home. They could truly appreciate the sunny Australian sky and relaxed atmosphere, even the Custom officers were viewed in a different and more affectionate light, after their ordeal in Northern Ireland. Kath smiled, carrying her vanity case through the airport terminal with Rachel in tow, so glad she ended up in Australia all those years ago. It was truly the land of opportunity, a multi-cultural melting pot, made up of people offering unique properties from their various backgrounds and cultures.

"What are you looking so pleased about?" Marcus questioned after catching up with her, half expecting her to be sad, because Margaret stuck with her decision to stay in Northern Ireland.

"I'm so glad to be home," she answered happily.

Making their way from the airport, the city seemed more alive somehow, more cosmopolitan and colourful than she had remembered.

Rachel couldn't wait to call her friends and have them around, thus giving her the opportunity to distribute her thoughtful presents, knowing her friends would simply adore them.

Brigee rushed to the door, as the entrance gates began to swing open at the bottom of the avenue. She had been waiting patiently for their arrival for the past thirty minutes and was now bubbling with excitement. She missed them all dreadfully, finding the days had been long and arduous when they were away in Ireland.

"Welcome home," she shouted cheerfully, when the car doors opened.

Rachel was the first to receive a hug, before they congregated in the kitchen over a cup of coffee, catching up on the latest gossip.

"Valerie said she'll pop around tomorrow," Brigee relayed happily, feeling her old self again, now that her family was back safely.

At dinner time she was absolutely flabbergasted, when Kath explained the horrific ordeal Margaret had been put through, during their holidays.

"Bloody idiots," she muttered "when will they ever come to their senses?" shaking her head in disgust.

"I don't think they ever will," Kath added bitterly, knowing full well how terrorism destroyed her family's life.

Everyone retired to bed early shortly afterwards, a mixture of sheer exhaustion and jet lag, had hit them all at once.

The following day Valerie arrived as promised, bringing her happy cheery disposition with her. She was in the midst of renovating her home at present and up to her eyeballs in dust, she reiterated, raising her eyes skyward. Her eyes sparkled as she broke into a huge smile, describing the new sunken spa currently being installed. Lunch was a casual relaxed affair and Rachel's young friends came over later in the afternoon. Matt joined everyone in the evening for dinner. He was filling them in on Valerie's extravagant renovations, explaining all about her fussing and shenanigans, generating fits of laughter from everyone.

"Hush now darling," Valerie teased. "It's a girl's thing and we gotta do it our way," she laughed, prodding him jovially in the ribs to distract him.

"She was simply bored, because you weren't here Kath," he joked.

The evening slipped away in a relaxed, humorous manner, mixed with fine wine and interesting conversation. After they had left, Kath and Marcus headed off to bed, thrilled how the day unfolded, delighted to be home and settled but most of all, pleased to have such dear friends.

A few days later, everything settled back into some sort of normality. Rachel was attending school, Brigee was back on kitchen duties, while Kath and Marcus were up to their eyes in it at work.

Deadlines were fast approaching. "Everyone wants everything at once," Kath lamented to Marcus, holding on the line for Harvey, who was one of their chief editors.

"Take on less my darling," Marcus chided. "You do the work of three people as it is."

Putting her hand over the mouth piece "well, who else is going to do it?" she queried, rolling her eyes.

"Delegate my darling, you must learn to delegate more," Marcus responded, giving her a little peck on the cheek. He mentally noted, he would have to organise a long weekend away for the pair of them. Acknowledging that Ireland had taken a huge emotional toll on Kath and she obviously needed some time out.

Two weeks later, Rachel was hanging out of Valerie's car waving like crazy. "Don't worry mum, Valerie and I will have a ball," she shouted out, as Valerie drove down the avenue.

"Are you sure we can afford to have a few days off Marcus?" Kath queried, anxious about the launch of a new magazine due out next week.

"Everything's fine. Besides, the five days we are having off includes the weekend," he murmured, climbing into the stretch limousine behind Kath, before it made its way up the coast. "Do you fancy doing something naughty," he chuckled, popping open a bottle of champagne. He was

169

glad he organised a limousine, it saved them driving up to Nelson Bay, meaning their break could begin immediately. No fighting with the traffic, no stopping off for something to eat, everything was on board and all they had to do was enjoy it.

Sipping the champagne, Kath smiled. "This is a bit self indulgent Mr Garofoli, don't you think?" she purred.

"You bet it is," he grinned. "But you're worth it," answering in a husky voice, sliding across. He removed her empty glass, putting it back on the folding table, then pulled her up on to his knee and began kissing her passionately.

"What about the chauffer," she whispered, alarmed and embarrassed, feeling colour rising to her cheeks.

"Easily fixed," Marcus grinned, pushing a button near at hand, allowing the tinted glass behind the driver to slide up and close tightly, giving them complete privacy, as light relaxing music made its way through the stereo system.

She laughed out loud like a mischievous school girl, as he slowly unbuttoned her navy silk blouse. She closed her eyes, allowing herself to completely relax, allowing him to scan her body tenderly and seductively. Unclasping her black lacy bra, he slowly ran his hands up and along her shoulders, gently disposing her bra and blouse on to the back seat of the limo, while teasing and suckling her nipples. He was stimulating her, sending electrifying shockwaves racing up and down her spine.

Reciprocating, with her heart beating faster, she tore open his shirt, exposing his perfectly formed torso. Sweeping downwards, she ran her tongue over his broad smooth chest in soft feathery motions, teasing and biting, tantalising and arousing his innermost desires. All of a sudden, the car stopped. Panicking, she looked up.

"It's okay my darling," he growled softly "it's only the traffic lights."

"Aha," she smiled seductively, quickly recovering and continuing on her sensual journey.

Removing his belt, she quickly discarded the remainder of his clothing, before slowly removing her skirt and panties. Simply wearing her stockings and high heel shoes, amplified her sexiness as she sat on him, kissing him provocatively and deeply, as they were journeying north.

"If we're caught in an accident right now, god help us," she murmured.

She blatantly continued to tease him, going down on him again and again, deliberately driving him crazy.

Unable to restrain himself, Marcus stretched forward urgently, dragging her on to him more. Two hot and frantic bodies, desperately aching for one another, swirling and swaying together, were rapidly gaining momentum. His thrusts quickened and deepened, penetrating her innermost being through heightened emotions.

Breathing erratically and moaning in elation, Kath's agile, petite body was shimmering with perspiration. No longer willing or able to hold back any longer, she lost control, surrendering totally, completely letting go.

Marcus exploded, kissing and covering her sweet moist lips with his, burying into her intimately and drawing her in, as they melted together in a sweet and undeniable bliss.

Kath clung unto him, as she slowly began her descent, her body tingling, alight and ever so sensitive. He held on to her, as tiny tremors continued ricocheting throughout her body, with her loving arms wrapped around him, drawing him closer as sweet joyful tears trickled down her cheeks.

"I love you," she whispered tenderly, as he cupped her face in his hands.

Brushing away her tears, he looked directly into her eyes. "I couldn't survive without you my love," he confided, kissing her once more.

They managed to get dressed, before tucking hungrily into lunch.

"I was absolutely famished," Kath giggled, sipping her champagne.

"I'm not surprised you sexy little vixen who seems to have boundless energy, if I recall correctly," he teased.

"You're the one who started the shenanigans in the first place," she added laughing.

He instantly took her into his arms and they snuggled up together, for the remainder of the journey.

They arrived at the Shoal Bay Resort & Spa; the journey took approximately three hours by car. Both were thoroughly relaxed and sated, after their sexual encounter on the journey up. Marcus carefully helped Kath out of the limousine.

"So chivalry isn't dead after all," Kath joked, raising an eyebrow and laughing.

He automatically pinched her on the bottom.

"Ouch," she screamed. "I'll pay you back later," she purred.

"Why, am I going to get a beating," he hinted.

"You never know your luck," she chuckled, waltzing into the hotel, deliberately swaying her hips sexily, to tease him.

Running to catch up, he instantly took her hand. "Mmmm, interesting times lie ahead then," he grinned.

"Certainly does," she replied, smiling broadly.

Their suite was enormous and the bedroom contained a huge bed, draped in cream and gold embossed satin, creating a romantic feel. The bathroom contained an enormous spa fitted with gold taps, the opulence was simply overwhelming. Kath smiled inwardly, Marcus never failed when it came to booking venues. His standards were extremely high and so were the establishments he chose.

Their suitcases arrived and Kath was soon slipping out of her clothes to have a hot shower, before getting ready for dinner. In amongst the steam she unwound even further, smiling and thinking about their trip here. Marcus was certainly enamoured by her sexy antics and she felt more womanly and uninhibited, away from the atrocities of her homeland. Here she could be free, relaxed and sexy as all hell. Marcus, you'd better watch out, she mused, laughing instinctively.

Marcus called out and within a few minutes he joined her in the shower.

"That was quite a performance on the way over in the limousine Mrs Garofoli," he murmured in her ear.

"Why Mr Garofoli, it's one of many I can assure you," she playfully answered, enjoying the repartee between them.

They finished showering together and Marcus slowly dried her with an enormous fluffy towel, kissing her gently on her ear lobes, eyes, neck and breasts. "That's enough," she laughed "or we'll be late for dinner," pulling away from him and rushing quickly into the bedroom.

In one foul swoop he managed to grab her and sent her flying on to the bed, with him landing playfully on top. Grabbing her arms he anchored her down, leaving her totally powerless to move. Leaning over, ever so slowly, he kissed her deeply and she responded eagerly. "Now where was I," he enquired, raising an eyebrow and removing her towel, before kissing her on her tummy. She shivered in delight, anticipating what lay ahead.

Afterwards, they quickly rushed and had another shower, before dressing quickly. "Zip me up darling and by the way, it's your fault we're late," Kath laughed.

"I don't mind being late for the rest of eternity," he joked "especially if I get a reaction similar to what I just experienced," he grinned sexily, as he finished zipping up her dress.

Down in the restaurant the atmosphere was serene; the candlelit tables added a romantic atmosphere, accompanying the elegant décor and the beautiful panoramic views overlooking the magnificent, volcanic headlands and spectacular bay. They drank wine while mulling over the extensive menu, before deciding on a seafood platter for two. A pianist was playing soft, slow melodies on the far side of the room, as couples chatted harmoniously, enjoying the delicious food and intimate setting.

"Thank you for bringing me here Marcus; it was exactly what I needed. I've been uptight and cranky lately over Margaret but there's no point in worrying anymore. What's meant to be will be," shrugging her shoulders in acceptance.

"Exactly my darling, that's what I've been telling you all along," he added softly.

"I know," she sighed contently. "I'm a slow learner."

The music commenced again and Marcus took her hand in his. "Let's dance," he insisted.

They made an extraordinary couple on the dance floor, swaying to the music, appearing like young lovers, totally engrossed in each other with not a care in the world.

The following morning she was woken by Marcus. It was still pitch black outside, she noticed.

"What on earth is happening," she questioned, still groggy from sleep.

"Hurry up and get dressed," he appealed. "I've got a surprise waiting for you."

"My god," peering at the bedside clock. "It's 5am in the morning ... can't it wait?" she pleaded.

"No it can't," he whispered, handing her a pair of jeans and a warm woolly jumper.

There was no point in arguing she figured; obviously he had something definite in mind. Outside a Range Rover was waiting for them and soon they were heading towards the wineries.

"Don't you think it's a bit early in the morning to go wine tasting dear," she grumbled, not yet fully awake.

"Perhaps," he stated, keeping his face perfectly straight, determined not to divulge his surprise.

They were driven along the quiet still countryside, blanketed in early morning mist; Marcus had Kath cuddled up in his arms, which helped pacify her until they reached their destination. Exiting the four wheel drive, Kath discovered they were in the middle of no-where. No winery. No hotel. Zilch. Nothing.

Marcus laughed, catching her by the hand, before pulling her through some gates and into an open field. Her eyes widened and she grinned immediately, getting the biggest surprise of her life. The loud bellowing from the giant portable fan, made her jump straight away, as it began inflating the hot air balloon. She laughed out loud absolutely delighted, as she watched the burners being turned down lower, before the wicker basket was tipped up into an upright position. Her heart melted immediately, this was one of those things she always talked about and wanted to do but like many others, would probably never have got around to accomplishing it. Straight away, she woke up properly, excited and raring to go.

"Wow Marcus, I never would have guessed," she screamed happily over the loud burners, giving him an enormous hug.

The bright colourful balloon was fully inflated and the organiser joined them. "Everything's set and ready to go," he signalled to Marcus.

"What … you're going to fly it," Kath gulped in amazement.

"Considering I've held a licence for over ten years, I guess that's a yes," he laughed.

Shortly afterwards, Kath was helped into the basket where she proudly stood next to her man. Without saying a single word, Marcus adjusted the regulator on the burners allowing the flame to grow higher. Within seconds, they drifted silently and swiftly heavenwards.

The feeling was totally exhilarating, like a bird soaring she imagined, as the ground was left rapidly behind, far below. The balloon drifted eastwards ascending and descending in altitude, catching different wind currents. Kath felt a sense of weightlessness, a euphoric feeling rapidly filling her soul with an inner calmness.

"This is the weather window," Marcus told Kath, breaking into the silence, explaining the still morning air was best for flying conditions, hence the early morning start.

An early mist was shrouding the great Australian landscape in a fine ghostly blanket, as they floated silently above the treetops. Kath felt she could almost reach out and touch the branches, holding her breath in appreciation of the natural beauty surrounding her. The sky began to lighten and the great Australian sunrise began peeking over the nearby hills. Spreading her welcoming warmth and cheer in magnificent pink hues, across the great southern land. Kath was filled with happy emotions, as she took a deep breath of the fresh dew filled air, experiencing the sunrise was both mystical and ethereal. Glancing across at Marcus, he handed her a glass of champagne.

"Good morning my love, welcome to a brand new day."

She leant across and kissed him, tears of joy streaming down her cheeks, reflecting in the early morning light. "This is magical, romantic, an unforgettable experience my love and these memories will last me a lifetime."

He hugged her tightly, as the undulating valleys drifted silently pass far beneath them.

Passing farms, the sheepdogs commenced barking as they drifted overhead. They floated passed streams, spotting cars meandering along the twisty roads, appearing like small matchbox toys. Kath's heart soared, as she caught a glimpse of the ocean in the far distance, melting into the pale crimson horizon. Marcus stood proud, like a ship's captain on a new voyage of discovery, as they dipped and ebbed their way across the vast southern sky. A massive snowy white pelican flew past, not even acknowledging the brightly coloured balloon in its terrain, as Kath laughed spontaneously. She noticed a white Range Rover up front, parked conspicuously in the middle of a field.

"Time for us to land," Marcus called out, while fiddling with some gadgets.

Kath nodded serenely, lost in a silent beautiful world, thoroughly enjoying the moment, one which she would treasure forever.

The following day Marcus and Kath decided to head out to the Sahara Trails. Kath choose a beautiful chestnut mare to ride, while Marcus settled for a lean black stallion. The Aussie bush trail followed an old dried up creek, taking them through the Casuarina Forest. They spent an hour journeying along winding paths leisurely, sometimes stopping to have a drink of water beneath majestic grey gums. When they both reached the clearing they took off immediately, breaking their horses into a fast gallop, racing each other, allowing the morning breeze to cool and refresh their warm worn bodies.

Later in the afternoon they strolled along Fingal Bay, located south of Nelson Bay. It was here when they spotted two huge migrating humpback whales frolicking around, putting on an energetic and spectacular display, not far from the shoreline.

On the third day, Kath felt adventurous and booked a parasailing tandem flight, for both her and Marcus. Lunchtime arrived and they were taken out to sea by a speed boat. Here they were winched up into the air, wearing a secured safety harness. Before long they were suspended one hundred and fifty metres up in the air, viewing the massive bay lying far below, observed from a bird's eye point of view. Their ten minutes seemed much longer, before they were winched down slowly on to the boat.

In the evening at the Promenade Restaurant, they had a few drinks in the relaxing cocktail lounge, before tucking into the local cuisine. Both discovering the fresh oysters were scrumptious and the macadamias delectable, before sampling the fresh figs for dessert and enjoying the local wine from the Hunter Valley.

The following day, they drove up to Nelson Head Lighthouse, wrapped up in each other arms, embracing the sweeping panoramic view to the entrance of Port Stephens, which offered uncrowded sandy beaches, sheltered bays and unspoilt national parks.

On their final day, they decided to visit Anna Bay which hosted the Birubi Beach and Worimi conservation lands. This was part of the Stockton sand dunes, which stretched quite spectacularly along the coastline for thirty-three kilometres, supporting magnificent thirty metre high dunes.

They spent an entertaining day riding quad bikes over them, then went sand boarding afterwards, which was exhilarating but extremely exhausting. After a snack in the Anna Bay Tavern, they took a tranquil camel ride along the beach, as the sun set far out on the horizon.

Making their journey back by limousine, they felt peaceful. Both having been recharged and rejuvenated by this much needed short break. There was however no shenanigans on the way back home. Instead, they nestled quietly into each other's arms, happy, content and at peace with the world.

Brigee left a light on for their arrival home, along with a note advising she had left them a midnight snack.

Heading up to their room afterwards, both Kath and Marcus peeked into Rachel's room, discovering she was sound asleep and out for the count. They moseyed off to their room silently, before slipping into bed and falling fast asleep. They were now ready and well rested, prepared to meet the daily challenges of work once again.

Chapter Sixteen

Margaret and Paul's relationship was growing stronger by the day. Their secret lay hidden from staff members, their colleagues were accepting Paul's protectiveness simply as a precautionary measure, due to her kidnapping several months earlier.

Margaret excelled in her internship, revelling in the everyday challenges found in the hectic emergency department. The troubles as they were known, kept everyone extremely busy. Operating theatres were inundated with semi detached limbs, the outcome from senseless bombings, still taking place. Margaret never got used to the women and children being rushed in on trolleys, bloodied and seriously injured; relatives following close behind, crying and praying for their loved ones.

On their weekends off, they sometimes visited Portrush, both always enjoying the drive along the craggy and scenic Antrim Coast Road. They frequently stopped off at pubs and coffee shops on the way, chatting away to the locals and learning about the North's history. The locals were friendly, often volunteering historical facts after recognising Margaret's Aussie dialect. By being helpful and informative, they were negating the ugly terror which haunted the North.

Margaret would also laugh and scream riding the notorious roller coaster, at Barry's Amusements in Portrush. She would cling tightly to Paul travelling on the ghost train, until she hit daylight on the other side. They would share pink fluffy candyfloss sitting on a bench together, overlooking the blue-grey Atlantic Ocean.

Later in the evenings they would have a meal in a pub, washed down with a pint of Guinness, before participating in a karaoke evening, filled with laughter and love. Cuddling up in bed much later together, they would kiss ardently and make love, before falling asleep in each other's arms.

Margaret was participating in more operations these days and was recognised for her no nonsense approach. She initially settled her patients with her compassionate Aussie accent, informing them there was nothing to worry about, in a sincere and professional manner. Both the patient and their relatives always felt assured, confident, very much appreciating her gentle bedside manner. Frequently, Paul would stand back and watch silently from a nearby cubicle, smiling broadly, proud of her achievements to date. Peering from a distance, his heart was bursting with love, knowing she was the woman for him. Hoping one day, she would marry him.

The following weekend she was to meet Paul's mother and father, over at their residence on the Malone Road in Belfast. It was an extremely affluent area where several judges, head surgeons and successful business people resided.

The Honourable Mr Hagan was a well respected judge and one who didn't tolerate any nonsense in his courtroom. After many deliberations, his judgement and sentencing were always firmly delivered, granting the grieving families sitting in his courtroom some respite, by expediting the terrorists responsible for taking their children's lives, to a life in prison.

His mother Helen happily suggested they could go sailing that weekend. Margaret was really looking forward to it, reminiscing about the times she had gone out with her late stepfather Rod, back home.

The week flew by as always and the next thing she knew, there she was standing outside the prestigious double storied residence, waiting with Paul, as he rang the doorbell. Security had been severely heightened; this was sanctioned because of the recent number of local prominent judges being singled out by various terrorist groups lately.

Helen greeted them, dressed in designer jeans and an Aran sweater, displaying her neat lean figure. Her honey coloured hair was up in a pony tail, tied with a pale blue ribbon, matching the colour of her soft blue eyes. Automatically leaning forward, she gave Paul a kiss on the cheek, followed by a loving embrace.

"So this is the lovely Margaret you've been hiding from us," she stated, smiling across at her.

"Please to meet you Mrs Hagan."

"Oh Helen will do fine; there are no formalities here dear. Isn't that right son," she confided, ushering them down the hallway and into the huge family kitchen. "Would you like a coffee Margaret?"

"Yes, that would be nice thank you."

Paul automatically plonked himself down at the kitchen table, quickly pulling a chair out for Margaret, telling her to sit down and relax. Margaret straight away felt right at home and breathed much easier; pleased her fears were alleviated immediately, after meeting Paul's mother. There were no signs of snobbery or pompous behaviour whatsoever and Margaret was instantly drawn to her.

"Your father's in the study Paul, you know what he's like when he gets stuck into his files. Could you please tell him young Margaret's here and we're having a cuppa before we leave."

Paul got up and went to fetch his father, leaving Helen pottering around the kitchen.

"We're so pleased our Paul has met a pleasant young lady. I'm sure he's told you about young Violet already."

"Yes he did, it was extremely sad she died so young from cancer," Margaret confided, appreciating the openness and friendliness Helen was portraying.

The door opened and the Judge entered, immediately walking over to Margaret to introduce himself. "Please to meet you Margaret, I'm Henry. Our Paul has spoken most highly of you and I believe you're from Australia," he smiled.

"Yes I am indeed," she replied, appreciating the warm welcome.

Henry was tall like Paul, his dark hair had distinguishing grey streaks throughout and his huge brown eyes were warm and comforting, as he questioned her about sailing in Australia. Soon they were seated in his Mercedes, heading to the Carrickfergus Marina, where their yacht was moored.

It was a windy day, excellent for sailing with a westerly blowing in. Margaret was impressed with the eighty foot yacht named 'Memories' which she felt was romantic.

"All the family are members of the Royal Yachting Association," Helen stated, remarking how they didn't get out as much as they would like to, due to everyone's workload.

Inside was luxurious, cream leather seating that tied in beautifully with the heavily varnished walnut, running along the galley kitchen. The two bedrooms included en suites and were ample in size. The living area was tastefully decorated, with the latest navigation and chart plotting equipment, fitted out up on the top deck.

Paul and his father were working well together, untying the ropes and checking the instruments, while Margaret helped Helen unpack the groceries. Champagne and smoked salmon, along with other delicacies were packed away in the fridge in a warm and friendly manner, as the engines were started up, before edging their way out of the marina.

"When the boys were young, we use to take them sailing in Lough Neagh in the summer holidays," Helen volunteered happily. "Mind you Paul and Stephen, his younger brother; use to take it out on Strangford Lough quite regularly, when they were much older. However, now that Paul's in medicine and Stephen is following in his father's footsteps, there never seems to be enough time these days," she sighed.

They were all on deck after safely leaving the marina, pulling on the winch handles and jack lines, allowing the huge sails to open up in all her glory. Paul and Margaret were standing on the starboard side inhaling the fresh salty air, watching the yacht cut through the blue-grey choppy ocean as she picked up speed, leaving a turbulent frothy white wake behind them, as they sailed north.

"Glad you came?" Paul whispered.

"Most certainly am," Margaret replied, giving him a quick kiss. "Mind you, it's a hell of a lot colder out here, than back home," she laughed loudly, with rosy red cheeks.

The instruments were set as they headed north, keeping the shoreline port side. Shortly afterwards Helen reappeared, dispensing warm mugs of tomato soup which everyone drank gratefully, hugging the beverage snugly in their hands for added warmth.

They edged their way closer to the rugged coastline to view Giant's Causeway, which appeared even more spectacular and mystical from her ocean viewing position. They had arranged with the harbourmaster to moor their yacht at Portstewart Harbour for the evening and decided to dine out later in the local town. When everyone was ready, they walked along the seafront, admiring the magnificent view and sunset. They were ravenous, having contributed their skills to a strenuous and exhilarating day on the ocean.

Henry suggested having something to eat at the Seasplash, a local pub renowned for their Guinness pies and delicious Irish fare. All were dressed in jeans and warm woollen sweaters, blending in with the locals as they perused the menu, chatting harmoniously amongst themselves, unwinding in the warm relaxed atmosphere.

After a hearty meal, they headed downstairs. Paul ordered Irish malt whiskies for everyone, as they settled in a little nook in the corner of the pub. Tables were packed with small groups, chatting and laughing over pints of lager, munching into their Tayto potato crisps. Young couples were cuddled up close in the cosy nooks, oblivious to the rowdy patrons, Margaret noticed smiling.

The band arrived and the musicians began playing Irish ballads, complementing The Celtic Tales, a group of angelic singers, harmonising and singing beautifully in their thick Irish brogues. The crowd commenced clapping and singing, enhancing the atmosphere even more.

Paul hung his arm around Margaret's shoulder and drew her in closer. Smiling, he whispered "I love you."

"And I love you too," she responded gently, totally relaxed, enjoying the company.

The following morning on board the yacht, somebody was rattling around in the galley. "Bacon and eggs in fifteen minutes everyone," Helen called out from the kitchen.

As Paul drew closer to Margaret in bed, she turned around quickly to face him. "Shit … I better get up and help," she uttered loudly, obviously in a panic.

"Mmm, I was hoping for dessert," he murmured, nuzzling into her neck.

"No way Paul," Margaret stated wide eyed and astonished, pulling the sheets back quickly.

"I could always put a muzzle on you, so my parents don't hear," he laughed, catching her hand before she exited the bed.

"Paul, there's no way in hell I'm making love to you in here with your parents directly outside," she shot back, pulling away swiftly and running into the shower. A few minutes later Paul joined her, stroking her body tenderly while kissing her avidly, it was all he was allowed this morning. "You can wait until we get back to your place tonight," she murmured softly, aroused but determined to escape his seduction.

Margaret arrived in the galley kitchen, her cheeks rosy and her eyes sparkling, as Helen welcomed her with ease, pleased Paul had met such a beautiful down to earth young woman. Margaret immediately began making the coffee and preparing the toast, while Helen checked on the grilled bacon, which smelt absolutely delicious.

Paul ventured out and grabbed a mug of coffee, pinching Margaret cheekily on the bum, before heading up top to seek out his father.

Shortly they were nestled around the kitchen table, tucking into a hearty breakfast.

"I'll clean up afterwards," Margaret volunteered. "After all, you made a scrumptious breakfast for everyone Helen," Margaret said, smiling across at her.

"No ... I wouldn't hear tell of it dear but I'll compromise and we can do them together, because I have a funny feeling we're going to become great friends and we'll get to see a lot more of each other," her eyes smiling affectionately.

"Thank you," Margaret replied quietly, her eyes lighting up with joy, as Paul stretched across and gave his mum a kiss on the cheek.

"You're right mum, you will be seeing a lot more of Margaret and I'm pleased you both have made her feel so welcome."

"Well how could we not. It's not often we meet a fine Aussie sailor," Henry laughed loudly, as Helen poured everyone another coffee.

Soon they switched on the engines, following the harbourmaster's instructions, before merging their way out of the marina. Out at sea the sails filled quickly, bellowing in the gusty wind as they sailed up north past Portrush and Barry's Amusements, with its ferris wheel twirling away in the far distance. They ventured up to Carndonagh, before turning around and heading back to Carrickfergus.

They arrived back at their original departure point at dusk; everyone was physically exhausted but relaxed and feeling much more closer by the end of their voyage. Henry drove home as Margaret and Paul cuddled up in the back seat, pleased the trip had been successful, with everyone blending in beautifully.

"Why don't you stay for a while?" Helen enquired politely, when they exited the car.

"Can't mum," Paul announced. "We're both up early for work tomorrow morning but thanks for the offer."

"Well it's been lovely to meet you my dear," Helen said, giving Margaret an enormous hug and a tiny kiss on the cheek.

"Likewise," Margaret reiterated, smiling happily.

"Yes Margaret, you must join us again soon," Henry announced. "I'm a pretty good judge of character, pardon the pun," he laughed "and we're delighted Paul has met you. Now that you've been introduced to the family, we hope to see a lot more of you."

"You certainly will," Margaret beamed, before plonking into Paul's car and waving goodbye.

"At last," Paul shouted, as he drove down the avenue.

"What?" Margaret enquired laughing.

"Now that I have you all to myself, I will be able to finally seduce you," he exclaimed, in an exasperated voice.

"You're a horny devil," Margaret laughed, as Paul drove quickly back to his place.

Margaret had only got through the front door, having dropped her bags on the living room floor, when Paul lovingly attacked her from behind.

"Did you enjoy the weekend?"

"Immensely," Margaret replied, as Paul kissed her ravishingly.

Slipping his hand up under her sweater, he unclipped her bra and ran his hand seductively over her breasts. "Mmm I missed this," he murmured between kisses. In an instance he had her gathered up in his arms and carefully made his way upstairs.

"And where do you think you're going Dr Hagan," she whispered in anticipation.

"I'm taking my woman to bed and I'm going to seduce her from head to toe," he laughingly remarked loudly, smiling with his eyes, as he dropped her on his bed. Within a minute he had her undressed and was covering her in sweet, tender kisses.

She responded immediately, unable to resist his tenderness and urgency. She bit into her lower lip as he went down on her, instantly raising her body up in a rhythmic fashion, meeting his incredible sexual ambush.

Soon he was fully laying on top, his fingers intertwined and enclosed in hers, kissing her face, earlobes, neck and breasts. Swiftly entering her without any warning, he sent her body surging into an orgasm, while French kissing her hot sensitive body, alight and burning bright with an enormous and overwhelming desire. He changed positions, pulling her up into his arms into a sitting position, continuing to kiss her, while still penetrating her. Her body was electrified as the pressure began to build, holding on to him tightly, invading his ears with her tongue and working her way around his neck as he dug deeper and deeper inside of her. Unable to hold off any longer, she let out a guttural cry, her body, her mind, crying out in ecstasy. He immediately pulled her in closer yet again, exploding instantly, growling incoherently.

"Mmm I love you Margaret," he said, nuzzling into her neck. "I love you so much; you're sexy, intelligent and quirky." Lifting her chin up, gazing into her dark green eyes, he leant forward and kissed her, his heart filled with undying love and compassion.

Lying back on the bed, he lit up a cigarette that they shared together, both happy and euphoric. "Are you hungry?" he enquired gently.

"I most certainly am, especially after all that," Margaret laughed happily.

"Okay then, let's have a quick shower and we'll head down to the local Chinese for something to eat."

Sitting in the Red Lantern Restaurant, both were comfortable sipping on a glass of wine, as they tucked into their delicious chicken chow mien. Both were ravenous, yet extremely mellow in nature.

"Mum and dad were really taken with you," Paul announced, breaking into their mutual silence.

"I really liked them; they're very down to earth with no airs and graces and both made me feel welcome and part of the family," Margaret replied, carefree and relaxed, especially after their bedroom romp earlier on.

"Dad seemed pretty impressed with your sailing skills, while mum thinks you're adorable and loves your accent," he continued.

"That's enough compliments Dr Hagan. I'm beginning to get embarrassed," she chuckled; inwardly pleased, she was so well accepted by his parents.

It was bedlam as usual back at the Royal Victoria Hospital. Emergency wards were packed with car accident victims and acts of terrorism continued, adding to the fatality list. Margaret was certainly getting hands on experience; however it was a difficult role to fulfil.

She acknowledged the most horrific task for her, was delivering news to the anxious waiting parents. Explaining to them how their child had fought so bravely in the theatre but their struggle to survive against such high odds was unsuccessful, resulting in their loved ones having passed away.

The outpouring of grief was always shocking to her; no matter how prepared she felt she was. Family members were completely traumatised, after digesting and fully comprehending the terminal news. The twisted anguish etched upon their pale drawn faces, their dark solemn eyes escalating with tears, their bodies frequently collapsing under an overwhelming weight of hopelessness.

Her heart bled for them, knowing the surgeons involved were at the top of their league and tried their upmost to help but it didn't make it any easier for her to handle, each time she delivered the sad and gut wrenching news, the parents hoped they would never need to hear.

Paul was a great comfort to come home to in the evenings. She was spending four nights a week at his place now. Her grandparents were happy she had met such a wonderful young man, who clearly doted on her.

Snuggled up in bed together in the evenings, they often exchanged news as to what took place while they were on duty. Paul helped her immensely, comforting her recently, when she had lost a patient. He gently explained the ramifications, if her young patient who was suffering from severe brain damage, had survived surgery. It was a shocking and difficult injury, for anyone to endure. To watch a loved one lying in a vegetative state, hooked up to numerous machines, unable to communicate, unable to be the person they used to be. Sometimes as hard as it may seem, death was a much kinder option, for all the families involved.

Margaret resigned herself to the fact, that this was frequently the case. Margaret valued Paul's knowledge and explanation, enabling her to deal with the situation and accept death a little easier. Her growing hospital experiences made her more appreciative of life, encouraging her to live it to the fullest.

Christmas would soon be upon them and Paul was looking forward to sharing the time with Margaret's grandparents, as well as his own family. The weather was growing much colder of late and the meteorologists were predicting a white Christmas, which Paul felt would provide a wonderful experience for Margaret. He also knew he had to make a call to Australia shortly and speak with Margaret's parents. March was drawing closer, closer to the time he was dreading. It meant Margaret had to leave ... leave Ireland ... leave her friends ... and leave him. He couldn't bear to think of it anymore.

Chapter Seventeen

Back in Australia, Brigee was running around once again getting everything organised for Christmas. It was hard to believe another year had disappeared so quickly. Margaret of course wouldn't be home until the beginning of March but Kath, Marcus and Rachel were looking forward to her homecoming of course. Margaret's bubbly personality was very much missed by them all. Her friends used to visit, play loud music or laze around the pool and were often seen poking around in the kitchen for munchies, happily intermingling with the family.

Tinsel was being twisted and woven down the banisters in the hallway, sprinkled with laughter and bouts of giggles from Rachel and her friends, who volunteered to help.

"When you're finished girls you may get the decorations for the dining room, because the tree will be arriving this afternoon," Brigee bellowed from the kitchen. Shortly afterwards, the girls were bounding down the stairs two at a time, racing into the kitchen for some chocolate milk and cookies, before unravelling the hundreds of lights for the Christmas tree, along with the brightly coloured tinsel and baubles.

"Ready for lunch, love?" Marcus enquired, poking his head in through Kath's office door.

"Sounds good to me," Kath murmured, peering upwards and smiling, before throwing her pen down on top of the paperwork piled upon her desk.

Christmas was always a busy time of the year at Noblealert. Deadlines had to be met, bonuses sorted out and parties to attend, as the festivities grew closer. She rose from her office chair appearing immaculate, dressed in a navy blue linen suit and a white silk blouse, her hair styled in a French knot, with her demeanour portraying a smart and articulate business lady. Taking a few steps forward, she leant in closer and gave Marcus a kiss.

"What's that for?" he enquired happily.

"It doesn't have to be for anything," Kath replied. "It's simply because I love you and I think you're the sexiest man alive," laughing out loud.

He immediately pulled her into his arms. "Mmm Mrs Garofoli, compliments like that and I might be tempted to skip lunch, take you directly home and seduce you," kissing her once more.

"No way you cheapskate, besides which, Rachel and her friends wouldn't give us a moments peace, because our tree is being delivered this afternoon A-N-D I'm starving," she giggled, grabbing his hand and heading straight for the office door.

"Well I guess I'll have to take a rain check on that," arching an eyebrow. "But there's always this evening," he chuckled, giving her a quick pinch on the bum on the way out.

Glenda glanced up from her desk and smiled. Both Marcus and Kath were very much in love, acting like a young love struck couple who had only met and were enamoured with each other. Kath appeared much younger these days, outwardly more relaxed and carefree, Glenda thought. Kath relayed to her on the way out that she wouldn't be back for the rest of the day and if anything important popped up, she was to be contacted on her mobile.

"I'll finish typing these minutes up from this morning's meeting, then see to it that all the reports are completed and delivered to the editors this afternoon," Glenda announced efficiently.

"You work much too hard," Kath chided. "Just finish up the minutes and call it a day, go home or go Christmas shopping or something. The reports can wait until tomorrow, there's no great urgency on them Glenda," she smiled, closing the door behind her.

Glenda smiled inwardly; Kath was always a good boss, appreciating her hard working ethics and long hours dedicated to the company. She frequently gave Glenda half days off, to make up for her loyalty and effort. Quickly she resumed typing, deciding this afternoon she would finish off her last minute Christmas shopping, as Kath suggested.

Lunch was a relaxed affair for Kath and Marcus; both sat overlooking calm waters from the Banjo Paterson Cottage Restaurant, situated in Gladesville. The old sandstone building had the restaurant elegantly decorated for Christmas, which was frequently used for Christmas parties by local establishments. The five acres of parkland had beautifully landscaped gardens surrounding the restaurant, offering up a peacefulness and serenity along the water's edge. They ordered a light lunch, soaking up the serene atmosphere while exchanging news on the business front.

"It will seem strange. Margaret not being here with the family at Christmas," Kath mentioned casually, after ordering a coffee.

"She's a young woman Kath and needs to spread her wings and has independently managed well, venturing into the big wide world and making her mark," Marcus mentioned quietly.

"I think she has certainly accomplished that my darling. Belfast isn't exactly down the road," Kath asserted a little peeved.

Marcus searched her eyes knowingly, sensing Kath's insecurities and fears of losing her eldest daughter. Resting his hand on top of hers and peering into her eyes "it's okay Kath. She's growing up and will always love you but you must let her go to expand, explore and do all the things she wants to do."

"I know that love," Kath answered, swallowing hard with tears in her eyes. "It's just that I love her so much and I want to protect her, make sure no one hurts her, that she's safe and comes to no harm and …"

"Hush now darling and relax," Marcus interrupted. "You're her mother and I understand. However, think about what you came through and how you survived. Margaret will be exactly the same. Mind you, with a lot less drama, thank you very much."

Kath smiled, her spirits lifted. "You're right darling, she has to grow and learn to live her life. I simply must take a back seat from here on in and hopefully be there for her whenever she needs me."

"That's exactly right, remembering she's her mother's daughter, she's clever, extraordinarily beautiful and extremely street smart. Paul is now her protector and he'll take good care of her."

Just in time, the coffee arrived and Kath immediately perked up, appearing much happier, after sharing her thoughts with Marcus. He was right after all. Many years ago she had personally taken on some of the worst terrorists in Northern Ireland, managed to survive in another country with a young child, worked her way up into a well recognised successful business and above all, found happiness with a man she truly loved. What the hell was she getting so worked up about; Margaret had nothing to worry about … neither had she.

Arriving home, Rachel along with Tracy, Karen and her other school friends were caught giggling in the dining room, trying their best to unravel the Christmas tree lights. The aroma of freshly baked mince tarts drifted through the lower levels, as Kath and Marcus made their way into the kitchen. Trays of dainty mince pies were cooling on the granite island bench.

"My god, are you thinking of opening up a bakery Brigee?" Marcus questioned popping one into his mouth.

"Oy, hands off. I've been fending off Rachel and her friends all morning, the little devils have been in pinching them whenever I have my back turned," she laughed gaily. "It's a good job I baked an extra dozen or two, to cover for their thieving hands," she announced glaring at Marcus, gulping down his last bite.

"That's you told off," Kath joked, peering at Marcus while giving Brigee a hug. "They look and smell delicious Brigee and they always go down a treat at the Christmas party," Kath confided appreciatively.

Kath and Marcus quickly changed into casual attire, in time to help out when the Christmas tree arrived. It was then full on for young and old, as the tree got decorated in a happy festive mood.

The girls quickly got changed into their swimmers afterwards and rushed out to the pool to swim and splash around, after their eventful day. Kath and Marcus sat on the sun loungers sipping on their homemade lemonade, enjoying the shenanigans taking place in the pool. It was hard to believe Christmas was only two weeks away, yet here they were sitting beside the pool in a thirty-five degree heat; however according to Margaret, Northern Ireland was expecting a dreadfully cold spell and a traditional white Christmas.

"Mum, can we go to the movies this evening?" Rachel pleaded. "We've been good all day and extremely helpful. Besides which, it's the school holidays," she added.

Marcus peered across at Kath smiling and nodded. "Okay then, Marcus and I will get ready after dinner." Rachel and her friends immediately cheered in gratitude.

Brigee was given a reprieve, as Marcus decided to cook a barbeque for everyone. Kath helped Brigee conjure up a few salads and butter some rolls, before heading outside to join the family. The kids tucked into the food, obviously hungry from playing and racing around in the pool.

After dinner, Kath helped Brigee tidy up before she left for the evening. The girls rushed off to Rachel's room to ready themselves for the movies. Kath and Marcus changed into light weighted jeans and T-shirts, before promptly making their way downstairs.

By 8.30pm they were seated at the movies with popcorn, choc pops, lollies and drinks all lined up along the teenager's seats, ready to be devoured throughout the movie. Kath and Marcus held hands, glancing at each other happily. Kath was glad of the distraction, relieved from not having to think of her eldest daughter, tucked far way on the other side of the world, making a life for herself.

The next two weeks had flown by for everyone; it was Christmas Eve and Kath was on the phone to Margaret.

"It's beautiful here mum, it's exactly the same as you see on a Christmas card. The holly bushes are covered in red berries and the prickly green leaves are full of snow. The fields are gorgeous, like big fluffy white covers, glistening in the sunlight. I love it mum; it's absolutely stunning and so different from back home. What's the temperature like over there anyway?"

"Well, Rachel spends most of her time in the pool these days with her friends and it's been varying between thirty-two and thirty-nine degrees this week."

"Wow and here I am running around with winter coats, sweaters and boots," Margaret laughed down the phone, extremely relaxed and carefree.

"Did you receive our parcels yet?" Kath enquired.

"Yes mum, thanks; we've left them under the Christmas tree until tomorrow."

"What are you doing now?" Kath asked.

"I'm sitting in front of a beautiful blazing fire in the front room, sipping on some ginger beer which grandad made and nibbling on some of grannies gingerbread men."

Kath smiled, reminiscing about her Christmases whilst growing up in Northern Ireland, picturing the scene so vividly.

"Paul and I are going out for dinner later this evening, so I'll ring tomorrow morning and speak to the rest of the family then."

"Before you go, get your Gran for me and I'll have a few words."

"Okay, I love you and I'll catch you later," she beamed down the phone, handing the receiver over to her granny.

Paul was standing back, taking in the exchange between mother and daughter, pleased they had such a loving and close relationship. Tonight was going to be special, it was Christmas Eve and not many men get the opportunity to wine and dine a beautiful Australian lady, like he was this evening. Later on Margaret was helped into her coat by Paul and kisses were delivered to both grandparents, before they left.

Winding their way along the country roads at night was magical. The hedgerow and stone built walls were draped in a velvety white blanket, appearing ghostly and mysterious in the bright car headlights.

The heater in the car was pushed up to the max, as they made their way to the Burrendale Hotel. Both were relaxed having obtained a week off together, which was badly needed as it had been chaotic at the hospital. At Christmas time, people were always in a hurry and not paying attention to what they were doing, therefore having silly accidents and ending up in the hospital emergency rooms.

"Happy?" Paul enquired driving slowly, well aware of black ice, which could easily have you skidding into a ditch or into an oncoming car in seconds, due to loss of traction.

"Extremely," Margaret answered, very much looking forward to a quiet evening meal with Paul, after such a hectic week.

They arrived and were escorted to the dining room immediately. The log fire was burning and it added a romantic ambience to the candlelit restaurant. They ordered wine while perusing the menus together.

Margaret noticed Paul seemed a little on edge and appeared somewhat nervous, although she had heard he was involved in a major operation today, a car accident with young children implicated, which is normally horrendous on anyone. They both ordered and Margaret instantly reached out, laying her hand on top of Paul's.

"Is everything okay? I heard about the family brought in from a car accident," she enquired gently.

"Yes, yes everything's fine, it takes me a little while to wind down, especially when there are young children involved," he smiled reassuringly, taking another gulp of wine.

Their meals were served and they ate, making idle chit chat and exchanging news on their daily events. Dessert and coffee were served, while violinists entered the room. Paul initially looked startled and then relaxed down into his seat more. The musicians commenced playing, congregating around the fireplace while patrons looked on, relaxing and enjoying the romantic background melodies.

Slowly they edged their way across to Margaret and Paul's table. Standing close by, they commenced playing When Irish Eyes are Smiling.

Margaret's eyes glazed over. "That's my favourite Irish song," she whispered, glancing across at Paul.

"I know," he responded gently, without saying another word.

A young girl arrived at their table with a glorious bunch of daffodils.

"Did you do this Paul?" her eyes wide, filled with surprise and wonderment.

"Yes I did. I know they're your favourite flowers as well as your mum's," he grinned, as a bottle of champagne was brought to their table and popped open.

"Gosh I'm really getting spoilt aren't I," Margaret stated, feeling slightly embarrassed, as people were watching from nearby tables.

"You deserve to be," Paul replied huskily.

Quite unexpectedly, Paul dropped down beside her on one bent knee, producing a red velvet box. Opening it up immediately, a huge pale pink, square cut diamond ring, was sitting prominently inside, sparkling in the candlelight.

"Oh my god," Margaret gasped, taken completely by surprise.

"Will you marry me Margaret and make me the happiest man alive? I love you with all my heart. Please say yes ... my love"

"Yes, yes, YES," Margaret screamed, tears of joy streaming down her cheeks, as the people seated close by applauded with glee.

She held out her trembling left hand, as Paul shakily slid the ring on to her finger.

"Thank you," he whispered, kissing her tenderly.

The violinists played a few lines of the wedding march, bringing forth rapturous cheers and enthusiastic clapping from the patrons, before everything settled down again.

"I had no idea whatsoever," Margaret said, shaking her head in shock. "I thought something was wrong, because you appeared nervous and edgy all evening but I thought it was the accident. Gosh, I can't wait to tell mum and dad and ..."

"Your father already knows," Paul interrupted.

"But how ...? When ...?" Margaret questioned.

"I asked for his permission three weeks ago, after I purchased the pink diamond, which was shipped all the way out from Australia."

"Oh my goodness, you're unbelievable," she beamed from across the table, totally elated and pleased he had spoken to her father.

Looking down at her ring, she was amazed; the pink diamond was spectacular with a small cut white diamond resting on either side of the setting. It was an elegant design, set beautifully which was absolutely perfect for her.

"Margaret?" she looked up, as Paul handed her a glass of champagne. "To us and a wonderful future together," he murmured.

"To us," she sighed happily, taking a sip and smiling profusely. The bubbles were adding to her immense happiness, excitement and the love she was experiencing right at this very moment.

Margaret couldn't help smiling all the way back to her grandparent's house, with Paul negotiating his way cautiously along the minor roads, covered in immense heavy snowdrifts. He had only driven into the back yard, when Margaret literally jumped out of the car as he stopped, rushing into the house quickly to break the good news about their engagement.

When Paul arrived inside, he was greeted with gentle smiling faces.

"You couldn't have picked a better girl Paul. I'd say our Margaret has done pretty well for herself, as well. We're really pleased and extremely happy for you both," Joe remarked, rising out of his chair to shake Paul's hand. He gave him a huge endearing pat on the back, before heading over to the drinks cabinet.

"I'm also happy for you both," Mary chirped up, admiring the ring on Margaret's finger. "I see you've gone and spoilt her, it's a real beautiful ring 'n' you can see it sparklin' a mile off," she laughed happily. Standing up, she walked directly over to Paul with tears spilling from her eyes. "I'm so proud of you both, it's amazing how you work together to save lives, it's a credit to ya both. Joe and I see how much the pair of youse love each other and you couldn't make us any happier. Come here, ya big strappin' thing and give us a hug."

Leaning down, Paul took Mary in his arms giving her a heartfelt hug, laughing loudly before half squeezing the life out of her. With eyes glazed over with tears, he was grateful for the love and kindness they had shown him, from the very first time they met.

"Now that's enough Mary," Joe interrupted. "You're gettin' the big lad emotional 'n' all. Now let's all be havin' a wee drink."

Four glasses were raised and clinked together. "Here's to good health and happiness," Joe announced, grinning from ear to ear.

"I better ring mum and dad," Margaret sang out "to give them the good news. It will be about 9am over there."

Everyone instantly agreed, as they sipped on their celebratory drinks.

"Hello mum, is that you?" Margaret enquired, happily down the phone.

"Margaret my love, your father and I were only talking about you a few minutes ago."

"Nothing but good, I hope?" Margaret laughed.

"Yes, yes, of course my darling. I was only saying it will be March soon and before you know it, you'll be home again."

Margaret was extremely excited with her news and was unable to contain herself for one minute longer; as she burbled out her amazing news in one massive hit.

"Mum, you'll never guess what happened this evening at the restaurant. Paul got down on one knee and proposed. We're engaged! Can you believe it? You should see the ring mum, it's absolutely stunning, a pink diamond. I'm looking at it now and it's gorgeous."

Taken back and absolutely shocked, Kath quickly inhaled a deep breath. "Why that's wonderful news darling, you sound really happy."

"Yes, I'm absolutely over the moon."

"I guess it means you have no doubts and you must love him immensely," Kath murmured cautiously.

"From the very first time I set eyes on him," Kath expressed an audible sigh, as tears spilled down her cheeks.

"Well then, what more could a mother wish for," she replied gently. "Congratulations my love, I'm real happy for you."

"Mum ... can I speak with dad now please?"

"Yes of course my love, just hold for a second."

Marcus was standing close by grinning. "Hello love, how are you?"

"Great dad, I'm sooo H-A-P-P-Y, Paul and I got engaged."

"Well that's marvellous love, he's a good man Margaret and he obviously loves you to bits."

"I know and I love him dearly too."

"Well then, you can't go wrong with that. Love is a beautiful and precious gift, to be treasured and nourished. And if you're half as happy as your mother and I are, we couldn't ask for anything more."

Marcus then spoke to Paul for a few moments, congratulating him, before passing the phone back to Kath.

"You'll look after her, won't you Paul?" Kath questioned gently.

"I love her with all my heart and will protect her until my dying day," Paul replied strongly.

Kath smiled. "Thank you Paul, you're a good man and I'm genuinely happy for you both. Now could you put that excited daughter of mine back on the phone again ... and you take care."

"Mum, mum, isn't it great news. I still can't believe it. I was totally taken by surprise. There were daffodils, violinists and champagne and it was ever so romantic," she gushed.

Kath smiled inwardly and felt happy for her daughter, pleased she had met someone who she loved and cared for so deeply. It was a pity though he had to live in Northern Ireland.

"Okay love, you best get some sleep. Your father and I will ring you tonight, which will be Christmas morning over there."

"Oh that's right, Merry Christmas mum. I love you."

"And I love you too possum. Now go to bed, try and get some sleep and we'll catch up again tomorrow."

"Okay, goodnight, love you."

"Goodnight darling ... and I love you too," Kath replied, before hanging up the receiver.

Paul gave Margaret a goodnight kiss and her grandparents a huge hug each, before he set off home exhilarated, extremely happy and very content. Driving homewards along the road, he knew he loved Margaret more than life itself. She was so loving, kind, intelligent and so god-damn caring. She was absolutely beautiful, both inside and out.

His parents loved her deeply; she captured their hearts from day one, as well as his own. He was a happy man tonight. Happier than he have ever been, in a very long time.

Chapter Eighteen

Marcus stood nearby monitoring Kath, when she put the phone down. Looking up and biting her bottom lip, huge tears began spilling down her cheeks.

"Come here," Marcus whispered, standing with outstretched arms.

Overwhelmed with emotions, Kath gladly fell into his arms, automatically breaking down and crying.

"It was bound to happen sooner or later," Marcus confided, hugging Kath closely.

"I know, I know but it was so unexpected and I wasn't prepared," she sadly mumbled in between sobs.

"You might as well know my darling but Paul asked for my permission before proposing."

Kath instantly looked up. "But you didn't say anything Marcus … why?" she questioned.

"Because my darling, I knew exactly how you would react. She loves him deeply Kath and she's not stupid my love," peering into her eyes. "We of all people, should know how short life can be," gently wiping away her tears.

"I know Marcus but it came as a huge shock, that's all."

"The main thing is, she's deliriously happy, we've gained a son and you'll never lose your daughter. Paul is a good man, who respects the relationship you have with young Margaret."

Kath smiled, stretching upwards to give him a kiss. She was beginning to feel much better, wrapped safely in Marcus's arms, after sharing his pearls of wisdom. Marcus always knew what to say, offering her comfort and security, when she needed it most. Drawing a deep breath, she acknowledged Paul would always be there for Margaret, when she too ... needed comforting.

Marcus thought everything worked out perfectly. He suggested opening the Christmas presents, shortly after midnight on Christmas Eve and Rachel enthusiastically agreed. It proved to be a happy and successful evening, distracting Kath a little from missing Margaret, by partly breaking the traditional family Christmas routine. Needless to say everyone got to bed late and Rachel declared she was lying in bed until 10am. Marcus knew this would allow Kath time to receive the call from Margaret on Christmas morning, without any distractions.

Later, Rachel came rushing down the stairs urgently enquiring "did I miss speaking to Margaret, mum?"

"It's okay; it's Christmas Eve over there now love, due to the time difference. We'll be calling her back tonight, so we can wish everyone over there a Merry Christmas."

"Okay, I'll catch up with her then. By the way, what was dad congratulating her for?" raising an eyebrow, waiting expectantly for a reply.

Marcus laughed out loud. "You never miss a trick young lady, do you?" automatically swinging around. "Well Kath, would you like to do the honours or shall I?"

Kath smiled and began divulging the news of Margaret's engagement. Rachel stood transfixed, her mouth gaping and her eyes wide, entirely engrossed.

"Oh my gosh!" she gasped. "Will she marry him and live over there?" she queried instantly.

"I honestly don't know Rachel. I'm still trying to wrap my head around the news of her engagement, let alone try to figure out what plans they may have. I don't think they know themselves yet," Kath pondered.

"You give that head of yours far too much work, young lady," Marcus chided.

Hoping Rachel's blasé comments wouldn't unsettle Kath again, acknowledging it would take some adjusting emotionally, if Margaret did decide to stay in Northern Ireland with Paul.

They wandered into the kitchen and Kath made some fresh coffee, while Rachel made a Milo.

"Did you leave your Christmas presents up in your bedroom last night Rachel?" Kath queried, thoughtfully.

"Yes I did and thanks for all the lovely presents, especially the sports watch. All of my friends will want one when they see it next week."

Rachel stood in the kitchen smiling like the proverbial cat that ate the canary, wearing a chocolate moustache, making her appear even more mischievous than usual. She had excelled in her final year exams, according to her school reports Kath mused, watching her make some toast. However, her teachers noted she was one of the classroom larrikins, not appearing to take her work seriously, although they did acknowledge her academic success.

Rachel was a child, who was not unlike a salmon swimming upstream. Even as a young girl she would have challenged everyone and everything, opting to be independent, from such an early age. Kath clearly remembers having fought with her because she insisted on tying her own shoe laces and wouldn't let anyone else help, even Brigee, who she simply adored. Kath recognised as Rachel became older she would have to be kept on a fairly tight leash; she would have to be totally switched on, because Rachel was a different kettle of fish compared to Margaret.

Brigee arrived, along with Valerie and her family to exchange gifts at lunchtime. It was a traditional Christmas occurrence which eventuates every year, although this time around, Margaret was noticeably missing.

Richard and Rachel spent time together catching up on school yard gossip, while the adults sat outside enjoying the sunshine and serenity, before the party got underway. This year the gala event was being held at Marcus's parent's place, meaning it would be another grand affair, with no expense spared.

Brigee purchased a black sequinned cocktail dress for the occasion, mainly with the help of young Rachel, who seemingly had a good eye for fashion. Kath chose a dark green velvet gown, which showcased her lithe body to perfection. All the men would be dressed in formal attire, adding to the extravaganza.

"Thanks for a delicious lunch Kath," Valerie said, climbing out of her sun lounger. "We better make a move Matt. I will have to get all dolled up for this evening and not let our side down," Valerie laughed, smiling across at Kath. Valerie knew Marcus's mother Eleanor was always so competitive, trying hard to outdo everyone in so many ways.

Kath found it hard to warm to her; however she simply adored Carlos, showering him with sincere affection whenever she had the opportunity.

"I think I'll wear my ice blue satin dress this evening," Valerie whispered, smiling. Knowing full well Eleanor was wearing a similar colour this evening, acknowledging it would look much more spectacular on a slimmer and younger frame, which would obviously put Eleanor's nose out of joint.

"You naughty woman," Kath chided, aware Valerie hadn't taken to Eleanor either and was guilty of doing a little stirring now and again, as well.

Brigee tutted loudly, "Dr Valerie ... shame on you. I can see why you and Miss Rachel get on so well together, because one is as mischievous as the other."

All three of them burst out into laughter, comfortable with each other, having almost shared a lifetime together. Their friendships were woven together with a strong loving bond, which could never be broken.

"Okay then, let's make tracks," Matt interrupted their chatter, as Marcus gathered their gifts together to take to the car.

Brigee gave Kath an enormous hug, before leaving.

"Merry Christmas Kath and don't worry. Margaret's engagement is a blessing in disguise and I'm really glad she's met a nice young doctor. Your Marcus was telling me all about him and he's obviously madly in love with Margaret. So what more could a mother ask for."

"An Aussie one," Kath teased, half heartedly.

"Well, look at you and Marcus, you've done alright and Margaret is simply following in her mother's footsteps," Brigee shot back.

"Come on you old gasbag," Valerie interrupted, grabbing Brigee by the hand and leading her towards the door.

"We'll see you all tonight," Brigee called out happily, waving and smiling, as the car drove off.

"Valerie's so funny mum," Rachel chuckled on the way back into the house. "I love the fact she's wearing her ice blue dress this evening," Rachel piped up, not missing out on the conspiracy plan, to upstage Eleanor later.

"You behave yourself young lady and don't be getting any fancy ideas. Our Valerie's a bit of a wild one I'll have to admit," Kath answered, smiling inwardly.

Rachel entered her step-grandparent's home first and was given an impressive hug by Carlos. Of course Eleanor couldn't be found anywhere; apparently she had been hob- nobbing with the local Mayor earlier and with any luck she would spend half the evening with him, leaving Kath well enough alone.

The people aware of Kath's personal situation had forgiven her, recognising she staged her own death, to protect those who she loved dearly but not Eleanor. She forever held a grudge, making her feelings known to anyone who would listen, angering both Carlos and Marcus.

Kath and Marcus strolled in, both receiving admiring glances from the other guests, as they made their way to the bar. The elegant green velvet gown was stunning, making Kath appear almost like a younger version of the well-known Audrey Hepburn. Ladylike and poised, Kath strolled across the floor on the arm of the sexiest man present. Both were extremely glamorous and exceptionally approachable. This made them more appealing and attractive to the guests, as they mingled and chatted with them throughout the evening.

Valerie, along with Matt and Brigee, made their grand entrance thirty minutes later. Valerie appeared overwhelmingly beautiful this evening. Her light brown hair and stunning blue eyes, complimented the dress even further.

Kath almost choked on her champagne when she saw Eleanor staring at Valerie. The expressions etched upon her face, were worth a thousand words and believe you me; they wouldn't have been pleasant ones coming out of Eleanor's mouth.

Valerie straight away felt Eleanor's piercing gaze, so she immediately turned around and grinned, giving Eleanor a little curtsey, before quickly joining Kath at the bar.

"Well ... do you think I've made a statement?" Valerie enquired instantly, as Kath ordered her friend a drink.

"You most certainly did," Kath replied. "You should have seen the look on her face. As they would say in Ireland, she was certainly gobsmacked," Kath added gaily.

"The pair of us will go to hell you know, for all the crimes we've committed over the years," Valerie laughingly mentioned. Very pleased she had upstaged Eleanor, disliking her mainly because of her pompous mannerisms and the way she treated Kath with disdain.

Marcus and Matt were totally unaware of Valerie's antics, spending part of the evening mingling among some of their old friends, who they hadn't seen in quite a while.

Rachel was up dancing on the floor with some young guy who Kath didn't recognise but they seemed happy enough together and that was the main thing.

Carlos had a dance with Kath, which she enjoyed immensely. His dance moves were slow and elegant, never putting a foot wrong as he led her around the room, obviously proud of his young daughter-in-law, happy his son had found her again.

Eleanor watched from the sidelines, envious of Kath's beauty and demeanour. She felt Marcus had married beneath his standing; after all, she introduced him to rich attractive socialites over the years, which he showed no interest in, leaving her bitter and resentful.

"He could have done a lot better you know," the slightly intoxicated Eleanor, blabbered to Mayor Huxley.

"Who's that?" he enquired, half interested.

"My son Marcus," she repeated. "He could have done a lot better."

"Oh I don't know Eleanor dear. Kath is rather beautiful don't you think and extremely intelligent. I know Carlos speaks very highly of her"

"Never mind," Eleanor chided, shaking her head in disagreement, not at all impressed by the Mayor's comments. "I must go over and speak with Elizabeth," Eleanor stated, agitated and in an extremely bad mood. She waltzed off immediately with a scowl on her face, leaving the Mayor standing alone, somewhat disenchanted.

The music changed to a slow number, Marcus immediately sought out Kath to have a dance.

"Are you having a wonderful evening?" he whispered, with Kath wrapped up in his arms, swaying gently in rhythm to the music.

"I most certainly am and you?"

"Yes, I must admit I normally hate these formal evenings but I've caught up with a few friends I haven't seen in quite a while and enjoyed their company."

"I'm pleased," Kath sighed happily, leaning forward to give Marcus a quick kiss on the cheek.

"May I interrupt?" Kath knew who it was immediately, without having to turn around.

"Mother, must we?" Marcus stated.

"Yes we must and besides, it's not often I get to dance with my only son," Eleanor replied, giving one of her devious smiles.

"It's okay darling," Kath interjected. "I was about to suggest we get a drink," walking away swiftly.

Arriving at the bar Kath ordered a scotch and dry. Straight away she felt a hand grasp her shoulder.

"The old dragons up to her usual tricks I see," Valerie protested. "I swear to god; she's so jealous of you Kath. Remember to always watch your back."

"It's fine Valerie, it's nothing I can't handle," Kath sighed, before taking a sip of her drink.

"By the way, you best go and fetch Rachel. The last time I saw her she was smooching some spunky lad in the hallway and you certainly don't want the wicked old witch to catch her or you'll never hear the end of it," Valerie warned.

Automatically rolling her eyes, Kath quickly sculled her drink and thanked Valerie before heading off to search for her daughter.

True enough, she found the little imp locked in the lad's arms; the one Kath had seen her dancing with earlier on.

"Rachel ... come here now," Kath demanded. The lad looked up and blushed, as Kath made her way towards them.

"Mum ... we were only talking," Rachel replied defensively.

"Well you can talk your way back up the hall young lady. The last thing I need this evening is your grandmother making a fuss."

The lad scurried off rather quickly after Kath illustrated her disapproval, leaving Rachel stunned and unimpressed with her mother's intrusion.

"Mum, are you aware you totally embarrassed me in front of my friend a few moments ago," she declared moodily.

"Rachel, don't even go there," Kath grizzled, sighing loudly. Your grandmother is cornering your father over something. Valerie's getting tipsy and god only knows what she might say to Eleanor. And to crown things off, I can't find Brigee anywhere?" sounding frustrated.

Rachel instantly held back on her rebuttal, recognising straight away, her mother wasn't in a receptive mood.

After sending Rachel back to the ballroom, Kath made her way outside for some fresh air. It was a beautiful evening; the heavens were filled with bright twinkling stars, as the waves lapped idly upon the sandy beach, lying far below. Kath stood on the balcony inhaling the cool fresh sea air, looking out beyond the horizon, thinking about Margaret and her mother and father overseas.

Marcus interrupted the silence. "A penny for your thoughts." She smiled, turning around slowly. "I brought you out a drink," Marcus said, drawing her close. "Kath ... were you thinking about home?"

She nodded, as tears welled up in her eyes. "I know, it's terrible" she sighed. "Christmas is a time when I tend to think of my family more, especially when they're so far away," she sighed.

"You know what, I'm going to organise for Joe and Mary to be over here next year, to prevent you from feeling so sad."

Kath smiled. "I might hold you to that Mr Garofoli."

"You most certainly can," he said, kissing her tenderly.

It was approximately 2am in the morning when they travelled home in the limousine. It had been a pleasant evening and Kath had avoided any run-ins with her mother-in-law. She even managed to get Valerie into a taxi before she left, thus avoiding any awkward confrontations.

Arriving home, Rachel instantly grabbed the phone to ring her sister, as originally promised by her parents earlier that morning. On the third ring Mary answered the phone and she soon had Rachel in fits of laughter.

Rachel spent the next thirty minutes with her sister, discussing her engagement ring and extracting every possible detail about the initial proposal, made by Paul. Finally satisfied, she handed the phone over to her mother, stating she was retiring to bed.

"Good night love," Kath called out, before speaking with Margaret.

"What time is it over there mum?"

"Almost 3am but don't worry, your father and I will have a nice long lie in tomorrow morning."

"It is morning," Margaret chuckled down the phone.

"Well ... you know what I mean," Kath laughed. "Now tell me, did you both like your presents, I assume you have opened them."

"Yes we loved them, we unwrapped all of the pressies earlier this morning. Paul said you spoilt us and the matching Cartier watches are beautiful mum, we'll treasure them forever," Margaret joyfully cried down the phone.

"Tell me, did you get a white Christmas after all?" Kath enquired.

"Yes, the snow fell heavily last night and it's like a white winter wonderland, everything is glistening like diamonds in the morning sun. It's totally amazing, beautiful and special. I'm really glad to be here with my grandparents right now."

Kath smiled, feeling much more at ease having spoken with her eldest daughter. It must have made it special for her parents this morning, to be sharing the time with their granddaughter and her fiancé. She thought she must stop pining and be happy. She should be grateful her daughter is having the time of her life and is proving to be a highly independent young lady. "I'll have a word with your Gran … and you take care love."

"Hello luv, sure it's grand over here and yur dad is over the moon. This morning you'd have thought Santa had been, he was as excited as a little kid searching under the Christmas tree for his presents. It reminded us of years gone by pet."

Tears formed in Mary's eyes, as she recalled the happiness felt when Paul, Margaret and Joe sat under the tree, exchanging gifts earlier this morning. Knowing full well Declan and Michael were not around anymore. Both missed out on sharing so many Christmases with the family, both dead a long time ago and never comin' back like Kath, to provide them with more grandchildren.

"Mum, are you there?"

"Yes dear, I was gettin' all sentimental. Now, what did Santa bring you?" The next half hour was spent divulging the day's events.

Paul thanked Marcus for his presents and assured them both he was taking good care of Margaret.

After hanging up, Kath and Marcus climbed the stairs, undressed and clambered into bed together. Both were totally exhausted after an eventful day. Kath drifted into a satisfied and contented sleep having spoken with her family, giving her great peace of mind.

Chapter Nineteen

Time passed quickly as she lay silently, bathed in the afterglow from their lovemaking which had taken place a few hours earlier. She smiled, watching the sunbeams bursting through Paul's bedroom window, scooping up the minuscule dust particles in its path. Fully awake now, she observed them twisting and turning and dancing along the golden path, momentarily distracting her. She sighed heavily, with a tear trickling down the side of her cheek.

She turned around to her right and sat perched up on one elbow, peering down at her beloved Paul. His dark ruffled hair lay tousled upon the pillow giving him a child like appearance, while his swarthy unshaven face, perfectly moulded, added softness and a raw sexiness to his demeanour. The time had flown by so swiftly, smiling gently as she reminisced about the days spent together, her first time with him, occasions spent happily with his parents, her marriage proposal and now. Now it was time to leave, leave her sweetheart behind and head back home to Australia.

Almost as if sensing her distress, Paul's dark long eyelashes shielding his eyes, flickered slowly open. He swallowed hard, his large chocolate come-to-bed-eyes melted, as he gazed over at her. "Come over here my love," he whispered, stretching out his arms, pulling her gently towards him.

Margaret fell into them, as tears burbled out from deep within. "I miss you already," she said, breaking down emotionally, no longer willing or able to keep up a pretence.

"Margaret, you must realise it's not forever. I have already put in various submissions to hospitals in Australia and with the shortages over there at present; I really don't see any problem."

"I know ... I know what you're saying Paul but it doesn't stop the pain I'm experiencing right now," she groaned.

"By the time you get home and settle into a routine, then placed as a registrar, I'll be over there before you know it," he smiled, drawing her closer.

Appearing gloomy, she gave him a watery smile, yearning for him deeply. He caressed her gently, kissing her tenderly. And before long their bodies were entwined, seeking refuge in each other, seeking pleasure, relieving tensions and expressing their love for each other one last time, before she left.

Margaret said her goodbyes to the staff at the Royal Victoria Hospital, a few days ago. Her friends Daphne and Hazel decided to have an impromptu party for her at their flat the previous evening. Loud music was played, alcohol was consumed and good-natured remarks were exchanged, while small parting gifts were given to Margaret.

She had been well liked and respected by her comrades from the emergency ward. They were pleased she recovered from the horrendous kidnapping experience; her closest friends Daphne and Hazel were also delighted they had managed to keep her relationship with Paul a total secret.

Tears were shed when she made a final speech in the evening, thanking everyone for their cherished friendships, acknowledging their help over the past year. Goodbye hugs were dispersed haphazardly, when her friends had to leave, due to their early shift allocation the following morning. Margaret was also getting ready to leave the girls' flat, when both promised to visit Margaret within the next couple of years. She was deeply touched by the kind sentiments shown and was sad because she was leaving some beautiful friends behind.

Climbing out of the shower after their final lovemaking session, she looked around and smiled. Tiny mementos of hers could be seen splashed around Paul's bathroom such as her hand cream, deodorant, hair bands and feminine accessories, which gained access into Paul's masculine domain. She got ready, quickly tying her hair up into a ponytail, before applying some mascara and lip gloss, standing cosily wrapped up in one of his bath towels.

Paul was downstairs checking her suitcases one last time, before her imminent departure. "Breakfast will be ready in five minutes," he hollered up the stairs, as she hurriedly slipped into a pair of comfy jeans and sweater, before making her way downstairs.

"Wow!" Margaret gushed, taken totally by surprise. "My goodness, I should leave more often," she laughed playfully.

The kitchen table was dressed with a white tablecloth, set beautifully and decorated with a crystal vase, filled with elegant mixed roses. The aroma of bacon and eggs mingled with the percolated coffee, instantly reminding her of how famished she was.

"Please be seated Madame, we can't have you leaving Ireland without a good home cooked breakfast, now can we?" Paul said, gesturing for her to sit down to be waited upon.

She smiled; admiration and love filled her heart immediately. How is she ever going to leave this wonderful, kind hearted, human being? she thought.

"Hey, where did you get the roses from?" she questioned, determined to chase away any sadness she felt.

"Mrs Mackin from next door supplied them and sends her best wishes," he replied, dishing up the huge breakfast.

"My god Paul, there's enough on the plate to feed three people," Margaret giggled.

"Well, I didn't want you to waste away on your journey home," he laughed, giving her a quick peck on the cheek. Breakfast was eaten, both trying their best to make idle chit-chat, both fully aware by this afternoon, she would be long gone.

On their way over to her grandparents later that day, Margaret absorbed the busy landscape passing her by, as Paul drove south. The double storied, semi-detached, orange brick homes, lined the streets uniformly, almost all covering their windows with white netted curtains. Chimneys stood tall pointing skyward, assembled in neat rows with aerials attached, drawing attention to their smoky stained, chimney pots. Chemist shops, fruit and grocery stores and many others, displayed their wares in crates or on stalls outside on the pavement, tempting shoppers to purchase, before walking past.

Leaving Crossgar behind and heading towards Downpatrick, the green fields were stretched out on either side of the road. Undulating hills with oak, beech and sycamore trees were scattered precariously along fence lines or positioned near farm houses in the distance. Bright yellow daffodils swayed in the morning breeze, nestled neatly in their dark leafy green foliage, in garden corners, as well as stretching along windy paths to homesteads.

Margaret was going to miss all of this and the friendly familiar banter from the locals, whenever she went shopping for her groceries. She was amazed by the population's never dying optimism and how they viewed life, even when their land was troubled and torn.

"We're here," Paul broke into the silence, scattering Margaret's thoughts to the wind.

"Well ... I best get this over and done with quick," Margaret sighed.

Mary and Joe were waiting for her, both red eyed and visibly upset. They had grown extremely fond of young Margaret; she helped fill a void after Kath's and Marcus's last visit, breathing life back into the pair of them.

"I'll put the kettle on luv, yur mum's been on the phone and the plane will leave at 3 o'clock."

"Thanks," Margaret replied mundanely, acknowledging there was no turning back.

Joe chatted idly to Paul, exchanging news on the latest football results as Margaret popped upstairs to fetch a few things from her room. She picked up Raggedy Ann, the old rag doll which belonged to her mother. Sighing loudly, Margaret acknowledged her journey brought her an even greater understanding of what her mother and father had been through. Also realising it brought everyone so much closer together.

"Lunch is ready," Mary called out from the bottom of the stairs.

The table was set beautifully with sandwiches, cakes and homemade biscuits, even the best china had been brought out for her farewell.

Margaret gulped, as tears welled up in her eyes immediately. "You didn't have to," she croaked.

"Yes we did, now come and sit yurself down young lady."

Too soon, it was time to leave. The subject had already been discussed and organised, that Paul was to be the only one at the airport to say his last farewell.

Rising from her chair, Mary quietly retrieved a box and handed it to Margaret; she immediately opened it, discovering a solid gold bangle lying inside. On the outside of the bangle the words 'When Irish eyes are smiling' were engraved.

"Peek inside," Mary prompted Margaret quietly. 'Until we meet again' Margaret read out aloud the inscription, before rushing over to Mary and hugging her, whilst crying.

"Margaret darlin' you brought smiles to our faces and joy to our souls, now no frettin' child dear, 'cause I know we'll meet again and a lot sooner than you may think."

Joe and Paul stood back, observing the emotional scene.

"Well come here lass and give us a hug," Joe exclaimed. Grabbing her firmly, as huge round tears rolled down his cheeks freely. "You were like a breath of fresh air to us luv and we're so proud of youse both," while nodding across at Paul.

"Everything's in the car Margaret, it's time to go love," Paul interrupted, knowing it wasn't going to get any easier.

"Okay I gotta go," she stated, giving them both a final hug, before running out the door.

The car drove off, as Margaret peered behind sobbing. She watched the silhouette of her grandparents holding on to each other, waving frantically; disappearing as they rounded the corner, almost breaking Margaret's heart.

Paul grasped her hand, while steering with the other. "Are you okay? You do realise it's not forever my love," smiling sympathetically.

She nodded, retrieving a tissue from her pocket, before wiping away her spilt tears. Belfast International Airport was extremely busy; queues had escalated for Aer Lingus and British Airways departure check-ins. The

Noblealert jet had been in England for the past week, due to one of the chief editors visiting London on a business trip, making it much easier for Marcus to redirect the jet over to Belfast, before returning back to Australia.

Margaret's heart was racing, biting her bottom lip to refrain from sobbing, as she checked in her luggage, while her passport was being cleared. Their sad farewell was finally upon them. Fumbling to put her passport back into her handbag, massive tears began to fall, obstructing her view unexpectedly.

Paul pulled her into his arms. "Now young lass, it's not as if we're never going to see each other again, is it?" He lifted her chin upwards to face him, searching deeply in his coat pocket to retrieve a small box, quickly handing it to her.

She opened it to find a gold Claddagh ring inside that made her feel even more teary eyed.

"The hands on the ring holding the heart, denotes friendship and togetherness. The heart itself signifies love and the crown for loyalty," he grinned.

Margaret nodded, unable to speak.

"In other words my darling, we'll let love and friendship reign forever between us." He slipped it on her right hand with the point of the heart facing towards her wrist, depicting her heart had already been captured. Without another word said, he took her into his arms and kissed her passionately.

"I love you ..." she sobbed, before rushing towards the exit door.

"I love you too and I'll see you soon," he called out loudly, not caring who saw or heard him, his eyes already filling with sadness and longing.

The jet raced up the runway climbing swiftly heavenward, leaving the Harland and Wolfe cranes behind in its wake. Paul stood with his outstretched hand placed upon the viewing window, upset and broken. Standing alone, he watched the plane disappearing in to the horizon, with a heavy heart.

Margaret was sitting in the jet crying uncontrollably, feeling as if her heart had been torn out of her body, desperately missing Paul already.

Chapter Twenty

The arduous journey seemed to be taking an eternity. Margaret felt immensely distraught from having left Paul behind. The editor present on the homeward journey, kept his nose stuck in his paperwork, making the minimalist of conversations, appearing wary and out of his comfort zone.

Margaret merely picked at her food, supplied by an overzealous air hostess named Sandy. She wore her flaxen hair clipped into a neat French roll, her light blue eyes sparkling, accompanying a cheerful smiley face, depicting a happy demeanour. Frequently, in a high pitch manner she would begin babbling, delivering little antidotes and pearls of wisdom, fully aware of Margaret's red eyes and obvious distress.

"Don't worry, it's never as bad as it seems," or "cheer up, it's not the end of the world." The one which really grated on Margaret, the one she detested the most, was the typical cliché of "if it's in relation to a man, don't worry, you'll get over him love."

Margaret felt like screaming at her to shut up, telling her to mind her own god-damn business and leave her alone in peace. However, after reflecting inwardly, Margaret chastised herself for being so morose and self indulgent. After all, it wasn't the end of the world. Paul, her fiancé, would be in Australia as soon as physically possible, allowing them both to continue on from where they left off.

The welcome home was filled with so much love and enthusiasm, with everyone highly emotional. Rachel was all smiles, clasping banners and brightly coloured balloons. Kath stood with tears rolling down her cheeks, elated Margaret had returned. Brigee gave her massive hugs and Marcus her father, had relief palpably etched upon his face, pleased she was back in Australia.

The following two weeks passed in a whirlwind for Margaret. She rushed around familiarising herself with the hustle and bustle of the Sydney traffic and even got around to reorganising her bedroom. Time was spent meeting up with friends and family, exchanging news of what took place over the last twelve months, while she was gone. She spoke with Paul regularly, twice in one day on many occasions, missing him terribly and hoping he would get transferred to a Sydney hospital, as soon as possible.

Dinner in the evening was normally a family affair, a chance for everyone to catch up on the daily news and events. Margaret noticed Rachel had matured immensely, since leaving over a year ago. Growing into a confident young lady, she frequently wore her blonde hair carefree, allowing it to swing freely down and around her face and fall upon her shoulders, highlighting her splendid blue eyes, which were as mischievous as ever.

Mum and dad were as much in love now, as when she left over a year ago. Seemingly in sync with each other, frequently touching one another tenderly and smiling a lot, totally oblivious to her scrutiny.

Brigee was as kind hearted, loving and attentive as she had remembered. Margaret hadn't realised how much she missed her afternoon chats with Brigee. That was until they recommenced again. Brigee was her pillar of strength, her confidant, an old soul who offered her wisdom and unconditional love, exactly in the same way she had done for her mother.

"Margaret darling, could you pass me the salt?" Kath interrupted Margaret's reverie. "And tell us all, how did you go in relation to your job hunting? Brigee was telling me earlier, apparently you made quite a few phone calls today."

Margaret straightened up in her chair "yes, I did," passing the salt over. "I got in touch with quite a few agencies today and with the experience I gained over in Belfast, they were extremely impressed with my resume and references, which I received from the Royal Victoria Hospital," she asserted. "In fact, they are sorting through some relevant positions coming up shortly, as we speak."

"Did you have to sew on many limbs when you were over there?" Rachel quizzed unexpectedly.

Turning to face her, Margaret replied. "I watched quite a few remarkable operations taking place. However, it was an emergency ward and everyone would be rushed in from car accidents, domestic mishaps and such like. When it involved broken arms and other limbs, these normally consisted of school children arriving in with their distressed parents or teachers."

"Wow! It must have been exciting, never knowing what was happening next," Rachel continued.

"Yeah! You could say that, mind you it was extremely stressful; you've got to have your wits about you at all times. The programmes you see on TV are completely and utterly glamorised, where patients normally survive and are civil to their doctors and nurses. It's not like that in the real world Rachel, believe you me!" Margaret expressed with conviction.

"You seem reasonably interested, are you thinking of going down the medical path?" Kath enquired lightly.

"Oh gosh no," Rachel responded instantly. "I'm not willing or able to spend time at university to become a doctor mum but I do want to do something worthwhile, interesting and exhilarating though," she boasted.

This caused Marcus and Kath to raise an eyebrow and nod to each other silently, both deciding not to go down the career path talk yet, not at this early stage anyway.

Desserts arrived and the phone rang, Margaret immediately glanced at her watch and rose quickly from the table.

"S-o-r-r-y, I've got to go ... I'm sure it's Paul," she added hastily and without waiting for a reply she quickly exited the dining room.

Three months later, everyone seemed to be in a routine. Kath and Marcus were diligently upgrading and implementing new systems at Noblealert. Albeit to keep ahead of opposing companies.

Margaret was now working at the Concord Hospital on a full-time basis, moving between the emergency ward and the general surgery department. Her rosters were brutal due to being the new kid on the block, her hours long and unrelenting but she revelled in it. It helped to keep her distracted and missing Paul so much and her parents were pleased she was excelling in both theory and practical exams along the way.

"An excellent surgeon in the making," Dr Stevenson remarked to Marcus, on an evening when he had to pick her up late, because Margaret left her car in to get a service.

In regards to Rachel though, she was becoming extremely independent and more defiant of her mother and father's wishes, of late. She was frequently wagging school and partying with her friends, instead of knuckling down and studying. Margaret noticed even though her sister was only a teenager, going out dressed in the manner in which she did, she could easily have passed as an eighteen year old, which meant inviting trouble. Brigee had been known to have given her a few dressing downs of late but seemingly to no avail. Rachel challenged anyone and everyone and was proving to be a real handful.

Five months after leaving Northern Ireland, Margaret finally received the news she had been pining for since she left. "Really Paul, when did you get that piece of good news?" Margaret screamed down the phone.

"Approximately five minutes ago my love, I'm still buzzing and trying to let it all sink in," he laughed.

"That's fantastic my darling. The Royal North Shore is a terrific hospital, plus it's easy to get there and back from our place," Margaret added excitedly. "What did your parents think and say?" Margaret queried.

"I haven't informed them yet. I'll probably speak to them this evening though. The sooner the better I guess, so they can get used to the idea,"

Margaret all of a sudden went deadly silent.

"Hello, are you there?" Paul enquired.

"Yes!" Margaret sighed.

"Okay, what's up? You sound sad … I thought you would have been over the moon?"

"I am, I am Paul, it's just that, well … your parents might try and talk you out of it, that's all," she murmured.

"I love you Margaret" he insisted. "And nothing my love and I mean nothing; will ever stop me from coming to see you and spending a whole year over there. I can't wait, it's so exciting and I've missed you so much," he confided.

Tears instantly came to Margaret's eyes, she was elated, overwhelmed in fact. Her true and only love was coming half way across the world, to work in a strange land and in a new hospital for a full year, because he loved her.

"I got to go love," Paul sighed. "My pager has just gone off; we'll catch up again at the weekend ... okay. I love you!"

"And I love you too baby," Margaret whispered, hanging up the handset.

Everyone was delighted; Paul was coming to Australia in January. He had organised to spend Christmas at home with his family and head out shortly afterwards, before commencing his position at the Royal North Shore Hospital, at the beginning of February. Brigee had heard so much about the young man from Kath, Marcus and even Rachel, whenever she was in the mood to talk, which was becoming rather infrequent these days. Valerie had been updated with the details about the kidnapping of Margaret. Valerie instantly had huge respect for the young man, who helped save Margaret's life.

Christmas came and went, mixed in with other holiday festivities. Valerie and Matt had the Christmas party at their place this year, which was a grand celebration, with no expense spared. Even Eleanor couldn't fault the venue or the food, displaying five star qualities. The evening was spent mingling, dancing to the lively music, provided by a young group call 'The Sweet Serenades' which everyone enjoyed immensely.

Margaret recalled the Christmas party with horror, after catching Rachel up on the roof top with one of her so called friends, named Caroline. She instinctively knew this so called friend would be trouble, ever since the first day she was introduced to her.

Rachel went ballistic when sprung by her sister for smoking, automatically screaming obscenities at her. Margaret was furious to find her smoking in the first place but was absolutely devastated to discover it was a marijuana joint, fully aware of the health problems associated with drug use. She threatened Rachel immediately, stating she would be reporting the incident to her parents but Rachel relented tearfully, swearing it was a one off occasion.

Margaret reneged, deciding to let it go this time but intended to keep a closer eye on her little sister from here on in. The fact remained, Paul would be arriving soon and she didn't want any family dramas. As Rachel could easily act up and be a little demon to everyone.

3rd January 1996 at 6.30am, the plane landed at Sydney Airport. Margaret was ecstatic beyond words. She waited behind the arrivals barricade, counting down the minutes, finding it difficult to fully comprehend, Paul was actually here. Here in Australia, for the next twelve months. Before long she spotted him pushing his way through the crowd, dodging and weaving everyone, appearing anxious, trying to make his way to the top of the line.

Almost immediately he spotted her, releasing a joyous cry and waving straight away, he speedily made his way towards her. Within seconds, he had her wrapped up in his arms; suitcases had been left abandoned on a trolley, as he kissed her passionately.

Her heart soared as tears of joy trickled down her cheeks, fully comprehending how much she missed him and was absolutely thrilled to pieces he had finally arrived.

"I love you and missed you so much," he exclaimed, when he finally released her.

"Not half as much as I missed you," she confided, happier than she's been in a very long time.

Margaret began merging through the traffic, as Paul drunk in the scenery, completely and utterly intrigued. "What a journey love. I'm so glad I'm not heading back for another year," he laughed. He couldn't help glancing across at her, as she drove. Her long auburn hair tied up with a green ribbon accentuated her emerald green eyes. She was wearing a pale green dress which showed off her petite figure and he was absorbing every single detail, smiling, wanting to seduce her straight away.

"What are you thinking, right now?" she questioned him, laughing, sensing his eyes were fully scrutinising her.

"My god woman, I had forgotten how beautiful you are in real life," he answered, leaning over and giving her a kiss on the cheek. "I want to seduce you right now!" he shouted.

She giggled. "You'll have to wait until this evening, when everyone's gone to bed, I'm afraid. I think doing it in the middle of Victoria Road might draw too much attention to us. Although, I have seen the road much busier," she joked, pulling a face.

He instantly ran his hand up over her leg, towards her inner thigh.

"Dr Paul Hagan, keep that up and I'll definitely have an accident and we'll not make it home to bed."

He immediately withdrew, recognising it was going to be extremely hard to keep his hands to himself all day.

The gates swung open and as they made their way up the driveway, the whole family could be seen waiting outside for him; a huge welcome banner was hanging over the doorway with brightly coloured balloons attached. Hugs and kisses were forthcoming from Kath and Rachel; Marcus welcomed him with a warm handshake accompanied by a friendly pat on the back. Brigee, Matt and Valerie were introduced and greeted him pleasantly; all equally taken back on how handsome he was, straight away noticing his bubbly personality.

Paul was shown to his room, positioned on the southern side of the house, which was opposite to Margaret's; because her parents were well aware of what would take place.

"You live in a magnificent home Margaret, I had no idea you came from such an affluent family," he confided. "You never said anything and always appeared so grounded, so down to earth and I would never have guessed."

Margaret smiled. "Yes, mum and dad are directors and part owners in Noblealert, having worked extremely hard over the years, to help build a media empire. They believe in spending their spoils on the nicer things in life, both very much aware how short life can be but were determined not to have two spoilt little brats."

Paul having already met the family, previously establishing a relationship back in Northern Ireland, fitted in extremely well with everyone. Brigee took to him straight away and made him feel really welcome. Valerie found his medical skills extremely advanced, enjoying his long discussions late into the evenings on various new techniques, being tested back in the UK. In fact, this one particular test was being seriously reviewed and considered for use in Australia, within the next couple of years. His manners were impeccable, his knowledge extensive in every facet of life and more importantly, he loved Margaret with all his heart.

Two weeks had flown by and Paul respected the Australian people, finding them to be enormously relaxed and friendly. He became blatantly aware of the massive tension he had been living under; this was attributed from his homeland, subconsciously accumulated during his upbringing in a country, undoubtedly divided and anxious. A car back firing made him instantly grab Margaret, drawing her close for protection, an automated built-in response, leaving him laughing at his idiosyncrasies. However, he couldn't help but notice the police stations lacked any real security.

No high built walls were erected, supporting lethal barbed wire on top. And no sandbags banked up, offering a shield against potential reprisals or raids. Instead, he experienced a unique and relaxed environment evolving around him. Discovering it was one he could truly relax in and one which he really appreciated.

He loved the multi-cultural society offering such diversity, allowing him to sample numerous delicacies from around the world, in the heart of Sydney. He marvelled at the young pre-school children from different ethnic groups, forming friendships and playing together in the playground. These and many more were things Margaret and other Australians perhaps took for granted, not realising the freedom they had to wander safely and freely around, without the threat of terrorism.

As he stood with Margaret sightseeing, he came to realise the Sydney Harbour Bridge offered a massive gateway for cruise liners. He watched an enormous cruise ship making her way slowly out of the harbour, weighed down with eager passengers, sailing away to some exotic destination. Down at Bennelong Point he marvelled at the Sydney Opera House, the sunlight reflecting off its sophisticated angular cut sails. Only now, could he truly comprehend the iconic building and appreciate the architectural masterpiece, with her distinctive shell-like terraced roof. They wandered around Circular Quay, picking up postcards and taking photos, before heading further down to The Rocks. This was Sydney's oldest colonial district, filled with cobblestone streets and ancient, historic, sandstone buildings. Former warehouses and sailors' homes once stood overlooking Sydney Cove; now having been converted into modern pubs and eateries, catering for tourists visiting worldwide.

Paul had been taken out on the family yacht on the very first weekend when he arrived; he was totally in his element, impressing Marcus immensely with his seaworthy skills. Days floated passed while visiting the main tourist spots with Margaret, making him realise the photos he had seen, simply didn't do any justice to the beautiful city where Margaret was born.

"Are you happy my love?" Margaret queried, lying wrapped up within his arms, on a hot balmy night in her bedroom.

"I am the happiest man alive," he whispered, having finished making love to the most precious woman in his life.

It was a tranquil evening as they both lay awake; a slight breeze blew the sheer curtains in a soft wavelike motion, edging its way into Margaret's bedroom through the opened French doors.

Gliding his hands gently along her erogenous zones, was sending tiny slivers of shockwaves along her body, still energized from his extraordinary lovemaking, only moments earlier.

"We have to be careful we don't get caught," he soothed, nibbling on her ear.

She smiled broadly. "What do you think our parents did when they were young," she giggled.

"Well, I don't think they were clamped in chastity belts, if that's what you mean?"

"Exactly," Margaret groaned, as another tiny orgasm made her body shutter. "Now turn around so I can snuggle up to you," she whispered. "I'll wake you up early in the morning so you can sneak back to your room, before anyone rises."

"Have you been careful not to disturb the two lovebirds," Kath queried as Marcus got ready for bed.

"I'll make a point of not running into them, when they're sneaking back from each other's room," Marcus laughed.

"I know darling it's hilarious, they think they have everyone fooled," Kath replied, readjusting her pillows.

Marcus pounced on the bed without warning, giving her an instant kiss. "I think it's funny and it takes me back to our days back in Ireland, when you hid my shirt or something that was lying around your flat at the time, when your parents came to visit ... u-n-a-n-n-o-u-n-c-e-d," he taunted.

"I know my darling, can you believe that was over twenty years ago. I really don't know where time has disappeared to?"

Marcus slid under the sheets, dragging himself up close to Kath. "You're still as sexy as ever you know," he teased, before turning off the bedroom light.

Slowly in the moonlight, he made love to Kath in a gentle and relaxed manner. Tender caresses were exchanged and endearing, gentle, kisses, followed. Time was spent exploring each other's bodies, in a soft romantic approach. Kath's body rose up, meeting Marcus's strong masculine advances. Soon, unable to hold back any longer, an orgasm invaded her whole body, as he smothered her lips in deep meaningful kisses. In the moonlight she could make out his strong manly silhouette, his body still taut, trim and ever so sexy. She could feel him build up his momentum, quickening as he took her, filled with so much love and desire. She gripped on to him pulling him downwards; her arousal taking full control and within a few moments, there was no turning back. A deep passion took over, igniting their uncontrollable lust filled bodies, both pushing beyond their innate human boundaries, causing them to release a rasping cry, smothered in immense desire, as they clung heavily to one another. They collapsed in a tangled heap upon the bed, thoroughly spent and exhilarated.

"My god woman, are you trying to kill me?" Marcus chuckled, covered in beads of perspiration, making his body shimmer in the moonlight.

Kath laughed gaily. "My darling husband can't you remember, it was you who instigated the lovemaking in the first place?"

"Maybe so," he replied huskily. "Anyway, who could resist those beautiful green eyes smiling up at me in the evening light?"

They both snuggled up quietly together. Both captivated and happy, both still very much in love.

Marcus and Kath lent Paul their four wheel drive, allowing him to get to and from work easily. Trial runs had been made by Paul with Margaret accompanying him, giving him various routes in case of traffic jams or accidents, on his way to and from the Royal North Shore Hospital. He adapted extremely well to the driving conditions in Australia, although he did find the Sydney Harbour Bridge crossing rather hairy, having ended up on the Cahill Expressway inadvertently on several occasions, when out touring with Margaret in the city. This of course raised great hoots of laughter from them both, because he couldn't get back into the main stream of traffic and had to carry on with the crossing.

"Well at this rate," Margaret declared giggling "we've certainly established with all the extra tolls you're paying, you're definitely contributing to the maintenance of the Sydney Harbour Bridge," she laughingly said out loud.

He had made his way to the Royal North Shore Hospital a few days earlier, introducing himself and filling in the necessary paperwork, before commencing his employment. Name tags were ordered along with uniforms and surgical gowns, so when he took up his new position, no time would be lost over administrative duties, meaning he could commence his role immediately.

This was typical of Paul, Margaret reflected, fully aware of how conscientious he was. Extremely appreciative, he was given this opportunity and position at the Royal North Shore Hospital in the first place.

Chapter Twenty One

Paul's work ethics were outstanding; he was instantly respected amongst his peers at the Royal North Shore Hospital. Mixing in easily with the Australian staff, Paul's Irish lilt sounded much stronger than normal but this was welcomed by female patients and nursing personnel alike, who found it simply adorable. His skills as a surgeon were highly commended, attributed by his exceptional detail and experience. His stitching techniques were remarkable, microscopic and extremely precise, resulting in very little scarring for his patients. Dr John Hamilton, the head cardiologist at the Royal North Shore Hospital was highly impressed with Paul's surgical skills, his exceptionally organised conduct and his obvious enthusiasm.

Three weeks into the job and Paul was treated like an old veteran. Dr Peter Stevens from the Emergency Department formed a relationship with Paul; both were frequently caught sharing lunch together at the hospital cafeteria. Peter was originally from the Proserpine area, situated up in far north Queensland. His parents still owned a sugar cane plantation which he grew up on; they were working and maintaining it with his two younger brothers. Paul found himself fascinated listening to tales told by Peter, of when he was a teenager helping out on the plantation. He explained that coming across large hairy cane spiders was a regular occurrence, due to their excellent camouflage, created by their mottled brown coats.

"These spiders were unusual because they didn't build a web, which would have given us some sort of a warning," Peter informed him. "We use to catch them crawling over our backs or up our arms, when helping out in the cane fields."

Paul shivered.

"Don't worry mate, they're not poisonous and they live on insects and small skinks," Peter cackled, noticing the horrified expression on Paul's face.

This encouraged Peter to speak about the horrible cane toads which were the grossest, ugliest, creatures on earth he reckoned, with their grotesque warty looking skin. He explained how some grew up to a kilo in weight and was brought in to eat the scarab beetles but due to their breeding, they increased to epidemic proportions. At night, the cane toads were coming into back yards and pinching the food from their pet's dishes.

"The dirty little buggers could squirt their poison at you, native animals die from eating them and now they're a major pest. I take it you hear the cicadas at night here?" Peter questioned.

Paul grinned, nodding in response.

"Well, you should hear this lot croaking at night, there's normally hundreds of the little shits, sitting up in the front garden at home," he laughed loudly.

"I think I'll stick to touring the city," Paul interrupted, conjuring up an image of the horrible toads.

"It's not all bad mate," Peter snorted. "Coming up to harvest time between June and December, I remember watching my dad and his neighbours set the sugar cane alight. They would cut breaks in the fields about five metres apart to control the fires and then stroll along the break lines with a drip torch filled with petrol, setting it on fire as they walked, the whole lot would flare up in a matter of seconds. My father usually lit the fires in the early evening when the air was still. I heard him speak about my grandfather once, how he watched people being devoured by flames when the wind shifted unexpectedly. Ten hectares would go up in ten minutes and the flames would sometimes be as high as eight metres or more in height. As a child, I remember the red fiery path spreading across the vast horizon, the horrendous roar it would make when it took off into the night, towering over my father and engulfing the paddocks instantly. The spectacular cane fires will always remain in my memory," Peter trailed off.

"Why was the sugar cane burnt?" Paul questioned, enthralled by the tale.

"All the undergrowth such as leaves, weeds and trash needed to be burnt in order to get the machinery in to cut the cane, plus it replenishes the soil for the next crop."

"It's a tough country and you got to know what you're doing, I guess," Paul interjected. "When you mentioned the huge cane fires, I immediately thought of buildings being demolished by fires back home. Unfortunately it was the aftermath, due to bombs having been detonated," Paul added sadly.

They both quietly munched into their sandwiches, silently contemplating their dissimilar upbringing, their respective homelands and their extremely different childhoods.

Peter was approximately six foot four in stature, slim with white blond hair and friendly greyish-blue eyes. His skin was swarthy, tiny freckles were scattered over his nose and across the top of his cheeks, depicting a boyish charm. He was a county larrikin in nature, the sort of guy you could easily trust, with his honest and easy going nature.

His girlfriend Jan, a nurse also at the same hospital frequently joined them for lunch, on the days she was rostered on. She was a bubbly brunette with huge hazel eyes, always wearing a happy smile, whenever they caught up. Roughly five foot ten in height, Peter would tower over her when he greeted her.

His demeanour would change immediately, similar to a playful puppy, whenever she was in his presence. He was obviously head over heels in love with her and they appeared suitably matched. Both were good-natured, compassionate characters; who were immensely compatible and happy with each other and had been dating for over nine months.

Meanwhile, Paul found the night life in Sydney was casual and laid back. Sometimes on a weekend he and Margaret, along with Peter and Jan would go down to the city together. In the pub, Margaret and Jan would chat amicably, sharing their respective dramas, which proved to be extremely therapeutic after a hectic week at work. Paul and Peter would fetch the drinks, before blending in and relaxing. Paul discovered a lot of people had a relative of some description from the emerald isle and they all made him feel truly welcome. One of the surprising elements he discovered when visiting Australia, was the immense celebrations which took place on St Patrick's Day.

In Sydney with Margaret, he found the street parades impressive, as the highly decorative floats made their way up George Street. Irish dancers were jigging their merry little hearts out, followed by floats with the Book of Kells and such like, all heading purposely towards Hyde Park. Pipe bands followed behind, along with people wearing 'Kiss Me I'm Irish' badges, marching along with the Irish stilt walkers who were strolling throughout the Sydney streets. The Irish pubs were bursting with fun and laughter.

"Well, did ya ever have a green beer before?" Margaret shouted over the rowdy crowd, in an Irish brogue.

"No, however I may start the trend up when I go back home," Paul smiled, displaying a fine green moustache, after taking a sip.

"Come here you silly oul ijit, you're starting to look like a leprechaun," Margaret laughed, quickly wiping away the frothy green residue.

Traditional Irish breakfasts and lunches were being served up in pubs, clubs and cafes, located randomly throughout the crowded streets. Irish souvenirs were displayed in tent-like stalls and were being haggled over in a friendly manner. The sunny skies added to the happy and joyful environment, engulfing the streets of Sydney.

"Here, I bought you a small gift while you were away fetching some more beer," Margaret said, handing him a silver pen with shamrocks engraved upon it.

"Very nice, I'll use it at work and hopefully it will bring my patients good luck, when I'm updating their charts," he joked.

"Having you as their surgeon, they couldn't get any luckier," she added hastily, smiling broadly.

Later on, Margaret slowly drove back home to Gladesville. Paul sat in the car watching the people filtering along the busy streets. Young families with green, white and gold balloons attached to prams, smiling and laughing with not a care in the world. Why couldn't everyone celebrate back home together without any animosity and without the absence of tension etched upon their furrowed faces? he thought.

"What are you looking so serious about?" Margaret enquired.

"I'm thinking about back home and how wonderful it would be if everyone decided to put the past behind them and simply get along."

"Mum and dad frequently said the same but wounds run deep and the prejudices are almost hereditary. The only real possibility is the next generation; hopefully they will optimistically rise above it all and choose to move on and live peacefully together," Margaret stated, arriving home.

Paul and Margaret were both heavily involved at work, each as conscientious as the other. They would try and co-ordinate their shifts, granting them as much free time as possible with one another, allowing them to enjoy the sights of Sydney together.

Rachel was interested in Paul's homeland, fully aware the troubles were still continuing, having been there when Margaret went through her dilemma. She found the country's history quite fascinating.

Many barbeques were held at home for Paul, as well as at Valerie's and even Carlos's place.

Eleanor was suitably impressed with Paul's surgical status and immensely pleased with his father's judicial position. She approved of Margaret's choice; quickly disregarding the fact he came from Northern Ireland. Eleanor was fully aware a choice would have to be made one day, as to where a wedding would take place and where the young couple would settle. A fact she knew Kath was particularly anxious about but she viewed it secondary, much preferring to concentrate on the status of the family in general.

The following weekend, Margaret took Paul down the South Coast, as they both had time off. Kiama was their destination and the drive from Bowral to Fitzroy Falls was made up of beautiful farmland, which would stretch for miles into the distance, scattered with dairy cattle grazing lazily, in the bright green fields. Cutting through the Morton National Park, huge prehistoric ferns were nestled on either side of the winding road, their huge fronds uncurled and spread out, allowing the sunlight to filter through their furry foliage. Large Sydney gums and southern mahogany trees created a tall canopy along the route, as Margaret negotiated the horse shoe bends, concentrating hard, paying little attention to the high screeches of the endangered gang-gang cockatoos, as they wound their way down to Kangaroo Valley.

Fifteen minutes later they arrived at the Hampden Bridge, an old bridge suspended high above the Kangaroo River, possessing a medieval appearance, built like a castle curtain wall constructed from local sandstone.

Crossing the bridge, a tiny village lay sheltered from busy city life, offering up a slow and peaceful existence.

"Do you want to stop for a break?" Margaret enquired, noticing the cooler climate and the freshness in the air.

"I thought you would never ask?" Paul joked, amazed how the Australians travelled for hours and thought nothing of it. They visited a beautiful quaint café and indulged in Devonshire tea together. The steaming pot of Earl Grey washed down the hot scones, smothered in homemade strawberry jam and cream, beautifully.

They wandered along the main street stretching their legs, walking hand-in-hand as they visited the little shops. A carpenter was fully engrossed carving out an intricate face on a beautiful rocking horse, matching the standard of all the others on display; the smell of freshly carved timber filled the air with a warm, woody ambience.

The next shop visited, a leather craftsman was seen punching a hole in a belt to accommodate his current customer. Margaret purchased a handbag, while Paul bought himself a new leather wallet, which was hand stitched and crafted intricately, both recognising their purchases would last a lifetime.

All the other stores were just as quaint, offering homemade fare such as jams, pickles and chutneys. The lolly shop was an absolute delight and the haberdashery store offered everything from hand sewn beaded cushions, to quilted bedspreads, all crafted with love and devotion.

They both travelled up out of the valley and stopped for a few minutes at the Cambewarra Lookout, allowing them large sweeping views of the picturesque Shoalhaven River and the Jervis Bay area.

Travelling further south, they branched off left for Kiama and arrived shortly at the Sebel Harbourside Hotel, their accommodation booked for the next few days. After freshening up and having lunch, Margaret took the car up to the iconic blow-hole and Kiama's white lighthouse. Here, the majestic Norfolk Island pine trees lined the pathway to various picnic spots and the scenic lookout. Hand in hand they wandered up the path seeking out the blow-hole, created by mother nature. The rugged sea had etched away at the volcanic headland and eroded into the softer basalt rock, creating a tunnel. Over time the rock caved in, creating a spectacular blow-hole.

Children were standing close by, counting and waiting in anticipation. A loud roar could be heard as the sea came rushing in, beating harshly against the rocks and bellowing up the tunnel near the expectant crowd. Suddenly, a huge gush of water sprouted heavenwards almost like a sporadic fountain, bringing with it a boundless spray, cooling the waiting children and sending them into fits of laughter, as the seawater drenched the nearby pavement.

Photos were taken by tourists, as nearby seagulls were fed hot chips. They were swooping down haphazardly in the gusty wind, squawking loudly and swiftly grabbing their tasty morsels, before flying off again. Small children with ice cream covered faces were clutching their cones, licking their fast melting dollops with vigour. The light sea breeze was gentle and soothing as Paul and Margaret hugged each other, gazing out into the horizon, blue on blue, stretching out as far as the eyes could see.

"I love you," Paul whispered, kissing Margaret tenderly, truly touched by the natural beauty surrounding them.

Paul pleaded with her the following morning. "Do we really have to go out, couldn't I just lie snuggled up to you all day."

"Nooo way Dr Hagan," Margaret said as she laughed wildly. "Besides which, too much sex will make you go blind," she giggled. Hurriedly she escaped from his clutches and headed to the bathroom to take a shower.

Today they were heading down to Gerringong, a small coastal town blessed with a magnificent coastline. Later in the afternoon, together they would attempt windsurfing in the superb Horseshoe Bay. The weekend had been gloriously idyllic, allowing them both to reconnect, cherishing the precious time they had remaining.

The weeks and months flew by with Paul blending in as one of the family, as he frequently chatted to Brigee at breakfast time, before rushing off to the Royal North Shore Hospital. He also enjoyed his talks with Valerie in relation to medical research and his numerous conversations with Marcus in relation to sailing. He often spent quiet moments with Kath, simply sitting beside the pool and chatting about his visit, discussing the highs and lows of being a surgeon and discussing Margaret's medical achievements to date.

Time was slipping away quickly and Margaret's family were trying their upmost, to let Paul see as much of the country as possible. After many discussions, everyone reorganised their workloads in the middle of July, which resulted in the whole family packing up and heading down to the snowfields for four days. Paul was amazed as to what Australia had to offer. He never associated Australia with having snow, yet here he was after a six hour drive from Sydney, at Jindabyne, hiring out snow skis in the middle of their Aussie winter.

"Mum p-l-e-a-s-e let me hire out a snow board. Paul and Margaret can watch over me when you and dad go skiing," she begged.

"I don't know Rachel, it is pretty dangerous and I don't feel you have as much control on a board, as you do with skis," Kath replied.

"It's okay mum, Paul and I will watch and keep her out of trouble. Besides she's an avid skier and she should be okay," Margaret added.

"Thanks a million sis, p-l-e-a-s-e mum p-l-e-a-s-e, I'll be extremely careful," Rachel insisted.

Kath eventually gave in, praying she hadn't made a mistake. They made their way up to the Alpine Railway ski tube, situated in Kosciuszko National Park. Marcus and Paul parked the four wheel drives and everyone gathered up their luggage, before catching the tube up through Mount Blue Cow, Bullocks Flat and on to Perisher Valley Station.

The bright yellow snow-taxi ploughed through the magical snowy terrain, taking them to the luxury hired chalet in the heart of Perisher Valley. The three levelled chalet was perched high up facing north, allowing them to have a panoramic view of the ski slopes and lifts, lying directly down at the bottom of the hill. The chair-lifts were filled with skiers in their brightly coloured attire, forging their way up to the top of the mountain; where they would jump off quickly, before commencing a swift curvaceous descent.

Brigee served up lunch, shortly after the unpacking took place in the contemporary chalet, housing a massive spa bath in one of the bathrooms, overlooking the snowfields. The interior was lavishly furnished, matching the warm cedar walls, Marcus noticed. He lit the stacked timber in the stone fireplace, adding a glowing warmth to the living room straight away. Hot pumpkin soup and crusty bread rolls went down a treat, before the family headed outdoors. Brigee was happy tidying up and pottering around afterwards.

"There's no way you'll get me on a pair of skis," she chided. "God gave me two good feet and that's what I'm sticking to," she laughed, chasing them downstairs and out the door, after their numerous attempts of coaxing.

Collecting their skis from the racks on the porch, everyone left the drying room in extremely high spirits. Marcus and Kath deciding straight away, to head down the slope to the chair-lift, as they planned to do some cross-country skiing together.

Paul and Margret stayed with Rachel on the lower slopes, allowing her to get accustomed to the snow board, as promised. In no time at all she mastered it; her sense of balance was brilliant, with her ample skiing during her younger years having contributed.

Within an hour they were heading up the mountain top, their feet dangling midair on the chair-lift, skis attached ready for a quick exit. Rachel sat behind clutching on to her snow board, displaying rosy red cheeks and the biggest smile ever. Margaret and Paul kept an eye on Rachel when she began her wobbly decent, twisting and turning, kicking up the wispy dry snow, as they worked their way downhill.

It was an exhilarating afternoon for everyone. Marcus and Kath enjoyed the challenging cross country trail, sending their heart rates soaring, as they criss-crossed across the picturesque snowy mountains from Charlotte Pass across to Mount Sugarloaf. It was a well renowned, gruelling, five kilometre track. Paul, Margaret and Rachel weaved their way down the undulating hills, gathering speed, as they flew past the magical, snow gums, heavily laden with virgin white snow.

After arriving back in the late afternoon, they were exhausted and well pleased with their skiing accomplishments, enchanted by the magnificent winter wonderland. Brigee had a beautiful roast dinner ready which smelt delicious, as they arrived upstairs ravenous from the day's adventure.

After hot showers and dinner, they wandered down with Brigee to the lower hillside tavern to watch the fireworks, a regular weekly event which took place during the winter peak season. Everyone was mesmerised by the spectacular colours cascading downwards from the sky above. The snowy white landscape, illuminated and highlighted the fireworks display even more vibrantly, as the bright reds, greens and mauves splayed out, across the snow-capped mountainous landscape.

"Unbelievably beautiful," Brigee announced, clutching on to a hot toddy, wrapped up in her warmest winter woollies, as she peered across the snow filled mountains.

"This is something I'll never forget," Paul added, holding Margaret in his arms, instantly giving her a quick kiss on the cheek.

Everyone agreed it had been a magnificent day, as they climbed the hill back up to their chalet.

The following morning Paul and Margaret sat out on the front top deck, after devouring Brigee's delicious cooked breakfast. The landscape was silent, as the mottled grey and russet trunks of the distinctive snow gums, stretched out their windblown crooked limbs, heavily laden with the late night snow. Ice crystallised the snowy countryside scene lying before them and bringing with it, a peacefulness and serenity, duplicating a European Christmas-card-like scene. The sun rose from the mountain top, escaping into the crisp blue morning sky, sending forth warm slivers of sunlight, thawing the nearby icicles, hanging from the numerous gables and window ledges, close by.

The rest of the gang soon arrived out on deck, to observe their beautiful surroundings.

"Well, has anyone told Brigee what we're up to this morning?" Rachel enquired with excitement.

"No but I'm sure you're dying to, child dear," Kath replied, pleased everyone agreed to join in. Without another word said, everyone ventured inside to help Brigee tidy up.

"Off you go p-l-e-a-s-e everyone, I have until lunchtime to tidy up and then I'll potter about," she declared, trying to usher Margaret and Paul out of the kitchen.

"No you don't," Rachel stated "because we have a surprise for you."

"And what might that be young lady," Brigee enquired.

"Well I'm not telling you, because it wouldn't be a surprise then, would it?" Rachel laughed, teasing Brigee.

"Why don't you go and get your winter coat and boots on Brigee. We came up with a great idea yesterday and would like you to be part of it," Kath smiled warmly.

"A part of what?" Brigee enquired.

"Never you mind," Rachel cut in. "Come on Brigee, your red coat and fluffy white hat and gloves will be great for this morning, as you'll look like Santa Clause," she chirped, leading Brigee up the stairs to fetch her things.

Shortly afterwards, they were making their way up past the car park and towards Pipers Ridge.

"You've got to be joking," Brigee exclaimed, when they arrived at the toboggan slope.

"No we're not," Marcus called out, grabbing her hand quickly. "Come on Brigee, you can sit behind me and we'll race Paul and Margaret down the hill."

Before Brigee had a chance to object, Marcus had her on a toboggan and went flying down the slope. Everyone stood laughing, as Brigee went flying past gripping frantically on to Marcus, screaming the whole way down the slope.

More toboggans were hired and soon everyone joined in, whooping and shouting out in delight, acting like children with not a care in the world. Brigee relaxed and had fun, after making several trips down behind Margaret, Paul and Rachel. After a couple of hours, they headed down to the village for some hot chocolate, served up with delicious marshmallows floating on top. They built a snowman afterwards at the bottom of the ski slope, which brought admiring glances, especially with Rachel's purple hat and scarf added as a decorative feature. Later, they ate a nourishing lunch at the local restaurant at the bottom of the ski run, while watching the avid skiers speedily make their way down the mountain side.

"You can all head off and ski now. I'm bushed and heading back up to the chalet to relax and read a magazine," Brigee informed everyone gaily. She gave everyone a quick kiss on the cheek to thank them all, before heading off to put her feet up.

Rachel was staying with Kath and Marcus this afternoon, allowing Paul and Margaret time on their own. They took advantage of their alone time and caught the ski lifts to the very top, allowing them to work their way across and tackle difficult, snowy, terrain. Margaret was suitably impressed with Paul's skiing; having spent his youthful years in Austria, she was finding him difficult to keep up with. His parents had frequently visited Salzburg in the winter holidays, a resort where he had perfected his skills.

Another day passed and with everyone living in such close proximity, it brought the family much closer together, including Brigee and Paul, who built up a wonderful fun filled rapport.

On the third afternoon, Rachel followed Margaret and Paul up the mountain top, having mastered the snow board brilliantly by now. They set off downhill racing and cutting across the peaks. Rachel being as competitive as ever, began setting the pace quicker than usual. Margaret called out but her kid sister continued on heedlessly. Paul was having a tough time keeping up and was getting worried, because Rachel was travelling much faster, spending less time cutting across the snow, speeding downhill in a much straighter manner. Paul and Margaret were rushing down the snowy terrain, twisting and turning to keep up with Rachel, who was speeding ahead laughing with joy. Travelling speedily pass the trail boundaries, Rachel began swerving swiftly to avoid trees, as her adrenalin pumped on her rapid descent. Quickly rounding a bend, they came upon skiers blocking their path, appearing wide eyed and startled, frozen to the spot, like deers caught in headlights.

"Watch out," Margaret cried but it was too late.

Rachel hastily swerved to avoid a collision but by reacting too swiftly her weight shifted forwards, causing her to lose her balance and go plummeting downhill. Screaming loudly, she went tumbling faster and faster down the escarpment. Quickly stretching her hand out to break her fall, she went crashing heavily into the snow, before plunging into a clump of bushes, brutally bringing her to a sudden stop.

Paul and Margaret went rushing down after her, completely horrified, having witnessed the whole incident. Within minutes they were upon her, as she lay motionless in the snow.

"Rachel, Rachel," Margaret cried out, spotting blood trickling down her sister's face and on to the snow.

Paul turned deadly pale, observing Rachel's crumpled body, her arm was splayed in an awkward position and the gash on her forehead was bleeding profusely. Unexpectedly, Rachel released a loud guttural growl from deep within.

"Thank god," Margaret cried, instantly relieved.

"It wasn't my fault," Rachel moaned. "My arm really hurts though," she groaned in her next breath.

"Lie still Rachel," Paul ordered, examining various parts of her body, ensuring no other injuries had been sustained.

"My arm and wrist really really hurts. I tried to break my fall on the way down," Rachel grimaced.

Paul felt her wrist, noticing the instant swelling and without delay, he immersed it gently into the snow. "I believe you've broken your arm and fractured your wrist young lady," he sighed "and I'm sure your mother and father will not be impressed."

The gash on her forehead had been caused by the nearby bushes, which she had gone crashing into. Lifting Rachel up out of the snow, Paul used his scarf to make a sling for her, immediately packing it with ice and snow, to help ease the throbbing pain.

They made their way tediously down the side of the mountain. Margaret dragged the snow board and skis, following Paul, who carried Rachel to the medical centre, to get her arm and wrist assessed. All three praying they didn't run into Kath and Marcus on the way down.

After a few hours, they left the clinic with Rachel's arm in a proper sling. Paul had been right in his diagnosis; Rachel sustained a broken arm, along with a fractured wrist. They were informed it was a common injury amongst snow boarders, especially when they didn't wear wrist guards to protect against such accidents. They made their way up to the chalet, all a little worse for wear, dreading the response when Margaret and Rachel broke the news to their parents.

"I'm not at all surprised," Kath asserted, shaking her head in frustration, peering down at Rachel with her arm in plaster, held up by a sling.

"But it wasn't my fault," she pleaded. "Skiers were standing in the middle of the tracks when we came around a sharp bend," Rachel said "and …"

"Rachel dear, if you had been travelling at a sensible speed, there wouldn't have been a problem, r-i-g-h-t."

"But mum …"

"It could have been a lot worse," Marcus stated "and luckily it's your left arm and wrist, so it won't affect your school work Rachel, now will it?" Marcus smiled, winking at Rachel.

"Dad's right mum and it really wasn't Rachel's fault. It was a stupid spot for the other skiers to stop and congregate in the first place," Margaret added, sighing heavily.

"Well enough of all this chattering please," Brigee piped up. "I've got a lovely beef casserole in the oven, all ready to be served up. So if you three could please remove your coats, we can get seated, so I can serve dinner up straight away," she beamed.

Rachel smiled knowingly at Brigee, fully aware she was breaking up the interrogation and distracting everyone with her blasé happy manner. Everyone shuffled over to the dining table. Rachel was well pleased with Brigee's intrusion and extremely grateful that it was casserole for dinner tonight. A fork would be adequate on this occasion, meaning it would draw fewer frowns at the dinner table, when they were sitting down to eat.

After lunch on the fourth day it was time to leave, everything was organised and packed up, allowing the snow-taxi to take their luggage down to the Perisher Tube Station. Shortly afterwards they were at the car park, wiping the snow off their four wheel drive windscreens, before climbing on board to commence their arduous journey home.

Chapter Twenty Two

Paul's time flew by quicker than he and Margaret ever thought possible. Work was still hectic for them both; Margaret was enjoying working in the emergency department, which was chaotic, fast and totally unpredictable. Her experience was accumulating immensely and was highly respected amongst her peers.

Paul's intricate surgical skills, learnt from his initial training, by operating on multiple extensive wounds in Belfast, were proving to be exceedingly valuable within the surgical world. When a helicopter arrived on the rooftop, air lifted patients were immediately transported down to theatre.

Usually Paul was waiting, scrubbed up and ready to go. Limbs would have been ripped off by farm machinery or were mangled and disfigured in a car accident. Whatever the scenario, Paul delivered triumphant results, astounding families and friends with his surgical prowess. During their recovery, patients were forever indebted to him, truly thankful for his expertise.

Kath and Marcus organised a party on board their yacht, allowing Rachel who was overjoyed, to celebrate her fifteenth birthday in style. Paul and Margaret were given the task of sailing the yacht around Sydney Harbour, allowing her friends to view the city from another perspective. Caterers had been organised and canapés and fruit cocktails were served up on deck, with loud music blasting from the speakers. Rachel felt it was cool, especially not having her parents around to chaperone activities. Kath and Marcus were equally pleased to have time out on their own, both extremely comfortable with Paul and Margaret's sailing abilities. They sailed up to Balmoral Beach and the kids immediately dived into the cool Pacific Ocean, laughing and splashing before racing to the beach, while Paul and Margaret anchored off shore.

"Well, would you like to have half a dozen kids?" Paul questioned, out of the blue, catching Margaret totally unawares.

"Not if they're as rowdy as this bunch," she answered laughing.

"Well they would hardly be docile with a crazy, energetic, go getting mum like you," he answered, pulling her into his arms and kissing her.

There was no doubt about it; Margaret and Rachel enjoyed the spoils of their parent's hard labour and good fortunes. They were lavished with gifts but only on their birthdays and at Christmas. Both were taught to make their own way in life and not treated or encouraged to behave like spoilt little princesses. Paul openly admired the girl's upbringing and made his feelings known to both Kath and Marcus; the wealth surrounding them could easily have encouraged disrespectful and unappreciative behaviour. Both girls were extremely determined and grounded, knowing exactly what they wanted and didn't for one moment expect either parent to pitch in.

Time was slipping by furiously; Paul was having numerous conversations with Professor Andrews, the Chief Executive Officer of the Royal Victoria Hospital in Belfast. They wanted him back; he was sadly missed, both professionally and personally.

He and Margaret frequently lay awake in bed at night, discussing their future. They made their decision a long time ago, to be true to themselves, to live their lives and to follow their dreams, as they see fit. However, not everyone would agree with their plans, nor would everyone be pleased. One thing they both accepted was that they were very much in love.

It was not a quick holiday romance, nor a rushed engagement, through a bout of infatuation. No, this was the real deal; both working within the same fields certainly gave them a lot in common. Both endeavouring to aid the sick, to make a difference, both willing to compromise for each other and constantly put each other's needs before their own. They were deeply in love and hearts would be broken once again, on Paul's departure. They snuggled up tightly together in bed, dreading the day when Paul would leave.

Two weeks before Christmas, everyone was frantically running around completing last minute shopping. It was Paul's first Christmas celebration with Margaret's family and people were trying to figure out what to purchase for him.

Kath had secretly spoken to Margaret, deciding to have the Christmas party in Paul's honour, treating it as a farewell and allowing many of his work colleagues from the Royal North Shore Hospital to attend the extravaganza. Everyone knew it was only a matter of weeks, before he left the Australian shores to begin working again in Belfast. Kath was personally worried for Margaret's sake, as she could see and sense how besotted her daughter was. Marcus frequently past comments in relation to the two lovebirds, as they frequently reminded him, of his younger days with Kath.

Paul was very much one of the family, having spent almost a year in the Garofoli household.

Brigee treated him like a loving son and would miss him desperately.

Valerie was becoming anxious and very much looking forward to the party. It had been an extremely taxing year at work for her and it was proving to be enormously exhausting of late, although still incredibly rewarding.

Eleanor was going all out, shopping for Paul's Christmas present; as his father was a high court judge, a man of great standing and power. She frequently took great delight in relaying this information to her dear friends, mainly the ones who were impressed with such things.

Rachel knew she would miss Paul when he left. She treated him like a brother, a brother she never had and whom she had grown to respect enormously during his visit. He always offered her sincere advice, treating her as an adult, which she greatly appreciated.

Marcus having being surrounded with his five ladies, including Brigee and Valerie, appreciated the male testosterone around the household dinner table in the evenings. Paul frequently backed him up on many occasions, when the feminine party were having their say on certain manly topics. Marcus valued Paul's help in many instances, during his working holiday with them. Above all he was enormously happy, discovering his daughter was very much in love with a kind, generous and intelligent man.

"You look absolutely stunning my darling," Marcus gasped, as Kath made her way across the bedroom, her dress flowing gently around her ankles as she walked.

The long ivory coloured evening gown had a low V-neckline with a lace trimmed waistline embossed with sequins, contoured beautifully to fit her petite frame.

"There is something missing," Marcus whispered, reaching down into the top drawer of their dressing table, producing a large blue velvet box.

"Oh Marcus you haven't, you can't keep spoiling me my darling," she exclaimed.

"And why not?" he interrupted. "Now close your eyes." He swung her around and fastened the necklace around her neck. Standing behind her he glanced into the mirror, she appeared regal, with her diamond necklace sparkling in the evening light. "You may open your eyes now," he uttered softly, gently kissing her on the cheek.

"Oh my goodness Marcus, it's absolutely gorgeous," Kath replied as she took a sharp intake of breath, peering at her reflection in the dressing table mirror.

It was a shimmering square-cut diamond necklace, with forty-six small diamonds leading down to a much larger purple diamond, positioned in the centre of the exquisite piece of jewellery. The whole necklace consisted of fifty-two carats.

"The diamonds represents the years you have been on this earth my love and the purple one is extremely rare. Well … I simply couldn't resist it," he smiled sexily.

"It is absolutely spectacular Marcus; I really don't know what to say."

"You don't have to say anything my love, simply be. Enjoy the moment, because I have enjoyed every single, solitary moment I've ever spent with you," Marcus relayed, his eyes filling with tears.

"I couldn't begin to imagine my life without you Marcus and to think I was once distraught enough that I was prepared to throw it all away," Kath murmured.

"Hush my love; it was a long time ago when we stood on the cliff top at Bondi. Since then, I am truly grateful for every single day."

Kath's eyes were swimming with tears.

"Come here," he whispered, swallowing hard, drawing her into his arms and kissing her.

Making their way down the stairs, the couple drew admiring glances from their guests. Eleanor was as envious as ever, never really accepting her kind natured, beautiful daughter-in-law. She always felt Kath took her son away from her and was always competing for his attention, instead of accepting Kath fully and embracing her into the family.

"My dear, you look absolutely ravishing," Carlos sincerely complimented her when they met; irking Eleanor even more, before they began mingling amongst the other guests.

The Christmas decorations were elegantly hung throughout their home, extending out to the manicured lawns and around the gazebo near the water's edge. Soft music was being played and 'The Ladybirds' an all female band, were serenading everyone beautifully.

"Mum, there you are," Margaret declared, racing over straight away while clutching Paul's hand. "We've been looking all over for you," Margaret stated, appearing young, fresh and extremely sophisticated.

Her long auburn locks were gathered up and tied loosely in a knot at the back of her head, with wisps of curly tresses falling loosely down the sides of her face and around her neck. Her strapless gown was both elegant and striking; designed with a sweetheart neckline and the bodice finished in a deep lavender satin. The remainder of her dress fell softly down around her feet, in pale lilac chiffon, tailored in an A-Line design. Her drop diamond earrings, a Christmas present from Paul, further complimented the overall effect of romance.

"We wanted to thank you for such a wonderful evening, we've seen dad already and thanked him as well."

"That's okay sweetheart, it's our pleasure. I hope your work colleagues are enjoying themselves Paul?"

"They most certainly are, especially the ladies, who really enjoyed getting dressed up," Paul smiled, feeling guilty, knowing what lay ahead.

Margaret made up her mind as to her future and Paul knew from experience there was no budging her, as it was a huge sacrifice on her behalf but she didn't see it that way.

Eleanor abruptly interrupted them; "I hope you liked your gold pen Paul?" she smiled. "The fact you'll be leaving us soon, it was rather difficult to choose something keeping in mind the luggage restrictions, especially if you take Margaret with you," she laughed.

Paul's face reddened and Kath shuddered at the mere thought.

"No Eleanor, it was absolutely perfect," Margaret insisted, rapidly grabbing Paul by the arm. "Look, Geoffrey is standing over near the bar, we better catch up with him and have a quick word," Margaret added quickly, dragging him away.

"What did you do that for?" Paul questioned Margaret. "It may have been the opportune moment to bring the subject up."

"No way Paul," Margaret uttered. "Besides, it would ruin the whole party and upset mum. I told you it could keep until next week. Please trust me on this one."

Paul nodded reluctantly and hoped Margaret was right, as he knew the longer you left things, the harder it got.

The remainder of the evening went exceptionally well. Paul was very striking, dressed in his formal attire; his dark features and demeanour, made him appear extremely aristocratic.

Rachel was on her best behaviour and with her friends attending, she was in her element. The pale blue chiffon dress matched the colour of her eyes and the diamante shoe string straps sparkled in the evening light, as she made her way across the room, visibly attractive and feminine. Matured beyond her young years, she attracted many secret admirers, unwittingly.

She danced the night away, enjoying the whole gala affair, without showing favouritism to any male in particular.

Valerie and Matt were in a jovial mood, dancing frequently; enjoying the ambience and the wonderful company. Valerie however had been sinking quite a few martinis down throughout the evening and was appearing slightly intoxicated, when Kath caught up with her.

"Pray tell me, what are we celebrating?" Kath asked casually, watching everyone dancing and having a good time.

She was taken by surprise, when Valerie responded "more like drowning my sorrows," slightly slurring her words.

"Surely it can't be that bad?" Kath soothed, turning around to give her friend her undivided attention. She was instantly concerned when Valerie became all teary eyed.

Kath hurriedly took her hand and led her to the study, providing a sanctuary where they could talk without being interrupted. Valerie instantly broke down crying, no longer willing or able to keep up the charade.

"God Kath, I've been so exhausted of late. I've discovered a lump on my god-damn breast over a month ago and I'm too bloody scared to do anything about it."

Kath immediately took Valerie in her arms, hugging her deeply. "I'm so sorry Valerie," she murmured, clutching to her dear friend, struggling to fight back her own tears.

Inhaling deeply and pulling herself together, for her friend's sake, Kath automatically kicked into a positive mode.

"Okay Valerie, first of all you're the most positive person I know and it's not like you to look for the worst case scenario. The day after Boxing Day, I'm going to make an appointment for you with my doctor. I will be there with you Valerie, my dear beautiful friend, so we can go through this together. Okay!"

"Does Matt suspect anything?" Kath gently enquired.

"No, all he knows is I've been extremely tired of late and puts my moodiness down to working long hours but he doesn't have a clue."

"Well then, we'll keep it that way until we find out exactly what is going on," Kath stated, handing her friend a tissue.

Valerie gave her a watery smile, grateful for her friend's intervention. Recognising she could handle it all much better now, even if it was disastrous news, acknowledging she had the best friend in the world to help her get through it.

Kath tidied Valerie up, giving her a massive reassuring hug, before rejoining the party. They each sculled a stiff drink and found their respective partners to have a dance.

The evening had been a wonderful success. Speeches were made by Paul's work colleagues and he was presented with an Australian Rugby Union jersey, framed and signed by his workmates, which touched him deeply. He was an avid rugby union supporter and was involved in many discussions during his lunchbreak at work, especially when the Tri-Nations were being played; as a large number of British staff worked at the Royal North Shore Hospital.

A permit had been granted and the fireworks display complimented the extravagant gala evening, before everyone took their leave. Kath made a special point of saying farewell to Valerie, wishing her dear friend well, informing her quietly an appointment would be made as soon as possible, reassuring her; she would be in touch real soon.

Brigee noticed Kath and Valerie emerging from the study earlier and was fully aware something was terribly wrong but decided to leave them both alone, until they were ready to share what was happening.

Rachel waved goodbye to her friends, pleased they had a terrific time, before making her way upstairs after bidding everyone goodnight.

Kath stood in the moonlight undressing quietly, as Marcus watched her silently from their bed. She was so attractive and serene this evening and he wanted to feel her close. He craved for her intimacy, wishing to smother her in sweet blissful kisses. Without saying a word he was behind her, slipping her satin camisole straps down off her shoulder.

"Mmm, that's nice," she purred, willing him to comfort and seduce her, allowing her to forget about Valerie's news, granting her temporary relief.

Gradually, he removed her lingerie, as she stood transfixed in the moonlight, her eyes gently closed, as her whole body tingled in anticipation. He was edging his way along her body, caressing her ever so compassionately, while smothering her in soft sensual kisses. Slowly he picked her up and carried her elegant body over to their bed; her body was completely naked, except for her diamond necklace, glistening in the evening light.

Without saying a word, he leisurely made love to her. Capturing her soft graceful body within his, he tenderly entwined his long limbs around hers to masterly take her, encapsulating and signifying his love and desire for her, in that very moment. She devoured his gentle advances hungrily, responding ardently by surrendering completely to him, giving him her very all. Silently they kissed and caressed each other in the moonlit bedroom, nurturing the other's needs, tenderly. Their rhythm in sync, Kath's body swiftly surged upwards, erupting into multiple euphoric spasms, as Marcus continued his seduction. Unable to contain himself any longer, his momentum was building, building strongly, as he immersed himself fully in the moment, pouring out and expressing his undying love to his wife.

Allowing themselves to simply feel, they lay together quietly, wrapped up in each other's arms, not daring to say a word. Their bodies were tingling and ever so sensitive, heartbeats were racing rapidly, as both slowly recovered from their seduction. A tiny tear trickled down Kath's cheeks; Marcus drew her closer, kissing her on the forehead.

"Do you want to talk about it, my love?" he queried soothingly.

Kath gulped back more tears, before finally caving in. "It's Valerie," she whispered. "She may have breast cancer. I only found out this evening," breaking down immediately into a gentle sob.

"Hush now my love; remember to never meet trouble half way. Valerie is strong and with the technology available today, she'll probably be fine. That is, if the diagnosis confirms cancer in the first place and we don't know that yet. Now do we?"

Kath smiled up at him, as she lay wrapped up in his masculine arms, defeated by exhaustion. She felt his gentle kisses upon her eyelids, before sleep overtook her, causing her to sink reluctantly into a deep abyss.

Morning arrived; she was greeted with a breakfast tray filled with hot steaming coffee and delicious chocolate filled croissants. She sat up in bed instantly, as Marcus adjusted her pillow.

"My oh my, if the board of directors could see you now Mrs Garofoli, they certainly would not approve," he said, as he laughed out loud.

This is when she caught her own reflection in the dressing table mirror, situated opposite the bed. Her tousled hair was resting upon the pillows; while the top half of her body was naked, highlighting her exquisite diamond necklace.

"Well, I don't think I would get a part in a soap opera, that's for sure," she laughed, noticing her smudged eyeliner from the previous evening.

Rachel was already up, having eaten breakfast and was heading off to her friends place, as pre-arranged from the week before. Brigee was having a few friends over at her place on Boxing Day, with people she had known for many years from bingo. Margaret and Paul called out their goodbyes to Marcus, when he was heading down the stairs earlier, as they were going down to the city, so Paul could experience the Sydney to Hobart Yacht Race which was an annual event. Marcus would like to have joined them but their company didn't have an entry this year. However, given the current circumstances, now with Kath aware of Valerie's suspected breast cancer, it worked out well for them to have the day to themselves.

"Well sleepy head, the entire family has deserted us, leaving us on our own. Is there anything in particular you would like to do today, young lady?"

Kath smiled across at her handsome husband. The years had been kind to him and he still remained youthful in his appearance. Perhaps it was his Italian bloodline or his bewitching green eyes, which she still found tremendously appealing. His gentlemanly mannerisms were as impeccable as ever and he clearly loved her, as much as she adored him.

"Do you know what I really fancy doing today my darling?" she beamed.

"And what's that?"

"Absolutely nothing," she declared. "It's been quite a while since we've drifted around home and just lazed about. We could watch an old movie, nibble on some chocolates and perhaps even have a skinny dip later this afternoon, allowing the rest of the world to slip on by."

"Sounds good to me," Marcus readily agreed. Acknowledging it would do Kath a world of good, as life in the media industry was always stressful, with deadlines to be met, campaigns to be organised and budgets to be maintained.

Meanwhile, a party was underway at Caroline's parent's family home, unbeknown to Kath and Marcus. Rachel giggled, sucking on a bong, appearing like a regular drug addict, as she shouted across to Caroline to turn the music up.

It's been a long time since Rachel touched marijuana; in fact, it was Margaret who caught her at it a year ago at the last Christmas party and she was lucky her sister didn't tell their parents. Today she didn't want to appear like a nerd, everyone else seemed to be getting high and she badly wanted to fit in with Caroline and her friends. Internally, she justified it was only a harmless recreational drug, not like cocaine or heroin, which she swore she would never touch. Caroline's parents were away at Bowral for the day, visiting relatives and wouldn't be back until the following morning, unbeknown to Kath and Marcus.

Caroline was up dancing on the floor and her arms were moving like a butterfly, Rachel thought, continuing to giggle some more. Wow, the room was beginning to spin out again as euphoric feelings engulfed her entire body, before she passed the bong on to Jason, who spent most of his time with her today.

He was eighteen years old and a friend of Stephanie's brother, deciding to come along when he heard there was a party going on. Rachel found him quite attractive and intelligent, making a nice change for her, because as far as she was concerned, most of the other guys present were either immature or just plain dull and boring. Jason had sticky out brown hair, the cheekiest grin imaginable and amazing honey gold eyes which immediately lit up, whenever he was explaining something to her in great detail.

She felt grown up and told Jason she was eighteen, which seemingly attracted even more attention from him. His conversations were interesting, coming from a similar background to hers and having also travelled extensively, they discovered they had a lot in common.

"Do you fancy going out for a swim?" he smiled lazily, sitting cross legged next to her. Aiming to please, Rachel readily agreed, because she knew she would look exceptionally great in a bikini.

She made her way up the stairs slowly, as the drug kicked in. She was lacking co-ordination and found it hard to concentrate. Losing control, she found herself smiling a lot and drifting into a foggy haze. Reaching her friend's bedroom where she was supposedly staying the night, she managed to make her way over to the bed, before collapsing on it in a doped up manner. She closed her eyes momentarily, trying her best to cease the spinning from happening. She was burning up and longed for a large cool drink. The door slowly creaked open, immediately capturing Rachel's attention.

Jason appeared, instantly making a beeline towards her, before happily plonking himself down on the bed beside her, grinning from ear to ear. He immediately went to kiss her, catching her totally unawares. She was co-operative, acting fully grown up and experienced, revelling in his undivided attention, responding as though she was completely carefree. After what seemed like hours of endless kissing and cuddling, he blatantly ran his hand up under her top, manhandling her breast.

"Don't," she stammered trying to push his hand away.

"Don't what you little tease, you've been flirting with me all day," he jeered aggressively, pinning her hard down upon the bed, his eyes hostile and bloodshot.

Chapter Twenty Three

Margaret and Paul had a fantastic day. Paul was fascinated by the yachts, before they headed out of the iconic Sydney Harbour, followed by smaller vessels, honking their horns in celebration of the inaugural Sydney to Hobart Yacht Race. Team colours were displayed on masts and sails as they manoeuvred from port to starboard, tacking rapidly, as the yachts raced towards The Heads. The skippers on board would be appreciating the aerodynamic drag, while enthusiastic crowds lined the shore, catching a glimpse of the wondrous sight.

Later, Paul and Margaret decided to stop on the way home to dine at a little Italian Restaurant. Enjoying a glass of red wine, both sat chatting while waiting for their ravioli, which turned out to be an authentic home based recipe, with both readily agreeing it tasted absolutely delicious.

Margaret's telephone rang unexpectedly. "Oops sorry, I forgot to switch it off," Margaret apologised to Paul.

"Don't worry, no big deal anyway. It's hardly work that's for sure," he smiled.

"Oh hi mum, what's up?"

"Sorry for disturbing you sweetheart. I was wondering if you could do me a favour."

"Sure, just name it and consider it done."

"Your father and I had a wonderful relaxing day and we've had a few drinks. I was wondering if you could pick Rachel up from Caroline's on the way home."

"Just a second and I'll grab a pen and paper to scribble down the address; I kind of know where she lives."

"Okay love."

"By the way, are you sure she's not having a sleepover, mum?"

"I don't think so darling but now that you've come to mention it, she could be. I wasn't up this morning when she left."

"Don't worry, leave it with me. I'll call in anyhow and if she's staying the night that's fine, because it's on our way home," Margaret replied happily.

After mother and daughter hung up the phone from each other, Marcus entered the kitchen with another two glasses of wine in his hand. "What was that all about?" Marcus questioned happily.

"Oh nothing my love, I'm organising for Rachel to get picked up from Caroline's, that's all."

"I thought she was staying the night."

"Mmm, that's what Margaret said. To tell you the truth, after getting hit with the news from Valerie last night, I didn't really take in what Rachel had said to me, before retiring to bed."

"Come over here and stop looking so concerned. Margaret will pick her up and if she's staying the night, I'll pick her up at lunchtime tomorrow."

Reaching for the glass of wine, he kissed her gently on the lips.

"And what's that for," she asked.

"Well, it's still hot outside and if we're quick enough, we can have another skinny dip and make it back to the bedroom before the kids arrive home."

"Sounds good to me," Kath whispered, making her way to the French patio doors, dressed in nothing but one of Marcus's shirts, appearing as sexy as ever.

Meanwhile, Margaret and Paul were making their way across town to pick up Rachel. "It's the next street over," Paul directed Margaret, scrutinising the street directly in the dimly lit car.

"Thanks love, it won't take long and it gives me the opportunity to introduce you to Caroline's parents. They're nice folks, although Caroline's a bit of a worry. You know when you have a gut instinct about someone and it never quite goes away. That's the kind of wary feeling I've always had in relation to Caroline," Margaret confided.

"It's not like you to be cynical young lady," Paul laughed. "It's just kids growing up and experimenting," he said, remembering about the marijuana incident on the rooftop, that Margaret had told him about. "Holy hell, you should have seen the time when my folks had to deal with Stephen. My brother was a bit of a wild one but eventually he settled down and conformed in the end," Paul joked.

Every room in the house seemed to be lit up, when Margaret arrived at the double storied home, positioned at the bottom of a prestigious cul-de-sac. Music was blaring loudly and sounded like it was coming from the back yard, when Paul and her approached the front door.

"Sounds as if a party is going on," Paul remarked, as Margaret rang the door bell.

Before she could reply the front door swung open, a barefooted dude with denim jeans wearing no shirt, with his chest plastered in outlandish tattoos, stood grinning and staring up at them.

"Welcome man ... to the wildest party ever," he slurred, obviously drunk, stoned or something Margaret instantly thought, feeling the hairs on the back of her neck standing on end.

"We've come to pick up Rachel; do you know where she is?" Margaret enquired, trying her best to remain calm.

"No s-i-r-e-e," the young lad slurred, opening the door up wider "but you can come right in and chillax, because there's one hell of a party going on."

Margaret entered the hallway together with Paul; the music screamed much louder now, almost deafening. The dude was wandering off and Margaret kicked into action.

"Okay let's find her quick smart and get the hell out of here. Obviously the parents are away and Caroline is up to her usual antics," Margaret bitterly complained.

They both made their way to the back of the house and through to the kitchen, which appeared as if a bomb had hit it. Empty bottles of alcohol were scattered everywhere, half eaten pizzas were lying in open boxes and the stench of marijuana was hanging densely in the air. Out in the back yard the party was raging, about fifty kids were dancing to some grunge rock song dressed in swimming attire and many were in the swimming pool swilling bottles of alcohol, while others were sitting around inhaling drugs on bongs.

"Holy Hell," Margaret stammered, the anger building up rapidly.

Paul was obviously shocked, judging by the expression written on his face.

Suddenly a loud cheer went up. Glancing across to their left they noticed a girl was on the table, obviously stoned, dancing incoherently and making a god-damn spectacle of herself, with the partygoer's clapping and cheering her on.

"That's bloody Caroline," Margaret yelled, making her way across to the table with Paul following closely behind.

Within seconds, Margaret had Caroline pulled down off the table, instigating loud grunts and heckles of disapproval straight away, before Paul dispersed the crowd.

"Where the friggin' hell is Rachel?" Margaret demanded, immediately sensing her sister was in danger, glaring wildly at Caroline who was half out of her mind.

"I dunno," Caroline slurred, her eyes bloodshot to kingdom come and barely comprehensible.

"What do you mean you don't know? Apparently she's your god-damn best friend Caroline, who foolishly trusts and respects you," Margaret snapped, grabbing her momentarily and shaking her, half out of her mind.

"Okay, that's enough Margaret," Paul intercepted. "You're not going to get any sense out of her anyway; we'll split up and find Rachel ... Okay."

Frantically grabbing Margaret's hand, he tore her away from the scene. "It's okay, we'll find her and everything will be fine."

They made their way back into the dishevelled house and started searching the rooms downstairs, to no avail. Making their way upstairs, tears flooded down Margaret cheeks, as anger and fear invaded her heart causing it to race anxiously, all at the same time.

At the top of the landing, Paul shouted out instructions.

"You take the left and I'll take the right, then we'll search the backyard thoroughly if she's not up here."

Margaret nodded, swallowing hard, trying not to think the worst.

Rushing down the passageway she opened up bedroom doors, getting more hysterical as she encountered an orgy of young limbs, mixed and tangled up amongst each other. Stoned young couples were making out in Caroline's parents main bedroom. Her eyes were searching, searching for her sister. Praying she was okay, praying she hadn't done anything stupid. Hoping she was safe and had not come to any harm.

In the meantime, Paul was at the other side of the house seeking out Rachel.

"Get off me you drunken brute, I'm not that sort of a girl," she screamed, beating urgently upon Jason's chest with her bare fists, extremely frightened.

The bedroom door suddenly burst open.

"You better do what the lady says," Paul asserted, interrupting the brutal scene.

"Mind your own business mate, she's over eighteen and ..."

Not taking any notice and rapidly marching across the room, Paul immediately dragged the young lad off the young female.

"Rachel," Paul shouted in astonishment, flabbergasted to find her lying on the bed, totally dishevelled, with smudged black eyes highlighting the tears streaming down her face.

"Oh my god," Margaret screamed, rushing into the room after spotting her sister. She dropped down on to the bed, automatically taking her into her arms to comfort her.

Rachel began sobbing, never so glad to be seeing Paul and her sister in her whole life.

"Are you okay, did you get hurt ... please tell me nothing happened," Margaret questioned frantically.

"I'm okay," Rachel sobbed. "Jason wasn't listening and was beginning to frighten me," she stammered.

By this stage, white hot with anger and trying to valiantly contain himself, Paul had Jason pinned up against the wall.

"Do you know you can go to jail for attempted rape, especially when it comes to a minor. She's only fifteen years old for Christ sake!" Paul declared.

The blood literally drained from Jason's face. Snivelling he gasped "shit I'm sorry, I'm real sorry man, she told me she was eighteen and I kind of lost it."

"Stop Paul," Rachel protested, "it wasn't his fault and I did tell him I was eighteen. Please let him go."

Paul glared at Jason, then Rachel and finally back to Margaret, before he reluctantly released his grip.

"Get out of here now! I detest scumbags like you or so help me; I'll not be responsible for my actions," Paul spat, half pushing him out the door.

Jason fled, as Rachel sighed with relief, feeling such a fool, acknowledging she had been well and truly out of her depth and came close to being raped. Large round tears bubbled up again, cascading down her pale cheeks. Margaret cried also, hugging her sister urgently, relieved, beyond belief.

"Okay, I'm going to leave you ladies up here to get tidied up and I'll head downstairs to sort this mess out, before someone gets injured," Paul offered.

Margaret nodded, recognising the party would have to be called to a halt. With their medical experience they knew harder drugs were being used and if it persisted, god only knew what the outcome might be.

Paul made his way downstairs to find Caroline, who was calling out and craving attention. Pulling her to one side, he noticed she had sobered somewhat, as she glared up at him.

"What do you want now?" she protested.

"What I want is for you to call a halt to the party, as someone is going to get badly injured or die. Have you seen the drugs around you?"

"So what, it's none of your business," she snapped back.

"Do you realise your friend Rachel came close to getting raped," Paul seethed.

She answered slowly; seemingly unfazed. "She was probably asking for it, she was hanging out with Jason all day long, like a little lost puppy," she laughed cold-heartedly.

Exacerbated, Paul completely lost it. "Are you going to stop the party or not? I can help you remove the troublesome ones and Margaret and I can help tidy up, before your parents arrive home."

"Read my lips, it's got nothing to do with you, we're all having a GOOD TIME," staggering slightly, before continuing. "Sooo, why don't you take wimpy little Rachel with you and bugger off," she sniggered, completely belligerent.

Paul had only just replaced the phone back into the cradle, when Margaret and Rachel appeared at the top of the stairs.

"What's happening?" Margaret enquired, noticing the distraught look written upon his face.

"Haven't got time to explain now, let's go. I'll explain everything later when we get back home."

Margaret climbed into the back seat of the car with Rachel, who seemed somewhat subdued. Paul quickly got directions from Margaret on how to get back to Victoria Road, after which point, he would know his way back from there. On accomplishing this task, they had only travelled approximately half a kilometre up the road when a police car and truck went rushing past in the opposite direction.

"Must have been an accident," Margaret said quietly from the back seat, her arms protectively wrapped around her little sister.

"Or one about to happen," Paul sighed, knowing there had been no other option.

When they got home, the hall lights had been left on and obviously their parents had gone to bed.

"Thank the Lord," Margaret whispered "or Rachel would be in the biggest trouble ever and grounded for life."

All three sneaked upstairs quietly and Margaret went with Rachel to her room. "Are you sure you're okay sis," Margaret enquired quietly and Rachel nodded. "I know it's not time for a lecture but Rachel do you realise how close you came to getting raped and how swiftly things can escalate and get out of hand, through drug use."

"I know I was stupid, trying to fit in … belong … you know what I mean," Rachel cried.

"I know Rachel, I really do but I suggest you stay away from Caroline. She's bad news and tonight she made it damn clear to me, she didn't give a shit about you."

"What are you going to tell mum and dad?" Rachel sobbed.

"Don't worry you're safe. Paul and I will think of something and we'll talk again in the morning before you go downstairs. Okay."

"Thank you and thank Paul for me. I've never been so glad to see you both in my entire life and you're right; I'm ditching Caroline and never touching marijuana ever again. I promise."

"What a horrible way to learn a valuable lesson Rachel," Margaret sighed, tucking a piece of Rachel's damp hair behind her ear. "But at least you're okay and that's the main thing. I'm glad we were there to rescue you," she smiled, kissing Rachel on top of the head while tucking her into bed. "Now get some sleep and don't worry, we'll come up with a good story in the morning."

Rachel nodded and closed her eyes, falling into a deep dark sleep, straight away.

"How is she?" Paul asked, when Margaret crept into his room.

"Sound asleep, completely exhausted and totally repentant. I don't think she'll ever touch drugs again for as long as she lives and more importantly, she's giving Caroline the flick, thank heavens."

"I'm glad to hear that," Paul sighed. "She was a nasty little bitch this evening and didn't give a damn about Rachel or anyone else actually. I tried to help her you know. I suggested moving everyone out and help tidy up before her parents got home but she turned real nasty showing her true colours, so I gave up in the end."

Margaret lay next to him in bed, so happy he was with her this evening. She was also pleased how he rescued Rachel and maintained an amazing amount of self control, while pinning Jason to the wall.

"What if something happens to one of those kids at the party Paul?" Margaret asked, biting her bottom lip. "Let's face it, one could easily drown in the pool for god's sake; they were stoned enough and couldn't help themselves if they tried."

Tears began surfacing, as Paul took hold of her. "Don't worry my love, I've taken care of everything and everyone will be safe."

"How Paul, how can you say that?"

"Do you recall coming up Victoria Road and we sighted a police car and truck in a hell of a rush?"

"Yes, vaguely ... why?"

"I instigated it, by making an anonymous phone call to the local police station, reporting an underage drinking party, laced with drugs. I also informed them loud music was blaring obscenely from speakers, disturbing the whole neighbourhood. Finally before hanging up, I strongly voiced my medical opinion, recommending it should be shut down, before someone ended up badly injured or worse."

"Oh my goodness, what will happen to Caroline and her friends now?"

"Well, with any luck her parents are probably heading back home as we speak. The police will have issued major warnings and arrested those who became excessively aggressive," Paul advised.

"I can't say I feel sorry for her, in fact it could be a good thing in the long run," Margaret confided. "You may have saved her life Paul; hopefully her parents will seek clinical help and provide a means for her to break her addiction. Other parents will become aware these parties need strict supervision and their children monitored much more closely," Margaret insisted, yawning.

"Get some sleep young lady," Paul whispered "you look exhausted."

"I am but I'll have to help Rachel in the morning and explain things to mum and dad."

"Don't worry about that, I'll sort it out," Paul insisted, giving Margaret a quick kiss before switching off the light.

The morning sunlight crept into Rachel's bedroom, causing her to instantly squint in pain. Her head was throbbing massively, so she quickly swallowed a couple of painkillers Margaret had left out for her the night before. Margaret obviously understood how she would be feeling this morning. She pulled one of her pillows up over her head, blocking out the early morning light and lay perfectly still, reiterating over in her mind the events from the previous evening. Silent tears fell upon her pillow, depicting the sadness she felt. Fully acknowledging she had been extremely reckless and foolish; also coming to the realisation that Caroline wasn't a true friend, recognising her mean streaks, for what they were. She vowed inwardly to link up with Hannah and her friends who were sincere, kind and true. As for drugs, she was never really into them, it was her second attempt, which came about merely to fit in. Jason was only after one thing in the end, she concluded, as more tears spilled out, dampening her cheeks.

She got out of bed slowly, deciding to have a shower to wash away last night's events, determined to make a new start and to never mess up again, ever.

Shortly afterwards, a short rap on her door made her jump.

Margaret entered quietly. "How are you this morning?" she enquired gently, noticing the pastiness of Rachel's skin.

"I'm lucky to be home and have a great sister, as well as an understanding future brother-in-law. Above all, I'm pleased to be given the opportunity to review and change my life AND my so called friends." Peering at her sister, she tearfully continued "thank you Margaret ... I love you," Rachel choked, breaking down and crying again.

"My goodness Rachel, that's enough or you'll have me bawling my eyes out," Margaret appealed sympathetically, giving her a quick comforting hug. "Paul is going to speak with mum and dad this morning. He's going to explain how he found the party had got badly out of hand and offered to help shut it down, highlighting how Caroline objected. He'll also explain we got you out of there quick smart, before all hell broke loose or before someone got injured. He's not mentioning where we found you and who you were with and he'll inform them about calling the police."

"He called the police?" Rachel's eyes grew wider.

"Yes he did. He reported it as a concerned neighbour, because if he didn't someone could have got seriously injured or might even have died last night."

Rachel nodded silently, acknowledging her sister was right, fully aware there was no other alternative.

"Okay, everything will be fine when we meet you down at brekkie," Margaret assured her little sister, before closing the door on her way out.

True to their word, Paul explained everything at the breakfast table as Kath and Marcus listened attentively, shocked and alarmed by what they were hearing.

"Are you okay Rachel?" Kath asked. "It could have got real nasty."

"I'm fine mum, thanks to Margaret and Paul's timing, it couldn't have been more perfect," she grinned from ear to ear, peering across at them both.

"It certainly hasn't lessoned your appetite young lady," Kath laughed, noticing Rachel tucking into her second round of pancakes hungrily, unaware of the side effects from smoking marijuana.

"Well I must say, you handled the situation perfectly Paul and I would have done exactly the same, given the circumstances," Marcus announced.

"Poor Isobel and Tom, they will be absolutely devastated," Kath sighed. "But at least you stopped a major catastrophe from happening Paul," Kath confided, smiling across at him.

"Rachel, have you spoken with Caroline this morning?" Marcus enquired, stretching across and pouring himself another cup of coffee.

"No I haven't dad and after having a chat with Margaret and Paul last night, I am finished with her. Margaret warned me she was trouble last Christmas and she was right."

Kath raised an eyebrow, glancing across at Marcus who seemed as equally pleased as she was, both delighted at their daughter's maturity level and grateful she was distancing herself from enviable future trouble.

"If I receive a phone call from Isobel today, I will explain you were picked up by Paul and Margaret earlier and offer her my sympathy of course. She must be distressed and utterly ashamed. I'm sure Caroline will be grounded for a very long time."

"Grounding won't be enough mum," Margaret asserted. "Of what I could see from last night's performance, she is going to need professional help and a lot of counselling."

Brigee arrived in the room. "Does anyone want more bacon?"

"I do," Rachel spoke up.

"I don't know where you put it all, child dear" Brigee laughed, dishing some more on to her plate.

The subject changed when Brigee left the room and Rachel breathed a great sigh of relief, pleased everything had been covered. Margaret and Paul helped her enormously and she was forever in their debt.

Chapter Twenty Four

After breakfast, Kath was on the phone to Dr Lee whom she had known for years, trusting her impeccably, fully aware she had valuable contacts, which could be useful to Valerie.

"I would deeply appreciate your help in this matter, as my dear friend works within the medical fraternity and wishes to keep everything low key. That is, until she knows for certain what her diagnosis will reveal."

"Yes, I fully understand the predicament your friend is in at present Kath, now let me see." Kath could hear her flicking through her diary. "I can fit her in first thing Monday morning at nine, if that's suitable?" Dr Lee advised pleasantly.

"Yes, yes that's terrific, I'll be accompanying her for moral support of course and hopefully it's a false alarm," Kath confided and thanked Dr Lee, before setting the phone down quietly in her study. She didn't want either of her girls to know or be alarmed. Understandably, Valerie wanted everything kept under wraps, until she found out where she stood.

Immediately Kath glanced at her watch, deciding to ring Valerie straight away to give her the latest news. "Hi Matt, how are you managing the Christmas indulgences of late?" Kath enquired light heartedly, trying to sound her usual happy self.

"I swear, if I see another chocolate truffle or eat another mince pie, I think I'll explode," he laughed out loud. "I take it you want to speak to Valerie?" he enquired gently.

"Yes thank you, I hope I haven't disturbed you both at breakfast?"

"No, on the contrary she's still in bed having a lie in. I've been telling her to slow down lately but it's like talking to a brick wall," he chuckled, totally oblivious to the real cause of Valerie's fatigue.

"In that case I'll ring back later, it's not urgent. Whenever she gets up, you can let her know I rang," Kath casually replied. She was concerned, because Valerie was obviously much sicker than she had been letting on, Kath thought, as she hung up.

The remainder of the day was spent lazing around the pool with the family, which was proving to be ideal. Rachel invited Hannah and a few other friends around and they all were having a wonderful time together. This pleased Margaret and Paul immensely; both fully aware Rachel had definitely changed, after receiving the biggest scare of her life.

Paul and Margaret organised a barbeque for later on and made a refreshing jug of sangria between them, which would be refreshing for the adults to drink later on in the afternoon.

"There's going to be quite a temperature change for you in another twelve days time," Kath leisurely remarked to Paul, lying next to the young couple in the sun loungers.

"I spoke to my parents on Christmas Day. Apparently it's minus five degrees over there at present. So yes, it will take a while to get acclimatised again, I'm afraid," Paul countered.

"Come on, let's take a swim," Margaret suggested, grabbing Paul by the hand quickly before he could object.

"You better make the most of it," Marcus joked, carrying out a tray of cool drinks. "When you get back, you'll need your winter woollies."

"Brrr it makes me cold just thinking about it," Kath laughed, shivering. "Mind you, it is quite picturesque when it's been snowing, however I must admit, I much prefer the heat," she said, shifting the glasses and making room for Marcus to set the drinks tray down.

Paul and Margaret swam a few leisurely laps, before breaking into a race together, both as competitive as one another. Rachel and her friends followed behind laughing and splashing, as they sped at breakneck speed up the pool. Kath and Marcus looked on happy and content, both very much enjoying the relaxing family day together.

Later in the afternoon Brigee called out from the kitchen. "Valerie's on the phone for you Kath."

"Great I'll take it inside, besides I need another cool drink in this heat." She made her way casually indoors, before picking up the receiver.

"Hi Valerie, I take it you got my message then?"

"Yes ... sorry about this morning, I had a lazy fit and decided to stay in bed and read a few magazines, a luxury as you know."

Kath detected the anxiety in her voice. "Look I'll not keep you for long. I've got an appointment with my lady doctor on Monday morning at 9am, so I'll come and pick you up and we'll make out we're going shopping, okay."

"Thanks Kath," Valerie sighed. "I really appreciate what you're doing for me."

"Don't worry that's what friends are for, now go and enjoy your family. After a relaxing weekend Valerie, you'll feel much better and stop worrying for goodness sake. Everything will be fine on Monday. Give my love to Matt and Richard and I'll catch you later."

Kath hung up with tears stinging her eyes; she was immensely worried about her dear friend.

In that very moment, Brigee walked in on her unexpectedly, catching on straight away. "Do you want me to fetch you another drink?" she questioned softly, giving Kath one of her all knowing looks.

"Yes thanks ... that would be great," Kath replied, trying to sound blasé, fully aware it was going to be extremely difficult to keep this from Brigee.

As Brigee went to retrieve a cool drink from the fridge, out of the blue she simply asked "do you want to talk about it now or later?"

Kath quickly glanced over her shoulder, confirming her family were still outside relaxing and enjoying themselves.

Instantly clearing her throat, Kath announced rather quietly "it's Valerie, Brigee. She suspects she has breast cancer and I've arranged an appointment for her on Monday morning with Dr Lee."

"Holy hell, it's a lot worse than I expected," Brigee exclaimed, letting out a huge breath while grabbing hold of the kitchen barstool to steady herself. "How long has she known?" Brigee enquired, visibly upset.

"About a month apparently, she's been putting it off you see. Her family doesn't even know and she only informed me at the Christmas party."

"I knew something was going down. I saw the pair of you come out of the study and neither one of you appeared happy on leaving," Brigee confided. "Let her know her secret's safe with me and that I'm here for her. If there's anything I can do, please let me know straight away Kath," Brigee added solemnly.

"Thank you I will," Kath replied, gently giving Brigee an enormous hug, knowing in her heart of hearts, the two of them would get Valerie through this.

Brigee had gone home after the barbeque, bidding them all good night, before heading back to Bondi. The teenagers vacated to the bedroom playing music and trying on each other's clothes, doing what normal teenage girls do. Paul discreetly mentioned to Margaret several times during the course of the day, to speak with her parents, as it was only but right to allow them time to adjust and become familiar with their plans.

The adults were sitting outside on the patio, with the pool lights creating a serene atmosphere, as the coconut palms rustled gently in the light evening breeze. The stars were out in full force, as Margaret gazed up at the dark velvety sky.

"The Southern Cross always reminds me I'm home," Margaret confided, breaking into the peaceful surroundings, drawing everyone's attention to this fact. "And by the way, thanks mum and dad. We had a lovely day today but unfortunately I have some news for you both, which might come as a bit of a shock."

Kath and Marcus both sat up in their chairs casually, peering at one another, wondering what news Margaret was referring to.

"I'll give you the good news first," Margaret smiled. "Paul and I are getting married in September and we'll be having our honeymoon in New Zealand."

"That's wonderful," Kath beamed happily. "We're really happy for you both but it doesn't give you much time to organise a wedding."

"Well, the second part of our news is, we're getting married over in Northern Ireland. It makes more sense, because all of Paul's relations are over there and they couldn't all possibly come out to Australia for the event," Margaret relayed rather quickly.

"I agree whole heartily," Kath laughed "but how will you organise the wedding from here?"

"That's just it mum ... I can't. So I'm going back over with Paul and staying for another year."

Kath was silent, gobsmacked, knowing in her heart this day would arrive. However, she didn't realise it would be so soon.

"What about your work darling?" Kath enquired, trying to hide her disappointment.

"Everything is taken care of mum. I've resigned at the Concord Hospital and the Royal Victoria in Northern Ireland has a post all ready and waiting for me," Margaret smiled weakly.

"You certainly don't muck around, daughter dear," Marcus interrupted. "Of course we're happy for you both, as you're not kids anymore and obviously have your minds made up. Kath and I know you love each other deeply and it's not easy having parents on either side of the world but you have our blessing."

"Thanks dad," Margaret grinned, giving him a huge hug.

"Isn't that right Kath?" Marcus prompted.

"Yes, yes of course darling," Kath replied, fighting back tears.

"Kath why don't you bring out a bottle of champagne, as this definitely calls for a celebratory drink," Marcus added, recognising the devastation written in her eyes.

"Good idea," Kath retorted, promptly slipping out of her chair and heading straight towards the kitchen. She was glad Marcus created the opportunity for her to slip away. It allowed her the time to pull herself together and accept the news more graciously.

Later in bed wrapped up in Marcus's arms, Kath began to sob gently. "I'm going to miss them both desperately," she whispered. "If it's not one thing it's another," she sighed. "First it was Rachel attending the drug fuelled party, then Valerie and now this. Jeez they say things come in threes. This last one ... I could have done well without," she sighed, as Marcus gently appealed to her good sense.

"She loves him immensely Kath and really at the end of the day, true love is the greatest gift any human being can ever have."

"You're perfectly right my darling," Kath nodded, wiping away her tears. "I guess it's not forever," she added weakly.

Marcus smiled. "Who knows where the pair of them may end up; it wouldn't surprise me in the least if the two of them went to help in Africa or ended up doing a stint in some other third world country. The main thing is, as long as they've got each other and are deeply in love, everything else will fall into place," Marcus announced determinedly. "Now get some sleep my love, everything will appear so much better in the morning. After all, we're gaining a son and it's a good excuse to visit your parents more frequently."

Kath smiled up at him, appearing happier than before. It was true; they had the financial means to visit as often as they wanted. The other side of the world suddenly, didn't seem so far away after all.

The days were rushing by too quickly for Kath. She accompanied Valerie to visit Dr Lee and all the tests were being organised discreetly, pleasing Valerie immensely. A few days later Brigee met up with Valerie and Kath for lunch, down at the Bondi Surf Club. All of them sat with their lattes having indulged in a delicious lunch. The three of them sat silently and contentedly, gazing out into the sky-blue horizon watching the vibrant hues merging into one.

Quietly, Valerie held their hands unexpectedly. "Thank you my dear friends for all your kindness and love shown towards me over the years. My life would never have been the same without you both," she said calmly.

Brigee and Kath both choked up, as they listened to her words. "Now young lady, don't you go and get all morose on us now," Brigee chipped in. "We're the three musketeers and that's the way it will remain, for a very long time to come."

"Here, here," Kath interrupted. "We'll help you get through this Valerie and I know in our hearts, everything will turn out fine," she said, smiling warmly at Valerie.

"Now tell me, what's going on with your Margaret?" Brigee announced, deliberately changing the subject to lighten the mood, purposely not allowing Valerie to dwell on her predicament.

"Oh that," Kath sighed, rolling her eyes heavenward. "Where do I begin?"

Soon after, they departed the restaurant with the three of them feeling in high spirits; aware life had its ups and downs although all were fully conscious they had each other to lean on, whenever the going got tough.

Finally the sad day arrived. Margaret and Paul deliberately made it a midday departure. They felt it made it easier to leave then, because there was less available hours at that time of the day to drag on and consequently less tears would be shed.

Brigee was at the airport saying her farewells; she had grown extremely fond of young Paul over the past year and was delighted he was marrying Margaret. Valerie came along to say her goodbyes to them both as well, appearing excessively thin though, which worried Kath even more. Kath and Marcus both exchanged loving hugs and kisses with their daughter and her fiancé, before they marched off hand-in-hand towards the Customs gate.

"I love you both," Kath called out one last time, crying uncontrollaby, as they disappeared out of sight.

"It never gets any easier," Brigee reiterated, with red swollen eyes. Valerie blew her nose, remembering the day Margaret was born.

"Holy jeepers," Rachel joked. "Look at the three of them dad. You would think Margaret and Paul were dying."

Marcus laughed. "You're right young lady, now come along, we have a wedding to attend in nine months time and I guess there'll be a lot of shopping to be carried out in between times."

Kath smiled. "You're right my darling, there's nothing like a bit of retail therapy for a good pick me up."

Everyone laughed heartily, as they made their way towards the exit, knowing they would be catching up again real soon, for the wedding in Northern Ireland.

Chapter Twenty Five

The next few months were gruelling for Kath, between trying to consol herself in relation to Margaret's departure and dealing with the many specialists, surgeons and oncologists attended by Valerie and herself.

She was mentally and physically drained. Determined to retain her optimism, she took solace in realising Rachel had settled down quite considerably, there was less socialising and parties and evidently she was more studiously engaged at school. Her school reports depicted an ideal teenager who was excelling exponentially at a remarkable rate, as well as proving she was an extremely academically minded and conscientious young lady.

Kath inhaled a deep breath. "Let's get this over and done with and no matter the outcome, we will face it and fight it together," Kath reassured Valerie, before walking into Dr Henderson's surgery.

He was a small set gentleman in his mid forties, with mousy brown short hair, swept to one side. He also had kind eyes that were of a bluish-grey colour. As he gently indicated for the pair to be seated, Kath noticed his elongated slim hands, flicking nervously through the pathology reports, sitting upon his desk. He fretfully cleared his throat, before addressing Valerie. Kath held Valerie's hand tightly, waiting in anticipation for the verdict, acknowledging the past few months had been extremely taxing on Valerie, who sat next to her, frail and worn.

"I understand you have been to many specialists and have undergone numerous tests Mrs Lorino," he announced immediately.

Valerie nodded in response, not daring to speak, waiting for his imminent decision.

"Since your last visit, I've had time to peruse the latest CT scans taken by ourselves, as well as reviewing the mammograms, ultrasounds and biopsies you had carried out previously," he said.

Drawing his chair closer and sighing heavily, before making direct eye contact with Valerie, his features momentarily softened, depicting sadness, as Valerie braced herself for the news.

"However, from my experience in situations similar to yours, I feel we must proceed with the upmost urgency and operate immediately. A double mastectomy is my recommendation and I unequivocally stand by my choice, bearing in mind the major surgery required."

Valerie appeared shocked, inhaling a deep breath as tears trickled down her face unchecked, recognising deep down she expected nothing less.

"Don't you think a double mastectomy is rather extreme Dr Henderson," Kath interjected immediately.

She was trying to come to terms with the possible diagnosis over the past few months but was now confronted with the severity of the situation along with Valerie.

"I'm afraid we don't have any choice Mrs Garofoli," Dr Henderson curtly replied.

Prattling on in a monotone manner, he explained that Valerie had inherited the BRCA1 gene and that she would require chemotherapy, four weeks after the surgery. This would take place every two weeks, four to six rounds and would be administered to her as an out-patient within his clinic. This would result in removing recurrent cancer risks, by approximately ninety-seven percent. He further went on to explain the tumour was three centimetres in diameter and had spread to her lymph nodes. However, breathing a great sigh of relief, he informed them they had caught it early and it was classified as a grade 2 but also highlighted the necessary procedures were absolutely essential for Valerie's long term survival.

"It's okay Kath," Valerie half whispered, holding on to Kath's hand tighter. "I've been having sleepless nights over this and decided I am prepared to endure whatever is absolutely necessary, in order to increase my chances of beating this."

Kath immediately leant in and hugged her dear friend. "You're a very brave lady and I'm ever so proud of you," Kath confided.

Dr Henderson paused for a few moments, taking in the emotional scene, before he continued on with this explanation, referring to his meticulous notes on various occasions. He suggested by taking aggressive measures, she had a very high recovery rate. Not unlike some who had already progressed to the later and lethal stages, in this all too common disease.

"How soon can we expect the surgery?" Kath questioned, as Valerie sat close by, coming to grips with reality.

"I have made arrangements for Mrs Lorino to be admitted at the end of the week and I will be carrying out the operation personally," he smiled weakly. "I feel it is a very wise move on your behalf to hold back on any reconstruction implants, as it will greatly reduce the risk of infection and enhance your recovery rate immensely."

Valerie looked up complacently. "Thank you Dr Henderson, I really appreciate your honesty and your direct approach. My family is unaware of my situation, however, my husband Matt, will no doubt comply with my wishes."

"I'm sorry it couldn't have been better news but one must do whatever is necessary in order to save your life. My nurse will fill you in on the details and make arrangements before you leave but if there are any more questions, please feel free to talk to me and we can discuss them openly."

"Thank you," Valerie replied warmly "but I am fully aware there are no other viable options and at the end of the day, a set of breasts does not define who I really am," she added steadfastly.

After completing the necessary paperwork, the hospital staff requested Valerie to endorse them with her signature, before leaving the surgery.

Outside the sun shone brightly as they breathed in the fresh air, both glad to be mingling with the outside world again. The noisy traffic and the brightly dressed pedestrians served as a distraction, momentarily shifting their moods after such a bitter sweet outcome, in relation to Valerie's health.

"Do you fancy some lunch?" Kath questioned, standing in the middle of Macquarie Street, trying her upmost to remain positive and calm, for her dear friend.

"Actually a glass of red would be nice," instantly glancing down at her watch "and it's 12.30pm, so we don't have to look like a pair of alcoholics," she laughed, grabbing Kath's arm to cross the street.

Slowly walking down to the Sydney Mint Café, situated in the heritage listed Mint Building, both were surprised the lunchtime patrons were already fast accruing. Valerie sat at a small table on the balcony, overlooking the sandstone courtyard and lit up a cigarette, as Kath placed an order, before disappearing to the ladies.

Drawing on her cigarette, Valerie noticed two middle aged women close by. They were chatting amicably, unaware of her observation, unaware she was scrutinising their bodies and their exposed cleavages, unaware she wanted to scream so badly. Kath reappeared and noticed Valerie's eyes filling with tears. Catching on immediately she sat down quickly, blocking the view of the two women purposely. Valerie looked up, startled.

"With bazookas like those, their tits will be hitting their knees in five years time," Kath announced smiling, making Valerie giggle loudly.

"Shhh they might hear you!"

"Who cares?" Kath retorted cheekily, breaking the gloomy atmosphere immediately, before lifting her drink and clinking her friend's glass. "To good friends, an excellent outcome and a speedy recovery," she announced.

"Thank you Kath; I really don't know how I would have survived without you and Brigee over these past few months."

"We've not done anything you wouldn't have done for us," Kath interrupted, sipping her wine and lighting up a cigarette.

They spent the next two hours debriefing, allowing Valerie to come to terms with Dr Henderson's consultation. Slowly but surely, Valerie was recovering from the initial fear and shock. Kath also helped her friend through the guilt she felt, for keeping it a secret from her immediate family, she also noticed Valerie's anger was slowly dissipating as she relaxed more. They participated in a light lunch and made preparations for her hospital stay, both going over many different takes on how to present the news to Matt and her son.

"Are you okay or do you want me to come in with you?" Kath asked, dropping Valerie off at her home.

"I'll be fine," she smiled sweetly, appearing much calmer now, before closing the car door.

"If you need me, call anytime, day or night," Kath sung out the window, before driving off.

Two kilometres down the road, she pulled in kerbside and lit up another cigarette, huge tears formed and slid down her face, as she cried for her dear friend Valerie, for Matt and her young son Richard. She cried bitterly, acknowledging the journey Valerie must soon go through, the hair loss, the massive scarring, the gruelling pain management, the lack of confidence and muddled brain, inherited from the chemo treatment. She would also experience more weight loss and the dreaded look of sorrow and sympathy, to be endured from her family and friends. Kath drew down on her cigarette one more time, before wiping away her tears and taking in a deep breath, she made a firm resolution there and then, to maintain a normal and happy relationship with Valerie. No tears, only positivity, laughter and above all, sustaining some sort of normality in her life. Kath wanted to provide her with a shoulder to cry on when needed or give her a kick in the ass if she started to get depressed and wanted to give up. To be the person there for her, when Valerie felt like shouting or screaming, when everything became overwhelming for her. Yes, she would be resilient and practical and with Brigee helping her; they would be a force to be reckoned with.

Later in the evening, Valerie laid in bed wrapped up in Matt's arms, peaceful and content. "Richard took it rather well, don't you think?" she questioned Matt quietly.

"Yes he did. Admittedly, I didn't know his friend's mother had come through a similar ordeal, so that obviously helped," Matt answered, kissing her on top of the head.

Peering upwards directly into his eyes, she asked "are you okay with it all? I will lose my hair you know, feel tired and nauseous, not to mention the cognitive impairment received from chemo. Plus, I'm having both breasts removed and will probably look pretty damn ugly, with a lot of scar tissue," she confided, painting the worse scenario imaginable.

"Shhh my love, you can't get rid of me that easy if that's what you're trying to achieve. I didn't marry you for your breasts. I married you because I fell in love with your personality, your sense of humour and inner beauty, not to mention your intellect and courage. You are a beautiful, warm, human being Valerie and that will never change. I will love you for all eternity, with or without your breasts," he comforted.

She leant in and kissed him and he reciprocated, drawing her in even closer, proud of her bravery and humility.

The operation was taking place, as Kath and Brigee walked the corridors like caged animals. Numerous cups of coffee had been consumed; heaps of cigarettes were smoked outside in the garden and the proverbial clock watching had taken place. Finally, Dr Henderson entered the waiting room, still dressed in his blues and removing his cap, before approaching them.

"The operation has been a great success, with no complications whatsoever," he added proudly.

Further consultations would take place over the next few days, discussing the chemotherapy and reconstructive surgery but for now the news was great, resulting in a positive outcome. When Valerie was brought up from theatre, Matt was the first to visit. After ten minutes, Kath and Brigee entered her room laden with flowers, cards and teddies, which immediately brought tears to Valerie's eyes. They both stayed briefly, recognising how tired Valerie was, leaving shortly afterwards to allow her to rest.

"Bye," they called out in unison, pleased the operation went well and Dr Henderson was delighted with the results.

The days passed slowly for Valerie, as she lay recuperating on ward nine. She felt a bit raw and sore, suffering some pain, numbness and pinching sensations in her underarm area but that was to be expected. Hooked up to an intravenous drip administering medication, certainly helped and offered relief. The nurses were proving to be efficient and gentle, when checking on her dressing and assuring that all tubes and drains still fitted properly. Valerie found herself frequently glancing down at the bandages, drawn tightly across her now deflated chest. She often wondered what it looked like underneath, quickly discarding the thought whenever she became too distraught. She was aware it would take up to two weeks for the wounds to heal and twelve months for the scars to change from red to pink and then to her natural skin colour.

Matt, Kath, Brigee and Marcus had been spoiling her rotten. Baskets of flowers, bottles of perfume and toiletries were brought in each day. Soft furry toys always drew a smile from her and the magazines brought in were enough to open up a newsagency.

Valerie sat quietly with Matt, as Dr Henderson explained the chemotherapy treatment, highlighting the side effects and explaining the programme in great detail. They held hands, hopefully smiling in all the right places, as both Matt and Valerie were of the same mindset and were desperate to leave. After the medical jargon was explained, they stood up and shook hands, before leaving the methodical Dr Henderson behind them.

On the way home, Matt held his wife's hand several occasions, watching and scrutinising her at the traffic lights, whenever they came to a standstill. "You won't mollycoddle me, will you?" Valerie questioned Matt directly. "If you do, it will drive me insane my love and I will really resent it."

Matt faced her. "I will treat you as normal as possible, which will be extremely difficult, given the circumstances. However, if I do get out of line, you have my permission to give me a huge wack across the head and a good telling off," he announced, laughing loudly, before driving off in a cloud of smoke.

Valerie gave Kath and Brigee the same lecture the following day and they agreed readily, informing her promptly it was exactly what they had in mind, drawing great hoots of laughter from the three of them all at once.

It was two weeks later when Valerie got to remove the bandages, permanently. She had sighted her mutilated body in post operative visits before but today she stood alone, peering into the bathroom mirror, as she apprehensively unwrapped herself from her protective garment. Valerie struggled for breath, as tears sprung to her eyes, sighting the redness and rawness of it all. The scarring was horrendous, carved out jaggedly and haphazardly upon her chest, although smooth, as she ran her hand tenderly over her mutilated body, taking it all in. She forced herself not to concentrate on her loss but to focus on the positive. She was here ... alive, constantly surrounded by her loving family and friends and she must continue to be thankful for every god given day.

Kath, Brigee and Rachel included, arranged to go shopping with her the following day. Rachel was rather creative, choosing beautiful silk blouses with brightly coloured prints, deflecting from the flatness of Valerie's chest. Kaftans were ordered for Valerie, something for her to lounge around the house in, after her chemotherapy sessions.

Kath insisted on visiting the lingerie department, which Valerie initially found rather confronting, however she was pleasantly surprised by Kath and Brigee's inventiveness. Elegant satin pyjamas were purchased; with pockets appropriately positioned to hide any irregularities. Short nighties with frilly bust lines, disguised her lack of breasts, amazingly well. They sought to provide her with beautiful feminine apparel, allowing her to feel womanly, confident and normal.

They had lunch together down at The Rocks, enjoying the harbour breeze and the outdoor eatery. It was a refreshing and welcome change for Valerie, after being confined in hospital for the past twelve days straight. They were mindful not to overdo it, as she had a gruelling time ahead and was still recovering from her operation. No exercise was allowed for the next four to six weeks and once chemotherapy started, Valerie would have to take things much easier.

After lunch Valerie was clearly exhausted, so Kath suggested they head back home, on the pretence of having to make an important overseas business call. Brigee offered to stay at Valerie's to help out until the treatment was completed and only after Kath's persistence, did Valerie finally accept. Matt gladly accepted the kind gesture made during Valerie's hospitalisation, truly grateful and appreciative that she had such loving and caring friends around her.

As Kath was leaving, Valerie suddenly announced, "I'm back at work next week ladies. So I thought it was best to pre-warn you, in case you were organising more retail therapy for me."

Brigee stood with her mouth gaping open and was about to launch into a full scale debate. However, the expression on Kath's face directed her otherwise.

"I assume you're undertaking light duties?" Kath enquired gently, careful not to impose.

"Three days a week is what I agreed to with Matt and the hospital confirms, this would be perfectly viable for everyone concerned."

"That's marvellous," Brigee chirped up "we can't have you lying around feeling sorry for yourself or may the Lord forbid, you get bored!" rolling her eyes heavenward.

This caused everyone to laugh merrily, all equally accepting Valerie was as determined as ever, to proceed forward as normally as possible.

"Do you think Auntie Valerie will be okay?" Rachel enquired on the way home in the car.

"Of course my darling, she's very strong willed and an extremely determined individual, owning a tremendously positive mindset. And that my child, as any doctor or surgeon will tell you, is half the battle when it comes to dealing with cancer patients."

"I guess it's no longer a death sentence, the way it used to be," Rachel added, sounding extremely mature for her young years, seemingly taking everything in her stride.

Later that evening, Matt watched Valerie sitting at her dressing table, her face serenely peering in the mirror, as she peacefully removed her makeup. He noticed the pretty new nightie she was wearing and to an untrained eye, it camouflaged her deflated chest extremely well.

"You're looking very sexy this evening," he commented gently, smiling across at her from his bed.

"Mmm, one of the creations I picked up today when I was out shopping with the girls."

"You can tell them I approve immensely," he laughed, requesting her to come to bed immediately. She slipped in beside him and he reached across, pulling her into his arms and kissed her.

"You look amazing my darling," he said sincerely, aroused by her tender touch. Huge tears formed immediately, her emotions were all over the place of late. "What is it my sweet, have I done or said something wrong?" he questioned anxiously.

"No it's not you Matt, it's me!" she heaved a sigh. "I feel completely sexless and my body is like a pre-adolescent boy. Look!" she cried, pulling down the top of her nightie, totally disappointed and appalled.

He automatically pulled her much closer into his arms, as she sobbed incoherently, confiding how disenchanted she was of late. Matt lifted her tear drenched face upwards, so she could face him. "Look," he said gently, "now there's nothing to come between us," he gestured; highlighting no boobs were allowing them to come more closer than ever before, while hugging one another.

She giggled in delight, peering in absolute awe at the beautiful man wrapped up in her arms.

"And never forget, I'm always here for you and that will never change my love," he whispered, before leaning in and kissing her.

She returned his advances ardently and soon they were making love, like old times and she became the woman she once was. Driven by desire they pleased each other, meeting each other's needs, becoming inseparable as they climaxed together, before coming to rest in each other's arms and falling soundly asleep.

The following day Valerie rang Kath, happy and carefree, casually mentioning the lingerie department had been a great idea and a wonderful success. Kath smiled inwardly, pleased Valerie was still having an intimate relationship with Matt. Proving she hadn't lost her confidence or her way, during her cancerous journey, which hopefully will end successfully within the next six months.

Valerie did start back to work; three days were enough for her both physically and mentally. Too quickly, the time arrived for her chemotherapy treatment to begin and everyone held their breaths, praying for a successful outcome. Matt, Richard, Kath and Brigee took it in turns to be by her side, when she was fed the angiogenesis inhibitors through an IV drip.

Stories were shared, jokes were told and the view outside the North Shore Hospital ward, offered up a spectacular green haven, while treatment was being administered. Her friends would sit quietly overlooking the neatly manicured gardens, the carefully trimmed hedges and the small flowering shrubs, which also offered an ideal sanctuary for the adorable little wrens. They provided such a beautiful distraction, in the midst of all the chaos going on around them. Their little tails pointing heavenward, swaying and tottering in the morning breeze, as they nimbly fluttered from branch to branch, on the pale pink azalea bushes nearby. Mother nature was exceptionally stunning, providing such fascinating little creatures. Some had little sky blue crested breasts, embossed upon their fluffed up, feathery rounded bodies, distracting Valerie enormously, from her aggressively driven treatment. She normally had the next couple of days off after treatment, allowing her time to recover from her ordeal, before she commenced back to work on much lighter duties. Her white blood cells had to be reasonably high, before her chemotherapy could be administered each time. Although on a daily basis, she was being effectively micro-managed by Brigee at home.

She made sure Valerie received enough rest and was provided with light nutritious meals, as her appetite was slowly diminishing. Brigee even took it in her stride to supply her with many exotic homemade juices, providing her friend with extra minerals and vitamins, to help her body cope with the treatment she was receiving.

Kath kept Margaret fully informed in relation to Valerie's health, preventing her from worrying unnecessarily. Margaret and Paul both were distraught when they received the news, especially Margaret who was overcome with guilt, fully conscious she left at a most inopportune time, in both Valerie and her mother's life. Coming from the medical fraternity, she was fully aware of the symptoms, treatment and side effects, involved with breast cancer.

Valerie rang them both before commencing her treatment, sounding ever so positive, instantly putting them both at ease. She explained how successful the operation was and how Dr Henderson had high expectations in the overall result. Valerie reiterated on several occasions, why they were not allowed to come back for a visit, explaining she didn't want any fuss and that's why she didn't tell them before they left. She wished them both well, telling Margaret she was very much looking forward to seeing them both at their upcoming nuptials..

The months came and went for most people, as it normally did. However, Valerie's life as she knew it was completely topsy turvey. Appointments had to be made to check her white cell counts before the administration of the drugs. Schedules had to be slotted in for treatments and afterwards to follow up on reports. It was also important for Valerie to follow a healthy eating plan and swallow the anti-nausea medication, whenever things became unbearable. Coming to terms with her hair loss and her gaunt waif-like appearance, all took its toll. Her friends and family were Valerie's rock, her sounding board; she would continue to forge forward, recognising these were people close to her heart and worth fighting for.

Before long, she ceased taking any form of pain relief at home and refused the injections at the clinic, because she found she could manage without them. Dr Henderson saw this as a definite positive and was extremely pleased with her progress.

Two months later, the doctor ordered some more CT scans, blood tests and other necessary procedures, as he felt she was nearing the end of her treatment. Matt and Valerie were both requested to attend an appointment in his clinic, seven months since the day Kath sat with her, questioning his aggressive surgery.

The clock in the receptionist wall seemed to move endlessly slow. Both Valerie and Matt were agitated, acknowledging at this appointment they would be told if the cancer still remained within Valerie's system. The chemotherapy had taken its toll; Matt thought clutching her hand, praying there would be no need for anymore. Valerie didn't dare hope; this way with no expectations, there would be no disappointments. She must remain strong; her Kundalini yoga helped her immensely throughout her ordeal. She reminisced about the quiet serene moments in the early morning light, when she sat quietly and meditated, chanting lightly and utilising visualisation for self healing. This regularly removed the negativity from around her aura, rejuvenated her body, relaxed her mind and gave her an overwhelming sense of power, allowing her to cope and accept things so much easier. It taught her to live in the present moment, in a much more passive manner.

"Dr Henderson will see you both now," the young petite receptionist stated, breaking into Valerie's thoughts. Grabbing Matt's hand tightly, they approached the doctor's office with trepidation, not daring to say a word. After they were seated, Dr Henderson welcomed them both, before opening up his records.

"How have you been feeling over the past couple of weeks Valerie?" he enquired gravely.

A part of her wanted to scream who gives a shit how I feel, just give us the god-damn results. Have I still got cancer or not? Instead she smiled sweetly and replied "I wasn't as tired this week and notice I'm getting a regrowth of my hair" reaching up and touching the crown of her head, feeling the small fluffy spikes.

"As I'm sure you both can appreciate, I had to go through the latest tests checking the results thoroughly, as I couldn't begin to imagine how you would feel, if I delivered the wrong news," he conveyed in a monotone manner.

Both Valerie and Matt inhaled deeply, watching and waiting for Dr Henderson to continue.

"As predicted, the cancer has completely gone," he continued.

"GONE COMPLETELY?" Valerie interrupted, laughing out loudly, with tears of joy gushing and streaming down her cheeks.

"Yes indeed," Dr Henderson confirmed.

"FANTASTIC," Matt announced, jumping up out of his seat immediately and hugging Valerie.

The atmosphere was electric, filled with so much relief, laughter and love, Dr Henderson observed. He was extremely pleased his forecast had come to fruition, thankful he had preserved another young life. On days like these, he was enormously satisfied with his chosen career.

Needless to say, Kath, Brigee, Rachel and other family members were waiting back at Valerie's home to hear the great news. They all participated in her journey, recognising whatever the outcome was, they would either console her or gladly celebrate with her. The wait was agonising for everybody, especially for Kath and Brigee, who wouldn't even allow themselves to think of a negative result.

When Valerie and Matt arrived home, they made the announcement very quickly. The looks on their faces were euphoric, as everyone congratulated Valerie for her bravery. Stating they admired her resilience and above all, thankful she wasn't going to be one of the unfortunate statistics.

Everyone stayed for the lunch that Kath and Brigee prepared while waiting; at least it helped maintain their sanity or they both would have gone completely mad. Everyone lifted their glasses and toasted Valerie, who was overwhelmed with the end result.

Her friends started to leave at three that afternoon, with Brigee giving instructions to Valerie to take it easy for a while, reinforcing that she was not to be over doing things. Kath, Marcus and Rachel spent time congratulating her once again, before they made their departure. Valerie's mother Sylvia, followed very closely behind, smiling graciously and clearly elated, appearing much happier than they have seen her in a very long time.

Chapter Twenty Six

"Hi Paul its Kath here, by any chance is Margaret there?"

"Yes you're in luck; we're both working the 3pm shift this week."

"Great, can I have a word with her; I've got some good news to share."

"Just a moment I'll go and fetch her. Oh before I go, how's Valerie coping at present?"

In a low conspiratorial whisper, Kath explained. "Don't say anything to Margaret but she's got the all clear."

Paul could hear the happiness and relief in Kath's voice and he was absolutely delighted for Valerie.

"M-A-R-G-A-R-E-T," he shouted. "Hurry up, your mum's on the phone for you."

"How's everything going at work for the pair of you and dare I ask, how's the wedding arrangements coming along?" Kath enquired politely, while waiting for Margaret.

"Chaotic on both fronts," he answered, laughing out loud.

Margaret was bounding towards him fresh out of the shower, wrapped up in a short towel with her hair falling in a tousled curly mane, flowing around her elfin smiling face. A quick kiss was given, as he handed the phone over to her.

"Hi mum, what's up? You're not ringing with anymore wedding suggestions are you?" she joked cheerfully. Very much appreciating the fact her mother and father left them to the wedding arrangements, without any interference whatsoever.

"No, I'm sure you and Paul can manage the wedding plans and all the chaos that goes with it, all on your own," Kath announced laughing. "Actually, I've got some brilliant news for you my love. Rather than beating around the bush, it's in relation to Valerie. She's cancer free. We got the news today and we all celebrated together this afternoon."

"Oh my god, I'm so happy for her mum!" Margaret beamed legitimately, as tears unexpectedly spilled down her cheeks. She sat down on the edge of the sofa, stunned and overwhelmed by the good news. Paul automatically came across and put his arm around her.

"Margaret ... are you there?"

Swallowing hard, Margaret took a deep breath. "Yes mum, I'm still here. I just wish I was over there to give her the biggest hug ever. I was so worried, she's been a huge part of our lives and I love her to bits," she exclaimed.

"I know exactly what you mean my love," Kath soothed, touched by her daughter's sentiments. "Well, we can all get a good night's sleep from here on in," Kath added lightly.

"Give her our very best wishes mum and we'll give her a ring over the weekend."

"I'll tell her tomorrow. Now tell me, how are things going over there?"

"Well, considering there's only two months to go until the wedding, it's been hectic and I mean hectic. Paul's parents have been fantastic though. Helen has been an absolute god send and helps me enormously. Are you and dad still coming over a month beforehand with Rachel?"

"Yes of course we are, we'll be staying at your grandparents and the last time I spoke to mum she was so excited."

"So am I," Margaret retorted happily. "What about Valerie. Will she be able to make it?"

"With bells on my dear, I have never seen a braver and more determined woman in my life. Your father and I offered the company jet for them to fly over a week before the wedding and Brigee will be flying over with them."

"Oh mum I'm so excited. I'm so looking forward to seeing you all and you'll get to meet Paul's parents, they're lovely. They're real genuine people who are really down to earth. Even though Henry is a high court judge, there is no pomp or pageantry whatsoever with him."

Kath was pleased Margaret had fitted in with Paul's family; it meant a lot to her that her daughter was settled and happy. "Okay my love I best be going and let you get ready for work. I'll give Valerie your regards and tell her you'll catch up at the weekend. Give Paul our love and you take care sweetheart."

"Thanks for the call mum, I love you. Give dad and Rachel a big hug and kiss from me."

"I will dear, now you go and get ready for work and I'll ring you next week. Bye!" Kath hung up the phone peacefully, acknowledging she would be seeing her whole family in a month's time and was absolutely thrilled.

"Whoopee!" Margaret let out a joyful scream. Jumping around the living room like a loony bin, totally ecstatic. "Valerie's cancer free, cancer free, cancer free," she sang, laughed and giggled out loud.

Paul picked up this rapturous bundle of joy tightly in his loving arms immediately and began kissing her. "I love you, soon to be Mrs Hagan. Valerie's one hell of a woman and I'm so pleased with the positive outcome," he said, kissing her again.

"Here! Here!" Margaret softly murmured, as Paul headed towards the bedroom.

A month later, the young couple were waiting in the arrivals lounge. "I can't believe it!" Margaret declared with happiness, clutching on to Paul's hand, waiting in anticipation for her parents' arrival at the airport.

So much had happened over the past month. Flowers, cake, photographer and dresses, everything had been checked and rechecked umpteen times. She hoped Rachel loved her matron of honour dress and more importantly, it fitted her well, at least this way they still had time to make any alterations if any were required.

With no girls in Paul's family, Margaret and Paul decided to have one niece from his mum's side of the family and one from his father's, to be their bridesmaids. They also decided on Margaret's two best friends Hazel and Daphne, whom she befriended from day one when she first began working in the Royal Victoria Hospital. Paul's brother Stephen was best man and a few cousins and friends were the ushers. A wedding party of twelve including the bride and groom was what had been organised. Two hundred guests were attending, which was much larger than they anticipated but both sets of parents insisted money was not an issue, as they wanted the best for their children.

"They're here," Paul interrupted her thoughts, bringing her back to the present moment.

Tears stung her eyes whilst watching the jet taxi down the runway, coming to a slow stop, before rallying around and making its way back to the terminal. Gripping Paul's hand they made their way up to the arrivals lounge, to wait there and greet her family. The doors slid open and Rachel came bounding out, much taller and more beautiful than ever, Margaret observed, as she made a beeline towards her sister.

"Hi sis, did you miss me?" she questioned, laughing and hugging Margaret warmly.

"Like a hole in the head," Paul chuckled, giving her a quick hug as well.

Kath and Marcus followed shortly behind and all the formalities took place, including hugs and kisses, collecting and gathering up of the luggage, as well as snippets of conversations being shared with everyone, in relation to their journey on the way over. Margaret explained that Mary and Joe were really excited and looking forward to catching up with them all, as they made their way out of the terminal.

Kath soaked up the greenery, on the way up to her mum and dad's. She had always forgotten how green it was, until she was in the midst of it and then she knew she was home. Rachel chatted to Margaret in the back, as Paul drove the Range Rover with Marcus sitting next to him, taking in the view. Driving up the lane, Kath's heart rate quickened as she was enormously excited and so looking forward to seeing her parents again.

Sure enough, as soon as they arrived into the yard, Joe and Mary came rushing out the back door to greet them. Hugs and kisses were once again exchanged chaotically and randomly, with sheer exhilaration and joy.

They were soon congregated in the homely kitchen, the table was set and ready for lunch, as the old Aga stove sat burning and smouldering away in the corner, adding to the warmth already felt by the whole family. Lunch time was a mish mash of conversations, all catching up on lost time as they munched into the delicious homemade bread and scones, followed by shortbread, apple pies and buns, which would have left any patisserie chef standing in awe.

"I've been hanging out and craving for one of your currant squares for the past couple of months Mary," Marcus exclaimed, downing another one with a huge mug of tea.

Kath patted his tummy area affectionately. "Easy on darling, you have a month to go until the wedding and at this rate; you'll not be able to fit into your suit."

Everyone burst into playful laughter, enjoying each other's company with the warm loving atmosphere, permeating from within the room.

It had been arranged for Kath and Marcus to catch up with Paul's parents at their home in a few days, allowing them time to recover from any jetlag.

Rachel was already booked in the following day with Margaret for her dress fitting. This would put Margaret's mind at ease, knowing it would be another detail taken care of.

The day progressed to evening with everybody joyfully swapping stories. Paul and Margaret left with great reluctance, having been heartily fed, they could have easily settled down for the remainder of the night. However, they still had some final details to go over for their wedding and had promised to drop in to see Paul's parents for supper, before heading back home.

Rachel went with Margaret the following day to Belfast for her dress fitting and was introduced to the other girls from the wedding party. They all got on exceptionally well; with everybody adoring Rachel, all treating her like a younger sister. The dressmakers, took great pleasure in listening to her Aussie accent, which stood out palpably, in amongst the other dialects. Rachel's outfit needed a slight alteration at the bust and the length adjusted after slipping on her satin shoes, allowing them to get the precise measurement.

All the dresses were a dusty pink taffeta, complimenting all of the girl's fine figures and complexions. They were tailored meticulously, fashioned into a mermaid silhouette style, adorned with intricately designed and slimline beaded belts. That rested comfortably upon their tiny waists, stretching around to the back, before splaying out and tied into a huge extravagant taffeta bow. The edges of which were etched in fine crystallised beads that matched in perfectly with the belt. The gowns were both strapless and boned, providing an elegant dipped neckline and were all moulded perfectly to fit their mature young bodies. The girls were simply a picture of pure sophistication and grace.

"It's absolutely beautiful Margaret ... beyond words," Rachel exclaimed, peering at herself in the mirror, with the other girls openly admiring and complementing her. Her sun kissed skin, blond hair and light blue eyes enhanced the gown even more, making her appear like a young starlet, someone you would expect to see on the red carpet, at the Academy Awards.

After leaving the fashion studio, Margaret took the small group out to lunch, pleased with the final effect. It had been the first time she had seen the five girls dressed up together and the overall effect was stunning.

Helen had initially introduced Margaret to Francoise Bernard, who made and designed couture gowns for many of the dignitaries in the UK, America and Europe. Of French descent, Francoise was recognised for her intricate beading and original creations, one of which was her wedding dress, a true masterpiece.

"Hasn't anyone seen your wedding dress?" Rachel enquired, before biting into her sandwich hungrily.

"Nope," Margaret smiled, determined to keep the dress a complete secret from everyone, until the big reveal on her wedding day, on the 9th September.

"I know the groom isn't suppose to see it," Rachel continued "because apparently it brings bad luck but I reckon we're okay," grinning at the other girls.

Margaret laughed loudly. "Gee you're as persistent as ever Rachel. However, Hazel, Daphne, Fiona and Bernadette have been trying for the past five months to get the details but to no avail."

"That's right," Hazel interrupted "so we've all given up. We'll be like the guests on the wedding day and will only get to see it for the very first time then, like everybody else," she laughingly added.

After finishing lunch they attended Roberto's hair salon, to finalise details for the wedding day. Roberto was fussing over Rachel's hair, checking the length and condition, flicking it from side to side while muttering away in Spanish.

"Excellent," he smiles. "We can do," he said in broken English, grinning at Rachel and Margaret both in the mirror. "See you on the 9th at 9 o'clock" he sung out merrily, dressed in his frilly pink shirt and sprayed on black pants, with his slicked back hair, sitting immaculately. Groomed to perfection, Roberto and his team would deliver on the day. Margaret had been utilising his services for the past six months and acknowledged he was nothing less than a perfectionist.

"Okay ladies, thanks for your time and patience. We will catch up again in three weeks for rehearsals," Margaret beamed, giving each one a departing kiss and hug.

"Are you clocked on for work tomorrow?" Daphne enquired thoughtfully, knowing they were inundated of late, due to the recent spate of bombings.

"No, I've taken three days off to be with mum and dad, so I'll catch up with you again on Thursday."

"Okay see you then," Daphne replied, before heading to her car.

"Wow ... what a day," Rachel declared. "I am completely exhausted but truly the dresses are amazing sis, and the shoes and hairstyles are absolutely perfect. It's going to be a spectacular day. I can hardly wait and thank you ... thank you for making me part of it all," she tenderly confided.

Margaret gave her a firm hug, fighting back tears, touched by Rachel's loving sentiments.

When they arrived home, Kath and Mary put the kettle on before sitting down at the kitchen table to drink their tea, waiting patiently in anticipation for all of the day's news. Rachel was allowed to verbalise her findings, describing the dresses to perfection, in her optimistic and enthusiastic manner.

"They sound absolutely divine," Kath announced, peering across at Margaret lovingly.

"You're obviously extremely well organised, got exquisite taste and have carried out your research my love," smiling warmly at her eldest daughter.

"I can't give you any details on Margaret's dress though," Rachel confessed. "It's a total secret to everyone, until the big day," she added with a bewildered expression.

"Good for you," Mary confided. "It will give us something to really look forward to, on yur very special day luv."

"She will look stunning no matter what she wears," Kath interrupted, stretching across and taking her daughter's hand. "I know your wedding day will be spectacular Margaret, because observing you and Paul together would make anyone's heart melt. However, your marriage will be extraordinary and that's what counts at the end of the day."

"Thank you mum," Margaret replied softly, allowing the tender moment to resonate.

The following day, her mother was getting ready to meet Paul's parents for the very first time and she was obviously getting into a fluster, not knowing what was appropriate to wear.

"Jeans, blouse and a pair of loafers will be fine mum," Margaret reiterated for the third time, totally exasperated. "We're simply having some wine and cheese, so a cocktail dress would definitely be over the top … believe you me. It's simply a meet and greet mum, you'll understand when you get there," Margaret added reassuringly.

Kath settled on her Calvin Klein jeans, her Dolce & Gabbana blouse along with her navy loafers. This way at least, if Margaret got it all wrong, she had casual designer gear on and it wouldn't come across quite as bad.

Marcus shouted up the stairs, "come on honey or we'll be late, we certainly don't want to give a bad first impression, now do we?"

Mary laughed at them both, because they were equally in a pickle as one another, neither one of them knowing what to expect, with them both obviously wanting to make a good impression, for Margaret's sake.

They arrived at the entrance, located in a primarily affluent area of Belfast. Marcus and Kath were amazed by the amount of security cameras, positioned at the heavily built, controlled gates, before entering the meticulous grounds. Standing high on the Malone Road, the solidly built, three storied home, retained its Georgian style period features. It depicted grandeur, with its grand wide sweeping steps, leading up to the front entrance. Four huge columns stood on opposite sides of the porch, a mantle stretched across with 'Tonaghneave Manor' embellished upon it, etched out in stone, further adding to its stateliness. Elegant peaked gables and cream coloured architecture highlighted the top arched windows and complemented the bay windows on the lower level. Large concrete pots, supporting well manicured topiary trees, sat positioned on adjacent steps, leading up to the magnificently carved, cedar doors.

Upon arrival, the door was immediately opened by an elderly lady, who welcomed them inside. The entrance hall was enormous, decorated in ancient black and white marbled tiles; a massive sparkling chandelier was suspended from the ornate decorated ceiling, cascading downwards into the hall, in a bejewelled and dignified manner. A sweeping staircase carved intricately from dark polished oak, was guarded at the base by a suit of armour, standing upright proudly bearing a coat of arms, suitably positioned and blending in well with the stately mansion.

Marcus and Kath heard Paul and Margaret coming up the steps behind them, when a door on their left sprung open, sending a beam of warm orange light leaking into the hallway.

"I assume you're Margaret's parents?" a friendly, blue eyed, middle aged lady addressed them pleasantly.

Paul came up quickly from the rear. "Sorry mum, I would like to introduce you to Kath and Marcus Garofoli, Margaret's parents."

"Please to meet you," Helen beamed, kissing them both lightly on the cheeks, her eyes lighting up, portraying a gentle soul. "I've heard so many kind things about you both, from our Paul," she smiled compassionately. "I simply cannot thank you enough, for taking good care of him when he was in Australia last year," she confided benevolently.

"It was our pleasure Helen," Kath replied, returning her smile.

"Unfortunately, my husband Henry is currently on the phone with the Home Office at present, apparently he shouldn't be too much longer. I do apologise on his behalf. Now if you would like to follow me into the drawing room, there's a beautiful fire crackling in the hearth and I'll get Francis to bring us some wine and a few snacks."

"Thank you," Marcus answered "an open fire is one of the things I miss the most in Australia."

"I guess there's not much need for it over there, when it reaches forty degrees," Helen laughed lightly, leading them into the drawing room.

The large welcoming fire was enclosed with a huge marble surround; a solid teak mantelpiece showcased the gold, antique, carriage clock, perched on top, positioned in the middle of the fireplace. Two elegant Royal Doulton figurines sat on either side, adding to the serenity of the room. A large, well worn dark leather couch sat directly in front of the fire, adorned with deep red and mustard cushions. The unique Oriental rug in warm rich hues, blended in well, with the thick wool beige carpet. Large dominant brass fire irons were positioned to the left of the fireplace, resting upon the marble base, mirroring the flames burning away magnificently, radiating a glorious heat.

Several chintz lampshades, supported by sturdy brass stands, glowed on top of the ancient sideboard and ornate side tables, positioned near the two comfortable, high winged chairs. Once they were seated, Marcus and Kath both relaxed immediately, experiencing the warmth saturating the homely environment.

"I thought an Australian wine would be appropriate," Helen smiled. "Brown Brothers, red or white?" Helen offered, within the tranquil setting.

"White please," both Marcus and Kath answered in unison, causing everyone to laugh.

"I'll fetch it mum," Paul insisted immediately, before leaving the room.

"You've got a wonderful daughter," Helen confided, immediately glancing across at Margaret with pride.

"We can easily say the same in relation to your Paul. We enjoyed his company immensely, when he was staying with us last year," Kath replied politely.

The door reopened and Paul pranced in with a bottle of white wine, as Francis followed behind with a tray of glasses and some finger food. Paul was busy pouring the drinks out, when his father arrived.

Marcus automatically jumped to his feet, introduced himself and shook his hand, before introducing Kath.

"At last we meet," Henry smiled. "I see you've produced a damn good sailor within your family," glancing directly at Margaret. "So which one does she take after?"

"Marcus my husband," Kath replied. "I'm simply the galley kitchen cook."

"Same here," Helen interrupted, laughing gaily.

The night flew by for Kath and Marcus. It was an extremely relaxed evening and they felt very much at home, with Paul's parents. They both were so accommodating and exceptionally down to earth people. The parents discussed and shared their sailing expeditions and spoke about how they were enamoured by their respective future son and daughter-in-law. Discussions were held in relation to the up-and-coming wedding and it was well after midnight before Marcus and Kath left.

On their way home they were glad it turned out to be such a successful evening and Margaret had been perfectly correct, knowing it would go off without a hitch. Both Helen and Henry were wonderful individuals, who made them feel perfectly at home and a great evening was enjoyed by all.

During the coming weeks, Kath and Marcus spent quite a few days with Paul's parents and on one such occasion they went sailing with them on their yacht. In the meantime, both Mary and Joe had a delightful time spoiling Rachel and before they knew it, the rehearsals for the wedding had come around.

It all went exceptionally well, without any major dilemmas taking place. A celebrant was being used on the day, as the wedding was being held at Tonaghneave Manor. An enormous marquee was required, to seat the invited two hundred guests. This was being erected in the enclosed formal and rear garden, laid out on manicured lawns, which encompassed a large mosaic terrace. A solid timber platform was being especially built to create a dance floor for the wedding guests. Lighting technicians, photographers, caterers organising food deliveries and all the other usual wedding personnel were coming together, for the grand event. Waiters and waitresses were being hired for the occasion, also arranged by Helen. Kath was appreciative of Helen's generosity, having undertaken the enormous co-ordinating role, immediately relieving the young couple of any unnecessary stress, before their wedding day.

Margaret explained to her mother and father, that Helen was simply following the young couple's desires and instruction, highlighting it was both Paul's and her idea to have a celebrant. They didn't want to hurt anyone's feelings, as they had friends from many different cultures and denominations and wanted the occasion to be a happy carefree experience, with no one feeling awkward or out of place.

Neither Paul nor Margaret was involved in the internal politics or religious bickering, taking place in the North. They much preferred to practice a spiritual path, made up of love and understanding. Both were constantly trying their best to refrain from judging and condemning, by reacting compassionately and adapting the method of treating every human being, exactly the same. God knows, the pair of them had seen more than their fair share of horrendous injuries, incurred on both sides of the religious spectrum and treated all their patients with the same loving respect.

Both sets of parents were filled with admiration for the young couple's intellectual viewpoint, aware it wouldn't suit or be deemed as appropriate by everybody but chose to respect and work in partnership with the young couple's ideology and plans.

The following morning, Valerie and her family along with Brigee, were arriving in Belfast. Kath suggested to Margaret and Paul to go to the airport alone, to pick them up. Allowing them precious time together to express their feelings, something Margaret had been hoping for, since receiving the news about Valerie's health. Paul was very much looking forward to the occasion, as he was exceptionally fond of Valerie and could now give her a massive big hug, welcoming her to Ireland. They stood waiting at the airport, waiting for touchdown, both holding hands, totally unaware another surprise was in store for them.

The jet arrived at 1pm; the Noblealert logo emblazoned upon the jet's tail was gleaming in the autumn sunlight, as it slowly doubled back and taxied towards the terminal. Margaret could hardly contain herself; her emotions getting the better of her, as her eyes welled up standing there, waiting for Valerie to appear. They were pleased and relieved she got to make it this far, both conscious it was only through sheer determination; she got to attend their wedding, making it a double celebration from the young couple's perspective. The terminal doors slid open, both Margaret and Paul searched frantically for Valerie and her family, amongst the higgledy-piggledy crowd exiting at the same time. Tears flowed immediately as Margaret spotted her, before calling out her name.

Valerie had lost so much weight, although she disguised it rather well with a huge chunky sweater and jeans but her face was extremely thin, although beautifully made over. She wore a gorgeous brightly coloured turban on her head, appearing trendy and chic, it would have been thought of as an attractive accessory by many and not a necessity, due to the chemo. Margaret ran forward swiftly, greeting her anxiously. The couple instantly latched on to one another, hugging furiously, spilling tears of joy, jubilant they were given this opportunity to meet again, to celebrate Margaret's wedding.

"I'm so glad you could make it," Margaret sobbed openly, as Valerie hugged her even tighter.

"I told you from the very start; I'll be at your wedding, didn't I," Valerie beamed, as strong and resilient as ever.

Paul greeted Matt and Richard, before moving on to Valerie. "You had us worried for a while Valerie but thankfully Kath kept us well posted. Mind you, I had one hell of a job holding this one back over here," he smiled, peering across at Margaret, giving Valerie another massive bear hug.

"Now that's enough talk of this silly old nonsense. I'm here, I'm fit, I'm well and we're going to have a fantastic time," Valerie announced strongly. "So I think it's fitting to spring the surprise on them now," she announced, nodding across at Richard, who disappeared behind the doors again.

"Oh my god, I had forgotten about dear old Brigee in all the excitement," Margaret gushed, as she came out hand-in-hand with young Richard, now fifteen years old and appearing very handsome.

However from behind them, two familiar figures also strolled out, with smiles as big as Cheshire cats. It was Peter and Jan, Paul's good friends from the Royal North Shore Hospital, while he was working and holidaying in Australia.

Brigee then came rushing over to Margaret displaying loads of affection, before moving to Paul. Peter and Jan then hugged and kissed the young soon-to-be married couple, most grateful that Marcus and Kath had made it possible for them to attend their friends' wedding.

They were driven to Downpatrick to meet Kath and the remainder of the family. On the way over, everyone made comments about the spectacular scenery and the lush green fields.

"The Aussies would give their right arm to have rainfall to produce this amount of greenery, which would sure help feed their sheep," Peter commented, thinking about the many years of endless droughts, the cattle and sheep farmers had to tolerate back home.

"I notice they have many cute little villages which we've been passing through so quickly," Jan commented, happily from the back seat. "Yet at home, on the way up to Paul's homestead, you can drive for hours on end for hundreds of miles and not see a single soul or town."

They were equally amazed and intrigued by the huge hedgerows, merging on either side of the winding curvy lane, on the way up to Joe's and Mary's. "It's absolutely stunning," Brigee sighed, thinking about her ancestors leaving such a beautiful place behind, many generations ago.

The usual commotion took place, when they arrived in the back yard. Patch the collie barked loudly, wagging his tail and greeting everyone happily, while introductions were taking place. More hugs and kisses were enthusiastically exchanged, with everyone obviously delighted to be reuniting, once again. Mary had the table set up with sandwiches, cakes and pastries galore.

"You've cooked up a real storm here Mary," Margaret laughed joyously, touched by the trouble she had gone to, to make everyone who was arriving feel welcome.

"Well that's not completely true," Mary answered. "I've had a fine little helper, who's turning out to be an excellent wee cook," putting her arm lovingly over Rachel's shoulder and smiling proudly.

"Wait until you taste the currant squares," Rachel piped up. "I helped make the filling, "she beamed.

"That's my girl," Marcus laughed.

And so did everyone else when Kath announced, in a thick Irish brogue "he needs those like a hole in the head," Afterwards, everyone was taken back to the Europa Hotel where they decided to stay, making it much easier for travel arrangements, when it came to the wedding day. Marcus and Kath kept everyone entertained, having arranged visits to main tourist destinations, while Margaret and Paul got ready for their wedding, which was almost upon them. Mary and Joe joined in with the entertainment of the overseas visitors, both in their element, enjoying everyone's company enormously.

Their Australian accents drew attention wherever they went, especially by the curators at the Ulster Folk and Transport Museum. They took great pride in explaining ancient artefacts with significant historical importance, to the Australian visitors passing through. Happily everyone meandered along, discovering the volunteered information extremely interesting and educational, with them later agreeing they all found the Northern Irish accent adorable.

The day finally arrived, the day everyone had great expectations of. It was a special and momentous occasion, when a young couple would unite in holy matrimony. Both were promising to share their lives together, forever. It was a beautiful autumn morning and at midday, the guests began to arrive at the Hagan's home.

The massive wrought iron gates were decorated with garlands of cream roses, with fine threads of dusty pink satin, woven throughout. The guests were escorted to the front garden, positioned on the right hand side of the stately home. Two large platforms had been installed, which provided seating for over two hundred guests. These were divided by a luxurious red carpet, leading to an open gazebo, decorated in ribbons and flowers. The red carpet stretched up to the front entrance of the massive, Georgian style home, regally trailing up the steps. Large pots of cream standard roses were positioned on either side, decorated with dusty pink satin ribbons, attached half way down their trunks.

Behind the gazebo, the seating was arranged in a fashionable curve. Neatly dressed in dark blue uniforms, an orchestra was seated playing the music of Beethoven beautifully. This was Valerie and Matt's favourite composer, both having listened to many of his symphonies at the Sydney Opera House. Symphony No.3 titled 'Eroica' was being played and instantly, Valerie gripped Matt's hand, automatically tearing up under her wide brimmed hat. Straight away, she recognised the musical piece, while Matt nodded in response. It was a piece well renowned for depicting heroism and courage of the human spirit, both coming to the realisation what Margaret had meant yesterday, when she told them to pay particular attention to the music being played. They smiled knowingly, appreciating the subtle loving gesture, made by Margaret and Paul.

Brigee sat close by, dressed in a pale mint green suit appearing glamorous, while chatting to young Jan and Peter, when her eyes were drawn to the gazebo. She was admiring the roses and ribbons, before she gasped in surprise. There at the foot of the gazebo were hundreds of little snowdrops, tucked away in small pots, planted in the ground. She smiled proudly, her eyes glazing over as she told Jan how they were her favourite flowers; divulging how Margaret told her the day before, to look out for a pleasant surprise. Margaret and Paul arranged for the flowers to be grown in a greenhouse, allowing them to make a small gesture of love, inciting a tender moment for Brigee on their wedding day, contributing more beautiful memories to their special occasion.

The guests were fast arriving and getting settled in by the ushers, dressed in dark tails with dusty pink coloured cravats, with matching cream roses pinned to their jacket lapels. One uninvited guest sat quietly, observing everyone on Margaret's wedding day. Dressed to blend in with everybody, making minimum conversation, his eyes was forever scanning the area, searching for any dangerous and suspicious characters.

It was a huge publicised event; Paul after all was the son of a well respected high court judge. It was an ideal venue for either side of the terrorist groups, to grab the headlines. Sabotaging a momentous family occasion and turning it into a horrendous blood bath.

Looking around, the uninvited guest recognised there were ample opportunities for explosive devices to be set. He had already run criminal checks on the caterers, electricians and many of the others involved, who were instrumental in bringing the wedding together. A chill crept down his spine, imagining the chaos and human lives being lost, by a bomb being detonated in a densely populated area, such as this.

Kath and Helen were both inside, helping the bridal party since early morning. The hairdressers had been and as Margaret predicted, they carried out a professional and glamorous job, by arranging the hair up for the bridesmaids and Rachel. The romantic double braids were woven with fine dusty pink ribbons, secured discreetly with bobby pins, the ribbons matched perfectly with the elegant dresses, to be worn later.

The make-up artist had left the ladies appearing sensational, their faces visibly angelic in the tastefully applied, natural looking colours.

Before they dressed, Margaret presented each with a small velvet box, a gift for carrying out their roles on her wedding day. Opening their gifts together, they sighed with surprise, discovering pearl and diamond earrings displayed inside, to tie in with their elegantly designed dresses. All agreeing at once they were utterly spoilt, divulging their gifts would be treasured forever, before putting them on for the special event. Dressed and ready to go, the five girls appeared regal; personifying what was to follow, as they stood gazing in the tall mirror, amazed with the overall effect.

The two mothers then left and got changed, before making their way outside to take their respective seats. The orchestra continued playing gracefully, keeping the guests occupied, as Paul and the best man took their places.

Paul spent the night at the Europa Hotel, along with family members and others, excluding Margaret off course, who was a guest at the Hagan's household for the evening.

Meanwhile upstairs, the girls finally got to see Margaret's dress and were instantly overwhelmed by the intricate tailoring and beading, all chattering excitedly, exclaiming how spectacular it was, before helping her into it. Shortly afterwards, a quick knock upon the door alerted them. It was almost time for the ceremony, as Marcus entered the room. For one single, solitary moment, he stood perfectly still; amazed beyond words on how beautiful his young daughter appeared, a replica of her mother from over twenty years ago.

Marcus briskly walked over to her smiling. "These are for you Margaret; your mother said you should keep up some traditions." He handed over Kath's blue garter, instantly evoking great chuckles of delight from the young female wedding group standing close by and a smile from Margaret, who promptly put it on.

The young group left and Marcus reached into his coat pocket, retrieving a flat velvet box and two small velvet bags. He quickly poured out on to his hand a spectacular pair of diamond earrings. "And these are on loan from Valerie," he grinned, giving them to her. "While Brigee wants you to have this old antique bracelet to keep, as it was an heirloom kept within her family for years," he smiled, fastening the clip. "Finally, we had to think of something new which would be appropriate," Marcus beamed.

"I've got my dress dad, that's pretty new," Margaret replied automatically.

"We thought this might go with it extremely well," he beamed, showcasing a magnificent, fine pink, diamond necklace. "This is from both sets of parents for your special day."

Margaret was completely overwhelmed by the thoughtfulness of the extravagant gifts and began to cry immediately. Her father then gathered her in his arms, holding her momentarily.

"They're special gifts for a special young lady, who has done us all proud," he said, smiling down at her.

"Thanks dad," she replied emotionally. "I feel I'm the luckiest girl in the world right now and with you coming into my life, it has made my wedding day even more special," smiling serenely up at him, before he fastened the necklace around her neck.

Margaret then went to put the diamond earrings on. "I've got the most loving and caring family and friends that anyone could ever wish for," she said.

Marcus proudly smiled down at her. "I think it's time to go my love, you have a special young man waiting downstairs for you to spend the rest of your life with and your mother and I couldn't be happier."

The girls followed Margaret down the stairs, adjusting her train from behind, as she latched on to her father's arm. Taking a deep breath, everyone lined up; the ushers opened the front door wide, as the orchestra began playing the traditional wedding march.

All the guests immediately stilled their chatter and stood up respectfully, before turning around to view the young bride, descending the steps with her father. Everyone let out a gasp of disbelief, overwhelmed by the spectacular bride slowly approaching them. Paul turned around at this stage and was clearly overcome with emotion, tearing up along with Kath, Helen, Brigee and Valerie, as his wife-to-be, proudly walked towards him.

Chapter Twenty Seven

Margaret carefully edged her way down the steps, glowing in a spectacularly styled wedding dress. The bodice was intricately embroidered, blending in perfectly with the dramatic crystallised beading; with the overall shape and design of the outfit accentuating her petite figure, in the gorgeous strapless dress. The full ball gown skirt, revealed a soft romantic garment, tailored to perfection. Tulle shaped gum leaves were sewn into many delicate and intricate layers, gently cascading downward, sweeping softly to the ground. The whole effect was incredible and awe inspiring, making her appear as if she was floating, when strolling down the red carpet with her father.

"It's a wearable piece of art," Valerie whispered to Brigee, smiling graciously. Meanwhile, Kath stood mesmerised, watching her young daughter exude beauty and a luminous sensuality.

Margaret wore her hair up in a chic French twist, radiating sophistication and elegance. She carried an exquisite trail bouquet, made up of baby's breath and delicate cream vintage roses, their fragile petals tipped with a subtle dusty pink, adding to Margaret's soft, romantic and alluring presence. The ivory chapel length train, trailed along the red carpet, embellished with fine intricate beading garnishing its edges, adding to the glamorous effect.

Paul stood mesmerised beyond words, knowing he would remember this day, this very moment, for many decades to come. The bridesmaids and groomsmen followed behind Rachel and the best man, the ladies dressed in their dusty pink taffeta gowns, clutching their cream rose posies with engaging appeal, as they made their way elegantly down to the gazebo.

The exchange was made and Paul stood beside Margaret, glancing sideways on a frequent basis, overwhelmed by her sheer beauty.

The celebrant took his rightful place and conducted the wedding service, gracefully. Vows were exchanged, pledging to love, honour and encourage one another in their individual endeavours. Not a dry eye remained, when the bride and groom kissed tenderly. Everyone broke into a rapturous applause, appreciating the wonderful union of a truly beautiful couple.

A soloist sang Ave Maria while the registry was being signed and witnessed in the gazebo, as the uninvited guest breathed a sigh of relief when the wedding ceremony was completed.

Soon, people were rising and dispersing to different parts of the garden, sipping champagne and eating little hors-d'oeuvres.

The marquee would make an ideal target for terrorists to strike, he strategically thought, lighting up a cigarette before deciding to do a last minute check on the surroundings. The caterers had multiple gas cylinders sitting outside, guaranteed to exacerbate the effects of a fire-producing device, positioned for maximum damage. Thank god it was all clear, allowing the stranger to breathe a little easier, before voices began mingling close by. He quickly left the immediate vicinity, determined to check the grounds once again, discreetly.

He paused for a moment, as family photos were being taken, when Kath caught his attention. She was appearing as beautiful and radiant as ever. Her smile was infectious as she stood with her husband and eldest daughter, completely in her element, a picture of true happiness. He was pleased she had found joy again. Her parents were present too, obviously everyone having made their peace. Her young years were ripped away from her, with bloodshed and death.

He recalled Kath lying in his arms at Bondi Beach, young, pregnant and frightened. He smiled inwardly, surprised at how attracted and drawn he had been to her, back then. She was vulnerable, yet portrayed a tough exterior, to protect herself and her immediate family.

Jack Gillespie was pleased and relieved; everything was going as planned for Kath and her family today. He owed her much, a woman who had purposely saved multiple lives, by preventing a bomb being detonated in Belfast City Hall, as well as saving her own family. Finbar was finally brought to justice by a woman he admired greatly and one he secretly loved.

A sharp tap on his shoulder made him instantly jump. "Sorry, I didn't mean to startle you," a middle aged lady smiled. "They're all heading inside the marquee now and you seemed a little lost."

Jack put on a huge smile, lighting up his handsome rugged face immediately. "Thank you," he replied, briskly making his way to the marquee, determined not to draw anymore unnecessary attention to himself.

Fragrant rose garlands were draped beautifully, creating spectacular romantic pathways, leading to the marquee. Fairy lights and tiny lanterns were strategically positioned, wrapped around poles and nearby trees, enhancing the dance floor area to be used later on when darkness fell. Formal waiters and waitresses were busily tending to the guests, serving hors-d'oeuvres and glasses of French champagne, with everyone mixing and chatting happily.

Meanwhile out front, the photographer was capturing some beautiful moments on camera, of the happily married bride and groom, along with many photos of the bridal party and immediate family.

The marquee entrance had the traditional wedding bridal arch, decorated with vintage roses that perfectly matched Margaret's bridal bouquet. Inside, the silk roof lining fell in soft folds, which was attached above the clear arched windows, creating a serene romantic atmosphere. White Tiffany chairs embellished with a satin ribbon, rested upon the polished wooden floors, enhancing the beautifully decorated tables of gleaming crystal, shiny cutlery and crisp white linen tablecloths and napkins. Crystal chandeliers were suspended carefully from the false ceiling, together with white paper lanterns and balloons. And finally, tall crystal vases of dusty pink roses added a sense of indulgent opulence to the overall effect.

Hours later, after a six course perfectly prepared wedding luncheon, the speeches were made in a relaxed and happy demeanour. Paul stood up, peering down upon his stunning bride, confessed his never dying love for Margaret, reminiscent of the day they met; he spoke about chasing her halfway around the world and his enjoyable Australian experience. Paul also confided that he considered himself extremely blessed, in finding such a gorgeous and wonderful wife.

He thanked his parents for their love, respect and guidance, before thanking his respective mother and father-in-law, for creating a truly astonishing human being.

After the speeches were finished, the wedding cake was discreetly brought forward, to be cut by the young newlyweds. The traditional wedding cake was tiered into five layers, decorated with cream roses and dusty pink silk ribbons, encapsulating their special day. Camera flashbulbs lit up the whole marquee, as the young couple cut the cake, smiling copiously, while soaking up the wonderful loving atmosphere. Everyone enjoyed the whole spectacular experience, along with their family and friends.

Night soon fell and the music began to play. It was time for the bridal waltz. Paul eagerly took Margaret's hand, proudly leading her out of the marquee and on to the dance floor. The area was stunning, surrounded by thousands of magical fairy lights, draped beautifully over nearby trees. Romantically lit lanterns, swayed in the light evening breeze, as delicate fragrant roses punctuated the air with a sweet aroma. Margaret's dressed glittered, as she was gliding across the dance floor, elegantly with Paul, both appearing as one and very much in love.

They were joined shortly afterwards by both sets of parents, along with the bridal party, enhancing the glamorous and stylish setting. Guests began to join in, filling the evening air with laughter and joy, as everyone celebrated the young couple's marriage.

Positioned later at the end of the dance floor, eager and single ladies waited until Margaret participated in the wedding bouquet ritual; it was caught by one of Paul's cousins.

The young pair rushed off to get changed in the house, before heading off to their honeymoon suite, chosen by Paul. Margaret looked stunning in a pale lavender suit. The style was of the late forties, a knee length pencil skirt highlighted her slim long legs. The design also accentuated her perfectly formed body and was accessorised with a purple Hermes suede handbag and matching shoes. Paul had a similar coloured shirt on, blending with his light grey suit.

Whilst having a cigarette out near the front gates, Jack was relieved the day was almost over. All was well, having cased the place, twice. People were relaxed and a happy ambience was evident throughout the day. Drawing down on his cigarette, he noticed the music had stopped, thankful it had gone off without any cruelty or vengeance.

Then suddenly a huge and loud explosion took place, his heart plummeted as he turned around, running immediately towards the dance floor. His heart was thudding rapidly within his chest, as a large crackling noise followed and a bright light lit up the entire sky. He stopped instantly in his tracks, busting out into nervous laughter. You silly asshole Jack Gillespie, you're really losing the plot; he chastised himself, laughing some more, peering up at the humongous fireworks display, bursting across the dark velvety sky. All the guests coming into view were smiling, standing peering upwards in awe and wonderment, at the magical menagerie of sparkling colours, drifting gently down to earth.

A white limousine arrived to take the young couple away; the farewells took place rapidly, with well wishers having celebrated an exceptionally enjoyable day, cheering them as they made their grand exit.

"Let us know when you reach Australia," Kath called out happily before the limousine left with cans rattling noisily behind, displaying the 'Just Married' sign, stuck boldly on the back.

At 1.30am Jack slipped away, undetected. Relieved no reprisals had taken place and that Kath was experiencing happiness in her life, as she sure as hell deserved it.

"Did you enjoy your day Mrs Hagan?" Paul announced, breaking into the silence, as he poured two glasses of champagne.

"I most certainly did," Margaret replied smiling, peering across at her husband tenderly.

The limousine drove them to the Culloden Estate and Spa for the evening, allowing easy access to the airport the following day, to make their trip to Australia. After tipping the concierge, Paul carried Margaret over the threshold of their Palace Suite, quietly closing the door behind him.

The hotel was positioned in amongst twelve acres of beautifully manicured gardens, while their room overlooked Belfast Lough and the exquisite woodlands. The honeymoon suite was a romantic hide-a-way, palatial surroundings with candles already lit and flickering, adding to the ambience of the astonishingly elegant décor. Champagne was on ice, sitting next to the huge king size bed, draped in a luxurious faux fur cover.

Margaret loved the softness of it against her skin, as Paul began his unhurried, tantalising seduction. Peeling away her clothes and skimming his hands gently over her body, she bit her bottom lip, as he discarded her creamy lace camisole and briefs. He gently trailed his lips along her jaw line, drifting ever so slowly, down along her throat, stopping at her breasts. She melted, trembling in anticipation as he kissed her sweetly and seductively, escalating her passion and desire. Their kissing was building and intensifying, savouring one another ardently, arms wantonly wrapping around each other in passionate embraces, as molten skin came crashing together, flowing with lust. Driving her to unimaginable feverish heights, her fingers curled around his hands, as he finally gave in, smothering her body with his before he took her completely. Wrapping her arms around him tightly, she drew him down, her body smouldering with passion, every single nerve tingling as she cried out helplessly. Biting down hard on his shoulder, they swayed and bucked and rode in unison, their bodies rising upwards, surging forward and shuddering, reaching an unstoppable, earth shattering crescendo.

Holding one another in an amorous embrace with their hearts overflowing with love, they gradually drifted downwards, a mellowness enrapturing their minds, bodies and souls.

"Paul … I love you," Margaret barely whispered, filled with raw emotion, as tender tears fell upon her pillow.

Kissing her gently upon the eyelids, Paul smiled "and I love you Mrs Hagan," he whispered sexily. He stretched up, pulling her softly into his arms and caressed her.

"This whole day feels like a dream, a beautiful dream," Margaret sighed happily.

"And it's just the beginning," Paul confided tenderly, kissing her softly on top of her head, before drifting soundly to sleep and merging as one.

The following morning, the company jet flew the young couple out to Australia, allowing them two days to rest at Gladesville, before catching their cruise to circumnavigate New Zealand. A destination chosen by them both, as neither had visited before. Both looking forward to some downtime together, having spent many hectic hours in theatres and emergency wards, back at the Royal Victoria Hospital.

"Hello mum, I'm giving you a quick call to let you know all is well. We arrived safely this morning."

"Thanks for the call love; I'll inform your father. I think he requires one of his chief editors in London soon, so he can travel across when the jet makes its way back to collect us," Kath commented quickly.

"It's strange being at home, with the house being practically empty," Margaret said, as Paul sneaked up behind her.

"Enjoy the tranquillity my love, the cruise will be full on," Kath stated matter-of-factly, as Paul tantalisingly ran his hand down Margaret's spine, causing her to shudder in delight.

Margaret interrupted, "mum, I got to go. Heather's just arrived."

It was a fib, because Heather had already been and gone but Paul was driving her crazy, making it difficult to keep a steady conversation going.

"Okay sweetheart, enjoy your honeymoon and send Paul our love," Kath relayed, as Margaret quickly hung up.

"Paul Hagan, if my mother could see what you were up to, when she was speaking, she sure as hell would be blushing," she laughed gaily.

Immediately sweeping her off her feet with half of her bikini removed, Paul rapidly carried her out to the pool kicking and screaming, before throwing Margaret in.

"You're mad," she spluttered, coming up for air and was instantly smothered in kisses.

They made love again; languishing around on their honeymoon was immensely enjoyable, he noted, for both him and his sexy new wife. They were extremely relaxed, both looking forward to their cruise the following day.

Chapter Twenty Eight

After three days at sea, both were slowly unwinding, very much appreciating the tranquil atmosphere. Between the hectic organising of their wedding and their heavy work schedules, had greatly taken its toll on them both.

The cruise ship edged its way slowly along the Milford Sound in Fiordland National Park. Along New Zealand's rugged coastline, spectacular lakes and fiords were created, gouged out by glaciers, millions of years ago. Jagged steep mountain tops were blanketed in virgin white snow and the mist added an eerie mysterious veil, drifting midway below. The early morning air was cold and fresh, as other passengers made their way up deck, to view the impressive landscape. The mossy green, sloping escarpments were lined with rich hues of bottle green conifers, clinging to steep craggy faces of hard rock. A portion of barren wasteland could be seen, scarred and scraped away by a tree avalanche, lying almost vacant, pale yellow in colour, with broken twisted timber scattered, throughout the battered terrain.

"The water is so still, almost like a huge pond," Margaret whispered, breaking into the early morning silence, while both stood absorbing the tranquil and impressive surrounds.

Rugged up in jeans and jumpers, they made their way along the timber deck to various vantage points, taking photographs, to be added to their current album collection later.

"Happy?" Paul questioned, squeezing her hand.

"Very," Margaret replied, in total awe of nature's glory unfolding before them, as the cruise liner edged its way stealthily up the fiord.

Steep impressive waterfalls, gushed from sheer-sided mountains. Higher up, alpine daisies and snow tussocks were dominating the precipitous terrain, mixed in with buttercups which created a European feel.

Great white clouds began to form in the crystal clear blue sky, as a small flock of blue ducks flew overhead. Avid bird watchers up on deck recognised their speckled chestnut breasts and their unique bluish-slate grey colouring, as waiters poured hot coffee's for passengers, viewing the magnificent scenery.

Paul and Margaret decided to head inside to have breakfast and were greeted by warm welcoming staff, before finding a suitable seat near a window. Ravenous, Margaret scurried along the food aisle, the smell of warm bacon and eggs permeated the air, as she filled her plate from the delicious buffet.

"I was so ready for that," Paul declared, patting his stomach after devouring his hearty breakfast, washing it down quickly with a hot mug of coffee.

"So was I," Margaret announced, completely relaxed and sated. "We can have a lazy day today, I've booked a tour for Dunedin tomorrow," she informed Paul, smiling.

The remainder of the day was spent in the outdoor spa, soothing their tired muscles, after working out in the gym. They ate a light lunch and got dressed later on for the formal dinner, hosted at the Captain's table this evening.

Margaret decided to wear her black velvet gown, accentuating her dark auburn tresses and her vivid green eyes. Paul was dressed in his formal attire and appeared sophisticated, his dark chocolate brown eyes melted with love immediately after sighting Margaret, before leaving their stateroom.

"Come here," he appealed quietly, wrapping her up in his arms and kissing her passionately. "Do we r-e-a-l-l-y have to attend this evening's dinner?" he enquired, gently between kisses.

"Yes we do," Margaret laughed, knowing full well what he had in mind.

"But it's our honeymoon," Paul replied jokingly "and I'm sure the Captain would completely understand," he announced.

"I'm sure he would," Margaret smiled. "However, we can't have the rest of the passengers talking about us. God knows, at this rate, we'll end up with cabin fever," she chuckled.

"O-k-a-y you win," Paul reluctantly gave in, grabbing her hand and heading towards the door, to make their way to the dining room.

The Sea Goddess was a magnificent ship. The dining room ceiling was carved out of various timbers; tiny lights were sprinkled throughout the ceiling in tiny clusters, providing a soft glow and romantic atmosphere.

White linen tablecloths were laid out with solid silver cutlery and sparkling crystal glasses that added a certain amount of opulence, accompanying the finely dressed waiters serving everyone, with an air of decorum.

Champagne was put on ice and everyone became acquainted with their fellow guests, making light conversations before their entrees. Seafood terrine was served, along with a dainty salad and Melba toast, as Captain Sergeti explained the ship's capacity and the journey ahead. The lobster was scrumptious, served with a delectable exotic sauce, accompanying fresh vegetables and potato croquettes. Dessert was a spectacular culinary delight, with everyone indulging, while sipping upon their French champagne.

Later in the evening, they made their way down to the Queens Theatre to watch the final show. The theatre was already three quarters full, when Paul and Margaret entered. The dark red velvet seats and the intricately carved walls, added a Victorian charm. The patrons fell silent, as the lights dimmed and the curtains rose. Revealing a stage filled with brightly coloured dancers, performing a waltz with their elegantly dressed partners, as the lead singer began singing an old melody from the late 1940s. The cabaret show was a graceful performance, an entertaining affair enjoyed immensely by Margaret. Paul on the other hand, sat idly, playing with the nape of her neck, dying to get her back to their cabin.

After the show, Paul rushed out along the endless passageways, back towards their stateroom as quickly as humanly possible. Laughing loudly, as she was being dragged along, Margaret found the scenario absolutely hilarious. Entering their suite, he instantly smothered her in hot passionate kisses, quickly undoing the zipper on her dress.

Margaret giggled. "My god Paul you're horny tonight, anyone would think you've been practicing celibacy for the past six months."

"It's your entire fault," he murmured, covering her neck in adorable little kisses.

"How come?" Margaret questioned.

"Because you're so damn irresistible and you turn me on," he responded smiling.

Soon he was above her and taking charge. Pinning her down, he moved to the lower half of her body, allowing her to move in rhythm, until she could hold back no longer. Rising upwards, she cried out softly, deeply emotional, before dropping back down upon her pillow. Gently working his way upwards, he was taking great pleasure in arousing her, making her hot, raunchy and ready for him. Kissing her passionately, awakening all of her senses at once, he tenderly took her. He was encompassing her whole being with his maturity, moving sensually and softly, his hips gyrating deliberately in slow motion. Enticingly, he built up the momentum, lovingly drawing her in, encouraging her to surrender completely. He was nibbling on her ear, exploring and probing, acknowledging her sensations were intensifying. Internally her tremors were building, coming harder and faster, making her rise higher and higher, until no one or nothing could stop her.

Lost in an emotional whirlwind, her whole body began shuddering, escalating into mind blowing peaks, causing her to tremble and explode into a million little pieces. Overwhelmed, she pushed forcibly into him, drenched in undeniable desire, as she continued kissing her masterful lover, murmuring and groaning, encouraging him not to stop.

Following her signal he continued, as she was panting and writhing and heaving beneath him until he too, overwhelmed with sheer passion, could no longer hold back. With a rasping cry, he unleashed his passion, coming strongly and passionately, allowing his emotions to cut loose. Purring softly, he pulled her into him more, consumed with immense desire and love, as his plateau gradually descended.

"God Margaret I love you," he whispered hoarsely, emotionally spent. "You drive me absolutely crazy," he whispered, smiling sweetly down at her, his eyes glazed over with love.

"Paul," she sighed peacefully "when you make love to me, you drive me so swiftly beyond my limitations," she murmured gently.

Both automatically rolling on to their sides and facing each other, wrapped up in each other's arms as they kissed, both completely relaxed and blissful.

Later on they stood outside on their balcony, cuddled up in a huge blanket together, both exceptionally happy.

"The sky is beautiful this evening," Margaret softly confided, peering up at the twinkling stars buried in the dark velvety sky.

"It most certainly is," Paul agreed, passing Margaret a glass of champagne. Life was good Paul thought, standing overlooking the horizon, with Margaret wrapped up in his arms.

The ship sailed further north, leaving a huge frothy wake far behind in the distance. He lit up a cigarette, silently sharing it with Margaret before heading back inside. Lying in bed, they began drifting into a warm and welcoming sleep. Both were enjoying their honeymoon and were very much in love.

Dunedin was a quaint city with one of the steepest streets in the world but together, the pair of them managed to conquer it. They also visited the local museum, as well as the Dunedin Botanic Gardens, both mesmerised by the architectural grandeur, depicted in Dunedin's Railway Station.

They had lunch together, before joining the tour to Taiaroa Head. A small boat took the tourists out along the Otago Harbour, up past Port Chalmers and along the peninsula, to view the wild life in their natural habitats.

"Over there quick!" Margaret squealed in delight, allowing Paul to capture the little fur seals on camera. They were so small and fragile in appearance, sitting on the rocks alongside their mothers, baking in the afternoon sun. Their huge moon shaped eyes watched, as the boat drew closer, all squeezing closer to their mothers for protection and from the prying eyes of the curious tourists.

Up high on top of the steep cliffs, white capped albatrosses could be seen, perched on their nests protecting their young chicks. Their snowy white feathery bodies were humongous, in comparison to the red billed gulls, flying high above.

Drifting further around the peninsula they came upon little blue penguins, perched and nestled into the craggy basalt rocks. Hundreds of them were gathered like little dinner waiters, with their white crested chests, tiny in stature, busily preening themselves.

Heading back to the mainland, royal spoonbills and pied oystercatchers flew overhead in flocks, oblivious to the spectators on deck, peering through their binoculars from far below.

Cups of coffee and biscuits were distributed and it was warmly welcomed by the group, all ravenous from the salty sea air. Everyone tucked in hungrily, wholeheartedly sharing their adventures with one another. They were totally in awe with their journey, overwhelmed with the immense natural beauty surrounding them. Everybody was duly touched, after experiencing the marine mammals within their natural environment.

Paul and Margaret had dined casually that evening, retiring to bed early; both looking forward to their adventure tomorrow.

After finishing their Eggs Benedict, Margaret and Paul went to collect their tickets for the coach tour. It was a bright sunny morning as they clambered on board the ship's tender, both clad in jeans and jackets to keep them warm. The journey travelling towards the inlet was tranquilly smooth, taking only fifteen minutes to reach the shoreline.

The waiting coach filled up quickly and soon departed Akaroa, an old colonial village with charming Gallic architecture, carved out by French pioneers of long ago. Quaint weatherboard stores cluttered with lambskin souvenirs, blended delightfully with the ancient Customs and Court Houses. Victorian bungalows were painted delicately in pale and pleasing pastels, unifying the calm serenity of this beautiful haven. Homes were decorated with colourful flowering, hanging baskets, dangling from their pretty verandas.

The coach then climbed the bountiful hills, graced with bright emerald green pastures and vibrant yellow gorse bushes, splattered haphazardly amongst the landscape. Far below the harbour could be seen, stretching across in varying hues of blues and greens towards the Sea Goddess cruise liner, anchored on the eastern side of the bay.

The bus driver negotiated the hilly climb, manoeuvring around the twists and turns with expert precision, as the commentator delivered a brief history on Akaroa. Ninety minutes into their journey, the Southern Alps came into view, majestically dominating the horizon with its white capped peaks, contrasting against the clear blue skies.

Their journey continued, taking them across the famous Canterbury Plains, these flat lowlands stretched out as far as the eye could see. Its myriads of green were broken up by huge tall conifer windbreaks, preventing soil erosion by the strong westerly winds, a pastoral perfection resting between the Southern Alps and the Pacific Ocean.

Gigantic irrigation equipment was robotically crawling across the farming district, giving life to the planted fields of wheat and barley. Their large steel arms stretching out, as they gradually rolled along, sprinkling the earth with much needed water.

Huge Merino sheep were later seen on the hilly banks, scattered amongst the harsh and hauntingly beautiful landscape, accompanied by spirited spring lambs.

Deep purple velvety foxgloves and pale lemon lupins were spasmodically scattered along the road edges, as they travelled further north.

The coach progressed along a beaten stony track, getting closer to the snowy Southern Alps. It stopped off at Clearwater Lake, a holiday resort made up of small holiday cabins, built for the tourists, providing grand open views of Mount Cook.

"Do you want your coat?" Paul questioned Margaret, as she clambered down the coach steps, determined to take yet another photo of the snowy covered mountains.

"No, I'm fine," she replied. "It's only a ten minute photo stop," she added happily.

A young girl took a photo of them both, depicting the spectacular landscape towering behind them, before everyone clambered back on board again. Lunch was served up at an exquisite little lodge, set high in amongst the mountainous terrain.

Heading back on the coach everyone was exhausted, yet exhilarated by the beautiful landscape openly admired and appreciated by everyone. The fresh mountain air sent many to sleep, on their way home from the tour. Margaret leant into Paul, resting her head upon his shoulder, happy and content, pleased with having experienced the wonderful landscape with the man she loved so dearly.

Throughout the evening while everyone slept, the ship sailed silently towards the North Island. The next stop would be Wellington, where Margaret intended to do some shopping after their brief bus tour, highlighting the important buildings scattered throughout the city.

Their guide informed them that Wellington was known as 'Windy Wellington,' drawing laughter and amusement from the small group of tourists. The Cook Strait separating the two islands apparently funnelled the slightest breeze from the harbour, positioned in a basin of steep hills, transforming them into gusty winds.

They visited the Museum of New Zealand Te Papa Tongarewa seeped in Maori culture, before boarding the Wellington cable car. The views were spectacular from the pinnacle, overlooking the city and harbour. Breathtaking shots were captured on camera, preserving their memories on film.

Wellington Botanic Garden was irresistibly beautiful. The Lady Norwood Rose Garden was an array of vibrant and pastel colours, comprising of old favourites to the most recent rose additions, punctuating the air with a sweet fragrance, as the young couple strolled by. They ate lunch at the Picnic Café located beside Begonia House, filled abundantly with a myriad of lush tropical plants. Begonias, cyclamens and orchids produced a riot of colour, blooming profusely in the humid hot house, creating a pleasurable atmosphere for anyone entering.

Wellington's natural beauty, charm and culture were evident as the tour bus drove past numerous embassies, parliament buildings and cathedrals. They were dropped off in the Lambton Quarter of the city, the main shopping vicinity. Margaret purchased an original, tribal greenstone carving for her mother and some paua shell jewellery for Rachel, with Paul readily agreeing they would be delighted with their gifts.

Back on board again, they decided to have a casual evening and dined in the Steak House Restaurant, before heading off to bed.

Cuddled up blissfully together, Paul yawned. "Where are we off to tomorrow ... miss tourist organiser?" he whispered, in the darkened suite.

"Napier," Margaret replied sleepily, exhausted, soon dead to the world.

The following day Margaret and Paul discovered Napier, where 'the Art Deco City' truly lived up to its name. Rebuilt in the 1930's after a horrendous earthquake, they discovered the architecture was truly fascinating. Napier sat overlooking Hawke's Bay, teeming with a conglomeration of geometrical designs and bold colours. St John's Cathedral imitated the early English style architecture; however intricate leadlight windows in the Criterion Hotel were completely opposite to the Egyptian columns used on the Napier Municipal Theatre. They enjoyed wandering along Marine Parade, its shoreline edged with magnificent Norfolk Island pines leading to a magnificent statue of Pania, the legendary maiden of the sea from Maori mythology.

"Do you think Valerie would like this?" Margaret questioned Paul later on, holding up an art deco artefact, in a store on Emerson Street.

"Yes my darling she would love it, as Valerie likes quirky objects I've noticed. Now let's hurry. I'm dying for lunch and hopefully I'll get to sample some of the Hawke's Bay wines," he laughed out loud.

"Mum was right about the cruise being full on," Margaret sighed, breaking into their silence over dinner.

"Are you not enjoying yourself?" Paul enquired, smiling across at his gorgeous wife.

"Yes, I absolutely love it. I love the scenery, the Maori culture is intriguing and the wines are pretty spectacular," Margaret laughed, lifting and clinking her glass against his in a loving gesture.

"Well then, what's the problem?" having detected a slight hesitation earlier on.

"I was wondering, if you're okay with everything Paul? Are you as captivated and enthralled by it all, as much as I am?" she murmured, peering across at him sympathetically.

"I'm having an absolute ball my love, its great getting away from everyone, including the hectic dramas at the Royal. I love exploring new cultures and countries, especially with my wife, who I find simply irresistible," he replied, before tenderly running the back of his hand along her cheekbone.

She smiled contently, her heart bubbling with love, as they affectionately shared their dessert. Retiring to bed they made love gracefully, totally encapsulating their tranquil mood, before falling asleep together, happily wrapped in each others' arms.

The cruise liner crossed the Bay of Plenty and docked in Tauranga Harbour. Today they visited the Tamaki Maori Village and Margaret was totally captivated by the traditional Maori welcoming ceremony. Paul found the haka war challenge fascinating and they took great pleasure in listening to the customary Polynesian singing, as ancient Maori instruments were utilised during the performance. They sampled the succulent pork, cooked underground in the traditional hangi fashion; both were soaking up the wonderful Maori culture, delivered in a warm and welcoming manner.

In the afternoon they visited Wai-O-Tapu Geothermal Park, located near Rotorua. The Devil's Bath, was an astonishing, vivid green crater lake, due to the sulphur content and not filled with shamrocks, as Paul jokingly suggested.

Further down the track, the Rainbow Crater was an enchanting geological feature, releasing a huge amount of steam, with boiling mud and coloured water, lying in its base. They wandered along the sacred path together holding hands, both totally absorbed in the spectacular scenery. When crossing The Terrace, a magnificent photo was taken of them on the boardwalk, which would always be treasured. Champagne Pool was a crater, sixty-five metres in width, a terrestrial hot spring appearing like something from a moonscape. Its bright orange deposits appeared stark, against the pale greyish sinter, surrounding the searing, geothermal feature. Its copious effluxion of colourless atmospheric gas appeared similar to a freshly poured glass of bubbly champagne.

A small cascading thermal waterfall topped up Lake Ngakoro, as they strolled passed to access the active volcanic areas. Thermal sulphur hung heavily in the air, causing them to hold their noses and laugh, as it smelt similar to rotten eggs. Margaret and Paul both agreed, they were mesmerised by the uniquely eroded, large mud volcano. The sight and sounds were magical, as the large mud pool bubbled, swirled and gurgled quite strangely and eerily.

Needless to say, they arrived back at the ship late in the evening, both truly enthralled by the tours. They were much more appreciative of mother earth's natural wonders and the local Indigenous communities.

The following day, they discovered Auckland was the metropolitan hub of the North Island, positioned between the Tasman Sea and the Pacific Ocean. Known as the 'City of Sails', due to more boats per capita than any other city in the world, the overall ambience was peaceful, although it held over one million residents. They couldn't resist visiting the iconic Sky Tower interrupting the skyline, similar to their Centrepoint Tower in Sydney. From the observation decks, Margaret marvelled at the city sprawling far into the distance, with the Auckland Harbour Bridge stretching across the Waitemata Harbour, shimmering in the morning sunlight. Modern commercial buildings were mixed in with old Victorian ones and this was coupled with wide open spaces and parks, creating an overall relaxed atmosphere.

The two harbours in Auckland positioned on either side of the isthmus, provided huge marinas. They had afternoon coffee at the Westhaven Marina, discovering it was the largest in the southern hemisphere, where huge magnificent yachts were docked, allowing their pleasure-seeking owners to enjoy the spoils of the city.

With a wide choice of tourist attractions to choose from, they decided to venture to Waitomo Glowworm Grotto. The pair of them was in sync when it came to choosing tours, much preferring outdoor activities, experiencing natural beauty and geological features, which were unique to the area.

Edging their way down the steps they were handsomely rewarded, as the caves were illuminated by thousands of tiny glow worms, projecting a bluish, green, fluorescent glow. Margaret was awe struck cruising through the limestone formations in an open boat, soaking up the tour guide's repertoire about the oddity of nature and couldn't help smiling across at Paul, who was equally intrigued.

The days and evenings were passing quickly for the young married couple and today was their last stop in New Zealand. The ship anchored offshore, allowing the ship tenders to transfer them to Waitangi Wharf. From here, the coach delivered them to the Waitangi Treaty Grounds, a prominent historic New Zealand site, where British Rule was declared.

The intricately carved Maori Meeting House, displayed carvings from all the Maori tribes. Paul and Margaret were captivated by the world's largest ceremonial Maori war canoe made from giant kauri trees, as it significantly sat overlooking Hobson's Beach.

Afterwards they chartered a yacht with a skipper, who sailed them through the majestic 'Hole in the Rock'. This natural landmark had been created from centuries of erosion by sea and wind, carving a massive 210ft hole, which allowed tourists to pass through it on a sailing vessel. It was an amazing and unforgettable experience, as they passed the historic Cape Brett Lighthouse on their way back.

They kissed passionately, acknowledging they had experienced a truly unforgettable honeymoon and would be the envy of many, when they retold their adventures to family and friends, after arriving back home.

Margaret and Paul arrived back at Gladesville a few days later, discovering the whole family were back home from Northern Ireland. It was marvellous to catch up with everyone again, before heading back overseas. The main conversation pieces were centred on the wedding, allowing photos to be scrutinised and exchanged happily. The glamorous event was blissfully relived, through each other's different perspective. Paul and Margaret also shared photos of their magnificent honeymoon, regaling stories of the extraordinary scenery, the Maori culture and New Zealand's natural beauty.

"I think we ought to make a trip Marcus," Kath mentioned, during lunch. "It sounds absolutely amazing."

"You should go mum," Margaret added enthusiastically. "If you took the yacht, you could accomplish it all at a much slower pace and it would be absolutely perfect."

Marcus laughed. "And do you think I could tear your mother away from her work for a whole three months, to achieve this wonderful adventure?" he joked.

Peering across at Kath, Paul smiled. "You can always do it whenever you retire Kath, isn't that right." Recognising she was as dedicated to her work as he and Margaret were and respected her greatly for it.

"Why thank you Paul, at least someone's on my side," smiling broadly and raising her wine glass in a salute, before taking a sip.

Paul and Margaret enjoyed the last few of days of their holiday mingling with family and friends, before making their homeward journey. Kath had reconciled inwardly that her daughter had matured into a fine young lady, who found herself a wonderful and dedicated husband. Kath also recognised that no matter where they lived, they would always get to share wonderful days as they have done, over the past few days. Whether it was here or in Northern Ireland, it didn't really matter. The main thing was, they were a close knit family and that would never change, no matter where in the world they were.

Chapter Twenty Nine

The next few years past uneventfully, with Kath and Marcus making frequent trips over to Northern Ireland. It was becoming an annual, pleasurable event. Kath enjoyed the benefits of spending precious time with her parents, Margaret and her son-in-law, as well as Henry and Helen who became close friends with Kath and Marcus and had visited Australia on several occasions. Rachel always enjoyed her time with her grandparents in Ireland and the world didn't seem such a huge place after all.

The following year Mary and Joe were brought out for Christmas, this delighted both Brigee and Valerie, who found Mary absolutely hilarious. Joe and Marcus, along with Matt and Richard, would meet up at the weekends and play golf frequently. The girls would go shopping, visit museums and art galleries.

"I think that lassie could do with some clothes on," Mary shrieked, on one such outing. Immediately drawing disapproving looks, as she stood peering in disgust at 'The Nude Maja' by Francisco Goya. Causing Rachel to immediately burst out into convulsions of laughter, followed by Valerie, Brigee and Kath, before making a speedy departure.

It was a wonderful Christmas that year. Mary and Joe were also able to say their goodbyes, before Rachel commenced university. She was completing a Bachelor of Arts degree, not yet deciding what career path she wanted to follow. Sticking with her new found friends, she was proving to be a mature young adult, since the drug fuelled party incident at Caroline's. Marcus and Kath were pleased with her academically and Margaret regularly kept in touch with Rachel by phone, delighted she had settled down.

Rachel was completing her first semester at the University of Sydney; however, she was still inwardly unsettled. She was meeting the criteria academically but she was feeling unfulfilled and looking for something adventurous and compelling in her life. She was heavily involved with the University magazine, which she enjoyed, as well as working at Noblealert between semesters.

Rachel had been deeply occupied with her best friend Hannah recently, due to her being traumatised. Hannah's grandfather Eddie was living on his own, when he unfortunately disturbed some young intruders in the middle of the night, probably searching for cash and valuables to fuel their drug habit. He had been viciously truncheoned over the head and brutally left to die. Sadly Eddie died alone, lying in a pool of blood, as he met his maker. He was a solitary, gentle, human being and having no immediate help available, he was struck down, in a senseless cold-blooded murder.

Rachel being a supportive friend accompanied Hannah to one of the Victims of Crime meetings. Hannah could air her grievances here, expel her anger and speak with other victims who lost their loved ones, tragically.

Rachel sat in the room, traumatised, by the horrific stories that unfolded. She experienced a wrenched heart, while listening to the tale of a young teenager who had been stabbed to death. Wives brutally murdered by their husbands, leaving devastated young children behind trying to make sense of it all. Bodies were found in the boot of cars, unsolved murders and tragedies, infused the room with pain and sadness. Rachel sat silently, mourning for these lost souls, with every last one of them suffering beyond human comprehension. She clasped her friend's hand tightly, as Hannah unleashed her anger and distress, with tears stinging her cheeks, as the other victims sat listening and sympathising. All appeared sombre as they offered their condolences to Hannah, because they fully recognised the fresh raw wounds of trying to cope with a senseless and tragic loss of a loved one.

As Rachel sat in the crowded space, overwhelmed with grief, inhaling the fear and despair within the room, she began to angrily seethe. Who were representing these people? Who were allowing their voices to be heard? Sure, the media would have had a sensationalised spread at the time of the incident, grabbing headlines momentarily which attracted the public's attention. But now, these people were largely forgotten, left high and dry on top of a large pile of bureaucracy, trying to cope with life, while dealing with financial hardship, mental torture and physical pain.

Rachel sat silently making a sturdy resolve; overwhelmed with immense emotion, before arriving at her resolution. She knew, without a doubt, what her calling in life was. Unexpectedly, it all became blatantly clear. She wanted to become a journalist, to report on human stories and follow them through to a satisfactory conclusion; making the public aware of what is taking place within their society. Following up with victims' lives such as these and try to make amends for the tragedies they suffered. Using the media to highlight their stories, making sure they were dealt with fairly, to ensure proper compensation and counselling was provided for.

After all, any one of us could easily become a victim of crime. But the real underlying crime would be if humanity didn't do their utmost to help these human beings, in dire need.

On the way home, Rachel comforted Hannah the best way she could, sharing her new life goals with her dear friend, who was astounded by

Rachel's commitment and vigil. She was heading home this evening, to share her goals and ambition in life with her parents.

"Won't they be mad," Hannah asserted, wide eyed and shocked. "My mum would be raging mad if I declared I was quitting uni," she added, completely surprised by Rachel's conviction.

"I don't care." Rachel's rebuttal was strong and adamant. Hannah knew there would be fireworks this evening in the Garofoli household.

"How was your day Rachel?" Kath enquired at the dinner table, later that evening.

Brigee decided to stay and eat along with them tonight. Rachel saw this as an ideal opportunity to announce her news, reminding herself she must remain calm and refrain from becoming too hot headed and emotional.

"It was a great day mum and I discovered what I really want to do with my life, at long last," smiling benevolently at her parents.

Brigee was instantly alarmed and looked up, holding her breath. Rachel could easily be announcing she's dropping out of university and going to live in a hippie commune, as she was totally unpredictable and completely independent, Brigee thought.

"Mum and Marcus, please hear me out before you make any judgement. That's all I ask."

Marcus looked across at Kath, raised an eyebrow and nodded.

"Okay, we promise not to interrupt," Kath smiled weakly, inwardly praying for god's strength, sensing a drama unleashing.

Rachel divulged her story, explaining what took place with Hannah earlier that day. She was extremely emotional, enthusiastic, sensitive and highly animated, while explaining the scenario with conviction.

Finally Rachel concluded with "I want to quit uni and attend Macleay College instead. This is something I really want to do. I want to be a voice for these helpless, weak and distraught people mum. And Marcus, you're always telling me to follow my dreams. Well ... this is my dream. I know in my heart this is what I want to do, because this is my calling. Please give me your blessings and approval," she pleaded.

Kath lifted her wine glass, not saying a word, while Marcus and Brigee sat silently, quietly admiring a young girl who had now grown into a fine young woman. Kath looked at her young daughter, her heart filled with emotion. She knew exactly where she was coming from. It was similar to a plea she made to her own parents many years ago, when she wanted to drop out of law school, to take up employment with the Belfast Telegraph. Kath peered across at Marcus, who had given her hand a discreet squeeze and nodded knowingly. She ever so slowly put down her glass, as Rachel sat tense, peering from one parent to another. Hoping and praying they would understand. Brigee watched silently, not saying a solitary word.

"Rachel my darling, it's not ideal to cut uni and go off on some whim," Kath stated, as Rachel visibly recoiled and wanted to cry, sighing deeply. "However, I feel Marcus and I will agree that the conviction you demonstrated this evening leads us to believe you will make a damn good reporter."

Whoops of joy filled the air, as Rachel jumped up from the dinner table quickly, almost sending her dinner plate flying, before rushing over to her mother and Marcus, hugging them with gratitude.

"Thank god for that," Brigee exhaled, her eyes filling with tears, as the emotional scene unfolded. "I thought you were planning to run off to some hippie commune," Brigee declared.

Everyone broke out into laughter and during dessert; they began making plans for Rachel's new venture.

Rachel was soon enrolled at Macleay College in Sydney. She was quickly excelling in her chosen subject, because she was working extremely hard to obtain her Diploma of Journalism. Fitting in exceptionally well, Rachel always made new friends easily. Her enthusiasm and energy, coupled with her sheer determination was highly commendable and Kath, together with Marcus, were suitably impressed. Rachel was obviously enjoying her studies; finally discovering her niche in life was spurring her on and would no doubt make her successful because of it. She also discovered a boundless new lease for life; as her unbridled joy would spill out each evening at the dinner table, allowing her the opportunity to inform her parents of the media roles she was participating in each day.

Kath was delighted for her and Marcus secretly hoped that Rachel would enter into the family business one day, as he recognised she had the drive and capacity to run it.

Brigee noticed an enormous change in Rachel's demeanour and was extremely pleased with the overall outcome. She was especially delighted her parents had listened, both immediately responding to young Rachel's passion, encouraging her straight away. They reacted positively and sensibly, allowing Rachel to follow her dreams.

Chapter Thirty

Back in Northern Ireland, life was invariably busy for Margaret and Paul. Both frequently rotated their shifts to correspond with each other, allowing them a few days off together to enjoy married life, before heading back to the Royal Victoria Hospital.

Mary and Joe participated actively in their lives, admiring the young couple for their hard work and ethical behaviour. Mary frequently prepared delicious casseroles and soups, storing them away in the young couple's freezer, to help ease the burden when they were working night shifts. Joe would tend to their garden, tidying things up, acknowledging the time the young couple had off, could be best spent on relaxing and not on trivial chores.

Helen and Henry welcomed Margaret wholeheartedly into their family, treating her like one of their own. Margaret was completely at ease in Helen's kitchen, frequently rustling up a quick meal for his parents, when they got back from some charity event. Paul's brother Stephen simply adored Margaret, treating her like a sister, regularly seeking out her advice, when it came to choosing a present for his current girlfriend.

Cuddled up in bed, Paul snuggled a little closer to Margaret and began gently moving his hand over her tummy region, in a kind and loving gesture.

"Don't," Margaret snapped "I'm not in the mood."

Paul was taken aback, surprised by her rebuttal and inwardly a little hurt. "Do you want to talk about it," he gently soothed, acknowledging she had been a bit irritable and moody of late.

"There's nothing to discuss," she bit back instantly, pulling away from him.

"Is it Doc Saunders?" he enquired, prying a little more. He had heard some of the new interns talking about him in the lunchroom; apparently he was a tyrant, totally unhospitable and snapped the head of anyone, who came into his line of fire.

"No it's not Doc Saunders, if you must know," Margaret grizzled. "And yes, he has been extremely rude to me on several occasions, however it's nothing that I can't handle," she sighed loudly.

"Well, do you think you're taking too much on my love? You've been a bit under the weather of late and you look extremely tired."

"I've covered a couple of shifts for Daphne but you're as guilty as I am, when it comes to helping out friends," she murmured, wanting to be left alone so she could get some sleep, as she had a heavy schedule ahead of her tomorrow.

"Okay then, we'll get some sleep and we'll do something nice at the weekend, as it's been all work and no play lately," Paul added lightly, switching off the bedroom light. He lay there for a while; not daring to utter another word, recognising there was something going on and Margaret seemingly didn't want to talk about it.

Margaret lay next to him, ever so still, not wanting to encourage any further discussions. She wiped away a tear, reprimanding herself instantly. Lately she had been crying over the slightest little thing. And emotionally, she felt extremely distraught and could bite the head of anyone recently.

She lay next to Paul feeling guilty, as he was a good man but recently, even he was getting on her nerves.

Saturday came around and they took the yacht out together, the sea air was refreshing, allowing them to both relax and get away from the chaos at work. Having moored at the marina, they visited a quaint little pub in Portrush and after an evening meal, they joined in the sing-a-long, which took place later on. Getting away from everything and everyone turned out to be very successful and they made love later in the evening, pleased things were getting back to normality between them.

The following morning Paul rose early and made breakfast, while Margaret lay in bed sound asleep. She was exhausted and extremely tired of late, he noticed. He was thinking of organising a short break away for them both, as they had been working feverishly hard to meet hospital demands and the pair of them had hardly any time off.

"Wakey, wakey sleepy head," he announced, arousing Margaret from her sleep gently, clutching a tray laden with a delicious cooked breakfast.

"Mmm, I was away in never never land," Margaret smiled sleepily.

Rising up and gently adjusting her pillow, she turned around to retrieve her bacon and eggs, made lovingly by Paul. No sooner had the tray been laid on her lap, she suddenly felt sick and immediately wanted to spew. Quickly grabbing the tray and setting it down, out of her way, she instantly made a beeline to the bathroom. Reaching the toilet bowl, she vomited profusely, appearing absolutely miserable.

Paul arrived at the bathroom door. "Are you okay my love?" he asked, extremely concerned.

She looked up, a ghastly green in colour, before nodding sedately. "Oh my god, it must have been those pickled eggs I took a fancy to last night, when we were sitting down in the bar. Remember?" she groaned.

"I think I'll give brekkie a miss," she smiled benevolently, appearing pale and sickly.

"Why don't you pop into the shower? I'll make a fresh cuppa and get you some dry toast, to help soak up the acid in your stomach," Paul volunteered automatically.

"Thanks love," she murmured, dragging herself up off the floor before clambering into the shower. The rest of the day she was fine and she put the whole incident down to a slight stomach bug.

On Monday morning she found herself over the toilet bowl, yet again and Paul was now really worried.

"I don't care what you may have on today Margaret," he declared. "I'm heading into work and informing them you're sick and you'll not be in and that's that," he chided.

Margaret knew there was no point in arguing and clambered back into bed, visibly weak and exhausted.

Paul went to work, promising to pick something up from the chemist for her on his way home from the hospital.

Margaret meanwhile slept like a baby for most of the day and Paul was kept busy at work, as usual. On the way home he stopped off at a chemist and began checking the shelves for stomach remedies.

A young shop assistant approached him. "Can I help you?" she enquired politely and he automatically explained the situation. She smiled immediately. "She's not pregnant by any chance, is she?" she questioned.

It then hit him like a brick. Heavens above, he was a doctor and the symptoms Margaret had been presenting, fell directly under that category. Mood swings, weariness and morning sickness. How could he have been so blind?

"Bloody hell," he responded, shaking his head in utter disbelief, grinning broadly. "I think you could be right," he laughed, delighted at the prospect of it all.

Immediately the young assistant directed him to the home pregnancy test kits, leaving him to decide which one to choose.

Arriving home, he discovered Margaret was up and busy in the kitchen, preparing a delicious evening meal, going by the tantalising aromas.

"How are you sweetie?" he enquired grinning mischievously.

"Much better, thank you," Margaret replied happily, appearing radiant.

"I've got a surprise for you," Paul smiled "and I think you better sit down," he coaxed.

Margaret sat down on the kitchen stool, totally unaware of what was about to take place.

Paul set the bag down on the kitchen bench. "I think there's something in there you might need," he smiled happily.

Margaret opened up the bag and lifted out one of the boxes. "Oh my god," she gasped "you've got to be kidding me!"

"No I'm not," Paul answered. "All the symptoms are there," he openly confided.

Margaret swiftly vacated the kitchen stool and immediately went racing into the bathroom. Paul followed promptly behind, extremely excited.

"Get out Paul. I can't pee with you standing over me," she screamed.

"Well make it quick," he said, making his way to the door.

One minute later, she returned holding a stick, while holding her breath.

"How long does it normally take to get a result?" Paul questioned, barely able to contain himself.

"Soon Paul, soon," Margaret replied staring down at the stick, as a thin red line slowly began to appear on the indicator.

"Holy shit," Margaret declared. "I'm pregnant."

Paul automatically lifted her up off the ground and swung her around. "I love you Mrs Hagan. I'm going to be a dad," he announced with tears in his eyes, obviously overjoyed with the result.

"And I'm going to be a mum," Margaret whispered, turning pale. "What are we going to do?"

"Celebrate," Paul laughed cheerfully.

Margaret was still in a state of shock. "I had no idea," she declared.

They had been trying for the past three months but didn't expect it to happen so soon. Tears suddenly came to her eyes; she was surprised, delighted and overwhelmed.

"Let's tell mum and dad straight away," Paul stated.

"No please, not straight away. You're a doctor and are fully aware that we should wait until we reach twelve weeks," she protested.

"Okay, okay but you'll have to get a blood test carried out anyway and we'll take it from there," Paul conceded, before pulling her into his arms and kissing her.

She reciprocated happily, settling down, pleased with the outcome.

During dinner they made plans to organise a nursery. Together they agreed Helen could babysit two days a week, giving Margaret the opportunity to return to work again, following a six month break. They decided three days a week would be sufficient, allowing her to maintain her symmetry at work. They cuddled up closely later in the evening, bathed in each other's love, both looking forward to becoming new parents.

Paul watched over Margaret at work, fussing over her, making sure she wasn't overdoing things. She would tell him off on a regular basis, determined to keep the baby bump a secret, until they got the all clear. Margaret was relieved to discover she wasn't turning into a horrible old tyrant, pleased she was only suffering from hormonal changes, due to her pregnancy.

At work lately, she frequently visited the children's wards during her short breaks. The children seemed more animated and interesting, now that she was expecting one of her own. In the evenings, Paul would fuss over her like a clucky old hen. God love her, when the grandparents and great grandparents are delivered the news, she thought, as Paul appeared and started making the supper.

"I'm not an invalid you know," she laughed "and the more active I am during my pregnancy, the better it will be for mother and child during childbirth," she informed him pleasantly.

The weeks flew by and she found herself looking at little girl's clothes, when out shopping with her mother-in-law.

"Is there anything you and Paul are not telling me?" Helen enquired casually, on one such occasion.

Margaret found herself blushing and explained she was searching for a present for an expectant girl at work, who would soon be on maternity leave.

Helen smiled meekly, inwardly a little disappointed. Henry and she had frequently chatted about having a little grandchild running around their home. She would babysit of course, knowing it would bring so much joy to their home. It would certainly be a major distraction for Henry, as his career was rather taxing and tended to encourage a cynical outlook in life. How he kept abreast of it all and maintained a happy demeanour, amazed Helen on so many levels.

Margaret attended Dr Moore's surgery and it was confirmed through blood tests, she was approximately eight weeks pregnant. "I hope you intend to slow down a notch Margaret, as I'm aware the workload at the Royal is hectic at the best of times."

"Paul will be keeping his beady little eyes on me," Margaret said as she smiled at Dr Moore, who was a middle aged GP with a great mop of red hair and the palest skin imaginable.

Her greenish hazel eyes would sparkle and smile, whenever you entered her rooms. Gentle in her mannerisms, she was a godsend to her local community, offering good strong advice, backed up with terrific medical experience, coupled with a friendly and happy disposition.

"Everything seems to be in order," she announced, as Margaret climbed down off the bed, adjusting her clothing straight away. "Next visit, I'll get you organised and booked in for an ultrasound. We'll be able to determine if everything is growing according to plan and perhaps the baby's sex will be divulged. That is, if the pair of you wish to know before delivery"

"Paul would love a little girl and I must admit it would be nice. However, as long as it's healthy, that's the main thing," Margaret added happily.

Paul received the news over dinner; on what took place during her visit with Dr Moore. He was discovering it was becoming more and more difficult, not to tell his parents about their great news. Fully aware his mother was dying for a grandchild, he couldn't wait to see the expression on their faces, when they discovered the truth.

Work was full on at present and Margaret was coping enormously well. Her morning sickness had subsided, which she was most grateful for. Working alongside a team of medics, it would not have taken long for them to work out she was pregnant.

Paul would frequently have a casserole defrosted and heated up for her, when she got home late in the evenings. He was constantly spoiling her and surprised her by clearing out the spare bedroom to convert into a small nursery, as it was positioned next to their bedroom. Mint green and cream was the chosen décor, as it was a neutral colour and subsequently pink or blue accessories could be added later, depending upon the baby's sex. Paul would slip out early in the mornings to commence his shifts, making a point of not disturbing Margaret on the way out, as he figured she needed all the rest she could get.

They had a few senior patients in their wards at present requiring operations, which were proving to be rather taxing on them both. Many were suffering from dementia, meaning they would have to explain to them on several occasions, as to what taking place. On top of that, it meant close relatives had to be brought in and the procedure explained yet again, before the necessary documentation could be signed, allowing for the operation to go ahead.

One more week to go and Paul could announce to his family, they were going to be grandparents and Margaret could inform her parents and grandparents, who he knew would be absolutely ecstatic. Mum, dad and Rachel will probably fly over for the christening, Margaret thought, sitting at the lunch room table smiling, in a world of her own.

"What's that you're having?" Paul stated, plonking down at her table, breaking her reverie.

"A cheese and pickle sandwich," she replied happily.

"Are you sure you're not expecting a mouse," he whispered, laughing out loud. "You've been getting stuck into the old cheddar a lot lately," he added cheerfully.

"My body is obviously calling out for calcium," she replied casually, glad he could catch up for lunch with her, as it had been an extremely hectic week.

"Can we tell everyone the good news at the weekend?' Paul asked quietly, smiling across at his beautiful radiant wife from across the canteen table.

"Yes you can," Margaret replied, laying her hands on top of his, recognising the love and concern written in his smiling eyes.

"Thank goodness for that. I thought I was going to burst a blood vessel, containing myself for this long length of time," he smiled.

"You are absolutely hopeless Dr Paul Hagan," she laughed, shaking her head. "I can imagine you at Christmas time when Santa comes, you'll be more excited than the child," she rolled her eyes heavenward.

"Well one thing I promised myself, is that he or she will be getting a train set, that's for sure," he added enthusiastically, beaming like a Cheshire cat.

"You're a hopeless case," she laughed, before rising from the table and giving him a quick kiss. "See you at 3.30am. Oh by the way, I thought we might try the new Italian restaurant for dinner tonight," she added casually.

"Yep, sounds grand to me," Paul readily agreed, pulling his chair out, before heading off to complete his rounds.

Margaret was speaking with Mrs Simpson and going over her charts, a dear little thing in her mid eighties, admitted for a hip replacement. In the middle of their conversation, Margaret was distracted by a loud ruckus taking place, further down the corridor.

Intuitively drawing back the curtains, she went to investigate and found an intern struggling with a feisty male in his early twenties, in the emergency section. She noticed a huge gash on the patient's left arm that would require stitching immediately.

"What seems to be the problem here" she interjected in an authoritative manner, startling both the intern and patient alike.

"He doesn't want an injection," the intern replied frantically.

Assessing the situation, Margaret knew by working in emergency wards for years, the patient was obviously high and the injection would bring him back down to earth rather damn quickly. Margaret approached the trolley, picked up the needle and calmly walked towards the bed.

"If we don't get that arm of yours fixed up immediately, you may get an infection and you don't want to lose it," Margaret said in a soothing and therapeutic manner, deliberately using it as a tangible excuse. She hoped this would do the trick and makes the patient completely calm down to receive the injection, therefore empowering the intern and allowing the stitching to proceed.

The patient visibly relaxed a little, obviously in a quandary, allowing Margaret to take advantage of the situation. Tapping his left arm and allowing the vein to pop, she moved in closer to inject him, speaking in an automated, calm soothing manner.

Unexpectedly leaning forward, he punched her brutally in the torso with immeasurable force, sending her flying backwards into the trolley, with 'fuck off bitch' echoing in her head. Margaret and the trolley went crashing to the floor, hitting it hard, as the intern began screaming for help. Two security guards raced up the corridor straight away, entering the cubicle immediately and wrestled with the offender, before containing the aggressive patient.

Margaret slowly struggled to get up and instantly felt an excruciating pain ripping through her abdominals straight away. Her face paled significantly and huge tears bubbled down her cheeks after she sighted the bright red blood seeping out, creeping along the sterile tiled floor. Like a red river, slowly ebbing its way around the surgical instruments, lying scattered over the ground, dispersed from the trolley sent flying across the ward, now lying tilted upside down.

"Get Paul," she stammered weakly, deteriorating rapidly, trying her utmost to hold it together.

Within minutes, Paul arrived. He was completely gutted and devastated beyond belief, when he spotted Margaret lying there. Completely helpless, with her lower region saturated in blood. Tears filled his eyes and his heart broke in two, as he bent down to pick her up.

"I'm so sorry Paul," she sobbed. "I'm so sorry."

"It's okay my love," he comforted, drawing her in closer.

Walking down the corridor in a trance-like state, he headed towards the theatre with Margaret wrapped up in his arms, embracing her lovingly and compassionately, acknowledging what came next. Tears were rolling down his cheeks and dripping down upon Margaret's shoulders, as she clutched on to him desperately, weeping uncontrollably, consumed with immense grief and insurmountable guilt.

Waiting outside the theatre, Paul felt immensely alone. He had no one close to share his burden with. It would be unfair to speak with his parents, shattering their dreams and putting them through what he was experiencing right now. He dropped his head heavily into his hands, engulfed in immense sadness. He was anxious for Margaret and furious at the drug addict who was responsible for it all. Paul tightly clenched his fists, conscious he wanted to beat the living hell out of the abuser, for directing his aggressive behaviour towards Margaret. This complete stranger, had successfully shattered their lives and dreams.

He walked outside and lit up a cigarette, drawing down upon it hard. He must get himself sorted out quickly. Margaret would need him. He must remain strong for her, knowing she would be riddled with guilt, which could destroy her. She had enough to deal with, in trying to cope with the loss of their child.

Paul re-entered the ward and walked into Margaret's room. "Daffodils, they're so beautiful Paul," Margaret smiled, peering weakly up at him.

"They're bright and cheerful," he said forcefully. "All the things we must try and be, to survive this latest trauma my love," he added sedately.

She nodded, agreeing instantly, choking up with tears.

He sat down on the bed alongside her, hugging her deeply.

"It was a girl, wasn't it?" she sobbed.

"Yes," he stammered sadly.

"And I lost her," she cried. "I lost her, because I went to see what was going on and tried to help," she wept. "If I had stayed where I was? If I had walked away or got help or . . ."

"Don't do this to yourself Margaret," Paul interjected. "Please don't do this to yourself my love. I love you more than anything in this world and we'll get through this together. I promise."

He pulled her into his arms tightly and they wept together. Both of them cried for their enormous loss. Weeping, for what could have been. Everything had brutally been taken away in a matter of minutes, fuelled by a drug induced fury. Paul was empowered with a steely determination while sitting there, holding his devastated wife in his arms. He inwardly promised to remain close to Margaret, to demonstrate his deep love for her, vowing to help her as much as he could, to overcome this catastrophic personal disaster.

He swiftly organised two weeks off work. Management was completely understanding and sympathetic towards their plight. Teneriffe was ideal and offered them sunshine, along with some rest and relaxation. Paul unwound some more, watching Margaret relax as she swam in the hotel pool, soaking up the sun and indulging in a few Pina Colada's. The evenings were spent listening to the Spanish music playing in the local restaurants, while dining on Paella and sipping their sangria's. It was exactly what the young couple needed, allowing them to put the tragic incident behind them.

By facing the physical pain head on together, a deep benevolence ran between the young couple, allowing them to become stronger, with every passing day. Only by taking time out and having intimate discussions, they helped ease each other's suffering by demonstrating genuine kindness and understanding to one another. Both were fully accepting of their fate, concentrating on the fact they were still young and had plenty of time to try again. Many would have voiced blame and condemnation but not Paul. He loved Margaret immeasurably and was grateful she was recovering, both physically and emotionally.

Chapter Thirty One

Back in Australia, Kath and Marcus were unaware of their daughter's traumatic loss. The weekly phone calls ceased for a little while but Paul explained to them they had been rostered on very hectic shifts. He also informed them of their much needed holiday in Teneriffe, which probably added to their lack of communication and apologised profusely to them both.

Kath's mind was instantly put at ease, glad they had taken a break. Mary told her Margaret had looked extremely rundown and tired lately but obviously the holiday had done the pair of them good, when she had seen them last week.

Rachel had nearly completed her journalism course, with only a week remaining. Kath could not believe another year had disappeared so rapidly. Marcus and she were extremely busy at work, although they always made it a point of getting home in the evenings to share a family meal together, along with Rachel and frequently Brigee.

"Your father and I have arranged to take next Friday off to attend your graduation Rachel," Kath advised, smiling across at her daughter.

"And I've got a new outfit to attend the ceremony," Brigee announced, very much looking forward to the day.

"I cannot believe I have reached the end of my studies already," Rachel shrieked, obviously delighted.

"You've worked extremely hard child dear," Brigee added lovingly "and I know your parents are immensely proud of you and your achievements to date," she smiled humbly.

"It just goes to prove that if you find your vocation in life, there's no stopping you," Marcus added to the conversation.

"EXACTLY," Rachel added enthusiastically, peering from one parent to another. Deciding this was neither the time nor the place, to make them fully aware of her plans.

The week flew by and Rachel received numerous phone calls from Margaret and Paul, wishing her well on graduation day. Her grandparents had also sent a beautiful card congratulating her on this wonderful achievement, wishing her a brilliant and successful career.

Valerie and Matt also attended the ceremony with pride. Valerie was elegantly dressed in a pale blue floral dress, complementing her huge wide brimmed hat and matching white Gucci sandals and handbag. No one would ever have known that she suffered from breast cancer, even though Valerie never went through with the breast reconstructive surgery. As her mastectomy bra and prosthesis did the trick in disguising her slight disfiguration.

Eleanor was there as well, dressed up to the nines in all her finery. Carlos immediately gave Rachel a congratulatory hug, after sighting her.

Brigee was dressed in pale pink, complementing Kath's mauve suit, as they strolled along the grounds with Marcus, before entering the assembly hall, where the official ceremony was taking place.

Cheers of jubilation were voiced loudly when the ceremony came to an official end, with graduation hats automatically thrown high up into the air and caught by their respective graduates on their descent. Lunch was held in the beautiful grounds and everyone mingled casually, enjoying the ambience.

Dinner was held at Marcus and Kath's home later in the evening, allowing everyone to present their graduation presents to young Rachel. Carlos and Eleanor decided upon a Swiss Caran d'Ache rose gold pen, believing it was appropriate for a young journalist setting out on her new venture. Her name was neatly engraved upon it in italics, adding a personal touch.

"Thank you ever so much," Rachel smiled. "I will use it every day and it will allow me to write beautifully and responsibly. Hopefully wonderful stories and fascinating headlines will be written on my journey as a journalist," she laughed happily.

Valerie and Matt presented her with a beautiful leather Gucci briefcase; it was feminine and extremely practical for her new posting, wherever that may be.

"It's beautiful, exactly what I needed," Rachel exclaimed, giving them both massive hugs.

Brigee handed her a small box and inside laid a gold 'R' initial, encrusted with tiny diamonds on a gold chain.

Rachel thanked Brigee for her thoughtfulness. "I wanted one for years," she sang out elated, hanging it around her neck instantly.

"You'll get your surprise from us tomorrow," Kath advised, smiling across at Marcus, who was visibly excited.

Rachel headed out with her friends to celebrate, leaving the adults to retire to the patio to have their coffees.

"Well that went well," Valerie yawned; pleased Rachel liked her presents and had settled down, maturing nicely over the past few years.

"She's in for a huge surprise tomorrow I believe," Carlos laughed.

"Yes, she most certainly is," Marcus announced proudly "and Rachel's got absolutely no idea whatsoever," he confided.

On Saturday morning, Rachel rose at 9.30am and they all left the house shortly afterwards, as planned. She had no idea where they were going but suspected she would be taken to a jewellery store and allowed to choose a new Cartier watch and ring, as her mother dropped many hints, coming up close to her graduation. Marcus drove down to Rushcutters Bay and parked outside the BMW dealership, stating he wanted to look at the latest model, as one of the board members recently bought one and was suitably impressed.

"I'll come with you Marcus," Kath said nonchalantly "that way you won't be so long," she teased. "Are you coming Rachel?"

"Yep and while you're looking, I'll use the toilet," she replied, slipping off her seatbelt.

Marcus was greeted by a friendly sales consultant and explained who he was, as Rachel darted off to the ladies.

Upon her exit from the toilet, Rachel was greeted with a loud cheer and clapping. Kath and Marcus were standing adjacent to three small convertibles. A red, midnight blue and silver one, all with ribbons tied on them.

"Oh my god what have you done?" Rachel gasped eyes wide and mouth gaping open.

"Don't worry, we haven't purchased anything yet Rachel, because we didn't know which colour you would prefer," Marcus laughed, delighted at her response.

"Congratulations Rachel!" Kath beamed. "Marcus had this wonderful idea to completely surprise you. We wanted to acknowledge how hard you have worked over the past twelve months and decided to spoil you a little," she added.

Rachel felt intense emotion, as her complexion turned positively green.

"Are you okay love?" Kath instantly enquired.

"Nope, I feel really sick mum," Rachel retorted, running swiftly towards the toilets. She only just made it, vomiting immediately into the toilet bowl, her heart filled with enormous anxiety and remorse. Shit ... what was she going to do now? she thought.

Kath appeared shortly afterwards. "Are you okay Rachel?" she asked, appearing perplexed. "Valerie said there was an old stomach bug going around at present."

"Can I go home?" Rachel pleaded. "I'm r-e-a-l-l-y sorry but I feel absolutely awful, perhaps we could come back again another time."

"Yes, yes, of course Rachel. Marcus is not locked into anything today. We can come back anytime next week. Whatever suits you love," she smiled graciously, handing her daughter a tissue. Kath then left and subsequently explained to Marcus and the salesperson, what had taken place.

In the meantime, Rachel rinsed her face thoroughly with cold water, before leaving the ladies.

"Are you okay love?" Marcus enquired earnestly after sighting Rachel, who was presenting a sickly pallor.

"Yes," she nodded reluctantly, smiling weakly at everyone, before heading outside to the car.

Apologies were made, as Marcus and Kath re-entered their car and headed home. Rachel sat deadly quiet in the back seat, closing her eyes, not wanting to get into a conversation right now. Hell ... she felt really really bad, not realising it was going to be this difficult.

Arriving home, she informed them quietly she was heading upstairs to sleep for a while.

Both Kath and Marcus readily agreed, noticing she was extremely quiet and still awfully pale. "We'll see how you are by this afternoon and if there's no improvement, I'll call the doctor," Kath advised.

"I think it was the shock of it all," Marcus said, as soon as Rachel was heard closing her bedroom door upstairs.

"I tend to agree," Kath replied quietly. "You could tell by the look on her face, she was absolutely horrified."

"I don't think the poor girl knew what to say or do," Marcus added guiltily.

"Don't worry love; it was a lovely thought and gesture. Mind you, our Rachel was never one for surprises and always seemed to be overwhelmed, even when she was very young," Kath comforted.

"Never mind love, do you fancy a glass of wine before lunch?"

"I would love one," Marcus replied, following Kath into the kitchen.

It was about 5 o'clock in the afternoon when Rachel reappeared; she had a healthy colour in her cheeks again and looked heaps better.

"How are you feeling?" Kath enquired when Rachel wandered slowly into the lounge room.

"Much better ... thank you," she replied sedately. "Where's Marcus?" she asked her mother, hoping to get the worst over and done with quickly.

"He's in the study going over some reports I think," Kath answered.

"I need to speak with you both, it's in relation to the car," Rachel asserted, biting her bottom lip, dreading what lay ahead.

"Okay, I'll go and fetch him and don't worry love, if you don't like the make or model, we're not locked into any contract. So stop looking so worried," Kath insisted, happily rising from her seat and heading towards the door.

Rachel panicked, pacing the room when her mother left. There was no way to break the news gently and there was no way in hell she could delay it any longer. Her heart rate intensified and she felt sick again. The shit was going to well and truly hit the fan, she surmised, as her parents entered the room.

"My goodness, you look a lot better now Rachel than you did earlier this morning," Marcus confided, walking over to the couch. "Your mother said you wanted to have a word about the car," he stated, before sitting down and making himself comfortable. Kath sat down next to him and Rachel remained standing.

Inhaling a deep breath, Rachel immediately announced. "I cannot accept the car from you both. I really do appreciate the loving gesture and I don't want to hurt your feelings, knowing in my heart you both meant well. However, it's far too much and I won't be able to use it," she protested.

Marcus looked up at her; she was appearing much more mature than her young years pertained. "We're sorry for surprising you this morning, Rachel love. Maybe we should have discussed it with you first. Your mother seems to think you would prefer another make or model," Marcus announced, calmly and decisively.

"It's not that," Rachel groaned, dreading what had to come next. "There's no easy way of saying this, so I'm going to come right out with it," Rachel announced. "The car is beautiful; it was a wonderful gesture and an extremely generous gift from you both. However, I cannot possibly accept it, not for all the reasons you're probably thinking of right now." Peering from one to the other, she announced "I've got a job organised already but it's not here, it's overseas." She took a deep breath; visibly squirming "so I won't need the car," she trailed off, watching them both recoil.

Marcus and Kath sat momentarily without uttering a word; both were obviously shocked, having been taken totally unawares. Ironically, it was a repeat of this morning's shenanigans down at the BMW showroom but their roles had been reversed this time around.

Intuitively, Kath knew this was not going to turn out well but Marcus was the first to speak. "May we ask, who have you got a job organised with and where are they based?" he enquired cautiously.

Gulping nervously, Rachel retorted rather quickly. "The position is with the Telegraph. The Belfast Telegraph to be exact," she grimaced, praying they would not be too disappointed or angry.

The look on her mother's face however, reflected the very opposite. Sheer horror was written all over it, along with anger, disappointment and confusion.

"How could you Rachel?" Kath exploded, her jaw line drawing tighter, her eyes glaring straight at Rachel, illustrating her anger and immense disapproval. "In the name of heavens, whatever possessed you to even apply for a job over there?" she raged. "I am absolutely dumbfounded Rachel," she shouted. "I really don't know whether to laugh or cry," she stammered hysterically, nearly at her wits end. "Frankly, I'm finding this extremely difficult to even try and comprehend right now," she confessed, shaking her head in total frustration.

Rachel stood before them, growing angry and resentful, feeling she was being treated like a child. She was a grown woman for god's sake, with goals and ambitions. She wanted to travel the world. Enhance her career. To grow, learn and experience the world and write about it with undeniable emotion and conviction.

"This is the last thing Marcus and I ever expected Rachel," Kath announced angrily, breaking into her thoughts. "And for the record, it would have been the last place on earth Marcus and I would have ever wanted you to go," she chided.

"I don't give a damn what you and Marcus want," Rachel exploded, her eyes bulging and her teeth gritted, towering over them, as they sat firmly on the couch.

"Don't speak to your mother in that manner," Marcus bit back immediately, trying to get his head around the news.

"Rachel, I would consider us to be extremely broad minded. In fact, if I recall correctly, none of your other friends were allowed to quit university and attend Macleay College to obtain a Diploma. However, I am fully aware the college has won numerous industry awards. Therefore, it was a good choice," Kath stated calmly. It was much more calmly than she felt at that given moment in time. In fact, right now, she felt like grabbing her young nineteen year old daughter and shake some sense into her.

"Your point mother ... is?" Rachel retorted sarcastically.

"My point daughter dear is that Marcus encouraged me to allow you to quit university after only one semester. We paid for an intensive journalism course in order for you to fulfil your dream, HERE IN AUSTRALIA, not BELFAST."

"That may have been your dream M-O-T-H-E-R but it most certainly wasn't mine," Rachel countered.

"Well, if you had been up front and honest with us in the first place Rachel," Marcus interrupted "perhaps we would have considered a different path altogether."

"EXACTLY," Rachel spat back venomously. "What had you and mother planned exactly, a cushy little number in one of the local newspapers over here?" she shouted. "How boring would that be."

"Boring or not Rachel," Kath could feel her blood pressure rising. "At least you would be in a safer environment. Bloody hell, of all places, you had to go and choose BELFAST!" Kath shook her head in total disbelief.

"Well mum, it was good enough for you and Marcus and apparently it's good enough for our Margaret, so quite frankly, I can't see what the pair of you are getting so worked up about?"

Marcus stood up promptly, trying to remain calm, acknowledging how much Kath would be hurting by now. "No more shouting ... please" he pleaded with Rachel, trying to alleviate the tension in the room but to no avail.

"Don't you understand?" Rachel barked back immediately. "I was only asking out of courtesy. I am nineteen years of age and legally, I can do what I damn well please. And do you know what, it's my life ... not yours or mum's and I have a right to live it any way I see fit," she spluttered, her voice cracking as tears stung her eyes.

"Come over here love," Kath appealed, stretching out her arms to her rebellious young daughter.

"No mum," she instantly snapped back. "I'm going to bed. I'm completely exhausted," she asserted tearfully, bolting away quickly towards the door and heading upstairs.

"Well ... that went well," Marcus drawled, swinging around to find Kath filling up with tears. "Do you want a drink love?" he questioned tenderly.

Kath nodded in response, not daring to speak, knowing she would break down. She remained seated, telling herself she must remain strong, because she knew she would need all the strength she could get over the next few days.

Later they clambered into bed together, deflated and really depressed. Cuddling up to each other for comfort, both lay silent, both lost in their own thoughts, each trying to come to terms that their daughter had grown up immensely. The fact still remained however that Rachel was planning to leave her comfortable and safe nest, abandon her family and charge straight into unknown territory, right into the heart of Belfast to take on the role of a journalist.

Kath twisted and turned in her sleep all night, horrors from the past came rushing to the forefront of her mind. Pictures of Finbar and Mad Dog dominated her nightmares, causing her to call out on several occasions before bolting upright. Waking up absolutely petrified, she found her entire body drenched in a cold sweat, leaving her frightened and shivering in the dark, as Marcus slept.

Marcus also tossed and turned throughout the night, knowing full well the effect it would have on Kath. Conscious of the fact it would reignite old memories, memories which had long since been buried and should remain that way. He felt helpless because Rachel was right, she was a grown woman and there wasn't a damn thing they could do. The fact that Margaret and Paul were over there along with Kath's parents, hopefully would help ease Kath's mind a little, making life a bit easier. As hard as it may be, it was a question of Kath resigning herself to the fact, Rachel was definitely leaving. He moved closer to his beloved, feeling unhappy and finding it hard to comprehend this particular cruel twist of fate. The irony of it was both daughters had chosen careers which would rise rapidly, by gaining experience in a country, Kath left many years before, due to the imminent danger her family was exposed to. He kissed Kath lightly on the top of her forehead, closed his eyes and prayed for some sleep before morning.

Kath and Marcus didn't go to work the following day, both were worn out and on edge over last night's arguments, coupled with their early morning discussion. They always had been a close family, able to communicate with each other in a civil manner and avoided confrontation for the majority of the time. Brigee arrived during breakfast and sensed the sombre mood immediately.

"Well, you two look as if there's been a death in the family," she announced, making her way towards the kettle to make a cuppa.

"It feels that way I'm afraid," Kath sighed, setting down her coffee cup.

"It can't be that bad?" Brigee answered, bending over to retrieve some milk from the fridge.

"It's the travel bug, unfortunately," Marcus groaned.

"Rachel?" Brigee enquired.

"Most certainly is, "Marcus interjected.

"I could feel something was going on, especially the way she's been acting up of late," Brigee countered, stirring her tea. "Well I guess you have to let them grow up; spread their wings and all that. Where to by the way? Bali or Thailand, isn't that the norm these days," Brigee added.

"I wish but no, she's off to BELFAST to be a journalist," Kath interrupted, her face taut, pale and filled with anguish.

"Oh shit," Brigee gasped, obviously shocked, standing with her mouth wide open.

"I know," Marcus said. "It came as a huge shock to us both last night and we all had a massive argument over it."

Brigee slowly sat down on the kitchen stool, immediately grabbing one of Kath's hands. "You'll have to let her go with your blessing," she said quietly, with tears in her eyes.

"I know," Kath nodded, biting her bottom lip.

"There's never a dull moment in this house," Marcus confided. "On a positive note though, we've got Joe and Mary, as well as Margaret and Paul over there and Rachel's a sensible kid."

Brigee nodded slowly in agreement, peering across at Kath.

Marcus got up from the breakfast bar. "Kath, you know Brigee's right, there's nothing we can do, so I'll leave it up to you to tell Rachel this morning or whenever you think it's best to bring the subject up again. We've discussed it earlier this morning and gone over everything a million times love and you know the answer. It's going to take a while getting used to the idea, that's all," leaning in and giving her a quick kiss.

Kath reciprocated. "Thanks love, I know I'll have to sort it out quickly, because there's no point in delaying the agony," smiling weakly up at him.

"Okay then, I'm off to my study to make a few phone calls," Marcus said, acknowledging Kath would pour her heart out to Brigee, her dearest friend.

"Are you really okay?" Brigee coaxed gently, observing Kath closely.

Swallowing hard, Kath replied. "The joys of motherhood Brigee, it was a real shocker but I know we have to let her go. She said last night it was her life and of course she's perfectly right. We can't keep her wrapped up in cotton wool forever."

Brigee came from around the granite bench and gave Kath a huge hug. "It will be fine love, she just has to spread her wings and get it out of her system, that's all."

A few hours later, Rachel arrived downstairs looking like death warmed up. Her eyes were swollen red, her skin ever so pale through lack of sleep and she was the picture of pure misery.

Taking one look at her, Kath instantly felt bad for her daughter, before she went rushing over, hugging her tightly without saying a word. They both openly shed tears, clinging tightly to each other, utterly exhausted and saddened by the outburst which took place the previous evening.

"I'm sorry Rachel love," Kath murmured, holding her daughter tightly.

"I'm sorry too mum. I didn't know how to tell you and I didn't want to hurt you or Marcus."

"I know love ... it's okay. It was a huge shock that's all; we love you so much and try to protect you as much as we can. And the thought of you not being around, simply broke our hearts. But you're right Rachel, it is your life and you must follow your dreams sweetheart. Marcus and I discussed it further this morning and you have our blessings my love," tears streamed down Kath cheeks, as Rachel broke down into huge agonising sobs.

"Thanks mum, I knew you would understand. I'll be careful ... I PROMISE," she cried.

"I know you will darling, so don't go worrying your pretty little head anymore about it. It's just your silly old mum getting empty nest syndrome," she soothed.

Brigee left the room quietly, wiping a tear from her eye, evidently pleased mother and daughter had made up and all was well again in their world.

By the following evening, the family was back to normality. Rachel was thrilled and was already getting her clothes organised for Northern Ireland and had spent a considerable amount of time ringing her friends to tell them her awesome news. Kath and Marcus were happy to see their youngest daughter back to her usual self again. Rachel later confessed and explained how she had emotionally wrestled with the problem, confiding how difficult it was to determine when and how to break the news to them and it clearly had taken its toll.

Kath finally resigned herself to the fact that her two children would be living in Northern Ireland, her homeland of long ago and chose purposely to concentrate on the beautiful memories of her childhood. She smiled inwardly, thinking of the time when she had first met Marcus in Mount Stewart Gardens and also reminisced about her idyllic schoolyard days, blocking out her last years, before she fled her home country and the people that she loved.

On the weekend, Rachel rang Margaret to give her the good news and she was absolutely thrilled.

"I'll speak with mum quickly before you hang up," Margaret stated, having finished her conversation with her younger sister.

"Hi mum, how are you holding up?" she enquired sympathetically, remembering how they reacted when she first left to go to Ireland, fully recognising how her mother would be feeling right now.

"I'm fine love, although there's no point in denying it, it was one hell of a shock. Your father and I will miss her but it's comforting to know that you and Paul, as well as my parents, are over there with her."

"Don't worry mum, we'll keep our beady little eyes on her," Margaret chuckled. "And no boyfriends will definitely be allowed," she laughed. "If this should happen, we'll send her packing pronto, so she'll then have to find an Aussie one and then at least you'll have one of us over there with you."

"I'll inform your father," Kath chuckled "he'll be well pleased with the concept and will definitely insist that you keep your end of the bargain."

The chat with her eldest daughter cheered Kath to no end and as each new day passed, she slowly accepted Rachel was going overseas for a little while, to enhance her career.

The days sped by quickly; Kath enjoyed shopping with Rachel, reminiscing about the time when she had done the same for Margaret, many years ago. She didn't think for one solitary moment that she would be going through the whole scenario again with Rachel, her youngest child. But that's life; totally unpredictable Kath thought and sighed. She fully realised and accepted that one must simply go with the flow, as she continued with arrangements for her daughter's imminent departure.

Having accepted Rachel's decision, they decided to organise a farewell party, before she headed off on her new venture to Northern Ireland. In the meantime, several conversations had taken place between Kath and Margaret. Everyone was happy with what had been organised. Paul and Margaret agreed that Rachel could stay with them; making travelling back and forwards to work so much easier.

Over the past week, Marcus and Kath were taken aback by how resilient and remarkably methodical young Rachel had been. Proving to them both it was not a whimsical decision made on the spur of the moment. Rachel had taken time out to explain to them how she sent a copy of her diploma plus several references acquired from the college. She had also sent a couple of references obtained from two Noblealert employees. It was this that had got Rachel her journalist traineeship with the Belfast Telegraph and consequently hired on a trial basis. The college was known to obtain overseas placements for their students but Rachel being Rachel, accomplished it all on her own.

Rachel had been helping out at Noblealert for the past few years during her summer holidays and had a vast knowledge within the media industry, which no doubt enabled her to get the position overseas. Her volunteer work with the student magazine, coupled with other published works submitted to local newspapers, most likely contributed as well. Jane from production and Malcolm from the Editing Department had no idea when they were supplying her with references, she was applying for the Belfast Telegraph.

Rachel felt confident and prepared for the reporter's position; she had been taught extremely well by working journalists and had been given a practical and in-depth experience. Having trained extensively, she had learnt about news research, foreign correspondence and news production, while attending Macleay College. Obviously her conscientiousness paid off and she had dramatically increased her chances to gain a journalist position, after completing her diploma.

Before they knew it, the party was upon them and the caterers had done a remarkable job. All of Rachel's young friends would be dressed casually, because she didn't want a formal farewell. Her parents had prepared the dining room to be transformed into a make-believe nightclub. Special effects were added, which included strobe lighting, a trendy DJ with all the necessary gear and a dance platform was temporarily installed, allowing the party goers to dance the night away.

The kitchen was set up with trays of delicate finger food, placed strategically on the granite bench tops, so her friends could wander in and eat at their leisure.

In the entrance hall, Kath arranged for a mini cocktail bar to be set up, equipped with young bartenders, appropriate lighting and fast-tempo music. Young security personnel also had been hired for the evening to mingle undetected, among Rachel's friends and their respective partners. All were instructed to monitor if any excessive drinking was taking place and to remove the person or persons immediately, as they certainly didn't want a repeat of Margaret's twenty-third birthday party. A mini bus had been hired to take Rachel's friends home safely, leaving her absolutely ecstatic with the whole outcome.

"Thanks a million," Rachel beamed, giving them both massive bear hugs after inspecting everything, before her friends arrived for her farewell party.

"I really appreciate everything you have done for me over the years," she exclaimed, smiling at them both, her bright blue eyes were sparkling with joy. "I couldn't have asked for better parents and I will do you both proud," she added.

"You already have my dear child," Kath reciprocated.

Marcus began to feel emotional. "Although you may not be of my own flesh and blood Rachel, during the time I have spent with you, I always felt you were my daughter and one who I am exceptionally proud of," he said, smiling down at her. Marcus spoke from the heart and all three hugged, cherishing the moment, grateful for the blessings with which they had been given.

The guests began to arrive and Rachel enthusiastically hurried out to meet them. The music crept up louder, as more people started to show up.

The speakers were belting out the lyrics of the song Can't Get You Out of My Head when Kath and Marcus left to visit Valerie and Matt for the evening.

"Do you think everything will be okay?" Kath questioned on the drive over.

"Of course my love, everything will be fine. Don't forget we have security in place this time round," Marcus replied, very much looking forward to seeing Matt.

During dinner, the subject came up in relation to the skill set required for someone to excel in the world of journalism.

"Well, Rachel has always been inquisitive by nature," Kath smiled "which would help I guess."

"Going on last week's performance, she certainly challenges authority, is painfully honest, highly outspoken, determined and extremely persistent," Marcus added, picking up his glass of wine.

"It sounds like you have a very successful reporter on your hands," Valerie laughed. "Rachel has always been courageous and challenged the status quo, ever since the day she was born," she added.

Matt chuckled. "The main attributes Rachel has inherited are; she thinks fast on her feet, gets on well with everyone and I personally feel she couldn't have chosen a better career."

"I tend to agree," Kath smiled "however, it's a shame she has chosen to make her mark overseas."

"By the way, was she happy with the party arrangements?" Valerie enquired, deliberately changing the subject.

"The party was getting underway when we left and everyone seemed to be having a wonderful time," Kath replied.

"No phone calls yet, so obviously everyone are behaving themselves," Marcus teased.

The evening was a casual relaxed affair, which Kath and Marcus enjoyed immensely. They left at 1.30am and sneaked back into their home in the early hours of the morning, via the back entrance. The party seemed to be winding down when they climbed the stairs. Alex, who was the head of security informed them the party had been a wonderful success. He also assured them that everyone would be arriving home safely.

In a few days, Rachel would be making her way overseas. Unlike Margaret, she insisted on travelling to the UK on a domestic flight and had taken full responsibility in organising it herself.

"Independence is a great asset," Marcus murmured to Kath, gently reminding her to let her daughter make her own way in life.

Now they were all standing at Sydney Airport, suitcases already checked in and Rachel was ready to disappear through to Customs.

"Okay mum I've got to go, no teary farewells … please," Rachel insisted. "Marcus look after her," she laughed. "She'll drive you nuts, until I phone to say I've arrived over there safely," she smiled.

"Take care my love and live your dream," Kath added strongly, much more strongly than she felt right now, biting her bottom lip and putting on a brave face.

"Go set the world on fire Rachel," Marcus asserted, giving her one final hug.

Rachel took off fast, not daring to look behind her, not daring to say another word, tears trickling down her cheeks as she began making her way through to Customs.

"Come here," Marcus whispered quietly, wrapping Kath up in his arms, kissing her gently on the forehead and peering into her eyes. "It's not forever my love," he soothed, gently wiping away her tears, before taking her hand and leaving the airport.

Chapter Thirty Two

It was absolute mayhem at Belfast Airport, when Rachel was collected. Mary and Joe saturated her in hugs and kisses, along with Margaret and Paul, who arranged to take the day off from the Royal Victoria Hospital to be there.

Her luggage was picked up and taken to Paul's home at Knockbracken; here she had been allocated the huge spare bedroom at the back of the house. Blue cornflower walls, her favourite colour, complimented the pale blue and white chequered bedcover, smothered in fluffy white cushions and large linen pillows, resting invitingly against the shiny brass bed head. A set of white bedside cabinets were positioned on either side of the bed, supporting tall brass lamp stands with blue satin lampshades. A matching dressing table and wardrobe were positioned at the lower end of the room, allowing access to the huge bay window. This was decorated with crisp white curtains, trimmed with a delicate cornflower blue, blending in beautifully with the perfectly decorated room.

"It's simply divine," Rachel gushed, thrilled with the interior design and layout.

"We only finished it last week," Margaret replied, delighted with her sister's reaction. "By the way, how were mum and dad when you left?"

"Oh you know ... the usual. Marcus tries to distract mum at the airport, to prevent her from crying and me rushing through the gates as quickly as possible."

Margaret smiled lovingly across at her sister, before giving her another huge bear hug. "They'll miss you terribly but it's great having you here sis," Margaret confessed cheerfully.

Downstairs, everyone sat around the kitchen table having lunch together, enjoying the latest news from Australia. Mary enjoyed glancing through the photos Kath thoughtfully sent over, while Paul enquired about Valerie and Matt. Mary and Joe left later in the afternoon, noticing Rachel was yawning on several occasions, obviously exhausted and jet lagged from her trip. Margaret bid them farewell before tidying up, as Rachel proceeded upstairs to unpack her suitcases.

Peering down at the family photo taken in Australia, Rachel smiled, before gently setting it down on the bedside cabinet. Gazing around the room, it straight away felt cosy and welcoming. She was so pleased she made the journey. This is when the phone downstairs rang, startling her, drawing Rachel immediately away from her daydreaming. She smiled inwardly, as she made her way across the bedroom door, knowing instinctively, it would be her mother.

Rachel heard Margaret laughing as she made her way downstairs. "Yes mum, she's coming right now," Margaret relayed smiling, handing the phone over to Rachel.

"I'm here safe and sound mum, no need to panic," Rachel cheekily commented, prior to explaining about her journey on the way there and revealing how wonderful it had been, catching up with everyone at the airport. "The room's beautiful mum," she added softly, touched by her sister's loving act.

They chatted for another ten minutes, before the phone was handed back to Margaret, who no doubt would be given a list of things that Rachel would or would not be allowed to do.

At dinner, they ate a prepared chicken casserole, made and supplied by Mary. It was delicious, washed down with a glass of wine, before everyone went to bed.

"Goodnight sis," Margaret said, as Rachel got up to leave the room, appearing absolutely exhausted.

"Love you," Rachel replied openly, giving both Margaret and Paul a quick kiss on the cheek, before retiring for the evening. Clambering into bed, the fresh linen sheets felt good against her skin as she leaned across to turn off her bedside lamp. Yawning widely, she sunk down into her goose-down pillows and was out like a light.

Morning arrived and Margaret entered her room unexpectedly, carrying a breakfast tray. A blue stripy mug filled with steaming hot coffee, was a most welcoming sight for Rachel. Scrambled eggs on toast and a glass of orange juice was an added bonus, as her stomach suddenly began rumbling, extracting giggles from them both.

"Well, that was good timing," Margaret smiled, as Rachel sat up in bed feeling totally spoilt.

"And it's not even my birthday," Rachel exclaimed.

"Don't worry, you'll not be getting spoilt like this every morning," Margaret laughed. "I have the next few days off and simply wanted to surprise you."

"Thank you," Rachel replied warmly, feeling truly loved and appreciated.

The next few days were spent together, shopping in Belfast, gathering up winter woollies for Rachel. The people were friendly to Rachel, all commenting on her Australian accent, most finding it extremely difficult to comprehend, as to why Rachel would want to leave the glorious sunshine to visit Northern Ireland.

Margaret then took her to the Royal Victoria Hospital and caught up with Paul during his lunch break. She proudly introduced her to her friends and they too found Rachel simply adorable.

Rachel was later astounded by the security when entering the stores with her sister. Quite unceremoniously, everyone prised their handbags open for the proverbial military search, before continuing on their merry way. Soldiers kitted out in their camouflages were walking the streets, with their black shiny boots, guns at the ready. Barricades were set up at the top of major streets for more stringent searching, acting as a deterrent for potential terrorists. Yet the locals appeared somehow anaesthetised to it all, not batting an eyelid, seemingly unperturbed by the inconvenience. Sadness filled Rachel's heart. Inwardly, she acknowledged she took her freedom for granted back home in Australia but here in Northern Ireland, the population was not so fortunate.

On day three, Margaret visited her grandparents with Rachel not knowing what lay ahead. Rachel, not unlike her sister enjoyed the journey out to Downpatrick, soaking up the greenery on the way. She would be starting work in five days time and was very much looking forward to it. When they arrived, Patch the dog came rushing out to greet them both, manically barking and swishing his tail. Mary and Joe followed swiftly behind, both with smiles as big as Cheshire cats, obviously delighted with something.

"We've got something to show you," they both cried out in excitement, as soon as Rachel and Margaret alighted from the car. Without further ado, they grabbed Rachel's hand and winked at Margaret, who was fully aware of what was happening.

They made their way across to one of the old barns on the other side of the yard, before Joe moved up front to open up one of the doors. Rachel half expected to find a baby calf but got the shock of her life. Behind the barn doors, a shiny blue Honda Civic sat, with a huge ribbon tied on it.

"Oh my goodness," Rachel gasped, taken aback and obviously shocked.

"Mum and dad organised it, with us over here," Margaret beamed, as Joe and Mary automatically gave her a congratulatory hug.

"You obviously deserved it luv," Mary announced with tears in her eyes, happy for her young granddaughter.

"It will be great for work," Rachel squealed, rapidly pulling the ribbon off and plunking herself down inside. "It's gorgeous," she purred, as everyone admired the car both inside and out.

They had afternoon tea at Mary's, which was briefly interrupted by a phone call from overseas.

"I absolutely adore it mum," Rachel bubbled down the phone. "It was one heck of a surprise and the last thing I ever expected to see, especially after the last dealership fiasco at home," Rachel laughed.

"Marcus wanted to do something special for you my darling, making you fully aware that all is forgiven and forgotten. Quite frankly, it will be much easier for you to get to and from work," Kath replied, delighted the car was well received and a total surprise.

Rachel extended her appreciation to Marcus, before hanging up and joining everyone else. After tea she left her grandparents, following closely behind Margaret in her new Honda Civic, proud as punch and very much appreciating the independence the new set of wheels would give her.

Rachel spent the next couple of days driving in and around Belfast, familiarising herself with the streets and the nearby car parks, close to her new employment. She drove out and picked up Mary on one occasion, who was absolutely delighted with her unexpected visitor and they went shopping together, enjoying each other's company immensely.

At the weekend, she joined Paul and Margaret when they visited Helen and Henry, to participate in a traditional Sunday lunch. Rachel could see Margaret was the apple of Helen's eye, the two of them got on exceptionally well together and Rachel was extremely pleased. She thought Margaret had lost quite a bit of weight and put it down to her hectic life at the Royal but noticed Paul and her sister were still in love as much as ever.

"How are you enjoying Northern Ireland to date?" Helen enquired over lunch.

"I love it, however it seems strange seeing people being wrapped up in so many layers of warm clothing, compared to back home, where it's brightly coloured attire and short sleeves at present."

"What about sailing? Are you as competent as your sister?" Henry enquired politely.

"I'm afraid, not at all. I never really took an interest in boats," Rachel replied. "I must take after my mother in that regard," she laughed. It turned out a thoroughly relaxing day, ideal really, allowing her to unwind before commencing her new role at the Belfast Telegraph tomorrow.

Rachel was suitably impressed, with the solid stone building when she arrived at the huge front doors of her new employer. The Belfast Telegraph was established in 1870 and this was showcased on its landmark clock she noticed, before she headed indoors.

She was greeted by a receptionist and quickly directed into the main office. Immediately she was introduced to John Thompson, a young and confident journalist, nominated to show Rachel the ropes. His objective was to make Rachel feel welcome in her newly appointed position. By lunchtime, she had met the majority of the staff, finding everyone to be extremely friendly and wonderfully helpful. John, her newly appointed chaperone was tall and wiry, with a thick mop of short blond hair and deep blue, sea coloured eyes. He possessed a mesmerising smile and cheeky manner, which everyone readily accepted; whenever he was making the introductions he would mischievously goad or taunt the other employees, automatically receiving a quick rebuttal and smile. Rachel was eventually shown to her allocated desk, equipped with a computer, phone and all the mod cons, necessary to complete her work.

At 8.30am sharp, all the journalists flocked towards the boardroom in readiness for their Monday morning meeting, to ascertain what stories they were running with for the week. Sales consultants sat opposite the reporters, waiting to hear what special features would be implemented. Afterwards they would contact their regular advertisers, as well as seek out new business, to generate revenue for the company.

Rachel was introduced to everyone again by the manager, going by the name of Al, who had been working at the newspaper for over twenty five years. An excellent journalist in his day apparently, according to John.

On Friday evening, a week after Rachel began her work, she stood looking around at the familiar faces, acclimatising her ears to the rowdy racket, created by the regulars. The good majority of journalists already downed a pint or two at their local haunt, a typical watering hole to congregate at the end of the week, allowing them to catch up and congratulate each other, on another stressful and successful week.

Margaret and Paul were pleased Rachel had settled in well at work. She pulled her weight at home, frequently having dinner prepared for them when they arrived home in the evenings.

"We got our girl after all," Paul commented to Margaret, later in the evening when they were tucked up in bed together.

"Yes, this one cooks, cleans and there's no teething problems to deal with," Margaret joked. Both thoroughly at ease with one another, they decided to try for another child, considering six months had passed since the tragic incident. Margaret was physically fit and got the green light from her gynaecologist. Emotionally she was fine, having attended a psychologist for one brief session, illustrating she wasn't fostering any long term guilt or depression since the incident. Both communicated well and she maintained a positive outlook, enabling her to move forward, without suffering from any psychological torment.

Rachel enjoyed Henry's company, whenever she caught up with him when she was with Margaret and Paul. She found him to be extremely intelligent, noting he had a wickedly dry sense of humour which was quite endearing to her ears. Rachel had spoken to him regularly in relation to up and coming cases and was frequently given permission to sit in his courtroom. All the other journalists recognised, she was given preferential treatment when it came to an official interview, due to Henry's recommendations.

After two months of employment, Rachel was unexpectedly summoned to Al's office. He explained that he was suitably impressed with her work; commenting she had a good nose to sniff out a story and had the makings of a splendid journalist.

Rachel had just passed her three month trial with flying colours and was offered a full time position to continue her internship. Al was well aware her father and mother had expanded a media empire in Australia, surmising this probably attributed to Rachel's skill set. However, he was totally oblivious he worked with Kath, a very long time ago.

"Damn it," Paul stammered, rustling through the first aid box at home. "I thought we had some headache pills in here," he sung out to Margaret from the kitchen.

"We did," she looked up, completely mystified.

"Oops, that my fault," Rachel confessed openly. "I had a splitting headache the other morning and raided the box. I forgot and ended up leaving the packet at work," she grimaced.

"No big drama," Margaret replied. "I'll just nip down the street and get some from the chemist."

"I'll do it," Rachel interrupted, jumping up from the couch and heading towards the porch to grab her coat and handbag. Down at the chemist she decided to stock up, purchasing extra packets to keep on hand. She had been suffering massive migraines of late but didn't want to say anything to Margaret or Paul or they would fuss over her and then the whole family would be in on it and she would never hear the end of it.

Work was gathering momentum of late; Rachel was heavily involved in reporting on terrorist activities, discovering it was both challenging and harrowing. She was trying to come to terms with the heavily biased reporting from within the different media groups, noticing that one was as dogmatic as the other.

She wanted to report on human tragic incidents, without mentioning their religious or political backgrounds, allowing the public to view the devastation with complete empathy and without prejudice.

Rachel felt the various media groups should have banded together and signed an agreement to this effect. She strongly believed it would have led to less reprisal shootings and lessened the overall casualty rates.

Drugs were also another factor dominating the north, with multiple gangs running their areas, clearly demonstrating if anyone encroached upon their domain, they were not tolerated and viciously dealt with. Rachel had been involved in many late night stakeouts, trying to investigate and gather information, as to who were behind the brutal murders and organised crime. She mingled with the authorities, piecing evidence together to come up with interesting stories, written from a humane perspective, omitting a biased opinion. It was a responsible method of reporting, which she felt comfortable with and one which she was determined to stick to.

John at work had taken a real liking to young Rachel. He was twenty-two years old and his previous girlfriend had taken off to England, to further her computer programming career. He and Rachel would spend hours together in stakeouts, discussing their personal lives, both extremely comfortable with one another. He was fascinated by Rachel's bright outlook on life, attributing it to her carefree upbringing in sunny Australia.

"Would you like to come to a house warming party with me next Saturday night?" he casually asked, sitting opposite her at work on Wednesday.

"Is it a casual affair or do you have to get dressed up?" Rachel enquired innocently.

"Jeans and tops probably," John replied. "It's my sister's new place and she told me to bring a friend," he smiled cheerfully.

"Okay then, I haven't anything planned, so why not" she grinned. "Where is the party by the way and what time does it start?" she questioned.

"It's at Bangor and don't worry, I'll pick you up," he instantly volunteered.

"Sounds good to me," Rachel countered, before being interrupted with a phone call.

Saturday night rolled around and Rachel changed her top three times, trying to decide which one was more appropriate. Margaret was sitting on the edge of Rachel's bed scrutinising her, before bursting out into laughter.

"What's so funny sis?" she enquired lightly.

"You are," Margaret giggled. "Who is this John guy anyway? Should we be worried? Is he going to sweep you off your feet?" she joked.

"Of course not," Rachel replied, rather indignantly. "We're simply work mates who get on extremely well together, that's all," Rachel added, rolling her eyes, settling on the pale blue lamb's wool sweater, which matched her eyes perfectly.

At 7.30pm the door bell rang and Margaret went racing to the door, before Rachel could get down the stairs.

"Hi John, I'm Margaret, Rachel's older sister. Come on in, she's not ready yet but she should be down shortly," she smiled, escorting him into the lounge room.

"Would you like a beer or a coffee?" Paul called out from the kitchen.

"No I'm fine thanks, we'll have to make tracks shortly," John responded casually.

Paul came into the lounge room and formally introduced himself, instantly taking a liking to the tall lanky lad, after having a quick chat. Rachel came bounding down the stairs, quickly singing out her farewells, as she gathered John up to leave. Margaret mouthed 'very nice' to her sister, as she was closing the front door, resulting in Rachel shaking her head and blushing.

Later, Rachel was introduced to John's sister Patricia, who was extremely sociable and bubbly.

"So this is the lovely Rachel I've been hearing so much about," she smiled, peering directly at her brother, giving him an approving look.

John instantly appeared rattled as he looked in Rachel's direction. "Yes ... well we don't get to meet many Aussies over here," he stammered, blushing slightly.

Observing the situation, Rachel's heart instantly melted. Immediately recognising he had been exceptionally kind and attentive towards her, ever since she arrived at the Belfast Telegraph. He was easy to get along with, exceedingly attractive and the best chaperone anyone could ever ask for.

"Would you like a glass of wine?" Patricia interrupted her thoughts, deciding to let her little brother off the hook. She could see he was enamoured with Rachel, who seemed incredibly intelligent and confident, yet friendly and approachable. She smiled inwardly; recognising straight away that Rachel had no idea how much her brother adored her.

Rachel recognised quite a few of the party goers from her workplace and felt totally at ease throughout the evening. She danced with John frequently, finding him extremely funny and the most relaxed she had ever seen him, over the past five months.

The party started to wind down at 2am and John automatically suggested grabbing some kebabs, before heading home. They sat snuggled up on the seawall, devouring their freshly made kebabs served up from a local kiosk, positioned to catch the patrons exiting the local pubs, in the early hours of the morning. The street lights reflected brightly upon the dark tranquil sea, as the yachts tranquilly bobbed soothingly in rhythm to the tide.

Rachel shivered abruptly, quickly taking note John immediately removed his jacket and wrapped it around her, to provide some extra warmth.

"Don't you feel the cold?" Rachel broke into the stillness of the early morning.

"Not really, I suppose you grow up in it and think nothing of it," he laughed. "Come on, I better get you home before you catch your death," he added quickly, noticing Rachel shivering again.

He grabbed her hand, pulling her up and into his arms. Without saying a word, he noticed her innocent blue eyes sparkling under the street light; her face soft and serene. Slowly he leant in and gently closing his eyes, he kissed her. Rachel responded, slowly at first, initially taken back by his tenderness, before mellowing and melting into his arms. Withdrawing softly, he smiled, flicking a light golden curl behind her ear.

"I'm sorry," he whispered compassionately. "That wasn't meant to happen," peering into her soft blue eyes, holding his breath.

"It was unexpected," she replied tenderly, wrapping her arms around his neck to kiss him again.

Margaret heard Rachel arrive in at 3.30am and smiled contently, reminding herself to get all the gossip in the morning, before drifting back to sleep.

Rachel arrived downstairs at 11am to make herself a strong cup of coffee, before she was set upon and quizzed by her sister. Paul wasn't going to be finishing his shift until 3pm, giving Margaret ample time to interrogate her younger sibling. Margaret teased and goaded her sister, until she extracted every piece of news from the previous evening.

"You would have made a good reporter," Rachel joked, tucking into a toasted sandwich for lunch.

"The kiss, tell me all about the wonderful kiss again?" Margaret appealed, smiling enthusiastically; absolutely delighted Rachel had a liaison with John the previous evening.

"It just happened out of the blue," Rachel replied, shrugging her shoulders. "One minute he was helping me up. The next minute, I was wrapped up in his arms and his beautiful soft lips were brushing up against mine," she sighed dreamily.

"It sounds ever so romantic," Margaret cooed. "So when are you going out again?" she queried.

"Oh I don't know? And who knows, he might never want to see me again," Rachel joked, inwardly hoping there would be many more liaisons. Not daring to breathe a word of what she was wishing for, to Margaret. "Right, I'm going upstairs to tidy up my room sis and to catch up on some work," she insisted, bolting up out of the couch immediately and making her way towards the stairs.

Margaret wandered into the kitchen to prepare the evening meal, pleased Rachel had met a nice companion. She hoped John and Rachel would get to spend more leisure time together, secretly feeling they would make a lovely couple. The way Margaret figured it; he was in the same line of work and would fully understand her busy working schedules. The pair of them were charismatic together, both with strikingly blue eyes and light blond hair, lean figures and quietly confident. Yes, Margaret was determined to do everything in her power to encourage their relationship, knowing in her heart he would be good for her sister, Margaret thought, as she sought out the cutlery to set the dinner table.

Rachel was hanging her clothes up in her wardrobe; when suddenly; an excruciating pain struck her forcibly, causing her to collapse on the bed immediately. She sat perfectly still, deadly pale, clasping her head in her hands, as blinding pain pounded the back of her head. Damn it, I think I might be needing glasses, she thought, as her left eye went blurry. The throbbing pain continued, searing relentlessly within her skull. Stretching forward and grabbing her handbag, she rummaged through it quickly, swiftly retrieving the headache pills. She devoured nearly half a packet, washing them down rapidly with a glass of water sitting on the bedside table. Lying back down on top of her bed, she closed her eyes praying for a reprieve, scrunching up her face in absolute agony.

"Hey Rachel, are you okay?" Margaret inquired gently, as she walked into her sister's room some several hours later.

"Gosh, it's dark outside already," Rachel said, really surprised.

"It's seven o'clock love and I was wondering what you were up to?" Margaret smiled meekly, noticing her sister was exceedingly pale.

Recovering quickly, Rachel explained she lay down for a few minutes and must have fallen asleep.

"Too much alcohol and too much kissing," Margaret cheerfully reprimanded her sister.

Rachel went along with it, simply grateful her headache had disappeared. All three ate dinner together shortly afterwards, sitting around the kitchen table, while Paul explained a funny scenario which had taken place at work that day. John came up in the conversation during dessert, with Paul mentioning he was a nice young guy and he hoped to see more of him around, inwardly surmising he would.

Soon afterwards, Rachel left Paul and Margaret lounging on the couch together watching a Sunday night movie, as she headed off to her room to have an early night, knowing she had an early start the following day.

Chapter Thirty Three

John was waiting for her when she arrived at work. "Ready for a coffee?" he asked cheerfully.

Rachel nodded, automatically smiling, recognising he knew her Monday morning routine before the meetings. Rachel intuitively felt him looking at her as she was going through her notes, when he was making her coffee. Looking up, their eyes met, his were soft and full of longing.

"Are you okay," he enquired gently. "I mean, after what took place on Saturday night, I hope I didn't overstep the mark?"

"Not at all," Rachel smiled.

"I'm glad," he replied, exhaling loudly, appearing more relaxed. "I wanted to call you last night but I was scared of intruding," he confided.

"I wish you would have, as my sister was giving me the third degree," she laughed. "Apparently you've made a great impression on both her and Paul, in the whole ten minutes you had with them," she declared, arching an eyebrow and grinning widely.

"Well obviously, they're a good judge of character," he teased.

Karan walked into the canteen at that moment. "I'll have a coffee if you're making one," she interrupted "two sugars thanks," she smiled, walking over to retrieve the biscuit tin from the table.

Soon everyone was gathered in the boardroom and Al was allocating everybody their schedules. Rachel and John were assigned to write a piece on the guns and ammunition, uncovered in Armagh over the weekend. This area was known as bandit country, because a lot of illegal activities took place in these parts. It was renowned for numerous murders, with countless ones remaining unsolved. Rachel and John worked well together and their relationship grew.

They both started dating and gone out several times to the movies, visiting pubs and the odd nightclub or two, allowing them to relax and let their hair down. Their jobs were stressful and completely unpredictable, frequently not knowing where their stories would lead them, discovering sometimes, it was simply downright dangerous. Rachel thrived on the unpredictability and was meticulous in her reporting, gaining massive respect from many of her peers.

On a personal level, John and Rachel's rendezvous were becoming more heated. Their kissing was growing more passionate and serious, with neither of them wanting to part at the end of an evening. Paul and Margaret caught them several times in the front room in a loving embrace, causing them to straighten up immediately, both automatically blushing from having been sprung.

Rachel was invited to one of John's cousins wedding, which was taking place in Londonderry. John suggested they head up early Saturday morning and stay the night in a motel. Two separate rooms were booked but they both suspected they would end up together by the end of the evening.

The wedding took place with one hundred guests attending and it was a beautiful family affair. Fiona the bride was radiant on the day and Brendan was enamoured with his gorgeous new wife. Celebrations continued until midnight, before the guests wound down and headed to their respective hotels. Everyone was in high spirits after consuming loads of champagne. Most of the guests mingled happily during the reception and ended up dancing the majority of the night away.

Rachel and John caught a taxi back to their motel; Rachel enjoyed the day immensely and was in a happy relaxed state of mind. While kissing John goodnight, her hunger grew for him as they kissed passionately, both desiring one another. They ended up in her room. There was no going back, because she wanted him badly. Rachel wanted to feel him close, kissing him urgently and egging him on, driving him crazy with desire. Lying upon her bed, he ran his hand up under her satin blouse, unclipping her bra, as their breathing increased, becoming heavier and more laboured.

"I better stop," John whispered, swallowing hard, not wanting to leave. His heart was reeling but his mind was racing ahead, warning him not to ruin the relationship they had created to date.

"Don't stop," Rachel gasped, unbuttoning his shirt and running her hands up over his chest.

"But we must," John hesitated between kisses; "your sister would kill me."

"Never mind her ... I'll kill you with my own bare hands, if you dare stop now," Rachel groaned, undoing his belt buckle.

John moaned, fully aware he wanted her, knowing he craved her so badly. Within minutes, they were stripped naked, both entwined in each other's arms. Their desires were overwhelmingly strong, urgent and unstoppable. His eyes were full of love and passion as he feasted on Rachel's young body, fresh and beautiful, willing him on. Rolling her on to her back, he smothered her in kisses from head to toe, as she whimpered and crumpled, beneath his warm loving embrace. His touch was electrifying, as he covered her body in moist loving kisses.

Slowly, ever so slowly, he took Rachel. She trembled, evaporating into his hot loving embrace. Totally mesmerised and overcome by his gentleness and engaging desire. Accommodating him, ever so slowly, she began finding her rhythm and then he took her, completely. Together, they found one another in the dimly lit room, both giving themselves wholly and unconditionally. Both crying out in unison and climaxing together, before collapsing into each other's arms, liberated and exhausted. Both were lying together as one, having tenderly shared and cemented their deeply felt love for one another.

Holding her protectively within his embrace, he whispered "I began falling in love with you Rachel from the very first night we kissed and you've had my heart ever since."

Smiling graciously up at him, Rachel sighed contentedly, wrapped up in her lovers' arms. "I feel at peace with you John, it's almost as if I've known you all my life," she whispered, kissing him gently.

The young couple fell asleep snuggled up together, having affirmed their relationship, taking it to the next level, knowing they were following their hearts.

John could be found sleeping soundly the following morning, while Rachel was showering close by in a happy and peaceful mood. Out of nowhere, she felt a piercing hot pain shoot throughout her skull, blinding, intense, unbearable pain, bringing her instantly to her knees. She sat crumpled up in the shower corner, clenching her eyes tightly shut; her vision having badly deteriorated, since the excruciating attack struck. Letting the water wash over her, Rachel prayed it would chase away the dizziness and nauseous, trying her best to refrain from passing out, as she sat hunched over in excruciating agony.

"Shit Rachel, are you okay?" John stammered, immediately pulling the shower door open and turning off the taps, before stretching downward and wrapping her frail, pale body up in a towel. Carrying her over to her bed, he set her down gently. "My god, you look ghastly. What can I do?" he requested urgently.

"My handbag please," Rachel whimpered, pointing towards the floor, as the jackhammers continued thumping in her head. Fumbling around in her bag, she grabbed for the headache pills. "Water please," she pleaded miserably, desperately swallowing a handful, as John hurried to the bathroom to retrieve a glass of water. Upon his return, she extracted another two pills and swallowed them, washing them quickly and gratefully down.

"Migraine?" he questioned.

She nodded in response, wanting the persistent banging to stop.

"Okay, close your eyes and rest," he soothed, tucking her into bed and drawing the curtains, blocking out the early morning light. Crawling into bed he laid next to her. Slowly he began lightly massaging her forehead, trying his upmost to ease her pain, as she lay perfectly still in utter agony. She gradually drifted off to sleep and he was enormously relieved, watching the tension slowly ease from her face, allowing a serenity to slowly and gently evolve, before he slipped away himself in a deep slumber.

"Gosh what time is it?" Rachel bolted up in bed, relieved to find her headache had subsided.

"Three o'clock," John answered; pleased to see she had recovered completely. "Shit, you scared me Rachel. You looked as white as a ghost. Do you get migraines often?"

"No," she lied, immediately recognising straight away she would have to see a doctor urgently, to investigate what was going on.

"When you were sleeping, I went out and got some sandwiches for lunch," he smiled, retrieving them from the bedside table. They sat and tucked into their food; Rachel was starving and John was concerned.

Shortly afterwards, they packed their belongings and headed back to Knockbracken. Rachel was quiet in the car, subconsciously feeling guilty for spoiling their morning.

"What's with the long face?" John questioned, drawing Rachel instantly from her thoughts.

"I'm angry at myself for drinking too many champers yesterday. I should have known it would have an adverse effect. I really feel I spoilt our weekend and I'm truly sorry," she confided humbly.

"Last night was sensational Rachel and nothing could possibly have spoilt it," he confessed smiling. Taking her tiny hand in his, he inwardly took note, never to purchase champagne for Rachel ever again.

Arriving back at Paul and Margaret's place, Rachel made a hasty retreat, giving John a quick goodbye kiss, before thanking him again for a truly magnificent weekend.

He drove off happy, acknowledging Rachel had immense loving feelings for him, as he had for her. Life was grand he thought, making his way over to his sister's house, immensely pleased he could tell her, that he was officially now in a relationship with Rachel.

The following day Rachel visited a doctor's surgery during her lunch break; he checked her reflexes and had her carrying out some simple and compulsory mental exercises.

"Gee, I haven't worked with fractions since leaving high school," she laughed.

Dr Jamison was extremely cautious as he carried out further tests and insisted on a referral, enabling Rachel to visit a neurologist, which she felt was completely unnecessary. However, she was having difficulties remembering things of late, which is not characteristic of migraines and acknowledged she had to follow through with his recommendation.

The neurologist booked her in for a CT scan and one week later she was sent for a MRI. More diagnostic tests, she sighed. Thank goodness I'm not claustrophobic, she thought, lying in the rounded chamber perfectly still. She was still under the illusion it was totally unnecessary, as she marvelled at the technology being utilised, to examine her brain. She seriously considered sneaking her plastic kangaroo key ring in and hiding it amongst her hair but lying in the cold sterile room, she sensed the medical team would not have appreciated her joke. She suffered several migraines in between the appointments and consequently decided to behave herself.

In the meantime, John was spoiling her rotten and she had fallen completely head over heels in love with him. She loved his sense of humour, his inner strength and his gentle loving mannerisms, which were endearing and what she treasured the most. They had many intimate moments together, deeply forging their love and passion for one another, whenever they had the opportunity to get away.

Upon completion of her MRI, an appointment had been organised for her with Dr Finlay, a neurosurgeon working at the Royal Victoria Hospital. Rachel was concerned for two reasons. Firstly, she felt the neurologist was definitely overreacting and secondly, she didn't want to run into Margaret at the hospital or she would be given the proverbial third degree.

During this taxing and anxious period, she purposely didn't mention anything to John. Rachel hated unnecessary fussing and decided to go it alone, hoping to find out what the problem was and to find a solution quickly. In quiet contemplation, she mentally decided to inform her family members, John and her acquaintances when the matter was resolved and could see no real point in getting everyone involved at this early stage.

A time was arranged for the following Wednesday and Rachel being Rachel, decided to write a story on Colleen Ahearn, who was currently a patient at the Royal Victoria Hospital. She was one of the survivors from last week's bomb attack, a recovering amputee, who was thankful to be alive. Al had given Rachel clearance to carry out the interview, acknowledging this was her forte, fully aware she would produce a tangible piece. Rachel took her dictaphone in with her and was truly amazed by Colleen's enthusiasm for life.

"I've got a second chance you know," she relayed to Rachel "not like some of the others," shaking her head sorrowfully. Peering at Rachel momentarily, with her dark set serious eyes, she broke into their ghostly silence, announcing "and I'm gonna put it to good use," giving her a watery smile, letting go of her debilitating beliefs and patting Rachel's hand.

Rachel instinctively knew it would be an intriguing article, filled with inspirational antidotes, depicting a brave and powerful, human spirit. Rachel thanked Colleen profusely, before going off to find Dr Finlay's office, in order to collect her personal results.

Approaching the reception desk to relay her details and confirm her appointment, Rachel thought, perfect timing, whilst glancing down at her watch

"Could you take a seat please, Dr Finlay will be with you shortly," the dark haired, middle aged receptionist stated curtly, before answering her phone.

Opaque glass windows cluttered with numerous medical posters, blocked the area off from the main hospital corridor, Rachel noticed, sitting in the waiting room. Warnings were depicted in bold red and black writing, obsessively informing the public of the latest flu epidemic, symptoms of diabetes and potential heart attack symptoms. Engrossed in the world of posters, Rachel was startled when Dr Finlay walked towards her, formally calling out her name.

Rising from her well worn vinyl seat, she was suitably impressed to find Dr Finlay to be an eccentric middle aged gentleman, dressed in a light blue jacket with contrasting bowtie, accompanied by a matching handkerchief, tucked into his top pocket. He smiled benevolently; his light blue eyes and pale grey hair suggested he was an intelligent aristocrat, who no doubted accumulated a wealth of experience over his working career. Rachel followed him into his office and was offered a seat straight away.

His desk was well organised and immaculate, a bit like him really she surmised, smiling inwardly. His voice was a deep baritone, professional, comforting and precise.

Rachel was asked about her family's medical history and she explained her father's accidental death, stating it was the main reason for her lack of complete medical records. She collectively went over her symptoms yet again, as Dr Finlay fidgeted with her reports. Intuitively, she sensed he was making small talk and in true journalistic fashion, she questioned him directly.

"I feel I've been repeating myself over and over again, with the various specialists I've been seeing," Rachel asserted. "My health is obviously deteriorating and I would really appreciate it please if you could tell me what is causing these headaches and how do we move forwards from here?"

"Have you anyone attending the clinic with you today Rachel, as suggested?" Dr Finlay enquired calmly, depicting kindness and understanding, until sadness unexpectedly flickered within his eyes. Noticing his body language, one of her habitual traits picked up as a journalist, Rachel instinctively straightened up in her chair.

"I came alone on purpose," Rachel announced, deliberately eliminating any doubt, while making direct eye contact. She wanted him to divulge his diagnosis as quickly as possible, so she could leave immediately, before getting sprung by Margaret.

Glancing down at his notes and pathology reports, a subtle transformation was taking place, creating uneasiness between them. Dr Finlay was distant, sounding as if he had swallowed a medical journal. Immediately he robotically began revealing diagrams and test results, prattling on in his medical jargon, implicitly concentrating on tumour positioning within her brain. He carried on, differentiating between benign and malignant tumours and illustrating how prevalent it was in younger patients. At one stage, he went off in another tangent, questioning the usage of mobile phones and other advanced technology.

Rachel assimilated the overall outcome, picking up on bits and pieces as he continued his monologue. The bottom line was ... a malignant brain tumour was located in the centre of her brain. A grade three apparently. It was too risky to operate according to Dr Finlay, because she could suffer a brain haemorrhage, which could lead to a stroke if she was lucky but most likely would result in death. Hell, that's the good part, Rachel thought, while the other alternative was to endure immeasurable brain damage, resulting in loss of motor and cognitive skills, by not operating at all. Drawing in a deep breath, she instantly shuddered.

"STOP ..." Rachel put her hand up, her head was beginning to hurt, her mind spinning and racing manically out of control, fighting anxiously to comprehend and digest the news she had just been given.

She was mentally trying to put the pieces together, like an enormous jig-saw puzzle, trying frantically to make sense of it all. She was only nineteen years old ... for Christ's sake. It didn't make sense. She fought hard to maintain her equanimity.

Looking directly at Dr Finlay, she explicitly asked "If it's inoperable ... how long have I got?"

Dr Finlay lowered his eyes, hesitating slightly, before looking up and advising her gently. "It's hard to predict Rachel but going on your symptoms and my experience, I would say approximately six months to one year ... MAX."

This one remark sabotaged any remaining hope.

Rachel gulped in air, while perfectly motionless, not daring to move, nor speak or do anything. Holy shit, u-n-b-e-l-i-e-v-a-b-l-e, this is so unfair, vibrated hysterically around and around in her mind. Clenching her fists automatically, her knuckles turned white; she tried with all her might to hold back the massive tears forming but to no avail.

Dr Finlay automatically retrieved his decorative handkerchief from his top pocket and handed it to her, as tears spilled down her cheeks. "Rachel, I am truly sorry to be the bearer of devastating news, these particular cases are rare but unfortunately it can happen. Are you sure there is no one I can contact for you?" he enquired sympathetically.

"There is no one," Rachel cried, looking up through blotchy red eyes, wanting desperately to vacate the room, struggling for air while appearing suffocated and trapped.

"I will make another appointment to meet with you Rachel. By then you will have had time to digest the news fully and gain clarity," he suggested solemnly. Recognising only too well the signs of a trapped human being, who simply wanted to run and live in complete denial.

"That won't be necessary," her rebuttal was both cold and angry, taking Dr Finlay by surprise.

"I feel it's important to discuss treatments, such as radiotherapy and chemotherapy to slow things down and ..."

"It is totally unnecessary," Rachel interrupted belligerently, instantly standing up. "I have your number if I need to make another appointment. However, in the meantime, I will be seeking a second opinion," she added forcibly.

Complete denial, Dr Finlay thought and sighed heavily, peering at Rachel sympathetically, understandable of course, as she was only nineteen years old.

"Thank you for your time Dr Finlay," she smiled half heartedly, shaking his hand hurriedly before exiting his room, closing the door abruptly behind her. It was on days like these, Dr Finlay wished he had never chosen or studied to be a neurosurgeon. She was only a young woman … and it was a damn shame, he thought, sitting in quiet contemplation, shaking his head mournfully, before returning to his paperwork.

Rushing up the corridor completely overwhelmed and devastated by the horrifying news, she made her way blindly towards the exit. Rounding the next corner she accidentally ran into someone, the impact causing her to drop her handbag, sending the contents splattering across the floor.

"SHIT," Rachel lamented, breaking into huge sobs as Paul automatically bent down to retrieve the items, apologising along the way.

It was only when he looked up to return the handbag; that he was startled to see Rachel towering over him, crying uncontrollably, obviously heartbroken.

"Rachel, what on earth are you doing here? What's happened?" he questioned, genuinely concerned.

Rachel recoiled instantly and pulled herself together rather quickly. Holy hell, there was no way she wanted to divulge her devastating news to anyone, least of all now. Not until she got herself sorted, mentally and physically prepared. Her mind went into overdrive, searching frantically for a solution.

"Mrs Ahearn," she blurted out, immediately grabbing Paul by the arm to escort him outside. The last thing she needed was for Dr Finlay to arrive on the scene. Outside, she immediately requested a cigarette.

"I didn't know you smoked," Paul stated, recognising Rachel was really distressed.

"I have an odd one now and again," she retorted, wiping her face with her sleeve.

Lighting her cigarette, Paul noticed her hand trembling. Whatever was upsetting Rachel had her well and truly rattled.

"Do you want to talk about it?" Paul enquired gently.

"After I've had my smoke," Rachel stammered, trying to buy some time. They both dragged on their cigarettes, peering up at the mottled grey sky, as a light drizzle sprinkled from the heavens, contributing to the puddles scattered along the edge of the car park.

"I'm sorry Paul," Rachel spoke first, breaking into the stony silence. "Sometimes the stories I write are heart wrenching and Mrs Ahearn is a prime example. She was one of the survivors from last week's bomb attack and I interviewed her this morning. It would break anyone's heart."

"Is that the amputee who lost both legs?"

"Yes," Rachel nodded solemnly.

Paul sighed. "It was sad but at least she's still alive," he announced.

"That's exactly what she said," Rachel replied, giving him a watery smile.

"If it's any consolation Rachel, it will get easier. At times your sister gets overwhelmed by it all but our fates are written and there's not much we can do about it," he sighed.

"Don't say anything to Margaret, she'll only start to worry," Rachel said frowning, appearing extremely anxious.

"Don't worry, your secret's safe with me," Paul added gently. "Now let me buy you a coffee from the cafeteria," he smiled humbly.

Rachel grinned. "Thanks Paul but I really must leave or my boss will think I've got lost," she joked.

"Okay then but are you sure you're alright?"

"I'll be fine," Rachel persisted, giving him a quick peck on the cheek. "Don't worry I'll have dinner ready for tonight and I'll not sit around moping," she teased, before rushing off towards her car.

Paul stood momentarily, watching her drive off in the dismal rain. Poor kid, it couldn't be easy for a nineteen year old experiencing the atrocities of terrorism and having to write about them, he thought, before quickly heading back inside.

Chapter Thirty Four

A week passed and Rachel had not endeavoured to seek a second opinion, as there was no real point. Dr Finlay was a renowned professional within his field; she didn't doubt his expertise in any shape or form. She simply had to make out she was making other enquiries and seeking alternative help elsewhere. Because she was sure to run into Margaret next time around and she wouldn't get off the hook so easily, as she did with Paul.

She spent sleepless nights, regurgitating everything over and over in her muddled mind. Fully comprehending her illness was terminal. Researching intensively on the internet, she was becoming more knowledgeable on her deteriorating symptoms and was secretly preparing for her future. However long that may be.

Nothing in life is permanent, she reminded herself, acknowledging she would have to sacrifice all emotional ties and attachments. It was only but fair to protect those she loved, making it her last remaining gift to them, in order to lessen their pain. When it drew closer to the time she would inform her parents but not until then. She refused to be treated like an invalid. To be looked upon sympathetically and pitied. Instead, she made up her mind to live life to the fullest, like Colleen Ahearn.

As she lay in bed, the street lights cast dark shadows within her room, her eyes filled with tears. She made the heart wrenching decision to let

John go. It would be totally inhumane to engage and continue a loving relationship with him. No, she definitely had to end it no matter how painful it would be, bitterly fighting with herself internally. He would never understand when it came to breaking up with him. How could he, especially when he was not aware of her medical condition. This way, he would get over her quickly and meet someone else. Someone he could love dearly and grow old with, a beautiful loving wife who could provide him with children. A young intelligent woman, who wouldn't break his heart and die within a year. Tears trickled down upon her pillow in the dead of night, as she lay alone, lost and exhausted.

"What do you mean you're moving out?" Margaret exclaimed. "I thought you were happy here?" she complained, taken totally by surprise with Rachel's decision.

Rachel peered across at her sister the following morning, hating the road she had to take but there was no other option. No ties, no attachments and no heartaches, she reiterated over and over in her mind, methodically.

"I need my privacy sis," Rachel appealed, arching an eye brow. "I do have a life you know," she added smiling "and besides, I'm sick of your cooking," she joked.

Margaret instantly backed down. Reminiscing when Paul and her first met, remembering how they longed for their privacy, both wanting to spend as much time as possible together.

"Okay ... I get the message but where will you go?"

"I've found a small terrace house on Ormeau Road, it's much closer to work and the rent is really cheap," Rachel replied.

"Gee that was quick."

"You know me, I don't muck around," she grinned.

"When are you thinking of moving?"

"Next weekend," Rachel retorted.

"Sounds like you have your mind made up," Margaret said, accepting her little sister was growing up and needed her own space.

"Don't worry you can come around and visit," Rachel laughed; pleased Margaret accepted her decision and explanation so easily.

The following weekend Paul and Margaret helped her move in. They gave her the bedroom suite from her existing room, along with the curtains and lamps, under the pretence of wanting to redecorate and turn her old bedroom into a study.

"Are you sure?" Rachel questioned, feeling they were being far too generous.

"Yes, we most certainly are," Paul stated. "I wanted a study for years, so don't be changing your mind," he joked.

The remainder of the weekend was spent getting Rachel's new home ship shape. She purchased a new dark brown leather sofa and also managed to pick up two vintage arm chairs from a second hand shop, with them all blending in together beautifully. Margaret and Paul bought her a new rug and matching cushions, to make Rachel's place even more homely.

The fireplace in the small front room was still functioning, which Rachel simply adored. The kitchen was small and basic but functional, neat and tidy. The two bedrooms upstairs were separated by an average size bathroom containing an old four legged bath, which had been lovingly restored.

Margaret rummaged through her cupboards at home and Mary did as well. Both ended up supplying Rachel with tea sets and saucepans, along with cutlery and extra bed linen. Rachel was absolutely overwhelmed by their kindness and was pleased with the overall effect.

"Are you sure you'll be okay?" Margaret enquired again, as Rachel said goodnight to both her and Paul.

"Of course I will be," Rachel laughed.

"Well thanks for dinner and give us a call if you need anything," Paul added, grabbing Margaret by the arm, making his way to the front door.

"Goodnight then," Margaret replied reluctantly, somewhat subdued.

"I'll come over for dinner on Tuesday night," Rachel announced unexpectedly, causing Margaret to automatically smile.

"Great," she said straight away, giving her sister a quick kiss before leaving.

Rachel stood watching the car drive up the road, before retreating inside. The fire was flickering in the hearth, radiating a heart-warming amber glow, as Rachel stood taking in her comfy surroundings. Tears formed in her eyes immediately, as she realised that this was it, no ties, no attachments and no heartaches.

She climbed the stairs and jumped into bed, reviewing her situation once again, totally exhausted. Plan 'A' had gone according to her vision, now the next step was to set John free. She switched off her bedside lamp, appreciating the glow permeating from the streetlights, together with the sound of the traffic swishing through the puddles, as they drove passed in the street below. She lay praying for the confidence to carry out the remainder of her plan, before falling into a troubled sleep.

Arriving into work on Monday morning, John was there to greet her.

"How was your weekend?" he enquired lightly, treading warily, as Rachel had been much colder towards him lately.

"I've moved in and there was a lot of hard work involved but it was worth it," she smiled meekly.

"I told you I could've given you a hand," John replied appearing concerned, not understanding why she was moving out and why he wasn't allowed to help her in the process.

"I know you did but you know how stubborn and independent I am," she laughed lightly, grabbing her coffee mug and hugging it, taking brisk short sips, knowing what lay ahead.

"Yes I do," John replied quietly. "In fact, you're the most beautiful, independent woman I've ever had the pleasure of falling in love with."

Rachel strangled her coffee cup some more, recognising she had a difficult task ahead of her.

"The meeting is about to start," Bernadette cheerfully announced, poking her head in through the canteen doorway.

"Thanks," Rachel replied, glad of the reprieve, immediately rising from her seat.

The Monday morning meeting took place, with John sitting next to Rachel, as everyone avidly took notes, listening to their assignments and filling Al in as to what stories were ready for submission. Rachel was praised for her article on Mrs Ahearn and was officially given the opportunity to write a piece on victims of terrorism, taken from a judge's perspective. John was to investigate and report on the knee capping which took place over the weekend.

After the meeting, everyone dispersed rather quickly. Al was in one of his moods and anyone with an ounce of sense knew to clear out of the office straight away or risk becoming the next target to vent his anger and frustration on. Rachel was grabbing her coat and bag when John gripped her arm.

"We need to talk," he pleaded.

"Not now," Rachel instantly retorted, watching Al roam the office with a face like thunder.

"Tonight then ... I'll come around," he added hastily, before grabbing his gear and exiting quickly.

Rachel snatched up her dictaphone and left the office shortly afterwards. She was heading over to Paul's father's place, to carry out a pre-arranged interview for her next story. All the other reporters were aware she would receive this assignment, due to her ties with the family. Since her arrival, Rachel had been included in the family gatherings and had successfully built up a wonderful relationship with both Henry and Helen.

Arriving at the gates, security recognised her car immediately and carried out the compulsory search quickly, before allowing her access. Driving up the avenue she was smiling, subconsciously thinking about Margaret's wedding day and how happy everyone was, causing her to feel slightly emotional.

Pulling up outside the entrance, Lexi the golden Labrador greeted her excitedly, frantically wagging her tail and rushing over to the car as Rachel exited. Francis the housemaid greeted her with a friendly smile, before leading her into the library; Henry was already waiting with a welcoming pot of steaming hot tea, along with her favourite choc chip cookies. His smile was infectious and endearing as he patted a seat nearby, indicating for her to be seated.

"I thought you would appreciate morning tea before we started," he announced kindly. "Then we can commence the official interview afterwards," he winked mischievously.

Rachel felt right at home, enjoying the friendly banter taking place, during her unexpected tea break. It turned out to be a wonderful morning, acting as a major distraction, preventing her to brood about this evening's meeting with John.

Some hours later, it was time for Rachel to take her leave.

"We'll see you at Sunday lunch … I take it," Henry sung out from the top porch, smiling.

"You most certainly will," Rachel replied happily, before winding up her car door window, honking her horn and driving off. She smiled thoughtfully and was tremendously pleased with the material she had received from Henry.

It was 6.30pm and John would be arriving in thirty minutes. Rachel was finding it hard to keep her nerves intact. This was not going to be easy but she didn't have any other choice, as she recited her personal mantra of no ties, no attachments and no heartaches, knowing the latter wasn't entirely true.

A loud knock upon her door brought her quickly out of reverie. God he was early she thought nervously, instinctively straightening herself up, immediately walking towards the front door. Opening the door, she was surprised to see John clutching a massive bunch of red roses. Her heart instantly sunk as she welcomed him inside.

"Very impressive," John exclaimed, peering proudly around her front room, smiling warmly.

"Yes I must admit, I'm pleased with the overall effect," Rachel replied, wanting to throw her arms around him but knowing she couldn't. "I'll put these in water," she announced smiling humbly, referring to the spectacular bouquet. "I was about to have a drink, would you care to join me?"

"Yes, providing I get to sit in front of the fire," he laughed.

"Not a problem. I'm having a scotch, do you want one or would you prefer a beer? I've got some Harp Lager in the fridge."

"Yep ... sounds good to me," John confided, leaning forward and warming his hands at the fire.

Rachel left him, heading down to her kitchen straight away to fetch the drinks. Immediately pouring herself a scotch, she sculled it, before quickly filling her glass again. Hopefully it would give her some dutch courage, enabling her to make it through the evening, because it sure as hell wasn't going to be an easy one.

Arriving back up into the front room, she found John holding a silver photo frame, staring at a family photo blissfully, standing comfortably with his back against the fire. Looking up straight away, he said "you've got your mother's fine features. Hopefully I'll get to meet her one day," he added quietly.

Highly emotional, Rachel immediately felt tense and her eyes began to water; John instantly drew her into his arms, causing her to breakdown right away into heart wrenching sobs.

"It can't be that bad," he whispered, stroking her hair tenderly, before settling her down on the sofa. "Here take this," he said affectionately, handing over her scotch.

She smiled up at him gratefully, before taking a gulp. John opened his beer and sat down alongside her, drawing her in close. He sat silently, inhaling her sweet perfume, allowing Rachel to relax and sip her drink. Gradually her breathing slowed and she began to calm down, watching the flames flickering in the hearth. It was proving to be very therapeutic, feeling the warmth radiating outwards, watching the red hot coals being devoured, ablaze and dancing, creating soft shadows within the dimly lit room. She felt calm with John holding her lovingly within his arms but she couldn't allow herself this luxury for very long, she reprimanded herself harshly. It wouldn't be fair on him.

Looking up, she discovered he was also lost in the flames; he seemed content sitting with her, embracing her peacefully with such tenderness. Her heart was bursting with pain, sadness, confusion and love and above all, the realisation that their relationship must end this very evening. She must do it. She had to set him free. Allow him to live his life, with someone who would be around for an extremely long time. She took another gulp of her scotch, before she began.

"Please hear me out John, before you say anything. I've been agonising over this for weeks," she confided, peering up at him sadly. "You probably have already noticed, I've been avoiding you lately, so please understand, it's nothing you said or did. I cannot deny I have strong feelings for you but one thing has been largely eating at me," she sighed heavily. "I know I have to head back to Australia. I am truly sorry and I never wanted to hurt you but I must make the cut now or your heart will truly be broken and I refuse to do that to you." Watching the pain deepen within his eyes, tears straight away began flowing down her face. "The moments we've spent together has truly been a beautiful journey and will remain with me until I die," she sobbed. "It may not make sense to break up now but I cannot continue along this path my love, because it will become even more difficult and it is the best resolution for us both."

He sat perfectly still, not saying a word. Tears began welling up in her eyes, before he ran his hand gently along her cheek, wiping away her tears. "Come here," he whispered hoarsely and she leant into him. She sat clinging on to him, with John hugging her even tighter, as Rachel sobbed incoherently, hurting and drowning in an emotional turmoil.

"I knew this was coming," he confided, ever so gently. "Your mannerisms had changed towards me, almost as if you were trying to block me out over the past few weeks. I've laid awake at night, churning over and over in my mind, trying to figure out what I might have said or done to upset you." He looked down at her pleadingly. "Rachel, none of us know how long we may have with each other and I've cherished every precious moment I've ever spent with you. I really don't want to lose you, yet I see how vulnerable you are. I recognise how dreadfully painful this is for you and how it is tearing you up inside. I can't be angry at you Rachel, because I love you too much and as hard as it may seem ... I really do understand," he confessed. Looking into her pale blue eyes, he pleaded. "Would you lie with me and chase away this hurt, forgetting about everything and everyone, so that we may spend one last evening together. Please grant us this opportunity Rachel, allowing us to say our goodbyes properly and to share our love, one last time." He swallowed hard, before adding "knowing it will have to last us a lifetime."

Tears were streaming down Rachel's cheeks, as she nodded in answer to his plea. She was unable to speak; desperately needing him to hold her in his arms and tell her how much he loved her, eliminating her stress, worries and fears, temporarily. This opportunity would allow her to express her tender loving feelings for him, one final time. Love is a mysterious phenomenon, she thought, rising from the sofa and taking his hand, leading him towards the stairs.

He followed slowly, wishing with his whole heart that this wasn't happening but knowing Rachel intimately, he knew deep down from within, this was to be their final evening. Climbing the stairs, their mutual silence didn't need to be filled.

In her bedroom they lay and caressed each other, charged with pure emotion. Their kisses were deeply passionate and meaningful, knowing this would be their last. Both were soon stripped bare, releasing their heartfelt emotions. Their bodies intertwined, feeling, touching, cherishing each other's long embraces, smothering each other in deep loving affection. Rachel was carried away into another world, as John poured all his remaining love into her, driving her over the edge. She rose up buckling under him, welcoming his amorous love making, desiring him more and more. She cried out in ecstasy, as he made her come again and again, completely overwhelmed by his lustful and urgent advances.

She flicked him over, taking charge and slowing the pace. She began seducing him tenderly, with undeniable loving emotions. He pulled her down hard on top, urgently smothering her mouth with his. She responded, surrendering her total being as he released, crying out loudly, calling out her name and confessing his undying love for her. She hugged him desperately, not wanting the evening to end. Wishing John could fall asleep next to her every night, allowing her to spend the remainder of her days, with her one and only true love.

But life can be brutal and unrelenting, she laid thinking. Having no control over one's own fate, we must be accepting of whatever we are dealt, she consoled herself, making the most of whatever we are given and dealing with it in the best way we can.

Rachel lay silently upon his chest listening to his breathing, wrapped up in his arms, radiant from their lovemaking and yet somewhat subdued. Thankful for having spent one last time with him but also felt deeply saddened by the fact she could no longer continue along this particular path.

He held her closely, kissing her tenderly upon the forehead. "I love you Rachel and I always will. You are the most wonderful, gorgeous, amazing woman I've ever met," he whispered. Pulling her into his arms once more, he leant in and kissed her lovingly, before falling asleep.

Early morning sunlight began trickling softly through the window, as Rachel leisurely started to stir. Opening her eyes gradually, she gasped loudly, suddenly aware John had left. A solitary red rose lay upon his pillow, resting upon a hand written letter. She filled up immediately, as she slowly stretched across to retrieve it. She hesitated momentarily, burdened with a heavy heart, dreading his final written words as she slowly unfolded his letter, praying he would grant her forgiveness.

My Dearest Rachel,

I am struggling to write this but I could not say my farewell personally, as the pain would be too great. My love for you will never die Rachel. All of my being wants to fight for you but intuitively, I know I must not. Somehow I will find the inner strength, as difficult as it will be; to honour your decision Rachel.

I will always remember your effervescent smile, your kindness and how you made me laugh when I needed it the most. I pray you will have a wonderful and fulfilling life, as you will forever be a part of mine. Thank you ... for making me a part of yours Rachel.

Yours truly,

John x x x

Rachel's heart shattered into a million pieces, acknowledging how much he must be hurting right now. Huge rounded tears formed, sliding down her face rapidly, as a vast amount of remorse hit her so hard, she could barely breathe. She cried unashamedly for her loss, knowing their relationship could have stood the test of time. The epiphany was, she wouldn't be given the time. She clutched on to his pillow, inhaling his masculine aroma, wishing none of this was happening, wishing she would wake up to discover this was a nightmare. Rachel could already feel a part of John missing from within, as she cried some more, longing to feel his arms holding her.

Miserable, alone and extremely sad, she rang the office informing them she was feeling unwell, coming down with a flu most likely, she hinted, explaining she was unable to make it into work. The receptionist readily agreed, hearing her despondent scratchy voice and advised her to take as long as she needed, wishing her a fast recovery.

Hanging up, the receptionist recognised a bug of some sort was obviously going around, because she received a similar phone call from John only a few minutes earlier, sounding like death warmed up. She rose from her desk and entered Al's office, informing him of the situation. He seemed unconcerned, knowing their stories had already been submitted for the week and there was no need to re-organise or dig out another article, to cover their allocated columns.

Chapter Thirty Five

"Hi Margaret, how's everything going over there at present?" Kath enquired, trying to keep up-to-date with the latest news.

Margaret was instantly caught off guard, answering the phone and discovering her mother on the other end. Recovering quickly, she immediately decided not to mention Rachel moving out or her mother would be concerned straight away and would question what was going on.

"Oh the usual, it's been busy at work and the experience is phenomenal," she confided.

"I suppose Paul is working as hard as ever? On top of everything else, he probably has his hands full looking after you and your sister," Kath teased, smiling down the phone. "How's Rachel by the way, I haven't heard from her of late? Is everything okay? I hope she's pulling her weight at your place?" Kath queried.

Margaret felt uncomfortable lying to her mother, so she decided to use a distraction.

"Rachel is going extremely well, from what I can gather. The Telegraph team here in Belfast are extremely proud of her achievements to date. Al, the main boss, is suitably impressed, according to Rachel."

"Who?" Kath queried, her face paling significantly, as she enquired.

"Alistair Peak ... her boss but everyone calls him Al," Margaret prattled on, as Kath felt the very breath being sucked out of her. Finding it difficult to comprehend that after all these years, hearing an old name mentioned from her past could still affect her in this way. Al was the one who allowed her to meet up with Richard Tyler, also known as Mad Dog back then, when he was carrying out an interview. She slowly drifted back, thinking about how her whole life dramatically changed, ever since that day.

"MUM, mum ... are you still there?" Margaret asked.

"Yes dear, I got slightly distracted by Brigee," which wasn't quite true but it most certainly had to suffice, as it wasn't a subject she wanted to discuss in great detail with Margaret.

"Anyway, as I was saying mum, Rachel carried out an interview with Henry yesterday and the article will be in next week's paper. It's in relation to how a judge views the victims of terrorism and the article will be written from his perspective."

"Sounds intriguing," Kath replied, gaining her composure. "Is she pleased with her submission?"

"Oh I don't know yet," Margaret hesitated. "I haven't had a chance to speak to her in great detail about it," Margaret fumbled. "I'll keep you posted and send you a copy of the article, when it comes out next week."

"How are mum and dad by the way?" Kath said; pleased her children developed a relationship with them both and were cherishing their grandparents immensely.

"Mary's fussing over us as usual, baking cakes and biscuits, supplying us with casseroles continuously. We'll be as fat as fools soon," Margaret laughed, thinking about the supplies taken over to Rachel's place at the weekend.

"Well give them my love and tell Rachel to give me a tinkle whenever she gets the chance. I would love to hear how she got on with Henry."

"Okay mum, give our love to everyone at home. Brigee's probably at loose ends over there at present, I take it?"

"No, not really, she meets with her group and attends bingo twice a week. She also comes over here three days, to tidy up and prepare meals. In fact, she frequently dines with us and enjoys catching up with Valerie and Matt on a fortnightly basis."

"How is Valerie by the way? Did she get her results from her check-up last week?"

"Yes, everything's fine my love, it's simply follow ups and she got the all clear. Mind you, after a double mastectomy, I wouldn't expect anything less," Kath sighed.

"Great," Margaret replied. "Gee, I could do with some Aussie sunshine over here. I really miss you all at times, along with the hot tropical weather," Margaret confided.

"But not enough to come back home," Kath quickly replied, wanting to bite off her tongue, as soon as she said it.

"M-u-m."

"I know, I know, I've almost given you up as a lost cause but there's no harm in hoping," Kath laughed. "Besides it's not too bad, considering Rachel is almost halfway through her time. Come to think of it, I really don't know where the time has disappeared to recently. Okay darling I best be going, hopefully I'll catch up with Rachel next week. Love you."

"Love you to mum ... bye."

451

Margaret set the phone down, pleased she had side tracked her mother. She avoided telling her Rachel had moved out and as luck would have it, she didn't even ask if she had a boyfriend, which was a great relief.

Peering at the clock, she immediately decided to ring Rachel at work, warning her mum had been on the phone and to tell her to make a point of ringing their mum soon, to prevent her from worrying.

This is when she found out that Rachel was not at work that day.

"Oh I see," Margaret replied.

"Can anyone else help you perhaps?" the receptionist enquired politely.

"No, no it's fine; it was a quick personal call. I'll catch up with her later," Margaret replied, before saying goodbye and hanging up. It was unusual for Rachel to take a day off, Margaret surmised, dialling her home number instinctively.

"H-e-l-l-o."

"My goodness, you sound awful Rachel," Margaret stated anxiously. "Are you okay? Are you coming down with something? Have you seen your local GP?" she quizzed automatically.

"I'll be fine, just a few days rest is all that's required. I got soaked the other day and I've got a bit of a horrible cold, that's all," Rachel confided, trying to sound as positive as possible.

"Do you want me to come over?" Margaret asked.

"No it's fine and I've got enough food from Mary to last me a month," she added.

This immediately caused Margaret to laugh and to lighten up straight away. "Okay then, it was just a quick call to pre-warn you mum's been on the phone. I didn't tell her you moved out; you know what she's like. I bamboozled her in relation to Henry's interview. So whenever you get the chance to give her a tingle, you can tell her what took place and hopefully, it will prevent her from asking too many questions," Margaret laughed. "I love her to bits but she tends to worry too much, when we're over here," Margaret added. "Well, I best be going and let you get some rest. Give John our love and I'll catch up with you soon. Love you … bye."

After hanging up, Rachel immediately broke down again; she had been excessively teary since she broke up with John. I must pull myself together real soon; she berated herself, before crawling back into bed and pulling the blankets over her head.

The following morning, Rachel still didn't feel she was ready to head back into work. Instead, she decided to spend the day in bed in her PJs, eat junk food and watch the telly. She hadn't heard from John since but what else could she expect. She told the man she loved dearly; they could no longer be together, giving him some flimsy explanation. Why on earth would he call? Flicking on the TV, she switched manically from station to station, trying to keep occupied, trying to keep her mind busy. Trying anything to prevent her from thinking about John and how much she missed him already, now that she accomplished her so called mission.

John had gone to work and felt like shit. He was both relieved and saddened, when Rachel didn't make an appearance. He soon discovered she was staying away, under the pretence of dreadful flu like symptoms. He knew exactly why she wasn't at work, it had obviously hit her hard, as it did him and it would take a hell of a while for the wounds to heal. He missed her bubbly personality around the office and her infectious laughter, which always made him smile. He felt they were compatible and their relationship would have lasted. He acknowledged internally, with Rachel heading back to Australia it would have put a strain on their relationship but he still believed they could have worked through it, not unlike Margaret and Paul.

"Do you want a coffee?" Bernadette broke into his thoughts. "You look like you could do with a bit of cheering up," she soothed.

"Sorry, I was a million miles away. It's a piece I'm working on at present, it's proving a lot more difficult than I anticipated," John sighed, rising from his desk and following Bernadette into the canteen.

Henry lifted the phone and dialled the number given to him. "Rachel?"

"Yes ... can I help you?" Rachel answered tentatively.

"It's Henry here my dear. I had a bit of a job tracking you down. I hope you don't mind? I caught up with Margaret and she gave me your number."

"Not at all," Rachel replied, pleased it was Henry and glad for the distraction.

"I hope you're feeling much better? Your sister informed me you have an awful cold."

"I'm feeling much healthier now, thank you," Rachel lied, knowing she would have to push herself to work tomorrow. She couldn't stay hidden forever.

"I was tidying up some of my old files and I came upon an interesting case, which I strongly felt would be worth mentioning in your article. I've gone ahead and taken the liberty to speak with the existing family members and they have graciously given me the necessary clearance, in order that the transcripts may be used. So if you were up to it, perhaps we can catch up tomorrow morning at the courthouse, before I commence my judicial duties."

"Perfect," Rachel said. "Providing you have some choc chip cookies ready," she joked, delighted to have additional material to utilise for her article.

"I'll have a cup of tea ready to go with them," Henry countered, in his friendly down to earth manner. "Well, I best be going and head home, as it's 6 o'clock already and Helen will be wondering where I am. Oh by the way, will 9.30am be suitable for you?"

"Yes that will be fine," Rachel replied, appearing much happier.

"I will inform security you're expected and they will allow you to park in our car park, hopefully making life a little easier for you," Henry advised.

"Thank you," Rachel answered "and before you go, I want you to know how much I really appreciate the help you have been giving me Henry," Rachel confided.

"Not at all, it's my pleasure Rachel dear. I'll see you tomorrow morning then ... bye."

"Bye," Rachel replied, hanging up much more contented, recognising this was exactly the push she needed, to make her get up out of bed and get back into work. She sprung out of bed with renewed enthusiasm and headed down to the kitchen to prepare an evening meal. Everything was going to be okay she told herself, looking forward to tomorrow morning.

Henry said his goodbyes to various staff members, on his way out. Many of them were young and eager, prepared to put in long gruelling hours to make an impression, enabling them to climb the corporate ladder. He smiled inwardly as he walked to his car; it reminded him of many years ago when he was much younger, setting out energetically and fighting for justice, desperately wanting to make a difference.

Starting up his Mercedes, he proceeded out of the car park and smoothly entered into the flow of cars, wishing he had left a little earlier as the traffic was extremely heavy.

He could have sworn he had seen the brown metallic Rover several times this week on his way home, obviously they must live on the same route, Henry inwardly thought, as he continued up the Lisburn Road. He had been feeling much older and more weary these past few weeks; his courtroom had been proving to be extremely difficult and challenging, with more terrorists having to be sentenced. No matter how many times he presided and listened to different scenarios, the senseless brutal murders always impacted upon him, making him appreciate his dear wife Helen, when he arrived home late in the evenings.

Margaret and Paul were exceptionally happy these days and Helen simply adored Margaret popping in to visit her, disrupting her routine to have a chat or go shopping together, he correctly surmised. This young and vibrant young couple added much laughter and happiness to their household, frequently telling amusing stories over Sunday lunch, in relation to peculiar cases presenting themselves in the emergency department. Rachel also had a vivacious personality, adding amusement to this fun family mix. He was looking forward to arriving home, participating in having a glass of his favourite scotch, with Helen, the greatest love of his life. It was one of his many little rituals, which helped him to unwind before his evening meal; Henry smiled broadly at the comforting thought.

"Oh for goodness sake," he suddenly muttered out loud, peering in his rear view mirror as the Rover weaved its way in and out of the traffic, causing some irritable motorists to honk their horns in annoyance. Why can't people be more patient and tolerant on the roads these days? he thought, as he made a left turn on to Cranmore Park Road.

Glancing down at his clock on the dashboard, it read 6.30pm as he sighed visibly, resenting the cold dark wintery evenings setting in, now with a sprinkling of rain, made him reach forward to apply his windscreen wipers, adding further to his general irritation.

Out of nowhere, a horrendous clash of metal dominated the atmosphere. One, god awful thud impacted heavily upon Henry's car, making him automatically look up, while gripping his steering wheel to gain control. The brown Rover was obviously overtaking him and managed to hit the side of his car in the process.

"Bloody fool," Henry shouted out loud, as he went to hit his brakes but seconds before managing this task, he heard a muffled sound, not unlike fireworks exploding. His side windscreen suddenly came crashing in and around him.

"Shit," he yelled, turning towards his assailants, shocked, before three of the bullets from the automatic revolver, met their mark. The Mercedes Benz went careening out of control, its tyres hitting the gutter hard, sending the vehicle reeling up on to the pavement and crashing violently into a telegraph pole. The insistent blaring of an ear-piercing car horn copiously filled the air, as Henry lay slouched over the steering wheel, blood leaking profusely from his head, where one of the bullets impacted. His eyes were wide open. Deer like, staring straight ahead into oblivion. His crumpled body lay completely motionless, isolated, soaked in blood, cut off from his loving family. The car was a mangled smouldering mess, torn and twisted, riddled with bullet holes. Vehicles in both directions came screeching to a halt, their owner's traumatised and stunned, having witnessed the horrifying event. Residents from nearby homes immediately came pouring out on to the street to offer assistance.

The brown Rover went screeching down the road recklessly, making a quick getaway, as the occupants inside the vehicle were laughing. "Did you see his face Brendan?" Peter mocked in a hostile manner. "Holy shit, you thought he had seen a ghost," he laughed out loud, totally negating the cold blooded murder he just committed. Sirens were heard in the distance, as the brown Rover snaked its way back to headquarters, situated off Falls Road. Their mission had been successfully accomplished. Judge Hagan would not be sentencing anymore of Peter's lads and sending them to jail, ever again.

The funeral was attended by hundreds of mourners, paying their final respects to Judge Hagan, having sentenced many criminals to prison for horrendous crimes, carried out perpetually in the North. He was renowned for his tough sentencing, although he was also recognised for his non bias approach, dealing with each group or individual appropriately, no matter their religious upbringing or background.

Helen had been living on tranquillisers for the past five days, functioning in a trance-like state, trying to comprehend and come to terms with his horrific death. Images of his bullet riddled car dominated her mind; having been splashed across newspapers and making headlines, on every television channel available. Her family gathered swiftly around her, trying their upmost to comfort her but to no avail. Nothing prepared her for Henry's untimely death. He had been a fair man, simply carrying out his judicial duties and to be gunned down like a hardened criminal, was enormously difficult for Helen to bear. Dripping in perspiration, Helen would awaken in the middle of the night, crying out hysterically for her beloved Henry. With tears running down her cheeks, she thought of him being brutally murdered, leaving behind a huge void, no longer present on this earth.

Hundreds of wreaths inundated the coffin positioned in the hearse, as it slowly made its way up Malone Road, heading towards the Belfast City Cemetery, to Henry's final resting place. The service had taken its toll on everyone and the two sons equally shared the eulogy, leaving not a dry eye amongst the congregation.

At the burial site, when the roses were placed on top of the coffin by Henry's two sons, Helen collapsed in a lamentable heap, besieged by immense grief. Kath, Margaret and Rachel tried to comfort her as best they could, as Marcus stood by Paul and Stephen, red eyed, grief-stricken and drenched in anger.

A huge gathering made their way back to the Hagan's homestead; John paid his respects and refrained from going back to the house, at Rachel's request. Caterers had been organised for the wake by Margaret. The staff proved to be efficient and professional while attending to the heartbroken mourners. The Irish wake took place with everyone mingling, all trying to come to grips and fully comprehend the sudden and horrendous tragedy, bestowed upon the Hagan family.

"I understand you want to stay on and be here for Helen my love," Kath soothed "but surely you must realise, it's not the safest part of the world," Kath smiled weakly, deeply concerned for the welfare of both her daughters."

"I hear what you're saying mum," Margaret chided "but Paul's family needs us here at present. Plus, I'm heavily involved in work at present and there's no way I could possibly leave the Royal Victoria Hospital right now," she explained, heartbroken and torn.

Kath decided to drop the subject and comforted her daughter instead, knowing they would be heading back within the next eight weeks and she didn't want any animosity between them.

Margaret obtained a dual citizenship similar to Marcus's, permitting her to work in the United Kingdom. Margaret was excelling in surgery, due to the extensive work she was constantly exposed to in the North and wanted to remain there for as long as possible. Her superiors acknowledged and appreciated her exceptional skills and abilities, counting her as one of their own, as well as being an exceedingly valuable asset.

Kath almost got her head bitten off, after suggesting to Rachel to come home six months earlier than she was due to leave the Belfast Telegraph, as a result of Henry's vicious slaying.

"You can't wrap me up in cotton wool," Rachel screamed at her, suffering greatly from the impact of Henry's death. Although, Kath suspected something else was going on in her life but couldn't quite put her finger on it. Kath relinquished by bowing out gracefully, knowing there was no way she would have been able to convince her independent young daughter, otherwise.

Paul was exceptionally pale and fragile during his father's funeral; he was trying his best to maintain his equanimity, throughout the horrific day. Countless mourners sympathetically patted him on the back, offering up their personal heartfelt condolences, as the realisation slowly sunk in. His father was actually gone, brutally killed in cold blood and no longer coming back home. He fought bitterly hard to refrain from breaking down, especially when he watched his mother shaking hands with relatives. Gaunt, appearing a hundred years old, her face was hollow and lifeless, illustrating excruciating emotions, while accepting their expressions of support and grief.

When evening fell, Paul clung helplessly to Margaret. Wrapped within her comforting arms while lying in bed, she provided a safe haven for him, allowing him to drop his brave façade. Overwhelming sadness engulfed him; debilitating beliefs rose up from deep within, choking him with immense sorrow and hatred, all at the same time. He would never understand how anyone could take the life of another human being, least of all a respectable and honourable man like his father. Margaret would whisper gentle words of encouragement, empowering and comforting Paul, tenderly stroking his hair when he was absolutely exhausted, before he surrendered to sleep.

Rachel lay in bed tossing and turning, horrified and traumatised, by Henry's sudden death. How ironic, she thought, just as she was about to publish a piece on his views on victims of terrorism. Quite unbelievably, his family were now falling under this all too familiar category of crime.

"God-damn it," she raged, thumping her pillow, as tears flowed openly down her face. "It's so unfair," she called out in the dead of night, alone and desolate. Angry, lost and miserable, knowing she could make no sense of this reckless callous murder. A kind and gentle man, eradicated from his family, by some radical splinter group. Who would do such a thing? Who could be so cold blooded and evil?

As she lay in bed crying, she thought of Henry and her last words with him, swiftly making a promise to herself. Yes, a major promise. She was going to track the conspirators down and bring them to justice. Rachel was a reporter after all, a god-damn great investigative reporter. Now she had some real and legitimate work to carry out, she consoled herself, before drifting into a restless sleep.

Chapter Thirty Six

Rachel arrived at work the following week. She suffered a few major headaches of late, personally preferring to put it down to stress, opposed to her deteriorating medical condition. The drowsiness she was experiencing was conquered by numerous cups of coffee and she ascertained the irritability and mood swings were probably due to her mother who had been asking so many damn questions of late, wanting to know why she moved out on her own.

"How are you?" John enquired immediately.

"Fine," Rachel answered, looking up and smiling.

"Would you like a coffee?"

"I would love one," she replied gratefully, before following him down the corridor.

As John moved around the canteen, fetching the cups and preparing the coffee, Rachel silently sat watching him. Her heart was brimming over with love, wishing she could fling her arms around John and hug him tightly but it didn't fall under her original plan, she reminded herself. No ties, no attachment and no heartaches was her mantra but on days like these, it was extremely hard to keep. But keep them, she must.

"I suppose you've heard already. Al printed the story you completed on Henry and it was an enormous success. Apparently it was very well received throughout the business and community sectors."

Rachel nodded in response, her eyes automatically filling up with tears, as she reminisced about the morning spent with Henry, carrying out her very last interview.

"I'm sorry," John struggled vocally, gripping her hand, pulling her out of her sad memories straight away. "I shouldn't have mentioned it," he added, appearing concerned.

"No, it's okay. If it wasn't you, I'm sure someone else would have said something," Rachel replied, as a matter of fact. "Now where's my coffee?" she smiled, putting him immediately at ease.

Al called her into his office shortly afterwards and closed his door, indicating for her to take a seat. Without further ado he asked her straight out. "How are you holding up Rachel? Henry's death was a major shock to us all and I'm truly sorry for your loss. You're more than welcome to take a few extra weeks off or due to the tragic circumstances, you might want to contemplate forfeiting your position here."

Initially, Rachel stared at him in shock; her eyes were wide, accompanied by a stunned facial expression, before kicking into a defensive role.

"Are you not pleased with my work Al? Bloody hell, I've clocked up enough gruelling hours to prove to you I'm conscientious and extremely serious in relation to my position held here," she declared indignantly, appearing disenchanted.

"No, no you're getting the wrong end of the stick here," Al automatically countered. "I'm more than happy with your performance Rachel; in fact, you've demonstrated terrific potential and have the makings of a damn good journalist. After your year was up, I was going to offer you a full time position here," he smiled graciously.

"That's more like it," Rachel joked. "I thought you were trying to get rid of me."

"No, no, not at all, it was a case of not knowing how to handle the situation. Basically, I wanted you to know, whatever you decide to do, you have my own and the team's blessing, that's all."

"Thank you," Rachel replied sincerely. Sitting opposite Al, she was fully aware she caught him off guard and instantly decided to strike, before he could have a chance to think too much about it. "There is one favour, I would like to request," Rachel looked at him innocently, with her pale blue eyes.

"Name it and consider it done," Al replied confidently, trying to recover and make up any lost ground.

Rachel peered at him directly, without losing eye contact. "Henry's death was sudden and a shock to us all. However, I would like your permission to further investigate his murder. By allowing me to track them down, I will be able to pass the relevant information on to the authorities if I come anywhere close to discovering who they were."

Al was visibly shocked. "Rachel, I can't allow it. This is extremely personal for you and I can't afford to have any of my staff running off on a vigilante crusade . . ."

"You promised," Rachel abruptly interrupted "and it wouldn't be a crusade Al, it would be responsible reporting. It's something I would do anyway quite frankly, whether I was on your payroll or not," she said, staring belligerently. "More importantly, it is something I'm really passionate about and I want to do it out of respect for Henry," she added firmly.

Al hesitated briefly, acknowledging the determination written upon Rachel's young face. All of a sudden, it reminded him of a young woman called Caitlin, who he worked with over twenty-five years ago. She was equally as persistent and as fiery as Rachel was right now, perched in front of him. He recognised Rachel would carry out an investigation anyway, secretly admiring her for her guts and tenacity. He drew in a deep breath and stared at Rachel, sitting upright in her chair directly opposite, looking as if she was ready to pounce.

"Okay, you can allocate two days a week out of the five, to see what you can sniff out," he sighed heavily. "The other three days I'll expect to see your usual submissions, with no excuses," he asserted.

"Consider it done," Rachel insisted, rising from her chair, stretching across to shake his hand. "Thank you," she said confidently. "You'll not regret it."

"Let's hope not," Al bellowed, as Rachel made her way towards the door. "And Rachel ... be careful."

"Of course," she exclaimed smiling, closing the door behind her.

"Has Rachel been around much lately?" Kath enquired idly, watching her mother pour out a cup of tea.

"Not really but it's understandable love," Mary countered. "She was pretty close to Henry and I reckon she's burying herself in work, to get over it."

"Mmm, you're probably right mum. Although, I feel she's hiding something from me."

"Oh daughter dear, you're gettin' all paranoid. I know it must be hard on you with both daughters over here at present, never mind with what happened to Henry 'n' all. But you can't wrap them up in cotton wool luv."

Kath laughed. "That's exactly what Rachel said."

"Well there you go; your daughter hit the nail right on the head." Mary looked up "now where has Marcus and your dad disappeared to?"

"I think they're looking at some cattle in the shed."

"Would you be a wee dear, go out into the yard, give them a holler and tell them afternoon tea is ready."

Kath rose from the table, smiling outwardly. It was good to be home again; although sad it was due to unfortunate circumstances. Her mum never seemed to get her feathers ruffled and a strain of guilt suddenly ran through her, thinking about what she must have put them through, when she staged her own death.

Soon everyone was gathered around the kitchen table talking about old times, trying to chase away the violent act, surrounding Henry's death and prevent it from impacting too much upon their daily lives. It turned out to be a wonderful day, giving a reprieve to both Kath and Marcus, who was staying at Helen's in Tonaghneave Manor, both trying to assist her with her recovery, due to her tragic and significant loss.

"Helen you should have waited until we got back. I'm sure I could have helped you prepare dinner," Kath gently chided, noticing how much Helen had wasted away since her husband's murder.

She was forcibly pushing herself to complete her everyday chores, palpably lacking motivation or any sort of enthusiasm. Kath frequently heard her crying herself to sleep in the evenings; it was enough to break anyone's heart.

"It gives me something to do Kath, helping me to put in my day or I would go completely mad," Helen replied, smiling sweetly.

Kath wanted to hug her but she purposely held back, fully aware she couldn't smother her in kindness continuously or it would take longer for her to heal.

"Well at least allow me to set the table," Kath suggested and was straight away shown where the dinner set was kept. "What time are Margaret and Paul coming around?" she enquired, seeking out the cutlery.

"About six o'clock I think, I'll serve up dinner at 6.30pm, if that's okay?'

"Of course it is," Kath smiled, noticing Helen had lost her confident manner and was a mere shadow of her former self, due to Henry's harrowing and sudden death.

"It smells delicious Helen," Kath added gently, before fetching the wine glasses.

Dinner was eaten in the dining room, Francis the housemaid served it up, as Paul poured the wines filling everyone in, on his rather hectic day. Margaret appeared pale and drawn; she confessed to her mother how she missed Henry desperately and explained how devastated Paul was over the whole sad and sorry affair. Kath advised her to take one day at a time, clarifying they would heal slowly over time.

"The memories will be painful at first but by allowing the good ones to be revisited, it will slowly banish Henry's tragic last moments on earth," Kath advised.

Margaret and Kath persuaded Helen to go shopping with them at the weekend; Paul was looking on approvingly, admiring and respecting his wife and her family for their understanding and kindness.

Both Rachel and Stephen had not attended the evening meal. Rachel stayed away under the pretence of an extremely heavy workload and Stephen who missed his father greatly, copped out, under the pretence of studying for the judicial bar. How he was achieving this down at his local tavern, consuming a massive amount of alcohol, was a whole different story.

The weather hadn't let up once since Kath and Marcus flew over for the funeral and it wasn't helping Rachel much either, when it came to her stakeouts. She was slowly making progress received from potential witnesses, hoping it may help track down Henry's assassins. The brown Rover had been found in the Ardoyne area, left abandoned and incinerated, the following day after Henry's execution. She was retracing steps and following up on leads, although she was tired the past couple of days, due to terrible back and neck pains, which was leading to numbness in her right arm.

Kath rung her, insisting she came out shopping with them, which she needed like a hole in the head, although she privately acknowledged that she wouldn't be able to put her mother off this time around.

Paul and Marcus went to watch Stephen play football for some charity fundraiser. Meanwhile, the ladies met up to go shopping in Belfast. Kath treated the girls to a gorgeous pair of boots each and Helen was talked into purchasing a gorgeous, pale blue, cashmere sweater, matching her eyes beautifully, enhancing her pale complexion. Kath purchased several pairs of slacks, something she seldom wore back in Australia, due to the warmer climate.

Margaret later drove them to Botanic Gardens, to have lunch in a wonderful little restaurant. They spent the remainder of the afternoon exploring the Victorian Palm House. This glasshouse structure was made from original bevelled glass and cast iron, proudly displaying vibrantly coloured geraniums, begonias and fuchsias hanging from overflowing pots, instantly brightening all of their moods. They also explored the tropical ravine, wandering around the spectacular grounds incorporating twenty-eight acres, with everyone appreciating the serenity.

The weeks flew passed, with Kath slowly immersing Helen back into her everyday family life. She had been taken to Mary and Joe's home for the day which she enjoyed immensely, with the clean country air adding some colour to Helen's cheeks. Helen was also encouraged to help Rachel furnish her spare bedroom, which kept her busy and allowed her to feel useful. Margaret also asked for her assistance in making Rachel's old bedroom into a study and overall, slowly but surely, things were slowly improving.

A special commemorative service was held the following week, two months exactly after Henry's death. An extension had been added to the existing courthouse and they were naming a courtroom after Henry, honouring his years of service, dedicated to the judicial system. A golden plaque was mounted on the heavy teak doors, his name and years of service were embossed upon it, in neatly scripted calligraphy. Morning tea was served in the judge's quarter and was visited by many of his old contemporaries, which could not have been easy on Helen.

Afterwards, Marcus and Kath took the whole family out to lunch, including Mary and Joe who came to pay their respects. Rachel and Stephen got on exceptionally well, pleasing Kath immensely, because her daughter was definitely much more withdrawn since their arrival. However, she validated in her mind it was due to Henry's untimely death, as Mary suggested.

On Monday morning after the normal meeting had taken place, Rachel was called into the office by Al. She gave him a quick recount as to how far she had progressed, in relation to the cause of Henry's death. Informing him she was performing a stakeout in the Ardoyne area later in the evening and hopefully the tip-off would produce a good result, as the investigation was proving to be painstakingly slow and extremely difficult.

Before leaving the office in the afternoon, she received a call from Dr Finlay, which came as a complete and utter surprise. She forgot that she had given her mobile number to his receptionist, to confirm her appointment a while back and Dr Finlay, being exceptionally meticulous, had managed to track her down.

"Good afternoon, I'm dreadfully sorry for imposing Rachel. I sincerely hope I haven't caught you at an inconvenient time?" he enquired politely.

"No, its fine," Rachel replied quickly, biting her bottom lip, wondering why he decided to call. The last thing she needed right now, was more bad news. Mind you, how much more difficult could it get, she thought.

"I was phoning for two reasons really," he explained, in his deep baritone professional voice. "Firstly, may I enquire since your last appointment Rachel, have your symptoms increased dramatically? For example, are you having headaches every day?"

"No, not at all," Rachel replied "maybe three a week," she added, peering around the office, conscious someone might overhear.

"That's marvellous, I'm very glad to hear it," Dr Finlay replied. "It is in fact extremely encouraging news Rachel, considering the reason for my call."

"And what might that be?" Rachel questioned rapidly, feeling uneasy taking the call at work.

"I wish to inform you that since our last meeting, I've taken the liberty to forward your details to a dear colleague of mine, Professor Bartwell. He moved to America approximately seven years ago and he is exceedingly interested in your particular case. He feels enormously confident he could successfully operate on you, utilising a wonderful unique technique being trialled over in the United States. Obviously I don't want to get your hopes up but I must say, it sounds extremely promising," pleased he could present her with such a rare opportunity. "They have been obtaining some excellent results," he added cheerfully. "Would it be possible for you to speak to my receptionist tomorrow morning?" he enquired immediately.

"Yes, I will be able to ring her after 10am," Rachel replied graciously, shocked beyond belief. There was a chance, a glimmer of hope, she could possibly survive her ordeal, she thought, trying to contain herself while digesting the potentially good news.

"Wonderful. In the meantime, I will organise the necessary paperwork and arrange for some more tests to be carried out. You can obtain the details from my receptionist tomorrow."

Swiftly peering around the office, making sure it was completely clear, Rachel cleared her throat. Choking up with emotion she quickly stammered "thank you from the bottom of my heart, Dr Finlay. Words cannot express how indebted I am to you. Thank you for giving me this second chance in life," she confided, benevolently.

"It's my pleasure Rachel dear and I will be speaking with Professor Bartwell very soon, confirming I have a very strong candidate indeed. Unfortunately, I'm heading out of town for a few days but I will be able to fit you in early next week to see you. Goodbye Rachel, I look forward to catching up with you real soon."

"Goodbye," Rachel replied, setting down the phone, completely overwhelmed.

"What are you looking so pleased about?" John enquired, after watching Rachel mingle with other staff members, appearing really optimistic and in high spirits. The happiest he had seen her since their breakup, he surmised.

"A lost cause has been given some hope," Rachel beamed cheerfully "and if everything goes well, life will be grand Mr John Thompson," she laughed. "Perhaps, wishes can come true after all," she added tenderly, walking towards her own desk.

"I suppose you're not going to tell me, what's really going on," John smiled. He was pleased though, because she was obviously happy about something.

"You'll be the first to know, if it all comes to fruition," she giggled.

In that very moment, he wanted so badly to take her in his arms and kiss her, telling her how much he loved her, how he wanted to take care of her. But he couldn't, because he would drive her further away, back into the cocoon she was dwelling in, ever since their breakup. No, he would wait for as long as it took. Somehow and someday, he would win her back and on days like these, he was convinced even more so of this possibility becoming true.

Rachel finished her notes, submitted her necessary paperwork and left the office bidding John a special farewell, which pleased him immensely. She headed home to grab a bite to eat before setting off to Ardoyne. She was following up on a hot lead, prepared to carry out her surveillance, as initially planned.

It was 3am as Rachel lay low and silent, curled up on her car seat, wrapped up in a tonne of blankets, like a caterpillar smothered in a cocoon. This won't do my back any good, she thought, fighting to keep her eyes wide open.

She smiled, thinking about the times she sat in John's car, both carrying out surveillance for a potential story. They would organise and allocate different shifts, so at least they got some sleep throughout the evening. The majority of the time however, was spent sharing personal information and slowly falling in love, she realised. Pulling her blankets further up around her neck, she recognised she missed him dearly, especially tonight, because she desperately wanted to share the good news from Dr Finlay with him. Of course she couldn't, because they had broken up and he was totally unaware of her medical condition, she sighed, snuggling down into her blankets some more.

She noticed the house from across the street; the upstairs lights were being turned off, leaving only the tall street lights remaining, casting their dark eerie shadows upon the tightly parked cars, where she remained hidden. Looking down, she automatically set her watch for 5.30am which would allow her to waken early, in order for her to continue her surveillance. Rachel's eyes became extremely heavy and she closed them wearily; acknowledging nothing was happening across the street, granting her a reprieve and allowing her some much needed sleep.

Chapter Thirty Seven

It was a miserable wet Tuesday morning, when Rachel entered the little warm bakery on the corner of Saint Judes Parade and the Ormeau Road. She noticed the fine hazy vapours of steam rising from her damp coat, as she stood waiting patiently in the queue. A raindrop dribbled downwards along her nose, immediately plonking off the tip and landing on her front lapel, before being absorbed straight away into her cold sodden jacket. She stood idly, listening to the friendly banter taking place between the regular customers. Even on such a cold damp morning, she observed the cheery and welcoming atmosphere, extremely grateful for the heat inside. She was standing trying to decide between the steak and mushroom pies on display or perhaps she would choose one of the flaky sausage rolls to suffice her appetite on this cold, wintery, bleak morning.

The stake-out didn't go as planned last night. She spent hours upon hours camped out in her little Honda Civic, crouched up in a ball wrapped up in her blankets, until early morning light broke, bringing with it grey miserable skies and bucketfuls of rain. The tip offs were not always as good as she would have liked, she mused, staring up at the menu board, lost and wrapped up in her own little world.

She stood quietly, inhaling the delicious aromas of freshly baked soda bread and savoury meat pies, before shuffling up closer in the queue. She smiled momentarily, noticing the hand drawn picture stuck on the back of the bakery wall. It was a child's drawing; a wax crayon had etched a scrawny stick figure with a huge baker's hat on top, holding hands with three other similar figures. One had brightly coloured beads around her neck, which Rachel assumed was the mother. The other two smaller stick figures, had little round heads and huge smiley faces, with long sticky out hair, both wearing brightly coloured triangular skirts with polka dots. The words 'My family' was scrawled on the top of the page and the names Dan, Bea, Clare and Lela, were written under the cute stick figures. What drew Rachel's attention the most was the huge arrow pointing towards the last drawn figure, named Lela. It had a huge 'ME' written next to it, accompanying lots of little love hearts merging from it, winding around and around the young girl's family.

Tears began rolling down Rachel's cheeks unexpectedly and quickly using the sleeve of her jacket, she rapidly swept them away. She's been awfully teary of late, having no one to confide in, no one to share her dilemma with. Bloody hell, just suck it up she scolded herself, merging further up the line. She noticed she had been berating herself frequently of late, often in a quandary, not knowing what to do and what direction to take, in relation to her tumour. She was clueless on how to handle things, constantly churning over and over in her mind on how to go about it, continually trying to conjure up enough bravery to explain her wishes to her immediate family. She almost managed it last week but panic set in and she didn't want to spoil their day. Now everything has changed again, after her phone call with Dr Finlay. Perhaps he was giving her false hope or maybe, just maybe, there was a chance for her to survive. Hell, why did things have to be so damn difficult? Why couldn't life be simpler, less complex, she internally argued, approaching the counter.

"You're absolutely drenched," the shop assistant announced, with her bright orange hair and happy freckled face, genuinely looking concerned.

"That's why I've decided on a hot meat pie to cheer me up," Rachel hastily responded, smiling broadly.

"Well, you couldn't have picked a better bakery to come to," the young red head grinned, followed by mumbles of approval from the waiting regulars.

"It seems that way, if the queue is anything to go by," Rachel chuckled, deciding on the steak and mushroom.

The young assistant reached into the display cabinet to retrieve the pie, chatting merrily away during the process.

The shop door made a tingling sound as it was opened up wide, bringing forth with it, a massive blast of icy cold air. Rachel shivered, knowing she must get home and change out of her wet clothes or she would catch her death as her grandmother would frequently chastise her, after discovering her in a similar state.

A young bloke shuffled inside, roughly in his early twenties, kitted out in denim jeans and jacket, with rolled up sleeves displaying saturated arms soaked in ink. Wearing a maroon beanie pulled tightly down over his head, he roughly pushed his way up through the line, making his way up front. This instantly extracted a barrage of complaints from the other customers, who were standing patiently waiting in line.

Stopping next to Rachel, he grunted in a loud voice "is Dan Brennan in?"

The young assistant obviously not liking his mannerisms rolled her eyes heavenward. "And who might I ask is enquirin'?" sighing loudly.

"Tell him that Jessie Banks is here to see him," he declared bluntly.

"Well, he's out the back and pretty busy at present ..."

"Tell him it's urgent," cutting in rudely, the lanky figure asserted, obviously not prepared to accept any excuses. His eyes were black and beady, his breath reeking of stale cigarettes as he stood waiting impatiently, repetitively shifting from one foot to another, depicting a sinister demeanour.

Rachel watched him from side on, automatically holding her breath; as the hairs stood up on the back of her neck. He seemed somewhat agitated, downright nervous in fact. She hoped there wouldn't be a confrontation; she simply wanted to purchase her pie and head home.

The door behind the counter swung open wide and a tall middle aged man appeared. He was wearing a smile, his face and hands were lightly dusted in white powdery flour, as he made his way over to the counter. A look of confusion registered upon his face, as he drew closer.

"Dan Brennan?" Jessie demanded abruptly.

"That's me and what can I do to help?" the tall blonde, family baker enquired.

"You can do nothin' ... not now ... or ever," Jessie protested angrily.

Almost as if in slow motion, Rachel stood watching in absolute horror, as the stranger next to her pulled out a gun, aiming it directly at Dan, trembling noticeably.

"What the hell!" one of the female customers screeched loudly, instantly scrambling out of the shop, alerting the others of the imminent danger on her way out. All of them exited immediately, terrified, pouring out on to the street letting the door slam in their wake. The young red headed assistant paled significantly, not saying a word, standing transfixed to the spot, almost as if she was in a trance.

"Get out of here Josephine," Dan commanded, pushing her cautiously but quickly to the side, not taking his eyes off the gunman. Not for one solitary second, as Josephine made her exit.

"Don't do it," Rachel interrupted in an authoritative manner, swallowing hard, breaking into the deadly silence, her voice not sounding like her own.

"Shut up bitch and get out of here NOW!" Jessie snarled.

Not thinking rationally, Rachel continued. "He's got a family … " she stammered. "Dan's got a young family," she pleaded, her eyes filling with tears. "Look at the picture on the wall, sketched by his young daughter," she begged hysterically. "I know you don't want to do this …" she murmured, the roof of her mouth growing increasingly dryer, her mind racing frantically.

Silence reigned, without another solitary word being spoken. Dan stood transfixed, staring down the barrel of a revolver. Unable to move, he stood paralysed. His face deadly pale, etched with sheer horror. His frail slender body twitched anxiously, as the sound of his pee dribbled down upon the cold tiled floor, distracting the gunman temporarily.

Proving more than Rachel could stomach, something inside of her snapped and she furiously threw herself forcibly towards the gunman. A frantic struggle took precedence between the two; both were thrashing and rolling along the tiled floor, sending racks of loaves hurdling towards the ground, before the gun went off. It was almost like time stood still, as a deafening and echoing thud pounded ferociously in Rachel's head, as Jessie slowly struggled to his feet. Dazed and smeared in blood, he unsteadily forced the door half open, before staggering outside, leaving a trail of blood in his wake.

Ambulance sirens could be heard screeching along the street, drawing closer and closer, as Rachel lay deadly still, curled up in foetal position upon the cold tiled floor. The ringing in her ears was constant. Dan knelt down gripping her hand tightly; huge tears rapidly streaming down his cheeks.

"What did you do that for?" he reprimanded. "You're so young child dear! God ... you're so young and you don't even know me," he sobbed incoherently, utterly shocked, totally bewildered, unable to fully comprehend what actually had taken place. He cried some more, sobbing uncontrollably, gasping for breath. Peering down at the young blonde haired woman, suddenly noticing her abdominal area covered in blood. Her glazed blue eyes were staring up at him, as the ambulance pulled up outside together with the police.

"Okay, okay, everyone move out of the way please ..." The ambulance driver could be heard from outside, approaching swiftly. "Bloody hell," he gulped, surveying the scene immediately. "Get the god-damn stretcher in here urgently," he bellowed to his other crew member.

Within minutes, they lifted Rachel up on to the trolley. Dan was instructed to let her hand go. He felt reluctant; as this young woman had saved his life.

Then ... only then ... did Rachel squeeze his hand slightly, startling him. "Lela ..." she murmured faintly, almost in a whisper. "Lela ... had to keep her father," she choked, smiling weakly, as tears trickled down the side of her face.

Dan collapsed in a crumpled heap, as she was being wheeled out. He immediately began dry retching, before vomiting profusely over the bakery floor, appearing absolutely gutted, traumatised beyond belief.

A woman police officer approached him having witnessed the scene, fighting back tears, peering down at him sympathetically. Without delay, she retrieved a nearby blanket left by the ambulance driver and lovingly wrapped it around Dan shoulders, as he sat, a trembling blubbering mess.

The ambulance made its way rapidly through the streets of Belfast, heading directly towards the Royal Victoria Hospital. Its lights manically twirling and whirling, the ambulance driver Gary was blasting his horn and sirens in sheer frustration, at drivers taking too long to pull over. He was angry and resentful. He had been in this job for fifteen years and these troubles were still taking their toll. He was seething internally; nothing upset him more than to see a young person shot, no matter their faith, no matter their nationality.

"It's a shame, a god-damn crying shame," he lamented, knowing he wouldn't be in this job for much longer. Each day was becoming an uphill battle and it was during moments like these, he just wanted to quit. "How is she going?" he hollered to his partner Patrick, diligently working on Rachel in the back.

"It's not looking good I'm afraid but she's a fighter. YES ... she's definitely a fighter ... thank god!"

Margaret was heading towards the emergency exit. It had been a very long night and she was eager to go home and crawl into bed beside Paul. He was starting the three o'clock shift this afternoon and they were both looking forward to the weekend, as the whole family was meeting up at Helen's for lunch. God knows, with what she's been through over the past few months, she would really appreciate the company, Margaret thought. With the commemorative service taking place last Friday for Henry, it certainly stirred up the past for everyone.

It was great her mother and father had flown over from Australia to pay their respects and it touched both her and Paul's heart. Rachel was even joining them for Sunday lunch, although she seemed to be a bit grumpy and distant of late, Margaret noticed. However, it gave the whole family time to catch up and say their farewells to Kath and Marcus, who were heading back home on Tuesday.

"Okay I'm off now," she sang out to Bernadette, a competent nurse who she enjoyed working with immensely, over the past few months.

On her way out she was almost knocked over; when the emergency doors burst wide open without warning. Gary emerged, rapidly wheeling a trolley, appearing short-tempered and anxious.

"Bloomin' Nora, youse nearly keeled me over Gary," Margaret laughed, imitating a thick Irish brogue. Immediately shutting up after spotting blood, seep through the hospital's blanket. "Car accident?" she queried, trying not to pay too much attention as she was passing by, appearing absolutely exhausted after finishing her shift due to a chaotic and busy evening.

"No, a bloody shoot out on the Ormeau Road ... in a bakery of all places," Gary exploded. "I can't work it out, I really can't."

Suddenly the monitor went berserk; sending out a chillingly high pitched shrill out into the dimly lit corridor.

"Shit code blue," Margaret screamed, turning instantly and rushing back towards the patient. Jumping up on the trolley immediately, she frantically ripped the covers off to quickly access the patient's heart. She almost collapsed, as the shock registered upon her face.

"Oh my god, it's Rachel!" she shrieked, staring down at her lying upon the cold sterile trolley. "Holy shit Gary, it's my little sister," automatically screaming out instructions as her adrenalin was pumping. "Quick, get me a god-damn defibrillator NOW, she's flat lined for Christs sake," perspiration breaking out on her forehead. Rapidly tilting Rachel's head back "hurry up Gary, I need Epinephrine, we don't have much time," she instructed.

Pushing Rachel's chin up, automatically applying rescue breaths, as her sister's soft blonde tresses brushed against her face. She immediately began cardiopulmonary resuscitation, pumping on her chest, using the heel of her hand at the base of her sternum, as the trolley was wheeled rapidly towards the theatre. Alarm bells were exploding in Margaret's head, her heart pounding, as doctors and nurses came frantically and urgently rushing up the corridor.

"Don't you dare die on me Rachel. DO YOU HEAR ME!" she screamed, pumping her heart rapidly, tears streaming down her face. "DON'T YOU DARE!" she cried out loud, as the theatre doors swung wide open, allowing the emergency team to enter.

To be continued

Printed in Great Britain
by Amazon